St. Catherine's Crown

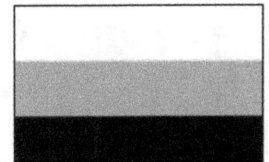  

A Novel
S. Martin Shelton

Inquiries should be addressed to the Publisher:
Lamplight Press
PO Box 82516
Austin, Texas 78708

ISBN: 978-0-9979774-0-0

Library of Congress Control Number
2013940389

Printed in the United States of America
by Lightning Source

Dedication

I dedicate this book to all those who fought Soviet Communist tyranny and defeated it, and to those who suffered and died under its despotic rule.

iii

Дскпошиеддментs

To many dear friends and colleagues, I extend grateful thanks for your sterling support in shaping this manuscript into the novel that it is. In particular, I acknowledge:

Ken Albright for his singular analysis of the military and intelligence scenes in this story, and for his overall cogent comments and keen editing skills.

Michael Cox for his superior skill in producing the maps in this book.

Margaret Dalrymple for her sage counsel and guidance on historical protocols of the times, perceptive concept editing, and patient understanding.

Danielle Hartman Acee for her energetic and earnest professionalism in preparing my manuscript for publication and for her cogent marketing strategy.

Stephen Hightower, M.D., for his professional guidance in rendering the medical scenes authentically.

Marta Galvan for their eagle-eye copy editing of the manuscript.

Sergeant George Trammell, USMC, for his expert contributions in describing the military procedures used during the regicide.

Cast of Characters

In order of first appearance or reference

Prologue

Senior Lieutenant Kirik Antonievich Pirogov. Veteran of the Galician Campaign and officer in the Czar's Imperial Guards.

Lieutenant Viktor Kuznetsov. Associate of Kirik Pirogov.

Chapter 1

Grand Duchess Olga Romanov (1895–1918). Oldest daughter.

Czar Nicholas ("Nicky") Romanov II (1868–1918). Autocrat of all the Russias. Married to Alexandra Fedorovna and father of Anastasia and four other children.

Empress Alexandra ("Alix") Feodorovna (1872–1918). Wife of the Czar and mother of his five children. Granddaughter of Queen Victoria (1810–1901), Regent of Great Britain.

Grand Duchess Tatiana Romanov (1897–1918). Second daughter.

Grand Duchess Maria Romanov (1899–1918). Third daughter.

Grand Duchess Anastasia ("Nastenka") Romanov (1901–1918). Fourth daughter.

Czarevich Alexei Nikolavich Romanov (1904-1918). Son of the Czar and Alexandra.

Colonel Carl Gustaf Mannerheim (1867–1951). Military attaché in the Swedish Embassy in Saint Petersburg. Leader of the Finnish Army in the 1939–1940 Russo-Finnish war.

Chapter 2

Countess Maria ("Masha") Pavlovna Pirogov. Mother of Kirik Pirogov, and close friend of and former lady-in-waiting to Empress Alexandra.

King George V (1865–1936). Regent of Great Britain. First cousin to Czar Nicholas II and second cousin to Empress Alexandra.

Grigori Pavlovich Cherkassky. Maria's brother, engineering surveyor on the Trans-Siberian Railway.

Chapter 3

Roman ("Dmitri") Malinovsky (1876–1918). Undercover Okhrana agent.

Vladimir Ilyich Lenin (1870–1924). Marxist revolutionary. In October 1917 was the Chairman of the Council of People's Commissars, and head of state of the Union of Soviet Socialists Republics.

Chapter 4

Anton Yureivich Andreev. Kirik Pirogov's *nom de guerre.*

Vaslav Nikolsky. Telegraph agent at Bolotnoye, Siberia

Chapter 5

Archbishop Benjamin Kazansky (1874–1922). Eparchy of Saint Petersburg.

Anna Bogrova. Anastasia's *nom de guerre.*

Chapter 7

Leon Trotsky (1897–1940). Socialist revolutionary and Commissar for Foreign Affairs for the USSR. Clashed with Lenin and Stalin. Assassinated in Mexico City.

Alexander Kerensky (1881–1970). People's Commissar for Foreign Affairs and later Commander of the Red Army. Interim head of government after the February 1917 revolution.

Major Fedor Linde. Commander of the Palace Guards.

Vladimir Suvorin. The Pirogovs' butler at Beryosha, the family manor house.

Chapter 8

Grand Duke Nikolai (1856–1929). Commander of the Russian Army and Czar Nicolas II's uncle.

Savva Morozov. Senior deputy of the Torzhok Soviet.

Felix Dzerzhinsky (1877–1926). Head of the Cheka (Soviet secret police) and leader of the Red Terror.

Chapter 9

Olga. Party apparatchik in charge of passports and visas in Torzhok.

Chapter 10

Boris Volodarsky. Conductor on the Trans-Siberian Railway train.

Nadia Azev. Hostess on the Trans-Siberian Railway train.

Vaslav Nikolsky. Telegraph agent in Bolotnoye, Siberia.

Chapter 12

Anatol Kavelin. Clerk at the White Russian Hotel in Peking.

Ivan Oretsky. Proprietor of Oretsky's Russian Teahouse in Peking.

Chapter 13

Grigory Zinoviev (1883–1936). Bolshevik revolutionary, close associate of Lenin, and Interior Minister of the USSR.

Chapter 14

Colonel Yakov Yurovsky (1878–1938). Cheka officer and leader of the Bolshevik cadre in Ekaterinburg.

Khina Demidova. Household maid and servant in the "House of Special Purpose," Ekaterinburg.

Chapter 15

Colonel Vaclav Zká. Commander of the Czech Legion in Russia.

General Aleksei Brusilov (1853–1926). Commander of the 8th Russian Army operating in Galicia in the Southwest Front.

Major Jan Klaus. Battalion commander in the Czech Legion.

Captain Doctor Jiri Litvak. Medical doctor in the Czech Legion.

Sergeant Rudolf Gadia. Medical corpsman in the Czech Legion.

Chapter 16

Tatiana Botkina. Russian nurse working with the Czech Legion.

Sergeant Major Serge Brusilov. Regimental top sergeant in the Czech Legion.

Chapter 18

Admiral Alexander Vasilyevich Kolchak (1874-1920). Commander of the White Russian Army in Siberia.

Chapter 19

Countess Magdalena Ivanovna Makarenko. White Russian *émigré*.

Chapter 21

Colonel Pare Lindstrom. Military attaché, Swedish Embassy in Peking.

Chapter 22

Lio Chung-k'ai. Proprietor of a pawnshop in Peking.

General Stanislaw Zinory Volosenkov. Okhrana agent.

Chapter 23

Colonel Kwei Yung-chen. Intelligence agent for the warlord General Wu Pei-fu.

Chan Sen-tao. Senior cashier at the China National Bank and Trust, Ltd. in Peking.

Major Kwan Soong-chow. Officer in the Nationalist Army.

Colonel Chiang Kai-shek (1887–1975). Nationalist military leader waging campaigns against warlords throughout China. Later, the Generalissimo of Nationalist China.

General Wu Pei-fu (1874-1939). Warlord of Kansu Province in northwestern China.

Chapter 24

Urumgi Ygur, or **Chen Tu-hsiu.** Leader of the Kirgiz tribe in Sinkiang Province and environs.

Chapter 25

Ivan Pashich. Head of the grave-digging detail in Ekaterinburg.

Chapter 27

Vaslav Nikolsky. Telegraph agent in Bolotnoye.
Katya Nikolsky. Wife of telegraph agent Vaslav Nikolsky.

Chapter 28

Ivan Vachot. Stationmaster in Duzhba, Siberia.

Chapter 29

Colonel Doctor Dmitri Markov. Physician at Yumin, Sinkiang Province.
Maxim Fedosov. Former accountant at House of Fabergé in Saint Petersburg.
Corporal Boreslav Tsigler. A corporal in the White Army.

Chapter 30

Yen Hei-lan (Black Orchid). Niece of Wuhan Wei-kuo who first appears in this story in March 1917. In 1933, she is twenty-nine years old and works in Wuhan's antique shop in Peking.
Madeleine de Boise. Daughter of the French chargé d'affaires in Peking.
Wuhan Wei-kuo. The premier antiques dealer in Peking.
Sister Mary Beatrice O'Hara. Headmistress of Saint Elizabeth's Academy for Young Ladies in Peking.
Brigadier Sir Malcolm Stanford-Brownsworth, VC, GBE. British military attaché in Peking.

Chapter 31

Nikolai Danilov. Former corpsman in the White Russian army who works in the infirmary at Yumin, Sinkiang Province, China.

Father Pavel Shubin. Priest of the Russian Orthodox church and member of the senior council in Yumin.

Chapter 35

Trevor Pryce. British photojournalist who works in Peking for several news media, including the Composite Press Service.

Dah Tung-lu. Barman in the Cygne Blanc Lounge, Hôtel de la Chine, in Peking.

Alexandra Marlowe. Daughter and only child of Samuel Marlowe. Executive Editor of the Composite Press Service.

Samuel Marlowe. Self-made multimillionaire capitalist and one of the richest men in New York.

Chapter 39

Sergeant Elena Vavilova. Sergeant-of-the-guard at the People's Hospital, Bolotnoye, Siberia.

Captain Yakov Prokoviev. Commanding Officer of the The People's Commissariat for Internal Affairs (NKVD) in Bolotnoye, Siberia.

Genrikh Yagoda (1891–1939). Director of the Commissariat for Internal Affairs.

Colonel General Yakov Yurosky (1878–1938). Assassin of the Russian Royal family. In 1933 the Leader of the Commissariat for Internal Affairs for all Siberia.

Chapter 40

Major Rodek. Aide to Colonel General Yurovsky.

Chapter 46

Mister Reginald Smyth-Lancaster. First vice-president at Barkley's Bank in Peking.

Chapter 49

Sergeant Bogdan Yezhov. NKVD soldier.

Preface

Welcome to *St. Catherine's Crown*

The basis of this yarn lies in the aftermath of the 1917 Bolshevik Revolution in Russia and the murder of Czar Nicholas II and his family on the night of 17 July 1918 at Ekaterinburg. To add authenticity, I have used actual historical figures as key Russian characters, and the major historical events and dates are accurate. I've maintained geographical accuracy and have set the narrative in the milieu of the times.

Any story dealing with Russian history is convoluted. Accordingly, I suggest that you consult the Cast of Characters to become familiar with the individuals involved in this narrative. Visit the Photographic Gallery at the end of the text to see portraits of the historic figures who appear as characters in this story.

To help you maintain geographic orientation, I have included two maps, which follow this Preface.

Finally, please review the Author's Notes at the end of the book for additional historical background related to this novel, the protocols I used, and a brief description of the various secret police organizations that were active in czarist Russia and the Soviet Union.

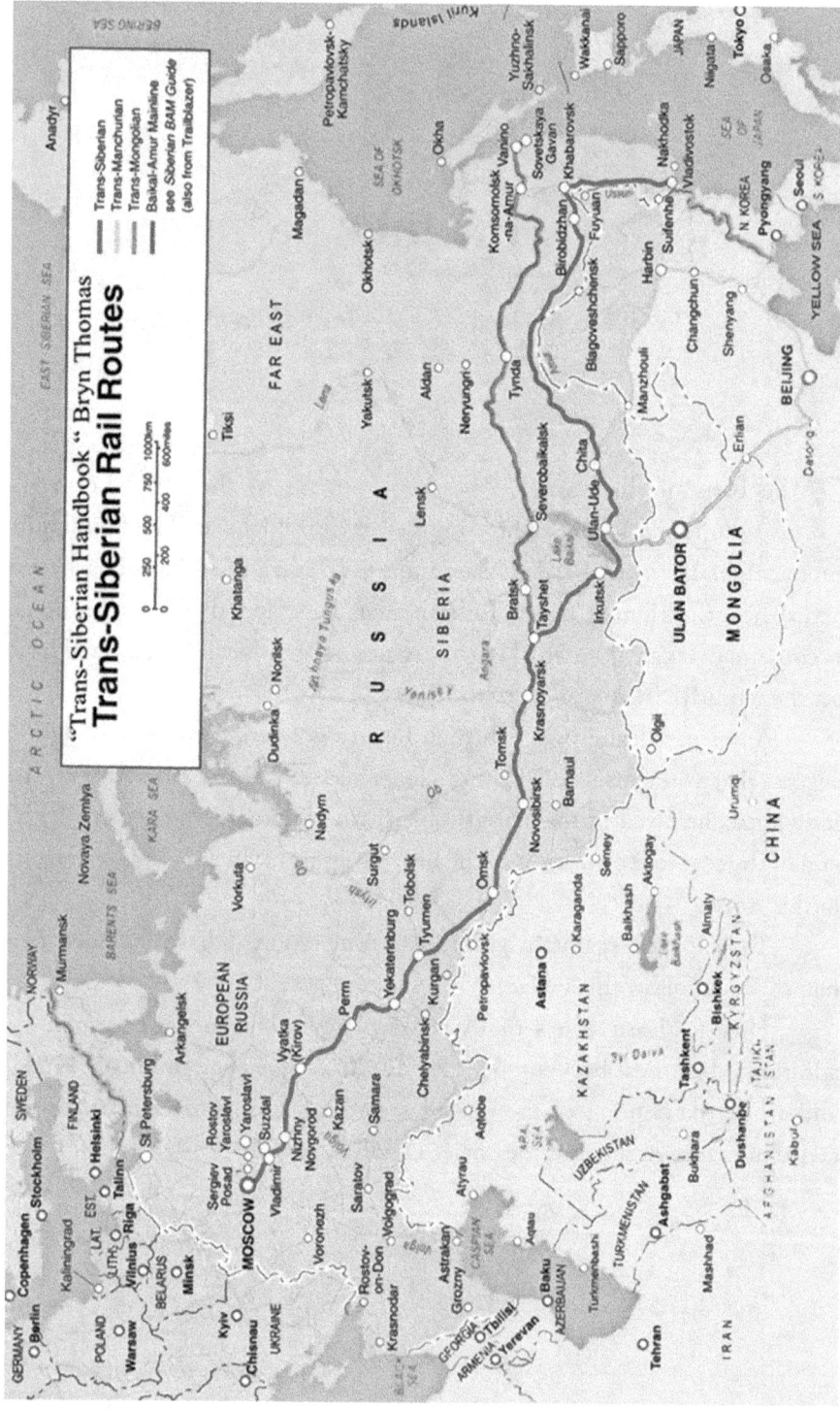

"Trans-Siberian Handbook " Bryn Thomas
Trans-Siberian Rail Routes

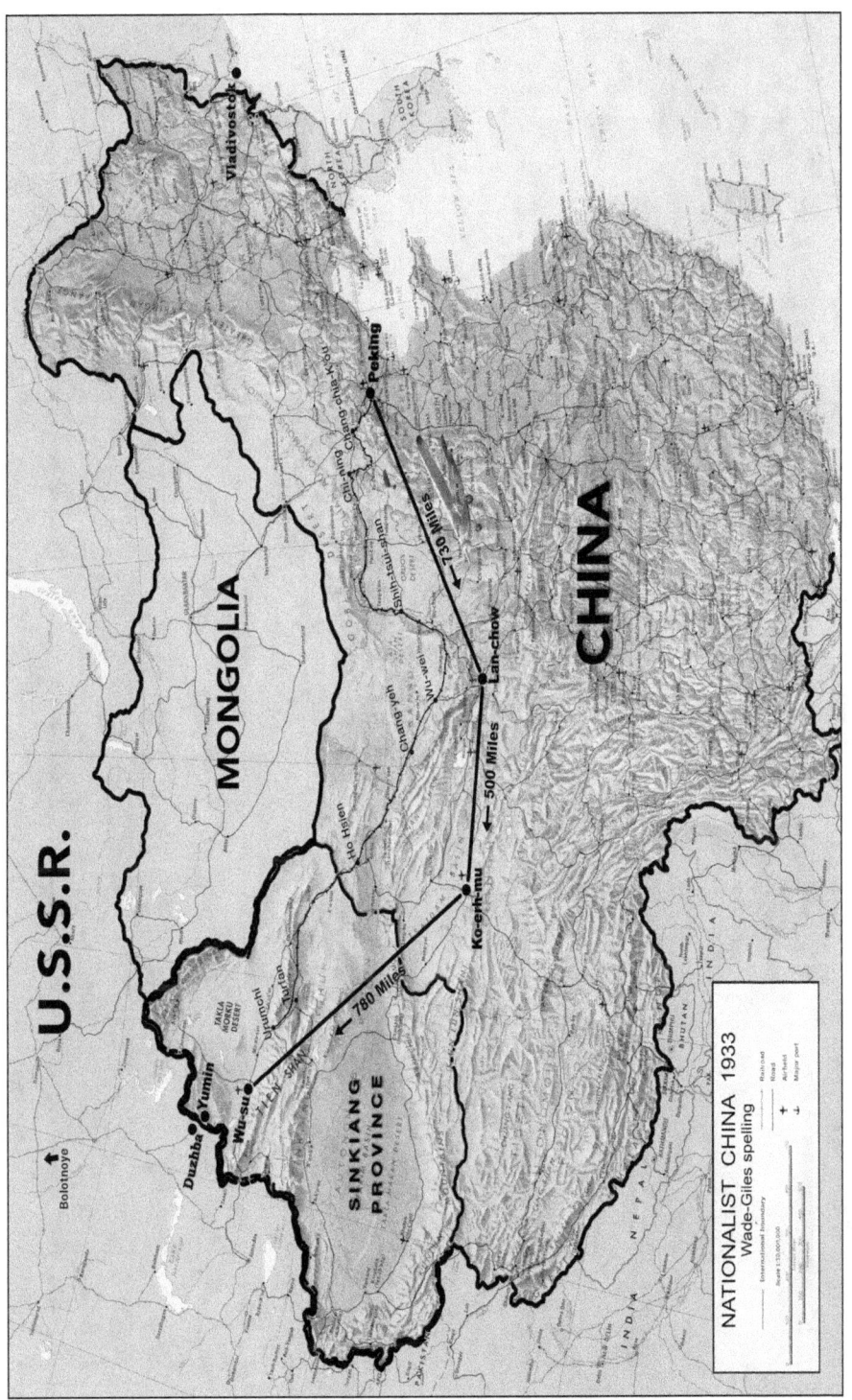

Prologue

Nevsky Prospect, Saint Petersburg, Russia
26 December 1916

Senior Lieutenant Kirik Pirogov ducks as a large stone whizzes past his head and smashes into the shop window behind him. Startled, he looks about to find the assailant.

His companion, Lieutenant Viktor Kuznetsov, shouts, "Red thugs. Get down!" He draws his pistol and scans the area.

Pirogov falls to his knees, draws his pistol, and responds, "Viktor, what do you see?"

"Nothing. But they're probably in that alley across the street."

Pirogov searches for the attacker but cannot see into the black void. "Viktor, I suspect that this attack is going to develop into serious trouble very soon. A rock fusillade is usually the opening gambit for a more violent assault. We've got to get out of here, or else find cover."

At this early hour in the morning, the streets of Saint Petersburg lie still and silent. A slight dusting of snow covers the area, and a bitter wind blows from the Baltic, dropping the temperature to several degrees below zero. In this disastrous third year of the World War, Red revolutionaries are stirring civil unrest and the general populace has become disheartened by the seemingly ceaseless slaughter of husbands, sons, relatives, and friends. Bolshevik agitators have incited thousands of soldiers to throw down their outdated weapons and desert the trenches. Sailors have mutinied and murdered their officers.

Incredible hardships and fear engulf the Russian people as they suffer in the bitter cold from the scarcity of coal, food, and other necessities. Resentment is growing rapidly against the Czar's imperialistic government and its increasingly violent response to protests.

Pirogov and Kuznetsov are returning from their regiment's three-hundredth anniversary soirée. Imprudently, they lingered far too long at the bar after the festivities had concluded. When they finally decided to leave, there was no transportation to take them to the Imperial Guards' barracks inside the grounds of the Czar's Winter Palace. The vicious winter weather is keeping people indoors, and taxicabs and carriages in their garages. Accordingly, their only option is to walk. The pair is well aware of the hazards of walking the streets of Saint Petersburg at this early hour, especially wearing their dress-blue uniforms, but the champagne had dulled their prudence.

Another rock knocks off Pirogov's uniform cap. He retrieves the cap, brushes off the snow, and points his pistol in the direction from which the rock came. Suddenly, a volley of stones pummels the pair. Pirogov shouts, "Fools, are you trying to kill us? Show yourselves and let's see what sort of noble fellows you are."

Several men burst out of the alley across the street and rush toward the two soldiers, shouting, "Death to the czarists!" In a few seconds, the gang is almost on Pirogov and Kuznetsov. In the faint moonlight, Pirogov sees that the leader has a dirk in his right hand and the others have cudgels ready to bludgeon them to death. With an automatic reaction, this combat veteran of the Austrian Front fires at the charging, knife-wielding Red thug. A neat red hole appears in the man's forehead and he crumbles to the street.

Kuznetsov fires at the next thug and drops him with a round in his chest. Realizing that these czarists are armed and determined, the remaining Reds scatter.

Pirogov and Kuznetsov stand, dust off their uniforms, and holster their pistols. Pirogov comments, "My friend, this attack is but one small incident in the revolution that is brewing in Russia. It bodes ill for our survival as a monarchy."

1

Winter Palace, Saint Petersburg, Russia
7 January 1917

Inter nights in northern Russia are frigid. Tonight, the dark sky glitters with cold stars, and the streets are paved with ice. Light from the windows of the Winter Palace casts a warm glow over the snow in the palace gardens, but beyond the glow, the garden is dark and the shrubbery lies buried under a blanket of snow. Inside, the ballroom is gaily lit for the Czar's annual Christmas Ball. The vast room is festooned with swags of balsam branches hung with golden ribbons and the flags of the provinces of the Russian Empire. At one end of the ballroom, an enormous tree is hung with shining ornaments and flickering candles. The ceiling glows with rococo tableaus of Louis XV's court in Versailles, surrounded by ornate gilt relief decorations, and crystal chandeliers cast a sparkling light over the festive scene. The forty-musician orchestra plays an endless repertoire of waltzes, occasionally a lively mazurka, and the polonaise processional parade at mid-evening.

Swirling around the room are the elite of Saint Petersburg society—aristocrats, government and military leaders, and the cream of the diplomatic corps. Grand ladies bedazzle in fashionable gowns and sparkling jewelry; military officers are resplendent in their colorful, bemedaled uniforms; and the diplomats add a note of sober elegance with their white ties and tailcoats. All are having a wonderful time, seemingly oblivious to the revolutionary chaos occurring beyond the barricades in Saint Petersburg.

Among the dancers are the four daughters of the Czar—Grand Duchesses Olga, Marie, Tatiana, and Anastasia—elegantly gowned and wearing fabulous jewels from the famed Romanov collection. In the center of the floor, Grand Duchess Anastasia dances with a senior lieutenant from the Palace Guard. She is aglow with pleasure and excitement at participating in her first ball. The sixteen-year-old Anastasia is short of stature and slightly overweight, with deep blue eyes, delicately shaped eyebrows, and a sensitive mouth.

Her mother, Empress Alexandra Fedorovna, says that Anastasia is stubborn, mischievous, and impertinent, the tomboy of the family. Nonetheless, she has a loving soul and is a devoted daughter. Tonight, Anastasia is the embodiment of a gracious lady. Her gown of Nile-green silk chiffon is trimmed in gold and edged in delicate lace. She also wears her mother's emerald and diamond necklace—Queen Victoria's wedding gift to her granddaughter Alexandra—and her curly strawberry-blonde hair is swept up and crowned with a glittering diamond tiara.

Her partner, Senior Lieutenant Kirik Pirogov, cuts a striking figure in his Palace Guard's dress uniform—a scarlet jacket with gold chain-cord piping and a stand-up blue collar trimmed in gold, worn with white trousers and black boots. Around his neck hangs a brilliant medal, the Order of Saint George, First Class, the Czar's highest award for heroism. He is twenty-seven years old, with broad shoulders, and almost six feet tall. He has brown eyes, dark curly hair, and a square chin. A deep, three-inch scar cuts vertically across his left cheekbone, put there by an Austrian grenadier's saber. There is a hardness about him and a haunted aspect to his gaze that is seen only in men who have known fierce and deadly trench warfare. After Pirogov was seriously wounded on the Galician Front, the Czar ordered him reassigned to the Palace Guard until he could heal. There, he has been able to continue his family's long history of personal service to the czars.

Pirogov holds Anastasia carefully and he is clearly enjoying her company. He gazes into her sparkling eyes and whispers, "Your eyes are so beautiful. They pull at my soul."

Anastasia blushes a bright scarlet. She has never had a man flatter her with such passion. She pulls away slightly and says, "Stop it, Senior Lieutenant

Kirik Antonievich Pirogov. You embarrass me." But her slightly upturned mouth and the sparkle in her eyes betray her delight.

As Pirogov spins her through the waltz, Anastasia giggles slightly. She has known her partner all her life. His mother, Maria Pavlovna Pirogov, is a former lady-in-waiting to the Empress, as well as Alexandra's closest friend. As a boy, Kirik often joined the imperial family at Tsarskoe Selo, the Czar's country retreat. He, like the Czar, is a keen hunter and an expert equestrian. When Anastasia was small, she idolized Pirogov as an older brother. Now she dances with him at her first ball, and she realizes that her feelings are no longer sisterly. She is dancing with a very handsome young man whose heroism is admired by everyone in the room, and he is flirting with her in a very unbrotherly way. Her excitement and delight bubble into another soft giggle.

"Do I amuse you, Your Highness?" Pirogov asks.

Anastasia smiles. "I'm just happy. The ball is wonderful and you, Kirik Antonievich, are an excellent dancer."

"I aim to please, Your Highness. You are looking very grown-up tonight and, if I may be permitted to say, very beautiful."

Anastasia blushes again, and Pirogov swirls them off into the swaying dancers.

Seated on the imperial dais at the end of the room are Anastasia's parents, Czar Nicholas II and the Empress Alexandra. The Czar, with a Van Dyke beard and wing mustache, wears a navy admiral's uniform and sports an array of unearned medals and badges awarded to him by visiting monarchs and foreign dignitaries. Alexandra is a handsome woman with strong blue eyes, golden-brown hair, a firm chin, and erect shoulders. She wears a midnight-blue velvet gown trimmed in silver brocade, a diamond-studded tiara, and a diamond and pearl necklace with a huge and brilliant diamond pendant.

Turning to her husband, she smiles. "I'm so glad you agreed to allow all the girls to attend the ball tonight, Nicky darling. With the war taking all the young men away and making everyone so serious, they need a bit of fun."

"I can't deny you anything, my dear Alix," the Czar responds, his eyes glinting warmly. "However, I still think our little Anastasia is too young for a ball. She won't be seventeen until the summer."

"But, darling, who knows how long this dreadful war will continue? By summer, we may not be able to have a ball. Nastenka deserves at least one grand ball to remember all her life. And doesn't she look lovely?" Alexandra smiles with maternal pride.

All the girls look so pretty tonight, she thinks to herself. *Such a delightful change from the nurses' uniforms the older girls wear every day when they go off to work at the soldiers' hospital. It's so refreshing to enjoy the colors and music of the ball, such a change from the Spartan lives the war has inflicted on everyone. Even their lives in the palace have become quieter and less comfortable since the Czar instituted limits on their meals, heating, and other comforts in a gesture of solidarity with his beloved military. The imperial women are all serving the war effort, the older girls as nurses, and all of them spending every spare moment rolling bandages and knitting piles of heavy woolen socks and drab scarves for the soldiers. Little Alexis, bless his heart, adores the quasi-military life his father has imposed on the family, but for the girls it's a different matter.*

Alexandra believes that girls need beauty and opportunities to enjoy life before they settle down to their royal obligations and eventually to appropriate marriages. She feels a quiver of pride at the willingness with which her daughters are supporting the war effort, but still.... *Well,* she sighs, *at least they have tonight. Whatever the future may bring*—even Alexandra realizes that the war and the spreading revolution threaten everything she values—*the girls have this grand ball to savor for a few hours.*

В друѓой рăз

Later in the evening, Pirogov takes a break from the dancing. Anastasia has been swept away by other partners, and he has danced with all her sisters and with many of the other women. As a special guest of the Czar and a highly decorated soldier, one of his duties this evening is to make sure that no lady who wishes to dance is left without a partner.

In an adjacent room, waiters are serving chilled champagne. Pirogov sips at his glass and watches the crowd milling around him. Through the wide doors into the ballroom he can see Anastasia dancing past in the arms of someone from the diplomatic corps. *Such a pretty girl*, he thinks. Amazing how she has grown up from that reckless tomboy he knew at Tsarskoe Selo, always clambering up a tree or racing across the grounds with her dogs. What delight she used to take in slamming his croquet ball far out of bounds! Now she is a lovely young lady, hovering at that magical moment between girlhood and womanhood. He smiles to himself, recalling the way her girlish giggles belied the regal poise of her head. *I wonder what kind of woman she'll be in five or ten years*, he asks himself. Anastasia was always his favorite of the imperial children, a bewitching and sometimes bewildering combination of princess and gamine, impudent, but blessed with a sweetness and kindness rarely seen in anyone, royalty or commoner. She might someday be a woman to be reckoned with.

"Senior Lieutenant Pirogov, I believe."

A slightly accented voice interrupts Pirogov's musing.

"May I congratulate you on your award of the Order of Saint George? And First Class besides!"

Pirogov turns to the speaker. "Thank you, sir."

"Allow me to introduce myself. I am Colonel Carl Gustaf Mannerheim, military attaché at the Swedish Embassy." Mannerheim is tall and stoutly built with a square face, bushy black hair, and a full beard. His soft grey eyes are wide-set and lighthearted. He wears the dark-blue dress uniform of his regiment and a few medals that indicate he had an active military career before assuming his embassy role.

The two men shake hands. "It's an honor to meet you, Senior Lieutenant. Stories of your exploits in Galicia have reached even my neutral embassy. The trench warfare being used these days is an abomination, the most brutal and degrading way to fight a war I've ever seen. Few men survive long enough to distinguish themselves in any way. But to rally your flagging troops and lead a second attack under a murderous Austrian fusillade while seriously wounded—ah, that is classic heroism."

"Thank you, Colonel. You are too generous."

"Well, young man, I salute you." Mannerheim clicks his glass against Pirogov's.

The two stand silently for a moment, watching the dancers and sipping their champagne. Mannerheim gives a snort of contempt. "There are several young officers, not unlike yourself, here this evening—aristocrats looking very dashing in their regimental uniforms and sparkling with medals, but most of them are completely worthless. Put these bold young studs in the trenches under heavy enemy fire, and most of them would just whimper and soil themselves. Nothing but a lot of toy soldiers!" He snorts again.

"We Swedes are blunt, so I'll get right to the point. Pirogov, your country is going to lose this war, no matter how hard you and other brave men try to win it. And the revolution cannot be stopped. Soon—a few months, next year at the latest—the Czar's government will fall, either because the war has been lost or because the revolutionaries have won. There will be no place for a man like you in the new Russia. Everything you are is anathema to the revolutionaries; and the Austrians, if they win the war, will want to punish those who fought hardest against them."

Pirogov raises his eyebrows and gazes silently at Colonel Mannerheim. He has heard the rumors, of course, that Russia's war effort is a debacle and that the revolutionaries are growing stronger each day, but he had believed them confined to the military barracks and centers of government power. He is not only somewhat stunned that a foreigner, a mere observer from a neutral country, has heard them, but that he has analyzed them so perceptively. For a moment, he is at a loss for words.

Mannerheim continues. "Young man, I respect your courage and loyalty. I would like to know you better. Perhaps we might dine together some evening? The chef at my embassy is very skilled, and we have an excellent wine cellar. I think that even in these dark days, we could enjoy an excellent meal."

"Thank you, sir." Pirogov bows slightly.

"Senior Lieutenant Pirogov, I want you to know that if I can ever be of service to you, I would be honored to do whatever I can. You need only contact me." Mannerheim drains his glass. "A pleasure to meet you, young man." He clicks his heels and bows, then turns and drifts away into the crowd.

Back in the ballroom, Pirogov is dancing again with Anastasia. He is still bemused by his conversation with Mannerheim, but the smiling girl in his arms holds all his attention. She is not the most beautiful girl in the room, but there is something about her that he finds far more enchanting than mere beauty—the happy sparkle of her blue eyes, the flicker of mischief in her smile that contradicts moments of girlish awkwardness. *She will one day be an easy woman to love.*

When Alexandra notices how Pirogov is looking at her daughter, she whispers to Nicholas, "Perhaps we have a small romance budding."

"Romance? Impossible!" snorts Nicholas. "Pirogov can flatter, and Nastenka can blush, but it goes no further. Our daughters will look much higher for their mates."

Alexandra turns to her husband. "Kirik is a brave and gallant young man, and he has known Nastenka since she was a small child."

"Our girls are imperial princesses. Pirogov is a mere count. Royalty marries royalty. My dear, forget this nonsense about a romance. When the war is over, our girls will make brilliant marriages with suitable young men of their own class. And remember that Cousin George in England has four fine boys who will be looking for appropriate wives. One of our daughters may well be the next queen of England." He shakes his head vigorously. "A mere count, indeed!"

Alexandra is silent for a moment, her face suddenly somber. She sighs deeply but silently, inhaling the gentle scent of the balsam swags and the sweet perfumes that permeate the ballroom. Then she murmurs softly, "When the war is over," and turns away to watch the dancers.

2

Winter Palace, Saint Petersburg
10 January 1917

Empress Alexandra moves to the rose window in her small, private boudoir and stares at the soft snow drifting lazily onto the rose garden. It is only four in the afternoon, yet the sky is nearly dark. From a distance come the faint sounds of another riot: people shouting, and occasional staccato bursts of small-arms fire. *What will happen to us?*

Alexandra's boudoir is her place of refuge in the vast palace; a room in which she can sit alone and think, read, and meet privately with her family. Here, she is protected from the endless streams of servants and bustling bureaucrats with their hectic missions.

The walls are covered with pale mauve silk damask and paintings. The furnishings include a small desk with ormolu fittings, a chaise longue covered with flowered English chintz, and several comfortable chairs—items that seem more suitable for a bourgeois parlor than the palace of an empress. A tall bookcase holds mostly novels and devotional books, and there are several étagères laden with bibelots and family photographs. A prie-dieu sits in one corner; above it hangs an icon of Saint Olga in a bejeweled frame. In a place of honor, next to the desk, hangs a large oil portrait of Alexandra's beloved grandmother, Queen Victoria.

Alexandra reflects on the Christmas Ball and finds herself wondering whether there will ever be another. Even though her husband tries to shield her, she knows that the war is going badly for Russia. The military hospitals overflow with wounded soldiers, and the servants in the palace seem glummer every day.

A soft knock at the door arouses Alexandra from her thoughts. A servant opens the door to admit Countess Maria Pavlovna Pirogov, Alexandra's closest friend.

"Your Imperial Majesty," murmurs Maria Pavlovna and drops into a deep curtsy. "Thank you for seeing me."

"You're always welcome here, my dear Masha." Alexandra draws her friend to her and the two women embrace warmly. "Come, sit down and warm yourself with some tea." The Empress turns to a bubbling samovar and pours a cup of tea for her friend.

"I'm so glad you asked to visit, Masha. With all the terrible war news, I am disheartened. Your company cheers me."

Maria is shorter than Alexandra, with a rounded, firmly corseted figure. She is fifty-seven, and her dark hair shows glints of silver. Faint lines around her eyes and mouth reflect a smiling personality. She wears a perfectly tailored dark woolen dress, relieved only by a heavy strand of pearls and a large, gold, religious medallion around her neck.

The two women sit, Maria Pavlovna on one of the soft chairs and Alexandra stretched out on her chaise longue to ease the constant sciatic pain in her back and legs. For a few minutes, they chatter about the ball, exchanging impressions of the gowns and the guests. Alexandra is pale with the exhaustion that afflicts her after any public event, and her mood is somber. Today, she wears a simple grey dress and no jewelry except for her wedding ring.

The tone of the conversation is casual, but Maria Pavlovna is carefully studying the Empress. She has known the Empress since Alexandra first arrived in Russia, a shy and painfully awkward Hessian princess. Several years older than the timid bride thrust so suddenly onto the imperial throne, Maria was appointed as one of Alexandra's first ladies-in-waiting. She took care to protect the young Empress from the worst of the jealous aristocrats, who made no effort to conceal their contempt for "the German," and she carefully mentored Alexandra on the elaborate protocols of the court, with its complicated hierarchies and Byzantine rivalries. A deep friendship grew between the women, stirred by Alexandra's gratitude and Maria's compassion. Maria has seen Alexandra through five difficult pregnancies, spells of debilitating ill health, and the despair of raising a son, the heir to the throne, who is afflicted with incurable hemophilia. She knows the Empress's every mood and can guess most of her thoughts.

Today, Maria sees new signs of stress on Alexandra's face. There are dark hollows under her eyes, and her mouth is tight with pain. Maria always feels a deep frustration at her inability to ease the heavy burdens of her friend's life—Alexandra's constant worry about little Grand Duke Alexis's fragile health, her mounting fears about the war and the spreading revolution, and her attempts to preserve a similitude of normalcy for her family as the world collapses around them.

At last, Maria puts down her cup and takes a deep breath. "My darling Alix, I must confess that I came for more than a pleasant chat." She is one of the few people outside the imperial family permitted to call Alexandra by her given name, a privilege given in recognition of the close friendship and trust between the two women. The friendship had continued even after Maria retired from her role at court to better care for her son and the country estate she inherited from her husband, an army general killed in the Russo-Japanese War. Alexandra had made a place for the fatherless young Kirik in her own family and guided his education. These days, the two women visit frequently, sharing the small confidences of loving mothers and women whose lives are divided between public and private responsibilities.

Alexandra stirs on her chaise longue. "And what troubles you, dear Masha? How can I help?"

"Alix, I have come to try to help you. But I must first ask you to promise me that our conversation will remain between the two of us. Please promise not to speak of what I am about to tell you to anyone. Not to your confessor. Not even to the Czar."

"But I tell Nicky everything," protests Alexandra.

"In this case, I must beg you to make an exception. Many lives depend upon your discretion."

"What lives? What are you talking about?"

"Trust me, as you have for so many years."

Alexandra reflects a moment, and nods solemnly. "Very well, I agree."

"Alix, you surely know that we are losing the war."

"Yes," the Empress sighs mournfully. "Every time I visit the military hospitals there are more wounded." She sighs again. "I feel so sorry for the poor souls. There is too much suffering, too many deaths."

Maria continues, "These are not the only losses. The military, in general, suffers from very poor morale. There have been many desertions; soldiers are simply putting down their weapons and walking away. Also, there have been mutinies and murdered officers."

"Nicky never mentioned this."

"Of course not. He wants to protect you from worry." Maria takes another deep breath and continues. "Alix, the war is lost. Oh, the fighting will continue for a while, because no one with the power to stop it is willing to admit defeat. But the war is lost."

Alexandra absorbs this information silently, her face a stiff mask of sorrow.

"Moreover, the revolutionaries are gaining strength every day. Throughout the country, there are riots, small worker rebellions, and bomb attacks on government offices. Here in Saint Petersburg, there are almost daily riots in the streets and in the factories. People are listening to the revolutionaries and accepting their message."

"But how can people believe that nonsense?" Alexandra protests indignantly. "Those horrid Bolsheviks are nothing but criminals and hooligans."

"The people are angry, Alix. For three years they've sent their husbands and brothers and sons off to war, knowing that many of them will never return. They see this war as a quarrel between a bunch of arrogant monarchs; a miserable slaughter being fought by poor people with no choice or stake in the matter. People are hungry, and cold, and tired. They are outraged that the Czar seems oblivious to their suffering."

"But Nicky loves them! He loves Russia with all his heart. How can they not know this?"

"Because what they see is their Czar living in comfort in his palace while they hope desperately to find a loaf of bread to feed their family and enough coal to keep themselves warm for one more night. They see the Czar sending their menfolk off to die in a hopeless war. The Bolsheviks and other revolutionaries promise them bread and coal and work for everyone. They promise them equality and peace. They are winning the trust and support of the masses."

Alexandra shakes her head. "How can you say these terrible things, Masha? They can't be true!"

"They are true. Alix, the war is lost, and the revolutionaries will win. And all of this will happen very soon. You and the Czar must leave Russia."

Alexandra glares at her friend, her face rigid with confusion and offense. However much she has mulled over the same thoughts herself, she resents hearing them from her friend. She sits stiffly.

"We cannot possibly leave Russia! How can you even suggest such a thing? Nicky would die before he would abandon his country. And I cannot abandon him."

Then, she collapses back onto the chaise and muffles a sob with her handkerchief. "And even if we were willing to leave, which we are not, where could we go? Who would offer us asylum? Our cousin, King George of England? I doubt it."

Puzzled by the Empress's statement, Maria asks, "Why would King George deny you and your family sanctuary?" She glances at the portrait of Queen Victoria. "You are Queen Victoria's granddaughter." She pauses to gather her thoughts. "He cannot refuse you. I do not understand."

"Masha, my dear, it's politics. Our ambassador in London has heard talk that it is the King's Prime Minister, David Lloyd George, who has demanded that the British government deny us refuge. He has MI5 intelligence that with the Russian royal family on British soil, the Communists would agitate the workers and start a revolution. Such a disruption could well cause Britain to withdraw from the war, and Germany and Austria would win by default."

Maria reaches out to take Alexandra's hand. For a moment she strokes it soothingly. "Alix darling, I am here to offer you another possibility."

Alexandra gradually relaxes and her sobs subside. She wipes her eyes and looks expectantly at Maria.

"The way to the east is still open. The Trans-Siberian trains run every day. Already many Russians are packing what they can carry and fleeing to the east, to China or Manchuria."

Alexandra snorts dismissively. "Cowards! Only cowards would abandon their country at a time like this." She pauses for a moment to reflect. "But even if we did flee, what would the Czar of All the Russias do in China? Open a shop? Peddle used clothes in the street?"

"There is yet another possibility for you. May I tell you about it? But please remember that many lives depend on your complete secrecy in this matter."

"I understand."

"Very well. Do you recall my brother Grigori, the engineer?"

Alexandra nods.

"Some years before the turn of this century, the transportation minister proposed creating a new railroad line south from the Trans-Siberian Railway into western China. Grigori was the head of the survey party sent to find a route. One day, a local tradesman invited him to go bear hunting in China. They discovered a long-abandoned lamasery in an isolated valley. The railroad line was never built, but Grigori always remembered that lamasery."

"Recently, as some of us who love Russia have seen the growing threat to its future, Grigori proposed the lamasery as a possible place of refuge for loyal Russians who see no future for themselves in a Bolshevik society. He returned there, with a few others, and little by little they have been restoring the buildings and creating a community. Others have joined them. People of many backgrounds, many skills. Among them are some people you know, members of the court, as well as retired military men, kulaks, professional people, and businessmen. There is even a priest. You and the Czar could go there. You would be safe in China, in this community of Russians entirely loyal to you, people who would give their lives to protect you."

Alexandra gazes silently at Maria, absorbing this information. Then she sighs and shakes her head. "The Czar will never leave Russia, and his family will never leave him. It is our sacred duty to stay."

Maria pauses a moment to gather her thoughts. Then she continues. "Alix, your sense of duty to Russia is one of your greatest strengths. But remember that you have another duty, one even more sacred than your obligations to your husband or your country. You are a mother, and it is your first duty to protect your children. That is the holy duty God has given you. You must protect your children at all costs. And never forget that your children are also the greatest hope that the Russia we both love will endure, after war and revolution. Whatever happens, it is they who will carry on the Romanov family, the great legacy of the czars. They must be saved."

Alexandra has dried her tears and recovered her calm. She looks at Maria doubtfully. "Masha, you make all this sound so dire. Surely you exaggerate."

"Before God, I assure you that I do not." Maria takes Alexandra's hand in both of hers. "You must understand that all will soon be lost, and that there will be no hope here for any of us."

"I cannot believe that."

"Then I beg you to listen to someone who knows far more about this than I do. We—that is, this silent group of Russians who want to preserve our Mother Russia, even if we have to leave her to do so—we have a contact, a man who is one of us but who has for some years been risking everything to serve as our eyes and ears inside the Bolshevik movement. He is close to the leaders and enjoys their confidence. Will you allow him to tell you what the Bolsheviks plan for our beloved Russia?"

Alexandra twists her handkerchief and stares out the window, as though she might see something there to contradict Maria's warnings. Her face is contorted with an agony of indecision. Some moments pass as Maria waits silently for a response. Then, suddenly, Alexandra speaks.

"Very well. I shall see him. Who is he?"

"He is called Dmitri. This is not his real name, which I do not know, nor the name he uses in his work, which I also don't know. May I arrange the meeting? Remember, absolute secrecy is paramount."

"You already have my promise of secrecy. Arrange the meeting." Alexandra sighs. "Oh, Masha, sometimes it feels like the whole world is collapsing under our feet. What is to become of us?"

"I don't know. But there is hope, even so. I shall pray that God will protect you and guide you in all things."

3

Winter Palace, Saint Petersburg
12 January 1917

Empress Alexandra is taking a late evening stroll in the palace rose garden. There is a biting chill in the air, and a promise of more snow to come. She can hear bursts of gunfire in the distance; the Bolsheviks and other revolutionaries are close to storming the city.

She pulls a heavy sable coat tighter around her shoulders and stuffs her chilled hands into a matching muff. She had explained her desire to walk alone on an impending migraine and the need for fresh air. There is no migraine, but she feels unbearably restless, a mass of irritable nerves and mental stress. Since her meeting with Maria Pavlovna she has been almost overwhelmed with worry and indecision. She wants more than anything to ignore Maria's warning, to retreat into her sheltered life in the palace. But she cannot ignore the hopeless faces of the bandaged soldiers at the hospital, nor the sporadic bursts of gunfire and the screams of mobs rioting around the city.

In the dusk, she spots a figure partially concealed in the shadows.

"Good evening, Your Majesty." He bows deeply as the Empress approaches. "I am Dmitri."

Dmitri is in reality Roman Malinovsky, a senior member of the Okhrana, the Czar's secret police, and an undercover agent. He is an innocuous-looking fellow of medium height and build, dressed in a long padded coat. A heavy fur Cossack hat covers his head and obscures most of his face. Several years before, he had joined the Bolshevik Party and participated in armed revolutionary activities. Through his apparent fervor, skill, and loyalty to the party he earned the trust of the Bolshevik leadership. Currently, Malinovsky is Lenin's aide-de-camp and communications director, a role awarded to him for his skills with Morse code and shortwave radio operation.

Alexandra nods graciously and extends her hand, which Dmitri grasps lightly and bends to kiss. "Your Majesty, my unswerving loyalties are always with you and the imperial family."

After a brief pause, he speaks softly. "Perhaps we might stroll through that little grove of pines. It will be more private there."

Alexandra is silent as they walk through the snow-covered garden. Dmitri awaits his cue from the Empress.

After a time she speaks. "I have great fear that our Imperial Russia is doomed. Our mutual friend, Maria Pavlovna Pirogov, has convinced me that the revolutionaries will soon take Saint Petersburg. Our pitiful army cannot fight the Germans, Austrians, and Lenin's ruffians simultaneously."

She walks silently for a few paces. "I received a letter earlier today from King George, telling me that there will be no help from England and her allies. They are stalemated on the Western Front. And the English are also waging campaigns in Palestine, Arabia, Persia, and East Africa." With a sigh, she continues, "The United States is unconcerned. President Wilson is an ostrich with his head in the academic trivia of democracy and his policy of 'peace at any price.'"

She sighs again, so deeply it sounds almost like a sob. "We are on our own, and completely isolated."

They continue to walk. After a moment, Dmitri pauses and turns to Alexandra. "I'm afraid that you're correct, Madam. Already Lenin is designing the form of the new socialist government, and naming his cronies as interim ministers. He has appointed me to be the People's Commissar in Charge of Post and Telegraph." He gazes at her for a long moment and then speaks, his voice low and choking with emotion. "Your Majesty, I implore you and your family to quit Saint Petersburg at once."

The shadows around them deepen and scattered flecks of snow begin to fall. The Empress and Dmitri silently continue their stroll. Around them the snow-covered trees and bushes loom like icy ghosts.

Finally, Alexandra responds, speaking with regal precision, "Dmitri, I appreciate your concern but the Romanovs will stay. Our duty is to our subjects." She pauses for a moment. "I have implored the Czar to send our children to England, but he will not even consider the idea. He is blindly optimistic and refuses to see what is happening. So we shall remain in Saint Petersburg and face the victorious Lenin and his Bolsheviks."

She falls silent, and they continue their walk. She murmurs softly, "So this is how it must be." Realizing that it is useless to continue his entreaty, Dmitri nods in acceptance. They continue their stroll in silence.

In a firmer voice, Alexandra says, "Maria Pavlovna told me that you have information about the Bolsheviks' plans for the future of our beloved Russia. What can you tell me?"

Dmitri turns away from the Empress and in a low, embarrassed voice says, "Forgive me, Your Majesty. I am reluctant to speak of this."

Alexandra grabs his shoulder and turns him to face her. "Come now, Dmitri. Tell me what the Bolsheviks are plotting."

He looks down and his words stumble. "The worst possible evil scheme." He stops speaking and looks into her eyes. "I have attended a secret meeting of the Bolshevik leaders. Lenin has drafted orders instructing his secret police to arrest the Czar, you, and the imperial family after he assumes control of the government. You will be sent to the Urals, to the town of Ekaterinburg, where you are to be held as prisoners in a dacha. He calls it the 'House of Special Purpose.'" He turns away from Alexandra, his face distorted with anguish.

Alexandra says, "It is as I suspected." She touches his shoulder and says, "Face me, Dmitri, and complete your report. There is more, is there not?"

He cannot look at her. With his head bowed and looking down, he speaks softly, "I am at your command, Your Majesty." Taking a deep breath, he continues. "No matter your status, or where you may be, the Czar and all the Romanov family are, and will always be, a threat to Lenin and his Communist movement. As Lenin's communications director, I am secretly charged with developing a secure code to transmit messages pertaining to the fate of the imperial family."

Dmitri pauses, as if seeking the courage to continue. Then he blurts out, "I am convinced, Madam, that when Lenin is firmly ensconced as the head of government, he will issue orders for the execution of the Czar, you, and even the children."

Alexandra gives a harsh gasp and stops abruptly, frozen with horror.

His voice thick with emotion, Dmitri continues. "I pray you forgive me, Your Majesty, for being the messenger of such morbid intelligence." Distraught, he kneels and kisses the hem of the Empress's gown.

В друго́й рắз

Late the following day, a heavy snow falls on Saint Petersburg. Alexandra paces the Aubusson carpet of her boudoir, her face ashen with fatigue and emotion. After receiving Dmitri's grim revelation of Lenin's murderous intentions, she had returned quickly to the palace, eager to flee to the only safety she knew, and eager to leave Dmitri, lest they be discovered and his life put into even greater danger. For the first time in her married life, she has kept an important secret from her husband, and the guilt gnaws viciously at her soul. Nonetheless, she reaffirms her vow of silence, though now she understands to the depth of her soul the egregious regicide the Bolsheviks have planned. So many lives around them, so many unknown lives could be at risk if she were to reveal anything. The burden of her new knowledge weighs intolerably on her frail shoulders. Never has she felt so alone, so helpless.

She has made it through the long day by pleading a severe migraine and begging her family and servants not to disturb her as she rests in her boudoir. The solicitous concern on their faces has only enhanced her misery and guilt at the terrible fate she is concealing from them.

There is a knock at the door, and a servant admits Maria Pavlovna. Forgetting imperial protocol, Alexandra flies into Maria's arms.

"Masha! Oh, Masha, Dmitri told me what Lenin plans for us. The worst thing possible! I don't know what to do." Alexandra bursts into tears, all the tension of the past twenty-four hours erupting from her tortured soul.

Maria guides the Empress to a chaise, sits beside her, holds her silently, and tries to ease Alexandra's wracking sobs. Maria rocks her soothingly, as she would a child, and softly strokes Alix's hair.

"Come now, Alix," she murmurs at last. "Tears won't help."

Gradually the Empress's sobs subside. "Masha, I had imagined what I thought was the worst—that the Czarist government would be overthrown and Nicky would lose his throne, but I had not even considered those diabolical Bolsheviks' bloodlust. They plan to murder us!"

"Regicide! Oh, my God!" Maria presses her fist against her lips, trying to stifle her shock and horror. "You and the children too? It cannot be!"

Alexandra clutches her friend with desperation. "What are we to do, Masha? How can we escape? King George has abandoned us. Our own cousin!" And she begins to sob again.

"Hush, Alix." Maria holds her close. "Remember what I told you the other day—there is still hope for you. For all of us."

"Not for us," Alexandra sobs. "Not for us. I spoke with Nicky again last night, not to reveal what you or Dmitri told me, but just to bring up again the possibility of our going into exile. And he refused even to listen. He is certain that the people of Russia love him so much, love the entire imperial family, that they would never allow harm to come to us. He will do nothing at all to save us. Nothing! We are doomed." She is overcome by her sobs.

"Oh, Alix." Maria holds her friend close, her own tears flowing freely. For several minutes the two women sit silently, unable to speak.

At last Alexandra stirs. "Masha, I couldn't sleep last night, thinking about the horror that awaits us, and trying, trying to think of a way to escape it. I had an idea. Please tell me what you think of this scheme."

Maria wipes away her tears and those on Alexandra's haggard face. "Of course, my dear. Tell me."

"Nicky will never leave Russia, and he will never allow me or the children to leave. But I wonder if there might be a way to save one of the children. Could I find a way to get one child out of here, one to go to that refuge in China that you told me about? Is that possible?"

Maria reflects for a moment. "It might be. But it would be much more difficult after the Bolsheviks are in power. However, if you move quickly, then perhaps with some help from our friends...."

She continues. "I can tell you only what I know myself, but it's enough to get someone to China, to safety." Maria moves to one of the chairs facing Alexandra's chaise. Leaning forward, she begins to speak softly. "Alix, you must remember that you have sworn yourself to secrecy. If you reveal what I am about to tell you to anyone, you will put many lives in peril and perhaps destroy all hope of an asylum for loyal Russians."

Alexandra nods solemnly. "I do understand, and I swear myself to secrecy."

Maria continues. "Grigori is a very clever and well-organized man. A true scientist, always thinking through every detail. Besides restoring the lamasery and creating orchards, agricultural fields, and herds of livestock to provide food, he has set up a clandestine escape route from the Trans-Siberian Railway into western China. It goes from Bolotnoye south into eastern Kyrgyzstan, and from there across the border into China. The lamasery is in a valley in the depths of the Altai Mountains. This is one of the most sparsely populated and unexplored places left on earth, and therefore one of the safest places for people like us to hide and plan for the future of our Russia."

Alexandra listens, wide-eyed.

"At each stage along the route, Grigori has established a guide, someone he can trust to make sure that travelers move safely to the next stop. They are all men completely loyal to us and to Mother Russia, men who for reasons of their own hate the Bolsheviks as much as we do. And their loyalty is well compensated—each receives payment in gold coin, usually Maria Theresa schillings, from every traveler who passes along the route. And all the guides are promised sanctuary for themselves and their families if they want it. "

"Grigori has devised a series of passwords and signals to allow travelers and guides to identify one another. Travelers bring whatever they can carry to start their new lives, as well as sufficient gold schillings to pay the guides.

There is no guarantee for your child's safety, but as far as I know, everyone has made it into China successfully."

She pauses and gazes at Alexandra, who seems fascinated by this information. Her face shows a bit of color, and her eyes are brighter with dawning hope. "Alix, I won't deceive you. Life at the lamasery is challenging. There are none of the comforts the imperial family is accustomed to. It's an agrarian community, and people there live very simply and work very hard. They grow their own food and make almost everything else they use. Whatever they cannot grow or make themselves, they enlist the aid of the local tribesmen to purchase quietly in the nearest Chinese town. But, they have a doctor—a retired army surgeon—and there are some well-educated people who have taken on the responsibility of teaching the children."

Alexandra listens intently, nodding with comprehension as she takes in the information.

Maria continues, "As I said, life there is Spartan, filled with work. But, for the inhabitants, there is the great comfort of knowing that they and their families are safe from the revolutionaries and the turmoil in Russia. They are living in what is really a Russian village, free of the godless viciousness preached by the Bolsheviks and other revolutionaries."

When Maria finishes speaking, Alexandra's face is serene. She breathes deeply, calmly.

"Masha, we Romanovs are not as pampered as we might seem, thanks to Nicky's simple tastes. The children have always been required to care for their own bedrooms and to maintain a plain diet and rigorous exercise. I think one of our children could adapt well enough. What matters is that one of them at least will survive."

"Are you quite certain, dear Alix, that you wish to do this?"

Alexandra sits up and reassumes the regal posture expected of her role. She raises her chin and her face assumes an expression of fierce determination. "Masha, my first duty is to save my children. And by God I shall save one of them at least!"

Maria sighs with relief. "Alix, if you can save only one, God will forgive His Majesty for his foolish optimism, his blithe disregard for his family's safety." Her voice is shaking with emotion. She reaches out to take Alexandra's hand, her eyes damp with sympathy.

"Then, dear Alix, let me give you these instructions. Here are all the stages of the route, along with the passwords and the identification signals. There is also the name of someone who can supply the necessary false documents in case your young traveler requires identification. Memorize every word, then burn the paper. Send with your child only what can be conveniently carried, and lots of gold. Demand absolute secrecy from the moment they leave the palace until they arrive at the lamasery. No display, no drama. He or she should leave the train quietly at Bolotnoye, then follow the stages of the route."

Alexandra nods. "What is the name of this place, Masha? Where precisely is it?"

"Alix, I can't tell you, even if I knew myself. It's too risky to allow so much information to circulate in these dangerous times. The information I have given you is sufficient to allow a traveler to arrive safely. That is all you or I need to know."

Alexandra nods again. "I understand. It just seems so far away, so hidden. I'm trying to imagine one of my children going there, to a place I can't even find on a map."

"Which child will you send?"

"I don't know." Alexandra shakes her head bleakly. "How can any mother make such a terrible choice? I would rather die right now than have to make this decision." Her eyes fill with tears.

She reaches out and grasps her friend's hands. "Pray for me, Masha," she pleads. "Pray that I have the strength to make this choice, and that I can save one child. Pray for us all, I beg of you."

"You are always in my prayers, Alix," Maria replies soothingly. "But you must move quickly. There is no knowing how much longer the route to the east will remain open. The revolutionaries will soon take Saint Petersburg. And once they are in control, it will be impossible to smuggle anyone out of the palace. You need to make your choice and all the arrangements as soon as possible."

"Yes, I understand," Alexandra responds wearily, but there is a spark of hope in her face. "I shall make the arrangements."

Maria stands and prepares to leave. "Alix, darling, I also came to tell you goodbye. All the turmoil here in Saint Petersburg is taking a severe toll on my nerves. I need to go home. In a few days I am leaving for Beryosha, my estate in the country. I want to immerse myself in the Russia I love, to live among the peasants and look out at the precious land of Mother Russia. I want to pray for Russia and make some decisions about my own future."

The two women embrace tearfully. "May God protect you and your family, dear Alix."

"And you as well, Masha. I pray that we shall meet again, in heaven if not here in Mother Russia."

4

Winter Palace, Saint Petersburg
18 January 1917

lexandra is sitting at her desk in her private sitting room. Hanging on the walls are oil portraits of the Czar and their five children. She is gazing at a silver-framed photograph of her grandmother, Queen Victoria, holding the infant Grand Duchess Olga. The Queen gazes lovingly at her great-granddaughter and newest godchild, Alexandra's first child.

The Empress is pale, with dark circles under her eyes. Her face is drawn with fatigue and stress, and her slim figure is almost gaunt. The stress of the past week is taking its toll on her frail constitution.

Since her last meeting with Maria Pavlovna, Alexandra has spent most of her time pondering the appalling choice she must make—which of her five children to try to save from the Bolsheviks' planned execution. She has tried to think of a way to save them all, somehow smuggling them out of the palace and sending them to China. But she can think of no way to accomplish this without arousing public suspicion. So, she has tried objectively to assess the qualities of each child to determine who might best be able to make an arduous and frightening journey alone, to a strange place far from the family.

Little Alexei is ruled out quickly. He is too young to undertake the journey alone or to maintain the necessary degree of secrecy. His fragile health and the constant threat of a hemophiliac episode would make any arduous journey a threat to his life. Between Alexei's childish impetuousness and his precarious physical condition, there are too many possibilities for exposure. No, Alexei wouldn't do.

The girls might manage better, but which of them to choose? Olga is level-headed, but she is so accustomed to her regal role as the eldest of the imperial children that it seems unlikely she could manage a clandestine escape without giving away her status. Tatiana is so affectionate and close to her family, and so tender toward her brother, she could never be persuaded to abandon the family. She has inherited Alexandra's timid nature and is never fully at ease outside the family circle. Marie, like Olga, takes her role as a Grand Duchess far too seriously to be able to travel inconspicuously or to relinquish it for life in a rough peasant community.

This leaves only Anastasia. The Empress's youngest daughter, her tomboy, her mischievous imp, just might succeed. Little Nastenka is the most daring and physically fearless of the imperial children. She is a gifted mimic and actress who delights in assuming other personalities and is the best performer in the little family theatricals that are such a pleasant part of palace life. Of all the children, she is the most independent and resourceful. To be sure, she would not willingly leave the family for a dangerous flight into the unknown, but perhaps she could be persuaded—somehow.

Alexandra sighs. The burden of secrecy weighs heavily on her, and even heavier is the abhorrent task of choosing one of her children for survival. And now she will have to add lies and manipulation to her litany of sins and secrets. The only way she will convince Anastasia to leave the family is to lie to her about the situation, to convince her that all the family will meet again at the end of the journey.

I've never lied to my children, Alexandra thinks to herself, *nor to my husband. But now I must weave a web of deceit in order to save one of them. Oh God, why must I bear this burden?* She sighs heavily.

Другое место

Alexandra turns off the electric lights, and lights a few candles that bathe her boudoir in chiaroscuro lighting for tonight's clandestine meeting. Shortly, she hears a soft knock on the door. "Enter." Senior Lieutenant Kirik Pirogov approaches and stands stiffly at attention. Alexandra leans forward and says, "Thank you for coming, Kirik. Please make yourself comfortable on that settee."

Pirogov bows, advances, and seats himself. "Thank you, Madam. I came as soon as my mid-watch was over. I am honored that you have asked me here. How may I be of service?"

Without ado, Alexandra focuses her sharp blue eyes directly on Pirogov. "Am I correct in believing that you have a special affection for Anastasia?"

Somewhat taken aback by the Empress's directness, Kirik replies sheepishly, "Yes, Madam. I know that I could never hope to ask for her hand in marriage, but I shall always have the deepest regard for her. I would give my life for her." Then, lest he be perceived as assuming too much, he hurriedly adds, "As I would for anyone in the imperial family. It is my honor and duty to serve the Czar."

"You are such a goose, Kirik." Alexandra is at her most imperious. She has shed her fatigue and sits erectly. Her voice is grave. "Tonight I don't need patriotic platitudes. We both know that Russia and our Romanov regime are lost. The revolutionaries will have Saint Petersburg in a few weeks. The guns to the southeast are sounding closer every day. The workers are rioting in the streets."

"I fear you are correct, Madam." Kirik sits straight, more confident now that the conversation has shifted away from his personal feelings. "Surely you and your family will escape. The Trans-Siberian Railway through the Ural Mountains remains open, but for how long, I cannot predict."

Alexandra interrupts him, "Kirik, enough! The Czar, the children, and I are staying here, in Saint Petersburg. Several times I have cautioned the Czar that we should leave, perhaps reestablish our regime east of the Urals. He refuses. He is stubborn and naïve. He is supremely confident that our army will defeat the Germans, the Austrians, and the Bolsheviks. I have implored him at least to send our children privately to England. Again, he refuses. He says, 'Our children are Mother Russia, and Czarevich Alexei is the next Romanov Czar. If the children leave, it would mean that we have conceded defeat and abandoned our sovereignty. And that we shall never do!'" Alexandra's face is grim.

"Because the Czar is both my husband and my sovereign, I must obey his wishes." She continues in a hushed tone, "I am resigned to the Czar's will." She stands and moves to the window, looking out over the dark, snow-covered gardens. Her posture is rigid, but her pale face, reflected in the glass panes, is distorted with anguish.

For a time, neither speaks. Then Alexandra continues in a more positive tone. "There are several actions we can take to save a part of the Romanov dynasty. Kirik, listen to me carefully. I have a secret mission for you. Only you and I will know of it. Do you understand? I demand your vow of complete secrecy in all that pertains to this mission. Do I have it?"

Kirik sits erect on the settee. "On my honor, I swear to secrecy. I will do anything you ask, Your Majesty."

"Very well. Of all my children, it is Anastasia, my lovely tomboy, my enfant terrible, who has the mental and physical strength to continue the Romanov succession in these troubled times. We must do what we can to ensure her safety."

"Madam, I will help in any way that I am able."

"Your mission has dual goals." Alexandra nods toward an ebony box on the corner of her desk. "In that coffer is a cache of some of our personal jewelry and the Romanov imperial crown that was designed for Empress Catherine the Second—Saint Catherine's Crown. I will not let these treasures of Mother Russia fall into the hands of those despicable Bolsheviks."

Realizing that the Empress probably will continue with details of his assignment, Pirogov leans forward slightly to insure that he hears precisely her forthcoming message.

"Senior Lieutenant Pirogov, your mission is to spirit this Crown and the Romanov jewels to safety outside of Russia." The Empress pauses. Then she speaks with spirited emphasis, "Over the past several months, some of our friends have left Saint Petersburg, Moscow, and other cities in Russia. They have traveled over a secret route to a place of refuge in western China—exactly where, I do not know. This place is a community wholly populated by Russians loyal to the Czar. You will travel with these royal treasures to this refuge, where you will be safe. Remain there until it is propitious to return to Russia."

She glances toward the window, sighs deeply, and says, "Within a few years, should it not be safe to return, take these royal treasures to the United States of America and donate them to the Smithsonian Institution."

Taken aback by this extraordinary task, Pirogov allows a deep and puzzling frown to leap across his brow. He envisions disaster. *I know nothing of such matters.* He turns to look at the coffer, and his latent resolve emerges with purpose. "I am honored that you trust me with this secret mission, your Majesty. But I'm at a loss as to how I can manage it. I have no experience in clandestine activities. I am only a line soldier."

"Nonsense," responds Alexandra curtly. "You come from one of the finest families in Russia. Your relatives and ancestors have served the czars and Mother Russia for centuries. Now it is your turn. An Okhrana general and I have made all the arrangements."

Pirogov, engulfed in apprehension, commands his resolve, stands, and makes a slight bow. He responds with military precision, "I am entirely at your command, your Majesty."

Alexandra smiles broadly, and nods. Her voice is clear and firm. "Return to the settee, Pirogov. There is more to your mission. I shall speak frankly." She looks directly at Pirogov to ensure that his attention is focused sharply on her. Satisfied, she continues, "I will send Grand Duchess Anastasia to that refuge in China as soon as I am able. She is the only one of my children who could engineer the trip successfully."

A thrilling shiver embraces Kirik. A slow smile creeps across his face as he realizes that he will be with the woman he loves.

Empress Alexandra continues, in her imperious voice. "Listen carefully, Kirik. You are to meet Anastasia in this refuge and, when appropriate, you are to produce a male child—a Romanov heir to the Crown of all the Russias. And you will name him after his grandfather, Nicholas Alexandrovich Romanov, III."

Clearly shaken and embarrassed by Her Majesty's inappropriate command, he avoids her eyes and stumbles to form a coherent response. "I understand, Your Majesty."

Alexandra relaxes in her chair and congratulates herself. Finally, she has said what must be said. She has rehearsed this scene in her mind many times, and now she feels a slight exhilaration that the Romanov direct line may well continue. Soon, the reality of the times overwhelms her optimism and she realizes that she will never hold her grandson to her bosom and shower him with kisses. A few slow tears slip down her cheeks.

Pirogov pretends not to notice.

The Empress gathers herself and exclaims, "Excellent, Kirik. That matter is closed." She looks at the closet and nods. "In that closet, you will find a suitcase containing the uniform of a Bolshevik political commissar attached to the headquarters of the Third Division—Lenin's own. Also, there are the clothes, apron, and coat of an ironworker, as well as a worn valise in which to carry the coffer." She opens the bottom drawer of her desk and withdraws a packet and a purse. She opens the purse and spreads the contents on her desktop. "Here are two dozen Maria Theresa gold schillings, several thousand rubles, and a thousand British pounds sterling."

Pirogov notes this currency without comment.

The Empress continues, "Here are forged papers that will let you pass as either a Bolshevik commissar or a worker from the Kirovsky Iron Foundry. The name on these documents is Anton Yureivich Andreev, your *nom de guerre*." She adds forcefully, "Whilst incognito, you are to purchase a ticket on the Trans-Siberian Railway to Bolotnoye, a modest town that lies about one hundred and twenty kilometers east of Novosibirsk."

With a potpourri of images whirling in his mind, he manages to say, "I understand, Madam."

"If I may be so bold, Madam, how trustworthy is this Nikolsky?"

"Enough that the Okhrana vouched for him." With a touch of pique, she continues, "Is that satisfactory?"

"My apologies, Empress Alexandra, if my question was inopportune."

She continues, "While there, discretely ask Nikolsky if a young woman named Anna Bogrova has contacted him and if he knows where she might be.

"May I ask, who is Anna Bogrova?"

"That name, my dear Kirik, is the *nom de guerre* of my daughter, Grand Duchess Anastasia Romanov."

Chagrined at his *faux pas*, he says, "Thank you, Madam."

"Do not trouble yourself, Kirik. It is nothing." Alexandra leans back in her chair and recalls the many times that she had rehearsed this scene in her mind. Now she is greatly pleased that her dual plan is in motion. Alexandra's voice is clear and firm. "Kirik, do you understand completely my mission? What questions have you?"

Pirogov gazes at the Empress. "None, Madam. I understand your instructions."

He maintains his military courtesy and does not voice his reservations at what seems a perilous and probably foolhardy mission. He stands and bows stiffly. "I will do my best, Madam."

"Best will not do, Senior Lieutenant Kirik Antonievich Pirogov. I demand total success." She pauses for effect. "I trust you to protect Anastasia—with your life if necessary—and to safeguard Russia's treasures."

Pirogov responds in his finest military voice, "You have my word as a Russian officer, Madam." Nonetheless, he is clearly shaken by the responsibilities with which the Empress has charged him.

Confident that Pirogov understands her orders and will execute them with consummate skill, she concludes, "Anton Yureivich Andreev, you are now a Bolshevik—a common laborer. Act like one. Void your aristocratic manners and your military bearing. You are a working man. Be one in body and soul. I have notified your watch commander that you are on special duty at the palace and not expected to return to your duty section. Take the coffer and those clothes. Leave now. God be with you."

5

Winter Palace, Saint Petersburg
19 January 1917

Alexandra smiles gently and shifts in her chair. "My dear, let us change the subject and discuss some matters of singular importance."

Anastasia squirms on the chaise. She is accustomed to the seriousness of her mother's voice.

"Nastenka, my dear vivacious tomboy, you are now an adult. Your childhood is over. As a grand duchess of the Russian Empire, a Romanov, you must accept wholeheartedly the responsibilities that God has bestowed on you in your royal station."

"I understand, Mamma." With a mischievous smile, Anastasia continues, "What is my first task? Do I charm the French ambassador's wife?" In a teasing voice, she purrs, "Do I flirt with the Italian ambassador? Do I write insolent letters to that horrid Lenin person?" In a pleading tone she asks, "Please, Mamma, what am I to do?"

Oh, my precious daughter. Alexandra gazes at her daughter's sweet face. *You are so untouched by life. How dare I send you away from us, from me?*

After a thoughtful pause, Alexandra responds more reproachfully than she intends. "Don't be frivolous, my dear. Today we must speak realistically. Your father and I have protected you from the fact that we are losing the war with Germany and Austria, and that we have failed to arrest the tide of the revolutionaries—the Bolsheviks and others." Alexandra sighs.

"On reflection, we probably should have been more forthright with our children."

"Mamma, you're the best mother in the entire world, and I know your intentions are kind, but I'm not uninformed about world affairs. I read the revolutionary pamphlets that are smuggled into the palace. I hear the servants and guards talking. I have some knowledge of what's happening in Russia."

Alexandra smiles faintly at her daughter's impertinent tone. *This is exactly the spirit of independence and curiosity that is essential for a survivor.* Inwardly, the Empress compliments herself on her choice.

"Nastenka, my task today is to acquaint you with the real world as it is now. Not in the careless prattle heard about the palace. Not in your papa's optimistic musings. Please listen carefully. What I am about to tell you is painfully true. There is no question of its veracity. By our love, mother to daughter, I vouch wholeheartedly for it. Take it entirely to your heart."

Anastasia is taken aback by the serious tone of her mother's voice, her intensity, and her obvious sincerity. She sits silently.

Alexandra continues, "Please understand to the depth of your soul that our Russian Empire is in perilous danger. In a few months, the Romanov dynasty will no longer rule Russia. We have lost. The Bolsheviks will have Saint Petersburg, our palace, everything. They will have total control of our empire. Political chaos will reign for months, probably years. Our family may be separated for a while." She looks to the window and sees soft snow falling. With enhanced courage, Alexandra lies. "I do not know what will happen to us."

"Oh, Mamma! How can this be true? Cannot the army and the police defeat those ruffians?" Anastasia begins to weep as she realizes the truth and gravity of her mother's comments.

Her sobs are knives that pierce Alexandra's heart and, for a moment, the Empress looks away, biting her lips to prevent herself from crying. In a few seconds, her self-control restored, she turns back to her daughter and says in a reproachful voice, "Stop your sobbing. You are an adult. A Romanov! I expect you to behave accordingly and face the real world with understanding and courage. Unfortunately, it's too late for our army to halt the Bolsheviks and the Germans."

Alexandra moves to the chaise and puts her arms around her daughter. "Be brave, my darling." Alexandra's heart is pounding and her mouth feels dry with tension. *Can I do this?* she asks herself. *Can I send my child away from me? Oh, God, please give me strength.*

When Anastasia recovers her composure, her mother continues. "Here is your first responsibility as a Romanov grand duchess. No matter what happens to our family, your duty is to survive—to continue the direct line of the Romanov dynasty." She pauses for emphasis. "To fulfill this responsibility in this hostile environment, you will have to leave Russia."

Anastasia interrupts her mother. "Dear mother, I do not know what you are telling me. I cannot leave you and our family. I belong in Saint Petersburg with you."

"Nastenka, enough. You are an adult Romanov. You will fulfill your royal obligations."

Unable to counter a royal command, Anastasia responds, "Yes, mamma. I will do as you demand." Still apprehensive, she says, "I am so troubled by all this talk of revolution, war, and our family being separated. How will it end?"

In a conciliatory voice, Alexandra says, "Nastenka, listen carefully, and I will explain." She pauses to gather her thoughts correctly. "The Germans and Austrians control the way to the west. The revolutionaries dominate the northern and southern routes. Only the way east is open. Hence, our only option is for you to travel through Siberia on the Trans-Siberian Railway to China."

Anastasia gasps and turns pale. She does not speak.

Alexandra notices but continues, "How long Czarist trains will operate, we cannot tell." She withdraws a map from the top desk drawer and places it on the desk. "Daughter, look at this map. I have marked your route."

"China!" Anastasia gazes at her mother with puzzled and fearful eyes. Her brain is reeling with the frightful news: her family is to be torn asunder, her sheltered and pampered life to vanish; Russia to be controlled by Bolsheviks, and more. She moves to the desk and glances at the map.

"Mamma, you frighten me. Go to China? I know nothing of China, Siberia, or how to travel. I have lived in our palaces all my life. I do not know how to purchase a ticket, buy a meal, or sleep in a strange bed. How am I to manage?" She embraces her mother. "How I am to accomplish your charge? One of my older sisters would achieve your tasks better than I. Choose Tatiana, she is the most capable." Slow tears embrace her cheeks.

With her arms around Alexandra, the Empress continues in a comforting voice, "Nastenka, I have the utmost confidence in you for this particular task. Your brashness and dauntless resolve convince me that you will accomplish my charge with singular spirit. I have other tasks for your sisters. Your father and Alexei will be with me." Alexandra struggles to form the next sham statement. "You will succeed, and we shall be a family again, perhaps in Great Britain with our cousins." She kisses Anastasia on her pale cheek.

"Is it true, mamma?" Anastasia says, her voice almost a whisper.

"Of course, my dear." *Mea culpa. Mea culpa.*

Shortly Anastasia, understanding that she has no options, says, "I will do as you ask."

Alexandra speaks with her full imperial authority. "This matter is settled." She retrieves the map and returns it to the drawer. She continues, "Over the next few days we will plan the details of your task." Looking directly into Anastasia's eyes, she demands, "What we have discussed today is confidential between you and me. And absolutely no one else. Not your sisters or Alexei, not even your father. Not Father Cyril either, not even in your confessions. This must be our special secret. Do you understand my charge to the depth of your soul?"

Still apprehensive that her family will be dispersed, Anastasia responds softly, "Yes, Mamma."

Alexandra goes to her desk and picks up a Bible. She places Anastasia's right hand on the heavy book. Sternly, she continues, "Swear on this Holy Bible, blessed by Archbishop Kazansky of Saint Petersburg, that your silence is sacred."

Anastasia stands slowly to face her mother. In a weak and wavering voice she says, "I do swear in my heart and soul."

"Swear on this Holy Bible that you accept the responsibilities I have detailed and that you will execute them with all the skill, industry, and responsibility you possess."

More forcefully this time, Anastasia proclaims, "I do swear in my heart and soul, so help me God."

"Thank you, my darling daughter. The die is cast." Placing the Bible back on the desk, Alexandra says, "Come and give your mother a big hug."

"Excellent." Alexandra pauses to squeeze her puzzled daughter. She picks up a small jewelry box and withdraws a silver ring mounted with Saint Olga's Cross. Taking Anastasia's right hand, she puts the ring on her index finger. "At all times keep this ring on your finger until we meet again after the war." *God help me. The lies flow from my heart without shame or regret.*

Anastasia gazes at the ring and wonders at its significance. She asks, "Why do you give me this ring? What is its purpose?"

"It is a recognition token for your journey to China. Loyal agents will identify it and help you on your journey along the Trans-Siberian Railway. We'll talk more about the ring tomorrow."

Alexandra braces to tell Nastenka her covert destination. With conviction, she begins, "In advance of the Bolsheviks' imminent overthrow of our Czarist government, a coup d'état in effect, Russians of all stripes have emigrated to a secret refuge in western China. They live in an isolated community where they will be secure from the coming chaos in Russia. The residents are loyal to our Czar, the Orthodox Church, and Mother Russia. I am asking you to travel to this refuge and live there. One day soon you will hear from your father or me, and we will become a family again." *My soul cries in shame for my lying sins.*

Weakly and without much conviction, Anastasia replies, "Yes, Mamma."

"A few moments ago we spoke about Lieutenant Pirogov. What I am going to tell you also is strictly confidential. Understand? "

"Yes, Mamma."

"I have sent Kirik on a special mission to China in my service. He is traveling under the *nom de guerre* Anton Yurievich Andreev. Store this name deep in your memory."

"I understand what you're saying, but it's all so confusing. Why does Kirik have to have a new name?"

"It's for his safety and the successful completion of his assignment. If you were to speak of his mission—to anyone—then you might well cost him his life."

Anastasia backs away from her mother, her face filled with shock and fear. "Cost him his life? What are you not telling me?"

"Secrets that you do not need to know for now—for Kirik's safety, yours, and that of many other loyal Russians."

"Why this secrecy? I'm so confused!" She pauses and crosses her arms across her bosom. "Does this have to do with that Lenin fellow?"

"In many ways it does," Alexandra says gently. "Nastenka, with all our love, trust your mother to know what is best for our family. Do I have your word of silence regarding Kirik?"

Weakly, Anastasia replies, "Of course, Mamma. I would do nothing to harm Kirik."

"Very well. I will outline the procedures for your travel and how to contact our agents in Siberia. What is critically important is that you must travel incognito. You will no longer be Grand Duchess Anastasia. You will use the passport and travel documents I have for you in the name of Anna Bogrova—your *nom de guerre*."

Resigned to the inevitable and now beginning to understand the scheme's *raison d'être*, she responds perfunctorily, "Yes, Mamma."

Alexandra stands. "I have one final charge, my darling." Opening the bottom drawer in her desk, Alexandra removes a leather pouch. She withdraws ten Maria Theresa gold schillings and a cache of several Western currencies. "Take these schillings and sew them into the hem of the dress you are wearing. Spread them so the skirt will hang evenly. Do this secretly, so that no one knows—not your sisters and especially none of the staff. When the Bolsheviks force us to leave the palace, put this dress in your luggage, and pack the currencies in your intimates. Do not wear the dress again until I give permission. One day, when I find it propitious, I will tell you to put it on. On that day, you will begin your journey. Use the currencies to pay your expenses as you make your way through Siberia and into China. The schillings are for payment to our agents, bribes, and extraordinary expenses."

"Mamma, I have no knowledge of the value of these things or what anything costs or how to pay for things. Will you teach me?"

Before answering, Alexandra recalls that she has had no experience with commerce. "Unfortunately, I cannot. I also have no information about the schillings' value or the prices of goods and services." Silence permeates the room. "I will hire a trustworthy tutor to teach your sisters and you about economics, money, and market values."

"An excellent idea, Mamma. I will learn quickly."

The Empress speaks in a precise and deliberate voice. "You are to leave the train at Bolotnoye, a small town in western Siberia. It is about five hundred miles north of the Chinese border. Find the telegraph agent at the railroad station. His name is Vaslav Nikolsky. Let him see the Saint Olga's ring. He will know that you are a loyal Russian. Give him one schilling and ask, 'When is the next train to Duzhba?' He will guide you to the Czarists' Russian refuge in China—either directly or through other agents."

"Also, discretely inquire from Nikolsky whether a Russian named Anton Andreev has been there and ask where he has gone. Kirik may have arranged to meet you somewhere along the railway. If not, you will meet Kirik in the Russian refuge in China."

A thin smile suffuses across Anastasia's face at the prospect of being with Kirik. The smile fades quickly as the reality of her task comes to the fore. Her voice has a tone of childish petulance. "You are asking so much of me! I need time to review your instructions. They are so many and so alien that they whirl in my brain."

Alexandra wants to weep with sympathy for her young daughter, so suddenly overwhelmed by new responsibilities. Once again, she exerts her steely self-control and speaks soothingly. "Nastenka, for the safety of the family, never attempt to contact any of us."

With a questioning eye, Anastasia responds, "Yes, Mamma."

"And never reveal your true identity. Should circumstances prevent us from uniting as a family, you should emigrate to the United States of

America. There, you may be the Russian Grand Duchess Anastasia Nikolaevna Romanov."

Alexandra waits for a response from Anastasia, which does not come. She continues, "Put all my instructions this evening in the back of your mind. Let them simmer there and meld slowly into your memory. When the time comes for you to act, they will spring to life and guide you correctly."

"Mamma, I am deeply stressed and tired."

After a deep sigh, Alexandra smiles. "That's enough for today." She embraces her daughter. "Go back to your rooms, my darling. And remember, what we have spoken of this morning must remain our secret. We shall speak of it again, and I shall try my best to answer your questions. In the meantime, steel yourself to the tasks I have outlined for you."

"Yes, Mamma." Anastasia kisses her mother and quietly leaves the room, her face solemn and thoughtful.

As the door closes behind Anastasia, Alexandra sinks exhausted onto her chaise, overcome by the burden of controlling her own fear and sorrow while starting her youngest daughter on the first steps of a still-dubious escape from the family's fate. *Am I doing the right thing?* she wonders. *And when shall I send her away?*

The questions swirl in Alexandra's troubled mind.

6

Guards' Barracks, Winter Palace, Saint Petersburg
19 January 1917

A concerned Kirik Pirogov enters his quarters in the palace's military bivouac. In his hands are a shabby valise containing the ebony box, the envelope of forged papers, and Alexandra's instructions. A worn suitcase holds the Bolshevik uniform and the ironworker's outfit. The gold schillings are in a purse attached to his belt.

His two-room apartment is austere, no more than a small bedroom and a bath. There is a single bed, a pine dresser and armoire, a straight-backed chair, and a small table that serves as a desk. On the stone-gray walls are photographs of his parents and the Czar.

For several hours, Pirogov sits and ponders his task and options. He is laced with fear and doubts about his abilities and how best to fulfill his tasks, and he feels burdened with misgivings about what lies ahead. Near dawn, he draws on all his inner strength and resolves to address Alexandra's assignment with all the courage and initiative he can muster.

One thing he has realized in his pondering is that no matter what he does, it is highly improbable that he can successfully deliver the box and its contents to a Russian compound somewhere in the interior of China. There are far too many unknown hazards lying between Saint Petersburg and the isolated émigré community. With chaos engulfing Russia, he speculates that it is unlikely he will even get to China. He studies this dilemma for a time but cannot resolve it. Fatigued, he finally lies down and sleeps.

Six hours later, Pirogov snaps awake with an idea. He recalls his meeting with Colonel Gustaf Mannerheim, the Swedish military *attaché*, at the Christmas Ball. Mannerheim, though from a neutral country, had suggested that Kirik join him for dinner one day soon and had offered his help in other matters.

Pirogov pulls the ebony box from the valise, drops a large bead of sealing wax on the lock, and then pushes his ring, bearing the family's coat of arms, into the soft wax. He puts on his dress-blue uniform, puts the box back in the valise, and hurries out of the barracks. Moving with purpose, and constantly alert to the people around him, he walks the eight blocks to the Swedish Embassy on Malya Konyshennays Street. At the reception desk, he asks to see Colonel Mannerheim. A Swedish army sergeant escorts him to Mannerheim's office.

Mannerheim is seated behind a large walnut desk scattered with papers. Pirogov enters and, standing at attention, salutes. "Good morning, Colonel Mannerheim."

Rising from his chair, Mannerheim returns the salute. "Ah, so it is Senior Lieutenant Pirogov, who so charmed the Grand Duchess Anastasia," Mannerheim says jovially. "It is a pleasure to see you again, young man. Relax, sit, and tell me what brings you to me."

Mannerheim's office is large, with plush carpets, four file cabinets, and a safe against the far wall. Behind the desk are the Swedish flag and a portrait of King Oscar Gustav V.

"Tell me, Pirogov, how may I be of service? From the serious look on your face, I know this is not a casual visit."

Pirogov leans forward and says, "Colonel, I am here to ask you a special favor in a matter of state that requires scrupulous discretion and maximum secrecy. I realize that what I am going to ask is a great imposition. Unfortunately, I am not authorized to discuss the details. Before I continue, may I have your word that you will erase all records showing that I was here today, and that you will keep my words confidential?"

Mannerheim puts both of his elbows on his desk and looks Pirogov square in his eyes. "You intrigue me, Senior Lieutenant. Yes, I will do as you have asked. But, please understand that whatever it is, this favor must not compromise Sweden's neutrality in this ghastly and nonsensical war of overblown egos."

Pirogov sits ramrod straight in his chair. Without blinking, he says, "Colonel, you have my word as an officer in the Czar's service and as a gentleman, that my request does not involve Sweden's neutrality." He twists in his chair and turns his eyes to the pen set on the desk. Returning his attention to Mannerheim, he continues, somewhat sheepishly, "Perhaps only tangentially."

Cocking an eyebrow, Mannerheim asks, "Just how tangentially, Senior Lieutenant Pirogov?"

Pirogov realizes he is in a quandary: he must either reveal the secret of the box or prevaricate. He tries to tread the middle of these two extremes. He responds, "If I proceed, I must have your assurance that what I tell you will remain your secret, and only your secret."

"You pique my interest mightily." Mannerheim leans back in his chair. "I agree to your terms, Pirogov. What is on your mind? I am always ready to listen to secrets." With an ironic smile, he adds, "That, after all, is my job as military attaché."

Pirogov removes the ebony box from his valise and puts it on the desk. "In this box are personal items of great value, and one state treasure. With the chaos in the streets and the future of the Russian Empire in flux, my principal has directed me to sequester these items in a secure environment. My request is that you put this box in your diplomatic pouch and send it to Stockholm. Then, have it sent in the diplomatic pouch to your counterpart in Peking. In two or three years, God willing, I will be at your embassy there to retrieve the box. I will not have any identification, but I will establish my bona fides with the code phrase 'Sophie Friederike Auguste von Anhalt-Zerbst, Catherine the Great.'"

Perplexed, Mannerheim says, "I'm impressed, Senior Lieutenant Pirogov. You spin an intriguing tale." After a moment of reflection, Mannerheim nods slightly. "Please write down that code phrase. I will never be able to remember it." As Pirogov hands him a slip of paper with the code phrase on it, Mannerheim asks, half seriously, "Tell me, is your assignment in the Royal Guard a cover for your activities as an Okhrana agent?"

Pirogov, with a touch of stiffness in his voice, responds, "I assure you, Colonel Mannerheim, that I am not an Okhrana agent. I have a critically important assignment to complete. And I need your help."

"Relax, Pirogov, I was teasing you." Mannerheim's face is coldly serious. "I will comply exactly with your request. You have my word of honor."

"Thank you. I have no way to repay this debt, but I assure you of my deepest gratitude." Pirogov continues, "One last thought. If I do not claim this box within four years, then it is to be sent to the Swedish Embassy in Washington, D.C. They are to send it to the Smithsonian Institution with instructions to hold it for twenty years. If, in that time, a White Russian female, about forty years old and with deep blue eyes, does not claim it by giving the correct password, the Smithsonian may keep it."

Mannerheim wonders how he can keep this deal with Pirogov off the record from his superiors and meddling government bureaucrats. He decides to put it into a sealed metal container with his own signet wax impression on the lock, and mark it "For Peking Military Attaché's Eyes Only."

"Indeed! Senior Lieutenant Pirogov, you have a shrewd scheme. It is just the type of mischief I like." Taking the box, he rises, goes to the safe, opens it, and puts the box on the bottom shelf. He snaps the door shut and spins the combination dial. "Your box will leave for Stockholm in tomorrow's pouch with my detailed instructions."

Resuming his seat, Mannerheim leans back and crosses his arms over his broad chest. "You realize, I expect, that my encounter with you at the Christmas Ball was not an accident. Your reputation, young man, is most impressive. And your future in your beloved Mother Russia is doubtful at best."

"What do you mean?" Pirogov asks suspiciously.

"We both know that Russia has lost the war, and the revolutionaries will soon be in control of the government. There will be no place in their Russia for a man like yourself—loyal, honorable, brave. These Bolsheviks, thugs all of them, will make the worst governments we have known so far seem absolutely benevolent by comparison. You understand that, I'm sure."

Pirogov nods solemnly. "Yes, of course I do. This situation is what lies behind my mission here today."

"And it's not only Russia that will suffer," Mannerheim continues. "These Bolsheviks plan to spread their poison all over the world. They're vicious thugs, and dangerous because some of them are very clever. Their victory in Russia will threaten all of Russia's neighbors—indeed, every civilized country in the world."

"I agree," Pirogov replies. Relieved of his concern about the safety of the coffer of jewels, he begins to relax in Mannerheim's friendly company. The Swedish Embassy feels like a peaceful haven away from the tempest outside in the streets.

"As I said, there will be no place for men like you in the Bolsheviks' Russia. But a man such as you might play a very important role in helping to prevent the contagion of Bolshevism from spreading into other countries." Mannerheim pulls himself up and leans forward over his desk. "Let me be blunt. The reason I sought you out at the ball was to look you over as a possible recruit to the Swedish secret service. We could use your courage and your knowledge of Russia. Are you interested?"

Pirogov is dumbstruck. The offer to continue battle against Russia's enemies, fighting from the safety of neutral Sweden, is deeply tempting. For a moment, he is pulled by the thought of an escape from the danger and madness that lie just outside the embassy walls.

"Thank you for the offer, Colonel." Pirogov breathes deeply, as though to rid himself of temptation. "But my visit here is only one part of a larger mission to which I am committed. It is my hope that in fulfilling this mission successfully, I will serve Mother Russia in another way."

"My offer stands. If you ever change your mind, just call at any Swedish embassy, anywhere in the world. Give them my name."

"Thank you, sir." Pirogov rises. "And now I must be on my way. I am grateful for your help."

Mannerheim stands. "My pleasure." The two men shake hands. "Good luck, Pirogov, and God be with you."

Другое место

Kirik Pirogov strolls along the crowded Nevsky Prospekt en route to his quarters. He is pleased that he has successfully accomplished the first phase of his overall plan to execute Empress Alexandra's instructions.

But, as an army officer trained to obey commands without question, and as a member of a family that had served the czars for generations, he is deeply troubled that he has disobeyed the Empress's express orders. He reasons that although he disregarded her charge to carry the box to China, he knows that sending it to Peking via the neutral Swedish diplomatic route ensures a much larger margin of success. At least the box will shortly be out of Russia and in safe hands. And, whatever happens to him, the box and its contents will be safe from the revolutionaries.

On the other hand, he has created another equally vexing problem. If he does not carry the box via the clandestine route from Bolotnoye that the Empress mapped for him, then he must make his way to Peking, retrieve the box, and smuggle it into the White Russian community somewhere in western China—exactly where in western China he does not know.

The trip to Peking will be difficult and perhaps dangerous. The entire area is rife with banditry and violence. If he reaches Peking, he will have to finesse information about the location of the White community in western China from the White Russians there.

Suddenly, a grungy fellow dressed as an ironworker comes from behind and walks beside him. "Do not look at me," he whispers. "Keep walking at your normal pace. I am Dmitri, an agent who knows the Empress. I have contacts within the senior leadership of the Bolshevik Party. Because of your close friendship with the imperial family, you are on their arrest list. Leave Saint Petersburg." The fellow drifts away.

Startled, Pirogov wonders if the encounter and the warning were sincere or some trick of an unknown enemy. He returns to his quarters, sits in his chair, and reviews the encounter. He cannot decide if this warning is genuine or spurious. Because he has been relieved of his military duties, the encounter with Dmitri influences him to immediately begin the second phase of his plan. If he is going to be a Bolshevik, he must look like one. He needs to change his appearance, toughen his hands, and learn to move and speak like a worker—beginning now.

7

Guards' Barracks, Winter Palace, Saint Petersburg
21 January 1917

At breakfast in the officers' mess, all the talk is about the Czar and his family decamping from the Winter Palace and moving to the elegant Alexander Palace at Tsarskoe Selo, about seventeen miles south of Saint Petersburg. Though no official explanation for this move is given, the reason is obvious: fear for the safety of the imperial family.

Angry crowds riot incessantly in the streets, egged on by fiery harangues from Lenin, Trotsky, Kerensky, and other revolutionaries. The people are exhausted after three years of a losing war, the Czarist government's totalitarianism, economic turmoil, and lack of food. Key members of the army and navy have deserted, engaged in sabotage, and mutinied against their officers. Mobs clamor at the palace gates, demanding that the Czar abdicate and surrender to their leaders for trial on charges of treason and murder. The Commander of the Palace Guard, Major Fedor Linde, orders his men not to fire, but they are strained to keep the mobs off the palace grounds.

As Pirogov goes through each day, his thoughts are mostly elsewhere. His first concern is for the imperial family, but he assures himself that they will be safe at Tsarskoe Selo. The family's move and the increasing chaos in the streets convince him that he himself must leave Saint Petersburg as soon as he can. The mysterious informant who accosted him on the street was correct—soon Saint Petersburg will no longer be safe for anyone who is not clearly allied with the revolutionaries. He had not foreseen the Czar abandoning the Winter Palace, nor the riots becoming so massive and rancorous. So far, the Imperial Guards, police, army, and mounted Cossacks have not exercised their full force to quell the riots. They have used their weapons only when threatened, and there have been only a few casualties among the rioters. But how long this quasi-truce can continue is impossible to predict.

As the days pass with mounting violence, Pirogov wonders how much longer the regime can last. He understands the vulnerability of his own position—an aristocrat such as himself would surely be singled out for punishment or death in the event of a complete collapse of order in the capital. But he has not yet had time to decide how best to make his way out of the chaos of the revolution and into China.

Alone each night in his quarters, Pirogov ponders his diminishing options. Finally, he decides his best course is to return to Beryosha, his family home in Torzhok. There, he can complete his travel plans and make his transformation from czarist officer to proletarian workman. He can also confer with his mother, who has already made her own retreat to the comparative safety of the countryside.

Because of the violence in the streets, Pirogov realizes, he cannot travel in his uniform or in civilian clothes because they would make him too conspicuous. Also, he knows that he cannot yet pass as an ironworker. His manner is too polished and his careful grooming and soft hands would betray him immediately to anyone who looked too closely. He needs a temporary disguise, something that will not only cover him as fully as possible but will discourage anyone from coming too near.

Late one evening, after the barracks had become quiet and most people had left the grounds, Pirogov moves stealthily to the head gardener's shed, slipping into the shadows whenever anyone approaches his path. Hanging on a peg are some bedraggled clothes that reek of manure, dirt, and sweat. On another peg is a large, badly worn, and very dirty wool coat. It's late January, and no one is about. Quickly, Pirogov wraps the clothes and coat into a tight bundle and leaves quietly.

For the next several days, Pirogov quietly settles his affairs and packs his well-traveled and much-battered valise. He makes no mention of his planned trip to his fellow officers. Recalling Alexandra's statement that he had been officially detailed to the palace, he sees no reason to explain his departure. His comrades' ignorance will protect him, and them, if he fails to make his escape.

В друго́й рӑз

It is early morning, long before the winter dawn in Saint Petersburg. Most of the city is still asleep, including the rioters who clog the streets during the day and evening hours. Pirogov rises and bathes, but omits his usual close shave, reasoning that a bit of scraggy beard will go better with the rough workingman's disguise. He puts the money belt around his waist, then dons the gardener's clothes to assume the identity of Anton Yurievich Andreev. After a final look at his officer's identification documents, he burns them in an ashtray. Watching the flame, he feels that he is also killing part of himself—the identity he has inhabited comfortably for so many years. After flushing the ashes down the toilet, he puts Anton Andreev's identification in the filthy coat's top pocket. As a final gesture to military discipline, he hangs his uniforms with meticulous care in the armoire.

Quietly exiting his quarters, he stops and looks wistfully at the palace. He recalls his time with Anastasia and her deep blue eyes, the Empress's mandate, the grand balls, and the jocund disposition of the privileged class. That life is over, he tells himself. Whatever happens to him, he knows with certainty that Russia's imperial might and the wealth it supported are finished. With resignation, he pulls on the gardener's cap, turns, and swiftly walks the twelve blocks to the Moskovsky train station on Plaschad Vosstanice. No one seems to notice him.

Despite the chaos in the streets, most of the trains are still running, although not always on time. The station is crowded with workers, peasants, kulaks, soldiers, and silk-stocking gentry surrounded by stacks of luggage. Pirogov is struck by the repugnant smell of this mass of people waiting for a train that will take them away from the turmoil in Saint Petersburg. The station floors are covered with trash and filth, and the benches are crowded with tired travelers. The world is truly changing, he reflects. If anything, the squalor in the once-grand station seems even more depressing than the violence in the streets.

Pirogov enters the long queue at the ticket window. After inching forward for almost an hour, he finally steps up to the window and buys a third-class ticket to Torzhok, giving the agent fourteen rubles. Then he finds a place on a grubby bench and patiently waits for departure time. For two hours, he does not speak, read, or move about. Outwardly bored, he constantly scrutinizes the crowd for any sign of recognition or unrest. He must not be discovered this close to his departure.

While his eyes move restlessly around the waiting room, Pirogov ponders how he will manage to recover Alexandra's box at the Swedish Embassy in Peking, then travel into the interior of China to a place he does not know. When he begins the next stage of his journey, he will travel from Torzhok to Moscow, where he will board the Trans-Siberian Railway. He tries to imagine what he will encounter on the seven-day trip to Peking.

With a shrill whistle, the stationmaster announces above the din that the Moscow local will leave in twenty minutes—almost on time. Pirogov is swept up in the crowd rushing to board. Entering a roach-infested third-class coach, he finds a seat next to a large, dark-bearded man who apparently has not bathed in weeks. Much relieved that his companion makes no attempt to strike up a conversation, Pirogov huddles deep in his large coat. The unheated coach is bitterly cold and stuffy with tobacco smoke. He tries to sleep but cannot. Four hours later, without incident, the train stops at Torzhok. Pirogov swings off with his possessions, the only one to depart the train.

Torzhok
28 February 1917

The station is nearly deserted and almost as dirty as the Saint Petersburg station. Even here in this quiet corner of Russia, he reflects, the national unrest is disturbing the once orderly management of a village train station. Grabbing his valise, he sets off down the long, icy road to Beryosha.

The countryside lies still in the deep Russian winter. The scattered farms seem deserted, although smoke rises from some of the farmhouses. Except for a single sleigh that passes him on the road, Pirogov sees no one. The hushed landscape seems to be waiting passively for whatever will come next.

Pirogov was born here, in this quiet corner of Russia, and he knows the landscape and the people as well as he knows his own hand. But unrest is spreading outward from the cities, and soon this part of his world will also be consumed by the radical ideas and relentless violence preached by the revolutionaries. For better or worse, his Russia is dying. Not a day has passed since his last meeting with Alexandra that he hasn't thought of the Empress and her family, but he is powerless to help them. All he can do now is ensure his mother's safety and do his utmost to carry out Alexandra's mission successfully.

Five miles later, Pirogov pauses at the iron gate that marks the entrance to his vast estate. Czar Alexander I awarded Beryosha to Pirogov's great-grandfather, Major General Ivan Pirogov, in 1815 as a reward for his military skills and valor in the Napoleonic War. Over the years, successive Pirogov generals willed the estate to their first-born male heirs. Kirik inherited it after his father, General Anton Simionovich Pirogov, was killed in 1904 by shrapnel from a shell fired from a Japanese cruiser during the siege of Port Arthur.

The estate consists of three prosperous peasant villages, large tracts of forest, and several thousand acres of wheat fields. Scattered copses of birch give the estate its name. The manor house lies a mile down a curved road, hidden by snow-draped spruce trees. Built at the end of the eighteenth century in the northern baroque style, the house was modernized in 1910 with electricity, indoor plumbing, and central heating.

As he walks down the lane that leads to the house, Pirogov recalls his loving father, who was all too frequently off on another campaign, and the happy days the family spent at Beryosha. He wonders if calm will ever be restored to his embattled country.

He walks to the front door and twists the doorbell twice. In a minute, the door opens and the butler stares incredulously at the filthy laborer who has the audacity to appear at the manor house's front door.

Vladimir Suvorin, who has served the Pirogov family most of his life, is of indeterminate age, a tall, lean man whose clothes fit him well. His high cheekbones and dark eyes reflect his Tartar heritage. He has thinning black hair with touches of gray, a strong, clean-shaven jaw, and a broad forehead. Wearing the formal tailcoat that is his usual butler's uniform, Suvorin looks better suited to his elegant surroundings than the shabby man at the door.

Pirogov says cheerily, "Good afternoon, Vladimir. Do you not recognize me?"

With slow recognition, Suvorin's response is a heartfelt "Welcome home, Master Kirik. My apologies for not recognizing you sooner. Your appearance confused my memory. It is so unlike you."

Entering the house and dropping his valise on the floor, Pirogov says, "No matter. I would not recognize myself in this masquerade. Please tell my mother that I am here."

"She is not here, Master Kirik."

"Where is she? And when will she return? I want to see her."

"Madam is not expected back at all. She said she was going to China."

Somewhat taken aback, Pirogov says, "What do you mean, Vladimir?"

The butler relieves Pirogov of his filthy coat, which he places gingerly on top of the valise. "For several months, Madam has been receiving a number of guests whom I did not know. They seemed to be of the gentry. She took them to the library and locked the door. After an hour or so, the guests left. Then she went to Saint Petersburg, alone, which is very unlike her because I normally travel with her and manage the townhouse for her. Then, several weeks ago, Madam returned here. She ordered me to sell or give away all our livestock, all the farm equipment, and the carriages. 'Get rid of everything, but do it quietly,' she told me. She gave no reason, and it was not my place to question her."

"She gave no advance notice when she would return, something she had never done before. She had her maid pack a large suitcase with plain and serviceable clothes and shoes, and a gripsack with personal items for a train journey. And Madam herself packed a valise with a few of her mementos and some jewelry. She dismissed the field hands and the household servants, giving them all a generous severance. She asked the chauffeur and me to remain in her employ. The following morning, the chauffeur parked the automobile at the front door and loaded her luggage."

"I don't understand," Pirogov says, bewildered.

"I don't understand either. She thanked me for my long service, gave me over a hundred thousand rubles, and said, 'Vladimir, take care of our home. I do not expect to return. When Master Kirik returns, give him this letter and tell him that I have gone to China.' The automobile left, and that is all I know about her. The chauffeur returned the automobile, parked it in the garage, demanded his wages, and departed in a huff, mumbling something about the fickleness of the aristocracy."

Forgetting his dirty clothes, Pirogov sits on a blue silk-covered divan, his eyes narrowed and his mouth firm. His mind is whirling at the cataclysm of revolution in his country. He struggles to understand that it has infected even the small town of Torzhok and caused the upheaval of his immediate family. He understands his mother's behavior, but is concerned that she did not write telling him of her plans. On quick reflection, he realizes why she did not—she would have been compromised if her letter had been intercepted. It becomes clear what the Empress meant when she said that some of their friends had left Russia and were now in China.

Coming to grips with these latest developments, Pirogov says, "I need a brandy, a stiff one. And please bring me my mother's letter."

A few minutes later, Pirogov is sipping his brandy and reading his mother's letter:

My dearest son,

When you read this letter, I shall be long gone.

Please forgive that I have left without telling you of my plans, but I'm sure you understand why discretion is necessary. These are confused and dangerous times.

I have left Suvorin in charge of the manor until you return, and I hope you will come soon. The city is far too dangerous for you these days. I don't know how much longer the countryside will be safe, but I hope that at least you will find some peace here at Beryosha. Perhaps you will consider leaving for China, as so many of our friends have done.

I cannot tell you where I have gone, lest this letter fall into the wrong hands and create further danger for other refugees. But I leave our beloved Beryosha in good health and expect to arrive at my destination in the same state.

I have given Suvorin money to support himself, but I ask you to protect him and see that he finds a safe haven. He has served our family loyally for so many years, and it is our duty to show him the same loyalty.

My dear Kirik, I pray that you will be safe and that you too will find a shelter in this national storm. And I pray that, above all, we shall one day be reunited.

In the meantime, I embrace you, I kiss you, precious son.
Mama

Pirogov swallows the last of his brandy and puts his mother's letter back in its envelope. He wonders, *Now what?*

Reflecting on the information Suvorin had given him, Pirogov wonders if his mother might be on her way to the White Russian enclave that is his ultimate destination. If she packed only what she could carry, and if she had only enough for a short train journey, she could not be on her way to Peking or Harbin. Her destination must be nearer, and northwestern China would be a good possibility. If so, he feels relief that eventually they will be reunited.

But before he can leave the comparative safety of Beryosha, he must transform himself into another man. It will likely require months of effort for him to shed his aristocrat's skin and grow a new one, better suited to the rough times he is living in.

8

Saint Petersburg
23 January to 19 July 1917

Knowing that the Czar is in near-isolation at Tsarskoe Selo and almost powerless, Lenin calls for a general strike. In response, tens of thousands of workers rally in the streets. The Bolsheviks seize the post and telegraph building and the police stations, railroad stations, and key government offices. Other revolutionaries establish armed blockades at major intersections. The city is paralyzed. Desperately, the Palace Guard counterattacks with machine guns, rifle fire, and bayonets. Mounted Cossacks slash with their sabers and fire their semi-automatic pistols, killing several thousand rioters and wounding many more. Briefly, both sides draw back to retrieve their dead and wounded, and to re-form their forces.

Lenin realizes that now he has the advantage and must seize the moment. From the steps of the post and telegraph building, he shouts the mantra of the Marxist revolution, "Workers of the world, unite! You have nothing to lose but your chains!" He tells the crowd, "You are the vanguard of the proletariat. Today, the armed revolution has begun. The Czar and his lackeys are doomed. We will have peace, land, and bread."

His cadres wave red flags emblazoned with the hammer and sickle ensign. Moving through the mobs, they distribute Red propaganda leaflets by the thousands. Lenin's fiery rhetoric inflames the mobs to insane fury.

Inside the telegraph building, telegraphers flood the wires with Lenin's words. Party lackeys order all primary stations to relay his message to minor stations, minor stations to relay it to the outposts. Radio operators send Lenin's words in International Morse Code via shortwave signals. By day's end, every Russian city, town, and village in the vast empire knows that the revolution is underway.

The next three days are relatively calm. There are sporadic clashes between the Reds and the Czar's forces but, under Lenin's guidance, the revolutionaries begin to consolidate their territorial and political gains. They organize governing Duma Councils of Workers' Deputies in the major cities.

Beryosha
 2 March 1917

It is early morning at Beryosha, and the low-angle sun is just clearing the windowsill of the spacious kitchen. Its bright golden light casts long shadows on the large walnut kitchen table. Pirogov, eschewing the formal customs of the household, is seated at the sunlit table, eating a leisurely breakfast of coffee, kippers, boiled eggs, black bread, and canned peaches. His red-and-gold silk smoking jacket covers a collarless white shirt. Earlier, he had asked Suvorin to move the Victrola from the sitting room into a corner of the kitchen. Playing now is a recording of Tchaikovsky's *Marche Slave*. The Victrola's large, curved speaker stretches almost three feet into the room.

Pirogov has not yet heard of the general strike in Saint Petersburg, but he is convinced that the Russia he knows is lost. With the intensity of the opposition building and spreading dramatically each day, he realizes that the czarist government will soon fall. Lenin and the revolutionaries will change his country into a socialist-totalitarian state. His mother has abandoned Beryosha, never to return, and he is alone. Reluctantly, he accepts that he is the last Pirogov who will ever live at Beryosha. But he cannot remain here indefinitely. His future lies in China where, God willing, he will be reunited with his mother and Anastasia.

Suvorin pours more coffee and says, "Every day I find it more difficult to buy food. There is no more bread. This bread is two days old. No one seems to work anymore. Most of the shops in the village are closed. The proprietors and customers are milling about in the street, all protesting something or other."

Pirogov nods with acceptance and sips his coffee. He looks at Suvorin and says, "Sit at the table with me and enjoy some of your excellent coffee."

Somewhat surprised that his employer would invite a servant to sit with him, Suvorin carefully pulls out a chair and slides his lean frame onto it. He pours coffee into the cup that Pirogov has placed in front of him. He sips, and there is a small light in his dark eyes.

"Vladimir," begins Pirogov, looking directly into the butler's eyes, "our Russia is dying. The war against Germany and Austria is lost, yet the army continues to send men to the trenches to die. The workers strike and riot in the streets, demanding that the Czar address their grievances. For reasons I do not understand, the Czar refuses to discuss these issues, which are destroying our country. Bolsheviks, Socialists, Mensheviks, Anarchists, and other revolutionaries strive to overthrow the Czar and replace our government with a communist-style dictatorship disguised as an elected Soviet Duma. I fear they will succeed."

He leans back in his chair and is silent for several seconds, then asks, "What are your plans, Vladimir? Would you like to join the revolutionaries?"

Suvorin puts down his cup and draws himself erect. "Never!" he replies vehemently. "Join that rabble?" His face is dark with contempt and disgust. "I have spent my life serving a great family in a great house, and I am not without pride. I will not lower myself to the ranks of those filthy revolutionaries. I shall remain here in Beryosha until you tell me to leave. This is my home, and you, Master Kirik, are the only family I have left."

Pirogov nods quietly, satisfied with his butler's loyalty. "Then we must make some plans for our life here, for however long we can remain. Tell me, Vladimir, how much food do we have in the pantry?"

Suvorin takes a careful sip of his coffee as he calculates his response. Then, placing his cup back in its saucer, he responds with a touch of pride.

"We have enough dry goods and canned food for many months. For the past year, I have seen the coming revolution, and I have been laying in supplies. Our root cellar is full of potatoes, carrots, turnips, onions, wheat, barley, rice, walnuts and hazelnuts, some salted beef, hams, pickled pork, jams, and dried fruit. The year-round temperature in the root cellar varies only three degrees, and the hygrometer consistently shows the humidity at about 90 percent. And, to ensure that the house continues to function, I have bought and stored almost a ton of coal for heating and the stoves, and about eight thousand gallons of diesel fuel in the underground storage tanks for our electric generator."

"Excellent!" Pirogov smiles. "It appears that you are much more than the butler of this household. You have assumed the role of estate manager. Your foresight and initiative are admirable. I'm indebted to you."

"Thank you, sir. Several months ago, I talked with our neighbors, and we struck a bargain. We can barter dry goods and vegetables for their eggs, butter, milk, and freshly butchered chicken, as well as fresh sausage and pork. Also, I have acquired stores of vegetable seeds, and in the spring we shall plant a garden."

Pirogov with a sudden burst of enthusiasm declares, "We have flour, salt, yeast, lard, and rye seeds, yes? We can bake our own bread."

Suvorin says, "Yes, sir." He sits straight in his chair. "It would appear that we can live here indefinitely. Provided, of course, that the Bolsheviks do not hector us."

Pirogov rises, and puts his napkin on the table. "Yes, Vladimir, that is the key. How long will it be before the Bolsheviks take complete control of the country and confiscate all private property?" Inwardly, he is calculating how long it will take for his beard and hair to grow sufficiently long and disheveled to help with his disguise. How much time and manual labor will it take to roughen his hands? Four or five months at least, he reckons.

He rises from the table, and with determined purpose walks into the dining room, where he carefully inspects every nook and cranny. He continues this inspection through the library, reception rooms, hallways, parlors, stairways, and bedrooms. In the late afternoon, he returns to the kitchen where Suvorin is preparing dinner. The Victrola is playing a recording of Mussorgsky's *Pictures at an Exhibition*. Pirogov gets Suvorin's attention by lifting the needle-arm from the record.

"Yes, Kirik Antonievich. How may I help you?"

"Vladimir, this house needs a complete renovation. There is dirt everywhere, the walls and ceilings need painting, the rugs should be beaten and cleaned, floors scrubbed and waxed. We need carpentry work to repair the stairs and roof, and the curtains and drapes must be cleaned. Everything needs work. Lots of hard work!"

Suvorin, puzzled at this sudden burst of industry and offended at his employer's criticism of his household management, stiffens. "As you say, sir. Shall I hire workers from the village? Wages for day labor are very low."

"No. Absolutely not. Hire no one. We, you and I, will clean and restore this house."

Raising his eyebrows at this pronouncement, Suvorin responds, "If I may say so, sir, the house was fully repainted just a few years ago; and, at your mother's orders, it has been kept in excellent condition."

"Yes, I understand, Vladimir." Pirogov pauses to consider how to rephrase his decision in a way that will not offend his butler's sense of propriety. "You have managed the house very well, and indeed everything is just as it should be. But I feel a great need for manual labor, and until we can put in the garden, I need some useful occupation. So, please humor me and allow us to pretend that the house needs restoration."

"As you wish, sir." Mollified, Suvorin turns back to his cooking.

The next afternoon, the pair is in town buying cleaning supplies, paint, lumber, and tools. Suvorin hires a horse-drawn wagon to haul their purchases to the estate. In the ensuing weeks, the dust flies. Pirogov presses himself harder than he has ever worked, tackling the manually intensive tasks with a driven passion. Suvorin continues his household duties and assists when needed. By the end of the second day, Pirogov is exhausted, every muscle in his body aching, and his hands are raw. He collapses onto a chaise. After a few seconds, he holds out his arm, and Suvorin hands him a snifter of brandy.

The weeks pass quickly. On his estate, which is far from town, Pirogov is still oblivious to the turmoil in Saint Petersburg and the spreading wildfire of armed revolution. He continues the cleaning and renovation of the house. It takes him five days to complete the master bedroom, which now sparkles with freshly painted walls, newly waxed floors, and freshly cleaned carpets. His body is gradually hardening, though his hands are cracked and bleeding from open wounds. His beard has grown about an inch. His military haircut is beginning to look shaggy. He tackles the renovation of each room with disciplined vigor.

Saint Petersburg
15 March 1917

On March 15, Czar Nicholas II abdicates his title as Emperor and Autocrat of All the Russias. His uncle, Grand Duke Nikolai, Commander of the Army, had urged his nephew to abdicate, as had several other generals and relatives. Additionally, the Duma had demanded the Czar abdicate. The provisional government, under Kerensky, isolates the Czar and his family at Tsarskoe Selo. On March 21, Kerensky places Czar Nicholas and his family under house arrest in the Alexander Palace.

Urged on by Lenin, Kerensky, and other leaders, thousands of workers, military deserters, anarchists, Bolsheviks, Mensheviks, Socialists, and other revolutionaries march in five columns and converge in the great square in front of the Winter Palace. Most of the army deserts to the revolutionaries.

Then, much to Lenin's chagrin, the Petrograd Soviet, with its Menshevik and Socialist majority, elects Alexander Kerensky as minister of justice and commander-in-chief of the army. In effect, Kerensky becomes the premier of the provisional government. He promises democracy, abolition of the death penalty, and a continuation of the war.

Throughout Russia there is sporadic fighting. Military units loyal to the Czar, the Orthodox Church, and some of the Asian minorities clash with Red units.

Eventually, fighting between the revolutionaries and czarists abates, and Kerensky continues to gain control over the disparate revolutionary forces inside Russia. Not over Lenin's Bolsheviks, however.

Beryosha
3 April 1917

A delegation of three deputies from the Torzhok Provisional Government Duma, riding in a two-horse wagon, arrives at the manor. Suvorin, responding to the doorbell, opens the front door.

Without any customary salutation, Savva Morozov, the leader, speaks. "In the name of the people's revolution, I demand to speak with Senior Lieutenant Kirik Pirogov. We know he's here. Weeks ago he was seen in town buying supplies." Morozov is a diminutive fellow with a high, squeaky voice; a bushy beard and mustache cover most of his face. His deep-set brown eyes have an ominous look of dark suspicion.

Suvorin is at a loss to know who these fellows are to demand anything of him. The butler of an aristocrat's manor does not bow to the proletariat. Knowing, however, that this delegation smells of revolutionary politics and that it would be judicious to behave civilly, he escorts them to the library. "I will fetch Senior Lieutenant Pirogov," he says, and leaves the room.

The delegates sink into the deep, leather-covered chairs. Silently, they are amazed at the opulence of this man's library. Tapestries hang from the wall facing the garden, and leather-bound books fill shelves from the floor to the high ceiling. On the floor are fine Persian rugs. Several standing lamps with pale-green silk shades flood the room with light. After luxuriating in the affluence around them, the delegation reverts to the appropriate revolutionary stance and condemns the decadence of the gentry.

In a few minutes, Pirogov enters the library. He is dressed in dirty, paint-smeared clothes, and his bushy hair and beard are unruly. He looks over the motley delegation and does not recognize any of them. He says, "Welcome to my home, Comrades. How may I be of service?"

Pirogov's disheveled appearance and ragtag clothing are not what the delegation expected. This fellow clearly is not a senior lieutenant of the Palace

Guard. The delegation looks at him with questioning eyes. Morozov, in a quizzical voice, asks, "You are Senior Lieutenant Kirik Pirogov?"

Pirogov responds. "No and yes. I deserted the army a couple of months ago, so I no longer have military rank and am a private citizen. And yes, I am Kirik Pirogov, the master here. Please tell me what brings you to my home."

Morozov asks, "Have you not heard the extraordinary news? The people's revolution has overthrown the czarist government. Czar Nicholas and his family are under arrest and in isolation at Tsarskoe Selo. The Petrograd Duma has elected the Socialist Alexander Kerensky as premier of our democratic provisional government. Local Dumas now rule under directions from Petrograd. We are senior members of the Torzhok Duma, and it is our charge to investigate all members of the czarist government and the bourgeois landowners."

With aplomb Pirogov responds, "I have not heard of these events, though I expect the Czar's government to fall soon. So be it." Mockingly he adds, "Only a hundred and twenty-five years after the French Revolution."

Pirogov pauses and walks over to one of the windows. He draws back the curtains as if to see what is happening outside. Then he turns to the delegates to gauge their reaction to his comment. They are stolidly silent.

After a couple of seconds, Pirogov continues, "Actually, I have been working here for these past several weeks refurbishing my home. I have not had any outside contact. Please understand that I have no politics. I did not and will not participate in any revolutionary activity, either for the Czar or for the provisional government. My goal is to live in my home in peace."

Morozov stares at Pirogov with his dark, penetrating eyes. "We know your late father and your mother, Maria Pavlovna. They were generous employers and treated their servants and the local peasants with respect and empathy. Is it your plan to continue this policy?"

Without hesitation and with firm resolve, Pirogov avers, "Of course! It's our family's custom, and I intend to honor it. You may be assured that I respect the rights of all people. Currently, I have no employees other than my butler, who has worked for my family for so long that I consider him my brother. Perhaps, sometime in the future, I may hire workers. If so, I will treat them respectfully as citizens of the new Russia."

"A few more questions, Comrade Pirogov. Will you share one-half of your harvest with our commune in Torzhok?"

"If I had a harvest, I certainly would. However, our fields lie fallow. They have not been worked for over a year."

"That is unfortunate. We were counting on your support. Perhaps you would share one-half of your newborn farm animals with the commune?"

"There are no such animals here. Last year, my mother either sold or gave away all our livestock. I do not even have a horse."

"Your answers are deeply disturbing." Morozov rises and prepares to leave with his delegation. "Thank you for receiving us with such courtesy." With no more said, they leave.

Suvorin, who has been eavesdropping, says, "Sir, may I ask, what was that about?"

Pirogov paces back and forth for a few seconds, then stops near the mahogany desk with his arms akimbo. "I'm not sure. However, I suspect that it was the opening gambit of things to come which will bode ill for us. It would be prudent for us to stay out of sight as much as we can, be respectful when dealing with the locals, and make no mention of politics."

He is silent for a moment, clearly considering further ramifications of their situation. "Vladimir, you mentioned some time ago that my mother gave you a hundred thousand rubles. I suspect that in a year or so the ruble will be worthless in the international market. My advice is to use those rubles to purchase some high-quality diamonds."

Petrograd
1 July 1917

Weeks earlier, Kerensky, keeping his vow to continue the war, had ordered his army to launch a massive offensive against the Austro-Hungarian and German forces in Galicia. In the early dawn, three Russian armies attack, achieving initial success and opening a broad gap in the Austro-Hungarian lines, soon reaching Lvov. However, the Germans hold fast and launch a counterattack, driving the Russians back and causing several hundred thousand casualties.

This failure is due to the Russian army's low morale, numerous mutinies and desertions, and an inept supply mechanism.

В другой рăз

In late October, the Bolsheviks launch a second revolution to overthrow Kerensky's provisional government. Bolshevik troops invade the Duma of Deputies in Petrograd and arrest the top two hundred leaders, including Kerensky and Leon Trotsky.

On November 8, the Bolsheviks' All-Russian Congress of Soviets elects Lenin chairman of the Council of People's Commissars—in essence, the head of government. Lenin announces, "Communism is Soviet power. Henceforth, the government of the Union of Soviet Socialist Republics will be totalitarian Communism." Bolshevik commissars throughout Russia establish socialist Soviet Councils of Workers' Deputies to govern provinces and cities. Felix Dzerzhinsky's secret police, the Cheka, begins the Red Terror.

On March 3, 1918, the Union of Soviet Socialist Republics signs the Treaty of Brest-Litovsk, ending its participation in the Great War. A week later, Lenin moves the government to Moscow to escape the continuing German threat to Petrograd.

On April 30, Lenin orders the Czar and his family moved to Ekaterinburg, a small town in western Siberia. There, they are confined to a dacha that is referred to in official documents as the "House of Special Purpose."

9

Torzhok
19 June 1918

During the past fifteen months, the Communists' revolutionary chaos has roiled the Union of Soviet Socialist Republics. With Lenin and his Bolsheviks in charge, local Soviet councils exert tyrannical control over every aspect of government, business, and citizens' activities. The Cheka's Red Terror rages on, unabated and unchecked. Its tentacles reach into every province of the Soviet Union. Red and White armies clash, with appalling casualties. Western and Japanese forces control the major seaports. The Czech Legion, an almost seventy-thousand-man volunteer army of expatriates from the Austro-Hungarian Empire, has formed into regiments and is fighting its way to Vladivostok. As the Legion moves east, it assumes control of sections of the Trans-Siberian Railway.

Suvorin, through his infrequent trips into town, keeps Pirogov informed of the political and military turmoil in the country. So far, such disquiet has been only minimally intrusive in this small town of no strategic importance. Keeping a low profile, Pirogov has not left the estate.

However, it is becoming clear that his time at Beryosha is limited. Two months earlier, the Cheka had established an office next to the Torzhok railroad station. Communist Party apparatchiks have formed a governing Soviet, and a Red Army company is bivouacked on the outskirts of town. Soon, Pirogov must resume his journey to China and recover the ebony box in

Peking. In the meantime, he continues the rehabilitation of the manor, which now shines as if it were almost new, inside and out.

Pirogov has gained eighteen pounds of muscle. His body is lean and sinewy, with a narrow waist and a wide chest. The skin on his hands is coarse and thickly callused. His face is tanned from long days in the sun working on exterior repairs to the house and in the garden, and it is etched with deep, narrow lines. His hair is shaggy, and his full beard and mustache are haphazardly trimmed.

Today, Pirogov's visitor, Savva Morozov, is standing a few steps inside the door of the library. Behind him stand two deputies and an armed Cheka officer. Armed Red guards are stationed at all entrances to the manor.

Morozov announces haughtily, "Comrade Pirogov, as the Commissar of the Torzhok Soviet Council of the Communist Party, I demand that you vacate this house and estate. Here are my eviction orders." He hands Pirogov a small packet of papers tied with a red ribbon. The cover of the packet is sealed in wax and deeply imprinted with the hammer and sickle symbol of the Communist Party. Morozov intones, "Directives from the Third International Congress of Soviets command the confiscation of all private property. The state will use this house to quarter landless peasants and to assemble a farm commune. Failure to comply will result in a visit from the Cheka."

Pirogov is dressed in the peasant attire he has adopted since returning to Beryosha—a white tunic, loose-fitting black trousers, and calf-high leather boots. Standing behind the mahogany desk, he puts his hands on the top and, with a glint of pride in his eyes, leans forward and looks at Morozov. He has expected this visit for some months and is mentally prepared to comply. He opens the eviction orders, scans the banner, and with restraint says, "I understand, Comrade Morozov. When do you expect me to leave?"

"Immediately." In a few seconds, seeing the impact of his statement has registered with Pirogov, Morozov says in a slightly more conciliatory tone, "However, because of your family's long tenure in this province, compassion for their workers, and service to our community for these many decades, you may have two days to vacate. I warn you not to remove any items from this house except a few of your personal belongings. The rest, as of now, are the property of the state."

Pirogov sits in the chair behind the desk and responds with a subtle tone of irony which escapes Morozov, "Thank you for your consideration, Comrade. My friend Vladimir Suvorin and I will be gone within the two-day grace period you have afforded us."

Without responding, Morozov turns and parades out of the house with his retinue in tow.

В другой ра́з

Later that day, Pirogov and Suvorin are sipping strong coffee at the kitchen table. The mellow afternoon light casts soft shadows and sets an almost serene tone. The gramophone is silent. They do not speak. Each is lost in his own thoughts. Suvorin puts his cup down and, breaking the silence, says, "We face a cruel irony. Now that you have almost completed the renovation of the house, we must abandon it." He pauses to sip his coffee. "I have understood for some time why you've devoted such energy to refurbishing this house. Look at you. You have accomplished your goal. You're a different man from that toy soldier who twisted the doorbell seventeen months ago."

Pirogov stares out the window at a fallow field. "Now that it's time to leave, I'm hoping that you're correct, Vladimir."

Continuing, Suvorin says, "And I knew that you would not remain here indefinitely. You're on a confidential quest of some kind. My only question is why you remained here so long."

Pirogov returns his gaze to Suvorin, takes a deliberate sip of coffee, and with the cup suspended in midair says, "I cannot answer your question. The less you know, the safer you will be." He sips more coffee. Then, in a burst of energy, he says, "Vladimir, we have lots to accomplish in the next few hours. Let's get busy. Build a fire in the library fireplace. I have a few items to destroy. After the fireplace has cooled, clean it."

Suvorin rises, heads for the library, and starts the fire. Shortly, Pirogov arrives, carrying the oil portraits of his family. One by one he tosses them into the fire. He mutters, "Those villainous Reds will not despoil my family." Next, he returns with his military records, the land title from Czar Alexander

I, his father's records, the estate's financial accounts, and various inventories of the treasures on the estate. The fire roars as he continues to feed it with the history of the Pirogov family, defying the dictates of Commissar Morozov. Finally, he tosses in the ironworker's clothes, but he keeps his identification papers as Anton Andreev.

In the pantry off the main dining room, Pirogov stares at the sterling silver service and flatware—over two thousand pieces, given to the family by Czar Paul I in 1799. He opens cabinet doors to view the thirty place settings of exquisite porcelain dinnerware, fired in pale blue and each hand-painted with the black double-eagle emblem of the Romanov Dynasty. In 1858, Czar Alexander II had awarded this dinnerware to Major General Anton Pirogov for his stunning victory over two British cavalry brigades at Balaclava during the Crimean War.

In the library, he sees the thousands of leather-bound books on the shelves. He scans the titles of a dozen or so. He tenderly withdraws Mark Twain's *Tom Sawyer*, flips open a page, and reads a few lines. His eyes brighten, and he breaks into a thin smile. With his handkerchief, he assiduously wipes the leather binding where his fingers have touched it. He carefully reshelves the book. His face is grim as he wanders through the house looking at, and mentally caressing, the treasures it contains, and letting their visual stimuli trigger treasured memories. Sharp furrows appear on his forehead as he imagines what the peasants who occupy this manor will do to these treasures. In a snap, his external distress is over.

He finds Suvorin in the kitchen preparing dinner. "Vladimir, tomorrow I shall travel to Moscow in today's garb. There, I shall change into my Bolshevik political commissar's uniform, and then I shall disappear on the Trans-Siberian Railway. Now that I am heavier and have a somewhat different physique, we must alter that uniform to fit."

The following morning, Pirogov and Suvorin are standing in the foyer prepared to leave. Each has a valise containing a few personal items and toilet articles. In Pirogov's, wrapped in his regular clothing is his Bolshevik uniform. As a precaution, he has taped the gold schillings to the lower calves of both his legs. His long trousers and boots effectively hide them. He has taped the remainder of the currency that Empress Alexandra gave him to his chest and back. His forged Bolshevik identification papers and travel documents, and Anton Yurievich Andreev's identification documents, are hidden inside the lining of his black leather cap. Suvorin has stitched a protective cover over them.

Pirogov turns to take a final view of the house's interior. With a deep sigh, he says, "Well, Vladimir, it is over. This is the end of the Pirogov family." He flexes his shoulders and stands stiffly erect. Then he snaps a salute and says in a loud, clear voice, "Goodbye, my dear family. I will keep our honor." He turns and pulls open the door.

The two men start to walk down the driveway. Pirogov breaks the silence. "Tell me, Vladimir, where are you going?"

"I have no relatives. My life has been with the Pirogov family here at Beryosha. There is no reason for me to stay in Torzhok and become one of the proletariat and labor on a farm commune. I could not tolerate watching this estate slowly decay as the Bolsheviks destroy it. Though I am not a czarist, I abhor what the Bolsheviks are doing." His face is dark with grief and contempt.

"I have heard that Admiral Kolchak is recruiting men for his army to fight the Bolsheviks. They're assembling in the Siberian town of Omsk. I'm inclined to join his forces."

The house shrinks behind them as they advance toward the iron gate. Pirogov slaps Vladimir on the back and says, "Capital, Vladimir. Capital." In a mirthful mood, Pirogov teases him, "Vladimir, do you think Admiral Kolchak will enlist an old man like you?"

"Perhaps not. But I know he will need a cook." They continue walking.

A few feet from the gate, Suvorin says, "Please take the diamonds I have purchased with your mother's rubles. They belong to you. I am resourceful and will survive. And it is foolish for me, a servant, to carry such a treasure. If someone found them, they would be my death warrant."

Realizing that Suvorin's reasoning is correct, Pirogov says, "Reluctantly, I accept. Have you rubles enough to sustain yourself and travel to Omsk?"

"Yes, I have several thousand."

Suvorin hands Pirogov a chamois bag that contains a small handful of diamonds. Pirogov puts them in a hidden compartment in his valise.

"And you, Kirik Antonievich, where are you going."

"Vladimir, my destination is confidential. Suffice it to say that I will never return to Torzhok. And certainly, I will never return to Russia."

They arrive at the gate. Pirogov hesitates, turns around, and looks back down the driveway. He says nothing as he takes one last look at what is now the Communist government's estate. He pauses for a time. Then, with a renewed vigor, he says, "Suvorin, we are not leaving, not just yet. Hurry back with me to the house."

At a trot, they burst through the main door. Pirogov exclaims, "We will not leave Beryosha to the Bolsheviks. Get all the coal oil we have and scatter it throughout the house. Start at the upstairs bedrooms. Soak the library liberally. We are going to burn this house to ashes as a pyre for the Pirogov name."

An hour later, Pirogov and Suvorin stand about a hundred yards down the driveway. Pirogov kneels and sets a lighted match to the coal-oil fuse. The flame speeds rapidly up the driveway and into the open main door. In seconds, the fire starts with a *whoof* and spreads quickly through the house. With angst, they watch as the raging fire rapidly engulfs the elegant old building. Quickly, the two men run among the outbuildings, which are also soaked with fuel. Within minutes, every structure around the house is in flames, even the empty chicken coops and dovecotes.

The two men hurry down the driveway, away from the heat of the burning house. Pirogov stares back at the inferno. There are small tears in his eyes. "Welcome to Beryosha, Bolsheviks."

He grabs Suvorin and says, "The deed is done. Let's take leave of this graveyard."

Torzhok
19 June 1918

It is early afternoon when Pirogov and Suvorin enter Torzhok. It is a bright, sunny day, the sky a crisp, dark blue. A few cotton-white altocumulus clouds add contrast. In the countryside between Beryosha and the outskirts of the town, crops rot in the fields because there is no one to harvest them, and neglected livestock wander around the barren landscape. In town, most of the shops are closed, having been expropriated by the local Soviet. The granary is abandoned.

The two men walk toward the railroad station. Trash litters the streets. Townspeople mill about and grumble. Some sit in doorways and stare blankly, others sob. A few express frustration and anger, but only in whispers to a trusted relative. The Cheka guards, in their olive-drab uniforms and budenovka caps with a large red star, seem to be everywhere.

Pirogov muses quietly to himself, *Welcome to the utopian world of change for workers who have shed the chains of their exploitative capitalist employers.*

The Communist Party and Cheka headquarters are located in a building that was formerly the police station. Standing in the doorway is Savva Morozov. He hails Pirogov and Suvorin as they walk by. "Come here, you two. I see that you are traveling. We have some business to conclude."

Pirogov stops and looks at Morozov. Annoyed, he asks, "What business can we possibly have with you? We have nothing with which to do business. The state now owns all our property." Behind his stern manner, he conceals a touch of anxiety, wondering whether Morozov knows about their arson.

With his arms akimbo, Morozov asks, "Where are you heading?"

"Moscow, to find work," responds Pirogov.

"Come inside. You need an internal passport and visas to travel anywhere in the country these days. The Party demands that all citizens carry such documents."

Inside, Morozov escorts them to the passport desk and tells the female clerk, "Take care of these two comrades. They need travel documents." He looks at Pirogov. "Comrade Olga will assist you." He turns and walks down a long gray hall to his office.

Olga is of indeterminate age and significantly overweight. Her olive-drab uniform bulges at critical points. Her pale hair is stringy, and her eyes are tired. She records their pertinent personal information, takes a photograph of each, and sends the plates to the darkroom for processing and printing. Pirogov and Suvorin sit quietly on the only bench in sight. After thirty minutes, the darkroom technician hands the portrait prints to Olga and she completes the passports. Then she begins to prepare the visas. "Where are you going, when, and for how long?"

"Moscow," Pirogov replies. "We will leave today, if we can catch the train that leaves shortly. And our stay is indefinite."

Olga looks up at Pirogov and in the most officious voice she can muster says, "One cannot stay anywhere indefinitely. To complete your visa, I need a return date. The Party must approve any permanent change of residence."

With resignation Pirogov mutters, "We will return on the tenth of July. Is that satisfactory, Comrade Olga?"

"Yes." Dutifully she completes the visas, stamps them with the official hammer and sickle seal of office, and hands them to Pirogov and Suvorin. "Do not overstay your visas. The Cheka will hunt you down if you do not appear here before they expire."

Without comment, they exit the building and head for the railroad station a few blocks away. The Moscow local train has just entered the station.

As they approach the entrance of the station, a Cheka guard demands to inspect their papers. Pirogov presents both sets of documents. The Cheka guard looks at the portraits, nods, and returns the documents. "Pass, comrades."

Walking to the train, Suvorin remarks, "That dolt can't read. Is this going to be the hallmark of our new Communist government?"

The four-hour journey to Moscow passes without incident. As the train approaches the Moscow station, Pirogov turns to Suvorin and says, "Vladimir, for your own safety from this point onward, we must not be seen together. Each of us must go his own way. I have a mission to accomplish, and I cannot involve you."

Suvorin nods. "I understand. Godspeed on your journey."

Pirogov shakes Suvorin's hand warmly, then the two men embrace. "Vladimir, my dear friend, thank you for your service, loyalty, and friendship. One day, God willing, we will meet again in a free country."

10

Moscow
20 June 1918

The Moscow train station is as squalid as the one in Torzhok. There is trash everywhere, and no one seems to be in charge. Travelers mill about trying to find train schedules and an agent to sell them a ticket.

Pirogov enters a stall in the men's room. Removing his peasant's clothing, he pulls a pair of small scissors from his valise and carefully trims his hair and beard to be more in keeping with his new role as a Bolshevik apparatchik. He changes into his political commissar's uniform, then snaps on the high-crowned pilotka cap with the large red star and engraved hammer and sickle. He stuffs his regular clothing into his valise. Carefully, he cuts the lining of his leather cap and retrieves his Bolshevik identification papers and travel orders. Standing in front of a cracked mirror, he stares at his new persona. He squares his shoulders, holds his head erect, and sees Anton Yurievich Andreev, Bolshevik.

Destroying all evidence of his previous life, Pirogov rips up the passport and visa he received in Torzhok, as well as the train ticket Alexandra gave him. He tosses them into the toilet and pulls the flush lever. Surprisingly, it works. Picking up his valise and the attaché case that holds his phony "official" documents, he leaves the restroom. With all the bravado he can muster, he intends to bluff his way onto the Trans-Siberian Railway with his forged documents.

There is only a short queue for the eastbound train. Two Cheka soldiers guard the turnstile entrance to the train platform. Pirogov bullies his way to the head of the queue and flashes his identification card before the Cheka can ask for his papers. The sergeant gives it a cursory look and waves him past.

Boarding the train, Pirogov enters the coach reserved for high-ranking Party members—formerly the first-class section. He chooses the first compartment on his left and finds it spotlessly clean and unoccupied. Upholstered chairs recline and have a footrest. The floor is covered with plush carpet, the walls with red silk brocade, and the ceiling is painted pastel blue. Victorian-style lighting fixtures illuminate the coach with a soft radiance. Pirogov marvels at the opulence around him and wonders if this is the ultimate fulfillment of the Marxists' maxim "From each according to his ability, to each according to his need." Stowing his valise on the rack overhead, he settles into his seat.

The conductor slides open the compartment door and says, "Good evening, Comrade. Welcome. I am Boris Volodarsky, the conductor on this train. We will do everything to make your journey comfortable. If I may ask, please show me your travel documents." The conductor is a short, overweight fellow with large, soft hands. His brown eyes are lifeless, and his long gray hair is combed with a part down the middle. His uniform is threadbare and wrinkled.

Pirogov forces a thin smile and hands the conductor his forged identification card and travel orders. The conductor glances at them, guesses that they are in order, and promptly returns them to Pirogov. "Thank you, Comrade. I see that you are traveling to Vladivostok and do not have a ticket."

With affected pomposity, Pirogov responds, "I am traveling on urgent, top-secret business for the Third Party International Congress." He pats the attaché case beside him on the seat. "Because of the pressing need for me to leave at once with the top-secret documents in this case, there was no time to bother with a ticket. I'm sure you understand. You can issue a ticket for me at your convenience."

"Of course, Comrade. I'll take care of it for you promptly."

On the platform, the conductor checks his vest-pocket watch, blows his whistle sharply three times, and swings aboard. Stragglers scramble to board and find a seat. The locomotive, with a burst of steam and the spinning screech of its drive wheels, slowly moves and gains momentum. With each passing second, the train accelerates faster and faster.

Pirogov relaxes into his seat, closes his eyes, and congratulates himself on his first successful bluff. Maybe impersonating a Bolshevik will not be so difficult after all. Then he wonders about the accommodations for the proletariat in the third-class coaches.

After several minutes, the door to his compartment slides open and he detects a faint aroma of French perfume. Startled, he snaps open his eyes and sees a gorgeous young woman standing in front of him. Her tailored, tightly fitted, railroad-employee's uniform is pale brown and trimmed in red. The skirt, slightly shorter than the usual style, shows off long, shapely legs, and the deep décolletage of her blouse exposes most of her substantial bosom. He guesses her age to be about twenty. She is tall, erect, and projects an easy mien. Her face is fresh and lovely, enhanced with deep, soft, blue eyes, dark auburn hair loosely knotted behind her head, high cheekbones, and a wide mouth with full lips.

"Good evening, Comrade Andreev. My name is Nadia Azeva. I am here to make your long journey less stressful. How may I be of service to you?" She leans over him to straighten the starched lace doily on his headrest, and her breast brushes against his cheek.

Pirogov slips down in his seat to avoid more contact. Nadia is certainly alluring and, after the long months at Beryosha, he feels himself respond immediately to her presence. But his mission must be his first priority, and he knows that he cannot afford any slips in his cover or his behavior. Not knowing what response is expected or proper, he mumbles, "Thank you, Comrade Nadia. Perhaps a touch of vodka would suffice."

She is keenly aware of his discomfort. "Of course, Comrade. I shall return with your order shortly." She smiles provocatively. "Is there anything else you desire?"

"No, thank you, Comrade Nadia."

She returns with an ice-cold bottle of Monopolowa vodka, two shot glasses, a small silver bowl of caviar, and toast points. When she takes the seat that faces Pirogov, her skirt moves provocatively up her legs. She pours the vodka, lifts her glass, and says *"Na zdorovje."* She smiles at him and tosses it down. "Your turn, Comrade." She dips a silver spoon into the caviar, places it on a piece of toast, and teasingly brings it to his lips. Understanding that he dare not refuse her invitation, he consumes it in one bite. Keenly aware of his fragile disguise, Pirogov resolves not to participate in Nadia's scheme. He lifts his glass, tosses down the vodka, and returns the glass to the tray. "Thank you, Comrade Nadia, for your kind hospitality. I am on serious Party business and I cannot be distracted. I have confidential work to do on papers in my attaché case. Please remove this tray. I will call you when I need something."

She rises, picks up the tray, and says with a pout, "Anytime, Comrade Andreev." As she exits the compartment, she turns and purrs throatily, "Anytime." She sashays away down the aisle, her hips swinging provocatively.

Pirogov leans back, props his feet on the footrest, closes his eyes, and wonders what this encounter portends.

The hours slowly turn into days of worry and pure tedium as the train continues monotonously eastward. Pirogov avoids his fellow passengers as much as possible. Fortunately for him, the coach is not crowded. It appears that few Party functionaries are traveling at this time. Occasionally, another traveler joins him in his compartment, and he feigns sleep until he is left alone again. He tries to take his meals at times when the dining car is mostly empty, in order to avoid having to share a table with other passengers. Such conversation as he must have he keeps brief, even curt. Occasionally, he is accosted by someone whose desire for conversation is relentless. To these people, he turns a witheringly cold gaze and informs them of his "serious Party business." The political climate has become sufficiently paranoid to make even the most determined chatterer turn away quickly. He has reasoned that the less he speaks or interacts with others, the less likely that he somehow unwittingly gives himself away.

Nadia continues to visit his compartment, and it becomes apparent that her "hospitality" role is very specialized. Her flirtation becomes more obvious with each encounter, and Pirogov is at pains to discourage her without offending her. His situation is too precarious to risk arousing her animosity or suspicions. When she approaches, he sometimes pretends to be sleeping.

When this is not possible, he opens his attaché case and keeps his head down, avoiding eye contact and pretending to be preoccupied with his top-secret Party business.

The towns become blurs: Novgorod, Perm, Ekaterinburg, Omsk, Novosibirsk. His days consist of meals, trips to the water closet, and long, solitary hours in his compartment. People come and go, and Nadia flashes by now and then. Feigning sleep or a semi-trance of boredom, he appears to notice nothing. In reality, every nerve is alert to possible discovery, and he grows weary from the stress. But no one bothers him, and he bothers no one.

Bolotnoye, Siberia
25 June 1918

After five days of travel and about two thousand miles, Pirogov is numb in body and mind. No one has yet questioned his identity or his reason for being on the train, and the more distance there is between him and Moscow, the better his odds of continuing his bluff and surviving. Still, he never allows himself to fully relax lest someone, somehow, take him by surprise and break his cover.

As Pirogov looks out his window at the bright morning light bouncing off the flickering leaves of a birch forest, the conductor opens his compartment door and says, "Comrade, Bolotnoye is our next stop. We will be at the station for ten minutes." This announcement rouses Pirogov from his daze. He sits erect in his chair as the train grinds to a jerky stop. People get off, some get on. Freight and mail are unloaded and more loaded. He leaves the train and pretends to stretch his legs as he walks smartly up and down the station platform.

Pirogov stops at the telegraph window in the ramshackle station. The clerk looks up from his duties inside the office and sees Pirogov in his Party uniform. He approaches the window and says, "Good morning, Comrade Commissar. Do you want to send a telegram?"

Pirogov reckons this fellow ought to be the Vaslav Nikolsky of whom Alexandra advised. He appears to be a kindly old fellow with a full head of gray hair and broad laborer's shoulders. He is clean shaven, and there is a vicious scar on his throat. He wears the dark-green uniform and visor cap of the State Communications Directorate.

Pirogov puts his elbows on the shelf and leans slightly into the window. "No," he responds softly. He reaches into his pocket, withdraws a gold schilling, and slips it to the clerk under a blank telegraph form. "I need to know when the next train to Duzhba is."

The clerk palms the schilling and stares at Pirogov. Then he responds in a husky, tense voice, "The next train to Duzhba is supposed to leave tomorrow morning at nine o'clock. Do you want to buy a ticket? It is ten kopecks."

"Maybe. But first, perhaps you have news of a colleague of mine—a young woman about eighteen or nineteen. Her name is Anna Bogrova. She also wants to go to Duzhba."

"My memory is short at my age." Nikolsky looks beseechingly at Pirogov. "I am having trouble recalling." He takes a step back into the telegraph office.

"Would another schilling stimulate your memory?" Pirogov asks with commanding authority.

"It will probably help."

"I don't have time to fool around. Here is another schilling. Obviously you are our contact. Get serious."

Nikolsky grabs the schilling and slips it into his pants pocket. "This woman, Anna Bogrova, has not been to my window. I would remember because she is supposed to give me a gold schilling for telling her the departure time for the Duzhba train." Then, with more confidence he continues, "I have not seen her, and I would have if she had arrived by train." In a softer tone he asks, "When do you expect her?"

Pirogov replies impatiently, "First, tell me where in China the White Russian émigrés are going."

"I am not sure that I recall."

Frustrated, Pirogov grabs him by his collar and pulls Nikolsky up into the window. In a penetrating whisper he demands, "Either you're with us, or against us. Which is it?"

"Turn me loose, fool. I'm neither. I am for myself."

Pirogov releases him, and stares at him.

"I hate the Bolsheviks as much as anyone," Nikolsky says as he points to the scar on his throat. "I'm just a simple man trying to gather enough wealth to escape this hellhole."

Pirogov hands him another schilling. With an apologetic voice he asks, "Where are my associates going?"

Nikolsky leans forward and whispers, "I have heard that they have formed a community in an abandoned lamasery in China."

"Where exactly is this lamasery?"

"I don't know, Comrade. No one has told me, and I haven't asked. And I don't want to know."

"Would another schilling help?"

"No. I'd love to have another schilling, but I really don't know."

Pirogov continues in a more conciliatory tone, "Here are your instructions. Remember them well. I do not know when Anna Bogrova will arrive. It could be soon, or in a year or two. When you see her, tell her that Anton Yurievich Andreev was here and that he asked for her. Tell her when he was here. Most important, tell her that Andreev will meet her at the lamasery."

"I understand, Comrade Andreev. I will carry out your instructions to the letter. My memory improves with each of you White Russian visitors."

In precisely ten minutes, the conductor announces, "All aboard! All aboard!" He blows his whistle three times and climbs into the first-class car. Pirogov rushes down the platform, grabs the boarding handle, and swings aboard. He nods to the conductor and settles into his compartment seat. Again, he is the only passenger in his compartment. In fact, he is the only passenger in this first-class coach.

With some apprehension, he reviews his meeting with Nikolsky. *Is this fellow trustworthy? Does his greed supersede his loyalties? Will he tell Anastasia what I asked?* After a time, he reasons that he must trust Nikolsky because that is his only option.

11

On the Trans-Siberian Railway
25 June 1918

As the train gains momentum, Pirogov begins to relax. He has managed the first leg of the journey without discovery, and he begins to feel confident that Nikolsky will relay his message to Anastasia when she arrives. He gives a deep sigh of relief.

Gazing out the window, he watches the scenery flash past. Not for the first time he thinks to himself that he is leaving his country, probably forever. He knows that the Russia he loved and served with such dedication is dead, but in his heart he feels the painful grief of loss. He prays for his mother's safe arrival at her destination, and for the safety of the imperial family, Suvorin, and his former comrades in the army. But even as he prays, he wonders if God still listens to the prayers of Russians. *Or do the Bolsheviks also control even the ears of God?*

A couple of hours after they leave Bolotnoye, Nadia enters his compartment and sits in the seat facing him. Her perfume is seductive. She smiles engagingly. "You have avoided me for days," she says reproachfully. "May I do something for you?"

"Yes, I would like some tea. If you please, Comrade Nadia."

"It will take a few minutes to brew it." She smiles coyly. "Is there nothing else I can do for you, Comrade?"

"No, not at this time. Please bring me the tea."

Nadia's soft hand idly strokes her neck and the white skin of her décolletage. "Am I not beautiful and desirable?" she asks. "Why do you avoid me?"

"Comrade Nadia, get the tea." Pirogov is eager to end the conversation and Nadia's aggressive sexuality.

But the woman doesn't move. Her eyes take on a crafty glint. "By the way, I saw that you had an extended conversation with the telegraph agent at Bolotnoye, and you gave him a gold coin. I did not see you draft a telegram for him to send, but I did see that you grabbed him by his collar. Pray tell, what business does a Party commissar have with such a fellow?"

With a hard edge to his voice, Pirogov replies coldly, "What I do and with whom I meet is no concern of yours."

Nadia, not a woman to waste a golden opportunity, looks at him with dramatic intensity. "But I could make it my concern," she says boldly. "Your behavior these past five days is abnormal for a Party functionary. I know. I've been working on this train for two years, and you're the only one who has not taken advantage of my personal services."

Pirogov leans forward. Facing her, his voice lowered, he warns, "Comrade, you are treading in dangerous waters. You would be wise to leave well enough alone. Is that clear?"

With her cool, arrogant eyes focused on him, she boastfully replies, "What is clear is that the Cheka would have interest in your strange behavior. Your persona. There is a bourgeois manner about you: the way you act, the way you speak, the way you say 'please' and 'thank you.' These things, and the way you avoid me, are out of context for the commissar you are supposed to be. Is that not so?"

Pirogov is stunned by Nadia's perception. He felt sure that he had shed his well-bred manners and that the Bolshevik uniform would sufficiently intimidate anyone inclined to question him too closely. In an instant, all the Empress's plans, Anastasia's fate, and that of the White Russian community are in peril. He is perplexed; what should he do? He cannot risk exposure this close to success.

Nadia leans forward, exposing her bosom. "I see that you are speechless. I can understand your dilemma. Perhaps we can reach an accommodation."

She leans back in her chair with her legs slightly apart. "Understand that I am not an employee of the railroad. Nor am I in the pay of the Cheka or the Party. I am a freelance operative, perhaps the only entrepreneur left in this shithole of a country. The Party ignores me with tacit approval. My services are conducive to the positive morale of their apparatchiks. And the conductor and I have a business arrangement. He lets me operate on a commission basis." She pauses and waits for Pirogov's response.

Leaning forward and looking into her eyes, Pirogov replies in a soft, obliging voice, "That story is most interesting, Nadia. Perhaps we can reach an accommodation. What do you have in mind?"

Realizing that she has her victim's acquiescence to her blackmail scheme, she smiles seductively. "For my silence, I will take all your remaining gold coins," she purrs. "Nothing less. How many do you have?"

"Five," he lies. "They are taped to my legs." He stands and straightens his jacket and trousers. "Where is the conductor?"

"He is attending to the peasants in the rear coaches. He will not return here for several hours, not until we reach our next stop."

Pirogov places his arms around her waist and whispers in her ear, "Do you have a place where I can remove my trousers to retrieve the gold coins? They are Maria Theresa gold schillings—an international currency of extreme value in these troubled times."

Nadia wriggles free and giggles. "Of course. That is my business. I have a compartment at the end of this coach. Follow me, kind sir." She leaves the compartment and begins to stride down the aisle, her *derrière* swaying in erotic syncopation.

Pirogov, knowing what he must do, steels himself as he moves closer to Nadia. They enter her compartment, and when she turns away to pull the door closed, he grabs her neck with his strong hands and squeezes with concentrated strength. In her desperation, she frantically clutches at his hands, trying to break his viselike grip. Her nails score the back of his hands. She gags. He puts his right knee at the base of her spine and pulls back with all his remaining power. There is a sharp snap, and Nadia goes limp. He releases his grip, and she slips to the floor lifeless.

He collapses on her bed and takes several deep breaths to regain his composure and renew his resolve. Pulling out his handkerchief, he wipes the blood from his hands and applies pressure to stop the bleeding. Though he is a soldier and has killed in the heat of battle, murder is not in the fabric of his soul. He rationalizes that its immorality pales next to the far larger morality of the Empress's plan. In war, what must be done, is done.

When his heart stops pounding, Pirogov peers out of the compartment to make certain that the corridor is empty. Then, he carries Nadia's body to the rear platform of the coach, opens the side door, and tosses the body from the fast-moving train. He immediately returns to his compartment and smoothes his rumpled clothes. He has frightful images of Nadia's body hitting the ground and tumbling into the tall grass.

Still breathless, Pirogov inspects himself. His clothing is in order, and no buttons or other pieces of his garments are missing. The deep scratches on the backs of his hands have stopped bleeding. He reminds himself to keep his hands concealed as much as possible and to dispose of the bloody handkerchief the next time he visits the water closet. Then, he leans back and tries to recover the guise of chilly calm that has served him well so far. But his hands are still shaking, and he feels the slight nausea that comes after an abrupt surge of adrenaline.

Three hours later, the conductor slides the door open and steps into Pirogov's compartment. "Have you seen Comrade Nadia? I can't find her."

"Yes, a couple of hours ago she went to fetch some tea. She hasn't returned." Pirogov feigns bemusement. "I've been wondering where she is."

Puzzled, the conductor responds, "Most unusual. She's supposed to remain in either this coach or the dining car."

"Don't be troubled," Pirogov replies. "I'm confident that Comrade Nadia will return shortly. She appears to take her work very seriously."

The conductor nods. "No doubt you're right, Comrade." He withdraws and continues down the corridor.

Near Ulan Ude
27 June 1918

Pirogov has passed a sleepless night and a troubled day. To avoid arousing suspicion about his possible role in Nadia's disappearance, he has kept to his usual routine: staying in his compartment, taking his meals at times when the dining car is mostly empty, and avoiding contact with other passengers.

He is still shaken from his final encounter with Nadia. He had carefully washed all traces of blood from his hands, but the scratches are still livid. At meals, he pushes the food around his plate, lacking any appetite. He feels almost ill with the fear of discovery.

He tries to reassure himself that there is little likelihood that Nadia's body will be found. The area where her body fell is far from any settlement, a wild region of the steppes avoided even by the locals. *The wolves ate well last night,* he reasons. Perhaps someday a few bones might be discovered, but they would be unrecognizable as the remains of Comrade Nadia. And it seems unlikely that she had a family or anyone else who might demand an investigation into her disappearance, particularly now when thousands of people are disappearing under the Red Terror. Her presence on the train was technically illicit, however it was condoned by the authorities. The conductor, who derived a financial benefit from Nadia's activities, would try to avoid official scrutiny of his private business pursuits, so even he would be reluctant to draw attention to Nadia's presence or absence on his train. But, however Pirogov rationalizes his crime or the improbability of discovery, he cannot relax.

It is now late afternoon, and Pirogov is gazing listlessly out the window. The conductor pokes his head into Pirogov's compartment. "Comrade Andreev, we're approaching Ulan Ude. We'll be there for thirty minutes." Pirogov stirs and gazes at the conductor. "There are bundles of freight and mail to transfer to the Mongolian Express to Peking. And we're expecting a delegation of Party officials en route to Vladivostok. They'll be disappointed that Comrade Nadia is not here to greet them and make them comfortable. Maybe you will know some of them."

Alarmed, Pirogov responds casually, "It's possible, but I doubt it. I've been on detached duty in Petrograd for several months." The conductor nods and returns to the rear of the coach to prepare for the upcoming stop.

Pirogov now makes a lightning-quick decision. He will leave this train at Ulan Ude and change to the Mongolian Express to Peking. The oncoming Party apparatchiks will surely want to talk with him. He sees no need to gamble on being exposed by his inexperience as a Party commissar.

And, although the conductor seems resigned to Nadia's absence, Pirogov cannot ignore his growing fear that someone may have observed him with Nadia or seen her body fall from the train. He also worries that he might unwittingly have left some evidence of his presence in her compartment. Certainly, the raw scratches on his hands would arouse the curiosity of anyone who looked at him too closely. He sees no other course than to leave the Trans-Siberian train now, while he still can.

It is not quite dark as the train begins to slow down. Pirogov picks up his valise and attaché case, walks to the front of the coach, exits onto the coach platform, and opens the door opposite the station. The train screeches to a jerking halt. Even before the train comes to a complete stop, he swings to the ground. All around him there is beehive-like activity as freight and mail are transferred and people leave and board the train. He walks around to the front of the engine, crosses the tracks, quickly climbs onto the station platform, and mingles with the crowd. He spots the conductor escorting the apparatchiks onto the Party coach, and gives a sigh of relief.

Pirogov enters the station. It is the same as the other stations on the line—dilapidated, littered with trash, its paint peeling, and smelling of unwashed peasants. At the concession stand, he asks for tea. The grubby attendant hands him a cup and says, "Two kopecks." Pirogov does not have kopecks, only rubles. He hands the attendant a ruble and says, "Unfortunately, I do not have any kopecks."

"I don't have enough kopecks to make change. But have the tea at no charge. You look tired from a long journey, Comrade."

Taking the tea, Pirogov says, "You are a good man and loyal to our revolution, no doubt."

The attendant looks at Pirogov with a cocked head. "No doubt."

The racket and clanking of the Trans-Siberian Railway train leaving the station stifle further conversation. When the din subsides, Pirogov comments,

"The station is empty. Where are the stationmaster, the telegraph clerk, the ticket agent? Are there no guards to check passengers' papers?"

The attendant closes the lid to his stand, removes his stained apron, takes his money box, and looks at Pirogov with curious eyes. "They've all gone home. There's nothing more to do here. The next train is the Mongolian Express, which should arrive tomorrow morning sometime. That's too early for the Red Guards. They'll be sleeping off another drunken binge."

"Sometime!" exclaims Pirogov. "Doesn't an express train have a schedule to keep?"

The attendant, clearly anxious to go home, responds, "Of course, there's a schedule. But this train comes from China through the Soviet province of Mongolia. It arrives when it gets here." He shrugs and exits through the side door.

Resigned, Pirogov cleans off a seat with his handkerchief and sits down to devise a plan in this lackadaisical outpost of civilization. But his internal stress and physical condition preclude rational thought. He is hungry. Dinner is now being served in the dining car on the train. He needs a bath; his clothes are filthy and stink. He is weary in body and mind. Guilt about having killed a foolish, opportunistic young woman still clouds his soul. As night envelops the area, he concludes that his best strategy is to remain in the station. Venturing into town in his uniform would be too risky. He spends a fitful night trying to sleep on a wooden bench.

About seven o'clock the next morning the stationmaster wakes him. "Good morning, Comrade. I expect that you're waiting for the Mongolian Express. It will be here in twenty minutes or so. It's almost on time today—only two hours late. You transferred from the Trans-Siberian Railway train last evening, did you not?" The stationmaster is about fifty years old, a large man with rough hands and two-day-old whiskers. His black eyes project a cold demeanor.

Pirogov stands and shakes off the stiffness in his muscles. He adjusts his soiled uniform as best he can. "Yes, I did. Thank you for waking me. I want to buy a ticket to Ulan Bator."

"Go to the ticket window."

Pirogov, still stiff, walks slowly to the window. The stationmaster looks at him dully. In a monotone he says, "Ten rubles."

Near Naushki, Siberia
27 June 1918

Pirogov has a window seat in the front coach. It is not as plush as the Trans-Siberian Railway train, but it is more comfortable and more private than the proletariat's coaches. No one had questioned him at the Ulan Ude station. There were no Red Guards on duty, and the civilians in the station were too preoccupied with their own concerns to pay him any attention. He wonders if he can survive the three days to Peking. It is almost 1,900 miles distant. Exhausted by the stress of the past few days, he takes refuge in a self-hypnotic state. The passing towns fade monotonously into blank memory.

Early the next day, the train arrives in Ulan Bator. Here on the rim of the Gobi Desert, the scorching heat is already stifling. Flies infest the foul-smelling, nearly deserted station. It is obvious that the building has not been cleaned since the revolution. The slow-motion activity of freight and mail transfer gives the station a modicum of life. The only passengers seem to be a small cadre of government bureaucrats and technocrats, a motley crew of Occidental and Tartar-type Russians, Mongols, Indians, and Chinese.

In the station's men's room, Pirogov locks the door, strips off his Party uniform, and jams it to the bottom of a trash receptacle that has not been emptied in days. Then he piles all the foul-smelling refuse on top. With scissors and razor he removes his beard and mustache, and cuts his hair as short as he can. He dons the civilian clothes from his valise and pulls his civilian identification papers from the inside lining of his cap. Wiping the grime from a section of a cracked mirror, he arranges his hat and sees Kirik Pirogov, newly formed.

The ticket to Peking costs twenty rubles. No one questions him or even seems to notice his presence. The ambience of the place appears to say, "It's too hot to bother. And why do we care that we have become a satellite of the Union of Soviet Socialist Republics?"

Only three hours late, the train pulls out of the station with the usual cacophony.

Now, Pirogov rides with the proletariat. Fortunately, the coach is not crowded and he has a window seat—narrow, upright, and hard. Again, he retreats into the appearance of mental torpor. He gazes listlessly at the passing countryside—the drab expanses of the Gobi Desert, then the eroded hills of north China. There is no dining car for third-class passengers, so he purchases tea, sausages, and bread from a cart that rolls back and forth through the coaches.

At the border, Chinese officials wander down the aisles in a perfunctory show of concern. They exit, and the train continues.

Pirogov speaks to no one, makes eye contact with no one, asks for nothing. But beneath his air of isolation and dullness his mind is seething, trying to plan his next steps.

Finally, after a painful journey of forty-six hours, the train enters Peking. Pirogov sits erect and looks out with interest as the shabby outskirts of the city gradually become denser and more urban. At crossings, he sees signs in Chinese characters, crowds of small people dressed in robes and dark workers' clothing, and carts pulled by horses or donkeys. The light is different here, softly diffused by the omnipresent dust. For the first time in over a week, Pirogov feels the burden of stress fall from his shoulders.

Finally, the train comes to a jarring halt in the Peking station.

12

White Russian Hotel, Peking
1 July 1918

A weary Pirogov, bedraggled and malodorous, is swept out of the Peking train station into a stew of jostling humanity. The seething city is hot, and the air is laden with moisture and dust. He knows there is no one here to befriend him or give him directions. Perplexed, not knowing which way to go, he stops and surveys the sprawling city around the station.

Never has he seen such a mass of humanity. The sidewalks are crowded with people jammed shoulder to shoulder, pushing past and around each other. Businessmen in long robes or Western suits mingle with workers and peasants carrying loads in baskets on their backs or dangling from a long pole resting on their shoulders. Dainty Chinese women in traditional dress slip quickly through the crowds, while Western women, larger and less agile, walk stolidly. Pirogov spots a pickpocket in a group of people waiting to cross the street. He's a slim boy, whose deft fingers relieve a beefy Western businessman of his wallet even as Pirogov watches.

The streets are congested with every imaginable kind of wheeled transport, from pushcarts and rickshaws to heavy trucks. Motorcycles dart between flashy automobiles. A weary horse pulls a large wagon loaded with sacks of coal. A bicycle carrying a family of four moves slowly along the gutter. The noise is an almost unbearable cacophony of horns, bells, motors of every size, and impatient shouts of drivers.

Eventually, he spots a large sign in Cyrillic lettering, highlighted by the setting sun. He has difficulty fathoming its message because it is partially obscured by a myriad of advertising banners blanketed with Chinese ideograms. The banners are dense enough to almost obscure the sky. He walks toward the sign, and in a few minutes he is close enough to read its message: "White Russian Hotel, Welcome."

The three-story hotel is squeezed between the One-Day White Laundry and Natasha's Entertainment Emporium. The entrance is a large, white-framed, double door, and the window sills and most of the trim are also painted a dingy white. The building is old, made of stone, and in need of major renovation and a thorough cleaning. Pirogov enters the miniscule lobby and steps up to the reception desk. A threadbare dark-blue carpet covers a creaky, much-scarred wood floor, and a single bare bulb hangs from the ceiling. The place exudes a musty atmosphere of long-dead cigars, stale rice wine, cheap cologne, and gamey sweat. He approaches the tattered birch desk and asks the clerk the price of a room.

The clerk, who's been checking accounts, puts down his pen, takes a long, piercing look at Pirogov, and eventually responds, "Depends."

Pirogov, with a hint of hostility, counters, "Depends on what?"

The clerk is a middle-aged Occidental with receding hair and a protruding chin. He projects a dour but honest bearing. "The posted rate is twenty-two Chinese dollars per night," he says in his growly voice. "However, the actual rate depends on how long you're going to stay, and what currency you've got. We don't ask questions here. We're flexible about trying to accommodate our guests, who are mostly White Russians like yourself. Lots of you people have been passing through here these past couple of years."

Pirogov, somewhat taken aback, puts his elbows on the counter and says, "I can pay in rubles."

The clerk leans back on his stool. "Rubles are no good anymore since the Bolsheviks took power. They won't buy a dead rat. What else you got?"

Frustrated, Pirogov rubs his face with both of his hands and kneads his head to ease the exhaustion that engulfs him. "What currency do you prefer? Or accept?"

"Gold! Always gold. You got gold?"

Not willing to reveal his stash of gold schillings, Pirogov says, "No, I don't have gold. What else?"

"British pounds sterling are satisfactory. Then Mexican silver pesos, American greenbacks, and lastly Chinese dollars. If I have to, I'll take Swiss francs. How long are you going to stay in our White Russian palace?"

"I'm not sure how long I'll be here. Perhaps a few weeks. I have some business to tend to, then I'll be on my way. I can pay in British pounds."

"You look like a soldier. Is that not so?"

Pirogov returns to his standing position now that the clerk shows some semblance of amity. "Yes, I was in the Palace Guards. I deserted shortly after the Czar abdicated," he lies.

"I thought so. Seen a lot of you Czarist soldiers lately. Me, I was a sailor, a gunner's mate, on Admiral Rozhestvensky's flagship *Suvorov* during the Tsushima Straits battle in May naught five. Caught a Japanese shell fragment in my right leg, still got it. Blown into the water and picked up by a Korean fishing boat looking for spoils. Eventually, I worked my way here, and here I remain." He waits for Pirogov's response. There is none. Pirogov fidgets, waiting for the clerk to continue.

After several seconds of awkward silence, the clerk says, "We have special rates for White soldiers. One British pound sterling for a week. Paid in advance."

"That is satisfactory." Pirogov reaches into his breast pocket, withdraws a five-pound note, and hands it to the clerk. "In case I have to remain longer than planned—and to avoid inquiries."

The clerk inspects the note carefully, especially the engraved portrait of George V, reckons that it is genuine, and stuffs it in his pocket. "My name is Anatol Kavelin. For the register, what is your name?"

Pirogov is somewhat chary of revealing his true identity. But by now he reckons that the Cheka is searching for Anton Andreev, the imposter. Having identification papers only in his false name, Pirogov says, "Kirik Pirogov."

Kavelin nods, puts Pirogov's name in the register, and with a sharp eye says, "Your real name or your *nom de guerre*?"

Pirogov looks down the long hallway and says with measured reserve, "You asked a question. Give me the key, if you please."

Kavelin hands him the key. "Room 223. Down the hall and up those back stairs."

Pirogov enters room 223. It is small, cheaply furnished, and none too clean. He shrugs. "It will do," he mutters to himself.

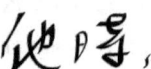

After several extended and restful nights of sleep, hot baths, and tasty Chinese meals, Pirogov's mental and physical vigor are restored. For the first time in many weeks, he feels relatively safe. Whatever chaos reigns in the Soviet Union, he is out of it. With renewed energy, he feels ready to deal with the next hurdles in his journey.

Occasionally, he wonders what has become of Vladimir Suvorin. He knows that Beryosha's former butler is a resourceful and highly intelligent man, but these qualities might not be enough to protect him from the murderous violence unleashed by the victorious Bolsheviks. In the months they spent together, Pirogov came to respect Vladimir's skills and enjoy his company. The man was as cultured as most of Pirogov's aristocratic friends, but also blessed with sound common sense and a sly wit that lightened their days. That the two had become friends, Pirogov felt, was more to his own credit than to Vladimir's, whose high standards of behavior would have been beyond the grasp of many of his aristocratic circle. Quietly, he prays for Vladimir's safety.

Once he is ready to continue his mission, Pirogov outlines three tasks for himself. First, he must somehow discover the precise location of the White Russian village. Second, he must equip himself for life in remote western China, in a place that he knows will offer few basic comforts or any convenient source of resupply. And, finally, he must retrieve the box containing Saint Catherine's Crown and the Romanov jewels from the Swedish Embassy. This third task should be left for last, he reasons, because the treasure will be more secure in the embassy safe than in his hotel room, which offers little protection from prying eyes or greedy hands.

He is busy in the ensuing days. The hotel clerk introduces him to members of the White Russian community, who help him find shops where he can replace the filthy peasant shirt and trousers he wore over the last leg of his journey to Peking. With a sigh of relief, he tosses the old clothes in the back of the small armoire in his room and puts on an inexpensive but serviceable three-piece suit that he deems suitable for wearing to conduct the rest of his business in Peking. He also buys clothing that he feels will be suitable for life in the White Russian village—heavy boots, work clothes, a warm coat for winter, as well as such basics as undergarments, soap, and a few essential medicines.

Pirogov asks the desk clerk if he knows of a restaurant where the White community congregates. Without hesitation, the clerk directs Pirogov to Oretsky's Teahouse, a Russian restaurant a few streets away. The place is small, obscure, and simply furnished with bare wood tables and chairs. It is spotlessly clean, serves hearty Russian food, and the samovar is always bubbling. It is quickly apparent to Pirogov that Oretsky's establishment is far more than a restaurant. It serves as a social center for Peking's White Russian community, and the place is occupied day and night by refugees sipping tea over a chessboard or reading the local Russian-language newspaper.

Oretsky's quickly becomes Pirogov's refuge as well, a place where he can rest between shopping and other errands, and where he can relax in the company of other Russians. Occasionally, a musician comes in with a balalaika or an accordion and spends the evening singing the sweet minor-key songs of Old Russia, and a hat is passed around the room to collect the coins that the musician depends on to keep himself alive.

Pirogov quickly decides that his best chance of discovering the name and location of the exiles' village may be from Oretsky's customers. Peking's White Russian community includes a couple of thousand refugees, and he reasons that surely among them there must be someone who knows of the village. For several days he loiters in the restaurant, sipping tea and pretending to read a newspaper while he eavesdrops on the conversations going on around him. But the talk focuses mainly on the speakers' daily lives or on the lives they left behind.

He must be more proactive, Pirogov reasons, but how can he ask questions without giving away the purpose of his mission? For several nights, he lies in his bed seeking a solution to this dilemma. Finally, he decides that an indirect question might serve his purpose and still protect his mission.

The next day, after a long shopping errand to buy heavy woolen socks for the coming winter, he stops at Oretsky's for his usual cup of tea and a session with the latest issue of the Russian-language newspaper. When the owner brings his tea, Pirogov tries his new approach.

"You've no doubt seen me here often," he tells Ivan Oretsky, a short, round man with a full beard and a slight limp. "It seems to me that many of the local Russian community come here. I wonder if you might be able to give me some information." Oretsky's eyebrows rise. He wears a traditional Russian shirt over dark trousers, the shirt frayed at the collar and cuffs, but all perfectly clean. "I'm looking for my mother. She left Russia just before the Czar abdicated, and all I know is that she was going to China."

"I might know her," Oretsky responds cautiously. "A lot of refugees ended up here in Peking. What's her name?"

Pirogov pauses, assessing the risk of revealing his mother's name. Deciding that he has little choice, he responds, "Maria Pavlovna Pirogov. She left Saint Petersburg in the spring of 1917. I was still in military service at that time and knew nothing of her departure until much later. Might she have come here, to Peking?"

"I don't know her."

Feigning disappointment, Pirogov continues, "Where else in China might she have gone?"

Oretsky, becoming interested in the conversation and enjoying his role as advisor, pulls out a chair and sits down. "Well, there are a lot of Russians in Shanghai, also a lot who made it to Canton, and some into British Hong Kong. And, of course, others went to Manchuria, to Harbin. There's a big Russian community there as well. But there are White Russians in almost every large town in China, although not so many as in the larger cities. It's hard enough for them to make a living here, in this big city. In the small towns and villages, it's impossible." He looks around the teahouse, filling now with customers at the end of the day. "Most of the people here have no work," he continues. "They live by selling off whatever possessions they brought with them. What they'll do when all their saleable items are gone, I don't know." He snorts. "Some of these people have never worked a day in their lives, have no skills except maybe for dancing at a ball or playing some bourgeois sport. They're fit for nothing but manual labor, but they think they're too good for that. So they starve and spend their days dreaming of the old days. Fools!"

Oretsky gets up to bring Pirogov another cup of tea, and a cup for himself. Setting down the cups, he looks Pirogov over closely. "You look handy enough. Done your share of hard work, I'd guess?"

"Some." Pirogov smiles slightly. The conversation is going well, and Oretsky seems eager to pass on information that might be helpful. "What about you?" he asks. "What brought you to Peking?"

"Oh, I've been here for years. I used to be a banker, came here from Moscow in 1905 to manage a branch of the Imperial Bank of Saint Petersburg. When the war started, the bank directed me to close the branch and return to Moscow. I'd been keeping a close eye on the political situation in Russia and decided there was no future there for me—or indeed for anyone not of the revolutionary persuasion. I closed the bank, took my savings, and bought this teahouse. It's not making me rich, but it's a living, and I get to hear all the latest gossip."

"Do you hear any gossip about other Russian communities in China? Is there any way I can find out where my mother is?"

"I'll keep my ears open." Oretsky sips from his cup. He leans closer to Pirogov. "But let me warn you. Be careful who you talk to. Most of the people here are decent folks, displaced Whites like yourself. But the Bolsheviks' secret police have ears everywhere. Don't say anything that you don't want to get back to Comrade Lenin's ears."

He points at the scar on Pirogov's cheek. "I'd guess you saw some time on the battlefield."

"Yes, I served on the Galician Front."

"Nasty fight, that. Too many good men died there."

"Yes," responds Pirogov, reluctant to discuss a topic that brings up painful memories.

Oretsky nods. "You should know that the Bolshies are looking for military men with White leanings. They're poking about everywhere. We discovered one of these fellows recently, hanging around the Orthodox Church. A few days later, he disappeared mysteriously. I understand that he fell into the river. Must have had too much to drink." He winks slyly.

"Watch yourself, young man. I'll keep my ears open in case I hear anything about your mother."

13

Kremlin, Moscow
16 July 1918

The afternoon is drab in the Kremlin. Vladimir Ilyich Lenin is writing at his desk with an intense focus. He wears a gray suit with a scarlet tie over his off-white shirt. On the walls are photographs and posters extolling the virtues of collectivism.

Lenin, the leader of the Russian Revolution, is now the Chairman of the People's Commissars of the Union of Soviet Socialist Republics. He is fifty-eight years old and bald, with a full mustache and a Van Dyke beard. His deep brown eyes are alive with passionate fervor.

He writes with slow precision on a paper bearing the official seal of the Soviet government—the hammer and sickle in yellow on a red background—then he puts down the pen and leans back in his chair. As he reads the document, spreads over his face.

Satisfied, he hands it to Felix Dzerzhinsky, the ruthless leader of the Cheka. He is exactly the kind of unbridled sociopath that Lenin wants as his lead henchman. Dzerzhinsky is a medium-size man with a brown, stony face and a fixed expression. He wears a walrus mustache and a short, pointed Van Dyke beard. Lenin leans forward and dictates, "Read it, Felix. Read it out loud. I want to hear how it sounds. I want the world to hear it!"

Dzerzhinsky looks mildly interested as he begins to read the short note aloud. Now, seriously interested, he reads it again, then once again. He looks up from the document to Lenin and tentatively asks him, "You are positive that this is the correct action? At this time?"

"Of course, I'm sure."

Dzerzhinsky, in a mild retort, suggests, "Comrade, my point is that I wonder if it would not be prudent to wait until we have consolidated more control over the country. Our political and military positions are perilously in flux."

Lenin snaps, "Comrade Dzerzhinsky, you keep the Cheka working to eliminate the counter-revolutionaries and I will lead our socialist country." Irritated, he shifts in his chair, then picks up a pen and taps it on his desk. He stares blankly out a window as the Kremlin glows scarlet in the dusk. Clearly, he is evaluating Dzerzhinsky's comments because they have a ring of truth. The *tap, tap, tap* of the pen continues. Lenin puzzles over the scarlet sunset. *Is it an omen—red for Red?*

After a minute or so, he shifts in his chair to face Grigory Zinoviev, the third man in the room. Lenin holds him in a thoughtful gaze for a few moments, then says in a spirited voice, "Let us hear what Comrade Zinoviev has to say."

Dzerzhinsky turns to Zinoviev, the Interior Minister, revolutionary, and close confidant to Lenin. Zinoviev is a big brute of a man with icy blue eyes and long, midnight-black hair. His face is littered with smallpox scars, but he is cleanshaven, almost proud of his disfigurement.

After a brief pause, and in a gruff bass voice, Zinoviev responds, "My respects, Comrade Lenin, but I ask you to reconsider. The majority of the proletariat still love their Czar, who is also the spiritual leader of the Orthodox Church. Such an audacious action will cause many loyal people to question your motives. I do not recommend this precipitous order. Over the next few months, let us reflect on some of the alternatives."

Lenin shouts, "Stop! Stop it, Zinoviev. Am I surrounded by naysayers? The Communist Party and the Third International Congress of Soviets made me Party Chairman and Head of State. I know what is best for our Soviet Union. The peasants will do as the State directs."

Zinoviev, who has remained standing, straightens his shoulders and responds deferentially, yet with conviction, "If you insist on this course of action, our socialist government will be in extreme peril and may well fall to the Western imperialists. We are fighting them on five fronts. The White Armies of General Denikin and Admiral Kolchak defeat our Red Army in every engagement. Our desertion rates are excessively high. The Northern Russian Expedition of fourteen battalions of British Commonwealth, American, and French colonial troops has occupied Murmansk and Archangel, and they are advancing into the interior."

Lenin is clearly annoyed that his old friend should question his judgment. He rises from his chair, glares at Zinoviev, shakes his closed fist at him, and snaps, "The Soviet Union will prevail over these Western interlopers. Our allies—the sharp winter and the vast steppes—ultimately will engulf and destroy them."

Zinoviev, stunned by Lenin's sharp rebuke, looks to Dzerzhinsky for support. Dzerzhinsky looks away and shakes his head from side to side. Then, he says, "Comrade Lenin has made his decision. I manage the Cheka on his authority."

Realizing that he is alone in this discussion, Zinoviev counters, "Comrade Lenin, we have been together for years. Please do not dismiss my report with such a cavalier comment, or underestimate the seriousness of these Westerners on our soil. Hear me out."

Lenin, still irritated, returns to his chair, and says, "Speak your piece, Grigory."

"There is more. American and Japanese troops have occupied Vladivostok, and the Japanese are moving inland. They have occupied all of Sakhalin Island. Elements of their Kwantung Army are assembling along the Khalkin Gol River at Nomonhan, threatening an incursion into our Mongolian province. The Japanese are continuing the war of 1904 unopposed, in violation of the Treaty of Portsmouth. British and Indian troops have invaded the Southern Caucasus. And perhaps most important, the Czech Legion has control of the Trans-Siberian Railway from Kazan to Novosibirsk."

Lenin snaps, "Your point, Comrade? Make it now. I have a country to run."

Zinoviev responds forcefully, "Comrade Lenin, my point is critical. We cannot defeat them all. We are isolated from the rest of the world. If our socialist government is to survive, then we must have peace—peace at any cost. We do not need more armed hostility. We need Western recognition and wheat, lots of wheat, if we are to survive this winter. I implore you to reconsider."

"Zinoviev, you were my loyal ally when our Bolshevik Revolution overthrew the Czar and his imperialist lackeys. Remain loyal to me now. Read my telegram. Read it out loud," demands Lenin.

With trepidation, Zinoviev whispers, "Your message is headed Top Secret. It reads:

To: Comrade Colonel Yakov Yurovsky, Commanding Officer, Cheka, Ekaterinburg. No later than tomorrow evening, you are to execute the prisoners held in the Ipatiev House. Specifically, I name the Romanov royal family of Imperial Russia: the Czar Nicholas, Empress Alexandra, Czarevich Alexei, and the Grand Duchesses Marie, Olga, Tatiana, and Anastasia. Confirm results. Lenin

Lenin smirks and tells Zinoviev, "Give this telegram to Comrade Roman Malinovsky, our new Commissar of Posts and Telegraphs. Have him encrypt it in our Omega code for immediate transmission."

14

Ipatiev House, Ekaterinburg, Siberia
17 July 1918

The corner windows on the second story are lit in the Ipatiev House, an elegant two-story dacha on several hundred acres of well-tended gardens, fountains, ponds, and virgin birch forest. The Bolsheviks have dubbed this dacha "The House of Special Purpose." It is shortly before midnight, but the house is astir with activity.

The imperial family have been prisoners of the Cheka in this house since April, closely confined and daily suffering the insults of their Red guards. Their only comfort is the fact that they are together. Rumors of impending rescue reach them periodically, but each time they wait in vain.

Anastasia is still with her family. After Alexandra's burst of courage and determination during the last days of the czarist regime, she was unable to follow through on her decision to send her youngest daughter away alone to the White Russian refuge in China. There were a few occasions when Anastasia could have escaped the scrutiny of the guards, but each time Alexandra hesitated, waiting for a better opportunity or for the desperately-hoped-for rescue that would allow the family to remain together. In truth, Alexandra could not bear to part with her child, even knowing the deadly fate that awaited them all if rescue did not come.

This evening the family had calmly retired at the usual time.

About an hour later, the sergeant of the guard arouses them and orders them to dress and hurry downstairs to the cellar. He explains that the Czech

Legion and a unit of the White Army are approaching Ekaterinburg, and the Regional Soviet has ordered that they be moved.

The family rushes to dress and pack a few personal belongings. "Put on your blue dress," Alexandra whispers to Anastasia as they pass in the upstairs hallway. When the family arrives in the cellar, the sergeant tells them that their transportation will arrive shortly. A Cheka guard brings a chair for the Empress. For a moment, Alexandra's heart fills with hope. If the Czech Legion and White Army are so near, rescue might be imminent. Soon they might all be free, on their way to England. She was right, she thinks, not to send Anastasia away on her own. Now the family will be together. She puts an arm around her youngest daughter's waist. *Thanks be to God.*

Suddenly, a squad of Cheka soldiers with their rifles at port arms marches single file and at double time into the cellar. After the last soldier is in position, the first sergeant commands, "Squad, halt! Right face." The soldiers turn to face the Romanovs. After a moment, the sergeant shouts, "Squad, ah-ten-hut!" The sound of rifle butts hitting the concrete floor reverberates throughout the cellar.

Several minutes later, Colonel Yakov Yurovsky enters. He is the senior Cheka officer in the area. He wears the summer gray, short-sleeved, tunic uniform with red piping and his colonel's pips on the shoulder boards.

"Present. Arms!" commands the first sergeant.

The soldiers bring their rifles to the present-arms position to salute their commanding officer.

In return, Colonel Yurovsky returns a snappy hand salute.

The Czarevich giggles in delight at the military prompt.

However, fear and concern race through the rest of the Romanov family. Alexandra knows exactly what is happening. The Czar, Anastasia, and her three sisters wonder what this military demonstration has to do with their rescue by the Whites or the Czech Legion.

"Order arms!" commands the sergeant. The soldiers return their rifles to the right side. The pounding of the rifle butts hitting the concrete floor sends chills through the Romanovs, causing them to wonder what is happening.

Yurovsky orders Alexandra to stand. The indignity of this crass Bolshevik officer ordering the Empress of All the Russias to comply with his command is unthinkable. She stares with smoldering hostility at Yurovsky. But, no longer enjoying the resources of royal status, she complies. After a moment or two she slowly moves a few paces to her left, next to Anastasia.

With his arms akimbo, Yurovsky walks down the line of the imperial family. He stops in front of each person and looks intently into his or her eyes. All but the Empress turn away from him. Summoning all her courage, she returns her most imperious glower of disdain.

He smiles faintly at her feeble attempt at bravado.

The Czarevich is dressed in his sailor uniform. Maintaining proper military protocol, he salutes Yurovsky. The colonel stares at him contemptuously and does not return the salute.

This military display does not look like a rescue to the four daughters. Extreme apprehension engulfs Maria and Tatiana. Unsure of what is happening and fearing the worst, they cannot control their fears and sob softly.

Colonel Yurovsky turns to the first sergeant and snaps, "On my orders!"

"As you say. Sir!"

Yurovsky moves to the concrete steps and climbs three. "Port arms!" he shouts. He surveys the scene to ensure that the Romanovs are positioned correctly and that his soldiers are ready.

Satisfied that the staging is correct, Yurovsky commands, "Fix bayonets!"

There is a loud clanging of metal as the soldiers snap their bayonets onto their rifles.

Anastasia now understands with crystal clarity the task that her mother assigned to her so long ago. They are not going to be rescued, and she and her family are going to be murdered by the Bolsheviks. An overwhelming fear of death engulfs her. Her family is in this cellar for an execution. She fights to be brave and to hold back her tears. Her mother cannot help her.

"Load!" The soldiers pull back the bolts of their rifles, then jam the bolts forward, loading a round into the rifles' chambers. The metal-on-metal clicking sends a vibration of horror through the cellar.

The other three daughters begin to sob and make the sign of the cross as they realize their fate is death. Alexandra commands, "Be brave. You are Romanovs. Saint Nicholas will guide you."

The Czar has been standing silently, as if he were in a dream. Aroused by the loud clicking of metal, he exclaims, "What!"

"Aim!" The riflemen select the nearest target.

The Romanovs see the loaded rifles with bayonets pointed at them. Their fate is all too clear.

Cries. Screams.

"Fire!"

The deafening thunder of the first volley reverberates through the cellar. Agonized screams! Another volley. Another. And another. Silence.

Colonel Yurovsky has complied with Lenin's orders with clinical efficiency. He cannot see clearly in the small, smoke-filled cellar. He checks the mutilated human forms askew on the concrete floor. There are no heartbeats. There is no light in any of the eyes. He grimaces at the bloody corpses. Even for a hardened Cheka officer it is a gruesome scene. In a few minutes, the basement window goes dark.

Satisfied that the regicide has been successfully executed, he orders his communications officer to send an encoded telegram.

To: VI Lenin and Felix Dzerzhinsky, in care of the Presidium of the Central Executive Council, Moscow: The Romanovs are dead this night. Yurovsky

In the upstairs lounge, he and his Cheka soldiers celebrate the foul deed well done, and toast frequently with shots of vodka.

В друго́й рӑз

Several hours later, one of the mangled Romanov bodies stirs and emits a low, painful moan. Anastasia, severely wounded, has survived assassination because her mother, knowing what was about to happen, stepped in front of her, knocking her to the floor as the firing began. The Empress took most of the bullets and bayonet thrusts intended for Anastasia.

Nonetheless, Anastasia has serious bullet wounds in her left shoulder and right thigh. She is in shock from the pain and loss of blood. The blood loss had depressed her blood pressure to the point that Yurovsky could not detect a heartbeat.

Near dawn, Anastasia regains partial consciousness. She crawls out of the cellar, across the kitchen, and out the back door. Moaning in pain, she slides down the rear steps head first. She is covered in blood, and delirious. She faints from the pain.

Khina Demidova, a local peasant and household servant at the Ipatiev House, has been cowering inside her hut since she and her family were awakened by the frightful din of the Chekas' guns about midnight. The subsequent uproar of the guards' celebration was even more frightening. She opens her front door just enough to peek outside. Demidova is a stocky, middle-aged woman with graying blonde hair and broad Slavic cheekbones. Over the past months, she has helped serve the imprisoned imperial family.

She spots someone lying on the ground outside the Ipatiev House at the foot of the back stairs. Fearful of the Cheka guards, she approaches cautiously. Recognizing the unconscious Anastasia, she makes the sign of the cross and runs to get her husband and sons to carry Anastasia to their small hut.

Not knowing what to do and fearful of retribution, the Demidov family tends to Anastasia as best they can. They place the girl in the marital bed. Demidova removes Anastasia's blue dress and her underclothes and bathes her, being careful not to go near the wounds, which are still oozing blood. As Demidova folds the blood-soaked blue dress, she notices that the hem is extraordinarily heavy. She cuts open the stitching on the hem and gold schillings spill to the floor. Astonished, she gasps. She has never seen so much wealth. Recovering, she gathers the schillings and puts them in a goatskin pouch. She continues bathing Anastasia and whispers a prayer for help to Saint Andrew, the patron saint of Russia.

Clearly, professional medical help is needed or Anastasia will die. But, there is no one in Ekaterinburg whom Demidova can trust. However, she knows what has to be done to protect her family and Anastasia from Cheka retribution. She gathers a bucket of water, scrub brush, and rags.

Cautiously, she enters the kitchen door of the dacha. The Chekas' drunken celebration has somewhat abated, as several of the guards have fallen into a drunken stupor. She follows Anastasia's blood trail to the basement.

She throws her hands to her face and stifles a cry as she sees the mutilated bodies of the imperial family. But, she is made of strong peasant stock, so she quickly controls her revulsion and turns away. Apprehensive that one of the Cheka executioners will find her, she begins her task. Working rapidly and quietly, she scrubs away the blood trail up the cellar stairs, through the kitchen, out the back door, and down the steps. Frequently, she refills her bucket with fresh water from the kitchen pump. She inspects her work and is satisfied that there is no trace of Anastasia's blood trail. She dumps the last bucket of blood-stained water in the closest flower bed.

Kneeling on the steps, she makes the sign of the cross and offers a prayer to Saint Olga to lead the souls of the royal family to heaven. Tears cascade down her cheeks. She rises to return to her house. In a flash, she realizes that she has left a clean trail on the somewhat soiled kitchen floor leading to the back door—a telltale sign that someone has been meddling. Refilling her bucket, she dashes back inside and begins scrubbing the entire kitchen floor. Working with harrowing fear in her heart, she completes her task with dispatch. She rises and inspects the floor; it is uniformly clean. She hurries home and sends a prayer of thanks to Saint Andrew for keeping her safe and guiding her to complete her task.

15

Railroad Station, Ekaterinburg, Siberia
19 July 1918

awn has broken into a crystal-clear day. A few puffy white clouds break the deep blue of the sky. The morning is cool for July. It is two days after the regicide. Anastasia is still in shock and slowly bleeding to death.

In the far distance, three Czech Legion armored trains on the Trans-Siberian Railway approach Ekaterinburg. Ahead of the first train's engine is a flatcar with a 76-millimeter turret rifle mounted on it. Behind the turret rifle is an armor-plated section supporting twelve Pulemyot Maxima 7.62-millimeter machine guns. Behind the engine are two freight cars and a dozen passenger cars full of veteran, well-armed Legionnaires. A few minutes behind is the command and control train with eight passenger cars, a communications car, and the command car. Following it is the hospital train. Each car is painted in various German camouflage lozenge patterns to disrupt its silhouette. Even the hospital train is painted in a hodgepodge of colors. White is used only for the circular backgrounds of the red crosses.

An hour or so prior to the first train's arrival, a vanguard consisting of a reinforced company had scouted the Ekaterinburg area. The Legionnaires surprised and overwhelmed a Cheka outpost in a brief firefight. As the vanguard advanced into the city, the remaining Chekas and Red Army Guards made a spirited resistance. Soon they realized that the Czech main force was just a few minutes away, and they fled to the southwest to avoid annihilation.

Shortly, the Czechs' armored trains arrived. The Legionnaires debarked and began to unload their equipment and set up bivouac.

Within a few hours, all three Czech armored trains are in Ekaterinburg. The fourth and fifth, the last trains, are due tomorrow. When they arrive, almost all of the Czech Legion will be marshaled in Ekaterinburg. The remaining Legionnaires are being evacuated out of Murmansk. After repairs and provisioning, the Legion will sally its trains into the depths of Siberia. Their destination is Vladivostok, over three thousand miles to the West. The way west is closed to the Czechs. Poland and the USSR are waging a brutal war that rages from the Baltic to the Ukraine, and there are several Red armies blocking any westward Czech passage. Their only exit is east. From Vladivostok, Western troop ships will ferry the Legionnaires to Europe, then transport them by train to their newly-created country, Czechoslovakia, carved out of the defunct Austro-Hungarian Empire by the Treaty of Versailles.

In one of the freight cars in the command and control train are several tons of gold bars "liberated" from the former Czar's State Treasury vault in Kazan. The Czechs are using this gold as a security warranty—a ransom, as it were—for a guaranteed unobstructed passage to Vladivostok. However, Lenin is furious that the Czechs stole this state treasure and refuses to submit to blackmail. He has ordered all Red armed forces along the Trans-Siberian Railway to seize the gold, "no matter the cost," and return it to Moscow. Accordingly, the Czechs have had several firefights with the Cheka and the Red Guards. They anticipate that their passage east will be fraught with further ambushes and obstructions.

Sergeants order the soldiers to leave the train and assemble. Company commanders call, "Attention" as the regimental commander, Colonel Václav Zak, approaches.

Zak assesses the situation and orders the Fourth Battalion to establish a perimeter defense. "Dig trenches facing west and south. Set up machine-gun nests on those three knobs. Ensure that the field of fire is covered with a devastating crossfire. When the Reds regroup and regain their courage, they will attack. The gold is their motivation."

Khina Demidova watches and waits until the Czech soldiers secure the town. Cautiously, she approaches one of the officers, a major who is supervising his battalion making bivouac close to the first train. She says in a low, tentative voice, "Sir, may I speak with you?" She pulls gently at the sleeve of his dark-gray coat to make sure she has his attention.

He turns to see who is bothering him. "Go away, woman. I'm busy organizing my men's camp. I have no time for peasants," Major Jan Klaus replies brusquely, as he wipes her hand away. Klaus is a tall, well-built man with bushy brown hair. His eyes are brown and tired—they have seen too much of the war and this Russian Revolution. His only goal is to get his men and himself out of Russia via Vladivostok and back to Czechoslovakia.

Not deterred, Demidova looks at him with pleading eyes. "Kind sir, in my home is a seriously wounded person—a young woman. A person of importance. She is dying. Will you help save her?"

Major Klaus again responds brusquely, "Peasant, we have little time to attend to every dying soul in this God-awful war. Leave me alone. I must work with my troops. We are expecting the Reds to attack." He turns and begins to walk toward a group of his men who are setting up a mess kitchen.

Demidova scampers after him. Within a few steps, she reaches the major and grabs his coat. Klaus spins around and pushes her hand away. "Go away, woman!"

Demidova implores Klaus, "In the name of the Holy Spirit, I beseech you to extend Christian mercy and charity to a dying woman." Again she touches his arm, and whispers, "This woman is a Romanov. She will be dead by tonight if she doesn't receive medical help."

"What? A Romanov?" Klaus stares at her with his eyes half-closed in a questioning look. Evaluating what she has said, he pulls a black Turkish cigarette from a worn case stowed in the depths of his coat and lights it with an exaggerated flourish. With a touch of patronization, he says, "Tell me, mother, who is she? From the war reports, we understand that the entire royal family was murdered and buried in unmarked pits in that graveyard across the tracks. Is this woman a cousin or some other minor relative?"

Cautiously, Demidova moves close to Klaus and whispers in his right ear, "No. No cousin. No relative. It is the Czar's youngest daughter, Grand Duchess Anastasia herself. Please, you must keep this secret. No one must know. If the Cheka finds out, they will institute a Red Terror in this area that will leave it a scorched earth. Everyone will be murdered—even the children."

His interest is piqued. "Remain here and be quiet." He leaves Demidova standing and at a semi-trot goes to the hospital train. The Czechs had captured it from the Austrians during the Russians' Brusilov Offensive in June 1916. This train is a complete hospital with all the latest medical devices and facilities, including x-ray machines, a medical laboratory, operating rooms, sterilizers, a hundred-bed ward, and a comprehensive pharmacy.

Klaus returns shortly with Captain Doctor Jiri Litvak. Litvak was a 1910 honors graduate from the Third Medical School of Charles University in Prague. He is a tall, lanky man with deep brown eyes, sandy hair, and a neatly trimmed Van Dyke beard and mustache. In his Don Cossack-style uniform, his mien is entirely professional. Over his uniform, he wears a fresh white coat with red crosses stitched on the sleeves and the left front.

Demidova, delighted to see that a doctor has come to help, greets him gratefully. "Good morning, Doctor. It is so good of you to come and save this dying woman. Come to my home and see."

Litvak responds forcefully, "I make no promises, woman. I must examine her and make an assessment. Proceed."

With Demidova leading the way, Klaus and Litvak enter her hut. She directs the pair to Anastasia lying on the bed covered with a thin wool blanket. Her hair is combed carefully, and her long curls are separated equally along each side of her face. She is ghastly pale.

Litvak carefully removes the blanket and makes a quick assessment of the nude woman. She is unresponsive. He finds that her airway is clear, but her breathing is fast and labored, her pulse is weak and rapid, and her blood pressure is dangerously low. Her temperature is several points below normal. He inspects the compound fracture of the femur and feels the damage to the muscle. Her right thigh is swollen from internal bleeding, and the wound is slowly oozing blood.

Next, Litvak inspects the bullet wound in her left shoulder. The shoulder is swollen, and her arm is ashen from lack of blood. The wound is narrow and torn. Blood oozes from the wound in a slight pumping motion. He suspects that an artery is nicked.

A great loss of blood is evident from the results of the assessment and the massive stains on the bedding. Litvak comments, "This woman, if it is Anastasia, will not live much longer without immediate medical care. The only positive we have is that her temperature is below normal, which indicates that she probably does not have an infection. Major, please stay with her while I get one of my corpsmen. If we are to save her, we must move her to our hospital train now."

Major Klaus, annoyed that he is diverted from his primary duty of soldiering, says, "I understand." Litvak leaves the hut and dashes back to the train, ignoring the military hubbub all around him.

While Klaus waits for Litvak's return, he wonders if this dying woman truly is Grand Duchess Anastasia Romanov. If she is, and the Czechs take her with them, then their goal of getting to Vladivostok will be seriously compromised if the Reds discover her presence on the train. To satisfy his doubts, he turns to Demidova and demands, "Why are you positive that this woman is Grand Duchess Anastasia? What proof do you have?"

With her chin quivering and her eyebrows furrowed, Demidova responds forcefully, "I served as Anastasia's household maid for months. I cleaned her clothes. I washed and combed her hair. I helped her dress. I consoled her when her fears were overwhelming. I wiped her tears. I hugged her with all my love. I know her as I would my own daughter, God help her. I have no proof, but here are ten gold schillings she had sewn in the hem of her dress." She pulls the pouch from a fold in her dress and hands it to Klaus. "Would I, a mere peasant, have such a treasure, Major?"

He opens the pouch and lets the coins spill onto the bloodstained bed. Amazed, he picks up one of the coins and inspects it closely. Satisfied, he returns the coins to the pouch and looks closely at the woman on the bed.

"This woman does have a resemblance to photographs of Anastasia as I remember them. I must say that the sincerity of your narrative is compelling.

Finally, these gold schillings add credence to your appeal." He leans over Anastasia and brushes aside a curl resting over her left eye. "I'm inclined to believe you, Demidova. You're a brave and honorable woman. I pledge to do what I can to help Anastasia, and I will return these coins to her when she is sufficiently recovered."

Demidova looks at Major Klaus briefly, then lowers her eyes as tears form. "Major, your kind words are not for me. I am none of those things. I am but a maid."

Inside the hospital car, Captain Litvak alerts his senior medical assistant, who is tending to a lance corporal wounded in the morning's action. "Sergeant Gadia, I need you now. Have another corpsman tend to your patient. Get a stretcher and follow me." Gadia is a tall, middle-aged, thick-bodied fellow with dusky features, thin brown hair, large, deep-set eyes, and a sharp chin.

Soon Anastasia is placed on a stretcher and carried to the emergency car of the hospital train. For now, the only Legionnaires who know this woman's true identity are Major Klaus and Captain Litvak.

Major Klaus, cognizant of his military duty, approaches Colonel Zak, his regimental commander. Zak is busy supervising the defensive deployment and billeting of his regiment and the refitting of his trains. Zak is a short, moderately built man of impeccable military bearing. With shoulders straight back, head erect, short-cropped gray hair, and steel-gray eyes, he projects the classic image of military command and attendant respect. Major Klaus snaps to attention, salutes, and says, "Good morning, Colonel Zak. May I have several minutes of your time on a matter of grave importance?"

"What have you got, Major Klaus? And make it quick. I'm overwhelmed with the details of this deployment. Our situation is perilous. We can't remain here more than a few days at best. As soon as the Reds get reinforcements and courage, they'll launch a fierce attack to get the gold and be rid of us."

Zak removes his cap and wipes his brow. "We can't be trapped here in Ekaterinburg. We've got to complete our resupply and get our trains moving to the east. Cryptographic intelligence tells me that elements of the Red Guard are assembling at key points along this railroad. We'll have to fight our way through Siberia to Vladivostok."

Major Klaus says, "I understand our situation. Sir, what I have to report is extremely sensitive and must be for your information only."

With a touch of desperation, Zak spouts, "Out with it."

Standing at stiff attention, Klaus continues. "We have found Grand Duchess Anastasia Romanov, fourth daughter of the Czar. She was in the hut of one of the maids. How Anastasia survived the regicide I don't know. However, she's wounded seriously and near death. Because of the urgency of the situation, Doctor Litvak has taken her to the hospital train and begun treatment. We ask for your understanding in taking this action without your permission."

Zak is taken aback by this singular report. After a brief time he says, "That's an amazing story, Major Klaus. I was led to believe that all the royal family was murdered two days ago. Have you confirmed that this woman is Grand Duchess Anastasia?"

"Yes, sir. I'm firmly convinced that this woman is Anastasia Romanov."

"Very well, Major Klaus. Stand easy." Colonel Zak stares at Klaus without expression. "What is your recommendation?"

Klaus relaxes and says with conviction, "We treat her. We keep her true identity secret. We can disguise her as a wounded Russian nurse working with the Legion and give her a fictitious name. I realize the possible consequences of this action. To keep her with us begs for serious trouble from the Reds if they find out that we have her. Conversely, with Grand Duchess Anastasia in good health and out of the Reds' grasp, there is a great opportunity for the Whites to bolster their cause to defeat the Bolsheviks. She could be a living icon for their cause."

Klaus pauses to form his next comments precisely and in a respectful tone. "Sir, do we continue medical treatment? Or do we return her to the maid's hut to let her die? I need your decision immediately."

Zak is not used to subordinates forcing him to make momentous decisions without careful reflection. Breaking his military mien, Zak shuffles as he evaluates Klaus's recommendation. He looks at his troops setting up the machine-gun nests. He looks down the trains and sees that servicing and repairs are proceeding. Finally, his gray eyes narrowed, his chin jutting, he speaks with a dull rasp, "Damn you, Klaus! As a senior officer in this regiment, your duty is to make my command function easier. I don't give a damn about the Whites, the Reds, or any of them. My goal is to get our men to Vladivostok and home. Now you force me to make a monumental decision that has worldwide political and military implications, a decision that could well jeopardize this entire mission."

As if on cue, an orderly brings a decoded message for Colonel Zak to read, respond to, and initial. Zak quickly scans the message and tells the orderly, "Send a message to Colonel Capec. I will meet with him tomorrow in the command car of his train when it arrives."

With his brow furrowed, Colonel Zak turns slowly to face Major Klaus. "We keep her. You're the Action Officer. Keep me informed. Dismissed."

16

Railroad Station, Ekaterinburg, Siberia
19 July 1918

The unconscious Anastasia lies on a litter in the emergency hospital car. Doctor Litvak makes a more comprehensive assessment of his patient. His conclusions are almost the same as they were in Demidova's hut.

Nurse Tatiana Botkina draws blood from a vein in Anastasia's right arm and sends it to the laboratory for typing. Botkina is a Russian working for the Czechs with the promise that she can evacuate with them to Central Europe. She is slightly overweight for her petite size and wears a dark-grey, ankle-length uniform covered with a white nurse's apron. She has a wide, kindly mouth with an easy smile; a small, straight nose; and large grey-green eyes hidden behind heavy bifocal glasses. Her thick brown hair is tied in a bun.

After Doctor Litvak completes his assesment of Grand Duchess Anastasia, he carefully enters his notes in the patient's chart. Meanwhile, nurse Botkina prepares Anastasia for surgery. She cleans the wounds in the patient's left shoulder and right thigh, and swabs them with a dilute iodine solution; applies compresses to the wounds to slow the bleeding; cuts her hair short, then shaves off her head and body hair; bathes the patient with Dakin solution—a potent disinfectant; and starts an infusion of saline solution. Lastly, she removes the silver ring from Anastasia's left hand and slips it into the pocket of her nurse's uniform.

Meanwhile, Litvak prepares the operating suite. He instructs two of his corpsmen to scrub up and then sterilize the surgical instruments. They will assist him today with the surgery.

Sergeant Rudolf Gadia brings the laboratory report—the patient's blood type is A-positive. Litvak tells Gadia to search the hospital's records to find soldiers with the same blood type. "We need an immediate transfusion of two liters. We'll need more during surgery. Get six donors here now, and have six or seven standing by. After you find the names, alert Regimental Sergeant Major Serge Brusilov to order these men to report to you here immediately—on the double, Sergeant."

Gadia dispatches several corpsmen to find the sergeant major, then he opens the patient records section and begins his hunt for potential blood donors. In a few minutes, he has identified a dozen who qualify. Soon Brusilov enters the car. He is a hulk of a man, standing ramrod straight and well over six feet tall, with wide shoulders and a large head with jet-black hair and a wisp of white on the sides. His handlebar mustache is finely waxed. He has ebony-black eyes and curved dark eyebrows. He has seen more soldiering than any man in his regiment. In his Cossack-style uniform, he embodies the ideal of the "top sergeant." He is seriously disturbed that he has been summoned away from his command duties getting the regiment ready to repel the expected Red attack.

He confronts Gadia in a slow, gruff voice. "What the hell is going on? I have important duties. I don't have the time or the inclination to play doctor."

Gadia responds forcefully, "Sergeant Major, your indulgence, please. We have an emergency and need your regimental knowledge and authority. We have a seriously wounded nurse who needs blood, and she needs it immediately. Captain Litvak wants you to find the men on this list, potential donors with A-positive blood, and escort them to the emergency car as fast as possible. It's a matter of life or death. Am I clear?"

The senior enlisted man in the regiment looks at Sergeant Gadia with shimmering eyes. "Whose life and death? We had only one corporal wounded this morning." No fool, he snarls, "We had no nurse wounded today or any time recently. Who is this nurse? What's going on?"

Gadia shifts uneasily and looks at Brusilov carefully as he forms his response. "Sergeant Major Brusilov, this matter is highly classified. All I am authorized to tell you is that Major Klaus is the Action Officer and is keeping Colonel Zak personally informed. Ask no questions. Do your duty and get these soldiers here. We'll begin surgery on this nurse as soon as we can."

Brusilov immediately understands that Gadia is passing on orders from higher command. "Very well. I'll return in a few minutes with these men." He bounds out of the car and heads off to search for the men on his list.

Meanwhile, Nurse Botkina has two corpsmen carry her patient to the X-ray section. As soon as the images are developed and dried, Doctor Litvak inspects them and spots exactly where the two bullets are. The one in her left shoulder is buried in the humerus near the joint—the source of the slowly oozing, pumping blood. Though he cannot see it on the x-ray images, Litvak suspects that the bullet has nicked an artery. In her right thigh, he locates the bullet that has broken the femur. Part of the bone has emerged through her skin.

Soon, three Legionnaires report to the emergency car. Sergeant Gadia tells Captain Litvak, "Here are three 'volunteers' for the blood transfusion. It will take me only a few minutes to double-check their blood type. The sergeant major is searching the regiment for more donors."

Within a few minutes, Anastasia is on the operating table in the surgery suite and covered with a sterile sheet. The first Legion volunteer lies on a table close by. Nurse Botkina rigs the blood transfer device, wipes the site on Anastasia's arm with alcohol, inserts a needle into her vein, and tapes it down. She duplicates the procedure on the Legionnaire. On Doctor Litvak's signal, she starts working the manual pump. In a second or two, the life-giving blood flows into Anastasia. The procedure is repeated with the second Legionnaire, and the third. A little color returns to Anastasia's face. Sergeant Gadia reports to Doctor Litvak that Sergeant Major Brusilov has fifteen volunteers standing by outside. "I'll have them ready for your call. Brusilov has told them that a nurse was wounded this morning and that blood donors are needed. Nothing else."

Litvak tells Gadia, "As soon as you confirm that their blood is A-positive, have the next two soldiers ready and waiting in the emergency car. Then, have the sergeant major attend to the other volunteers. I need you in the surgery."

Litvak dons his surgical gown and cap. Pulling on rubber gloves, he tells Nurse Botkina, "Get dressed and find a corpsman to handle the blood transfusions. Today you're my anesthetist. Hold a gauze pad soaked in ether over her nose and mouth to put her under. Then administer oxygen. This will be a long surgery. If she appears to awaken, apply more ether. Then oxygen. Continue this routine until we're finished. Gadia, you monitor her blood pressure every ten minutes. Tell me immediately if the systolic drops below 110 mm."

Litvak gives a comprehensive look around the surgery to ensure that all is prepared. A corpsman flicks on the overhead lighting directly above the operating table. In the background, the generator noise is a little louder. Litvak peruses the surgical instruments organized neatly on a sterile towel in an enamel tray. At his command, another corpsman removes the sheet that covers Anastasia. Litvak studies the backlit X-rays to confirm the location of the bullets and review the damage. Then he studies the patient's wounds. His movements are slow and thoughtful. Standing erect, he takes a couple of deep breaths as he builds his confidence for the delicate and critical surgery. His troubled brown eyes reflect his soul-searing anxiety. With a blast of bravado he exclaims, "Is everyone ready?" Without waiting for a reply, he says, "Here we go."

Two hours later, and after five more blood transfusions, Litvak finishes stitching the surgical wounds. He moves back a step to look at his patient. Her color is pale but much improved. Her breathing is almost regular. Her blood pressure is up, but still a little low. Her pulse is a little fast. Temperature is normal. Utterly exhausted, he tosses off his bloody gown, cap, and surgical gloves, and collapses in a chair. Anticipating his need, a corpsman hands him a snifter of brandy. Litvak, without flourish, tosses it down and lets the snifter fall to the floor.

Two badly distorted 7.62-millimeter bullets lie in a small tray by the operating table. As they tore through Anastasia's flesh and bone they expanded, twisted, and curled.

Litvak orders the corpsmen to bandage the incisions. "Tape her left arm across her chest to keep her shoulder immobile, and put a splint on her right leg that runs from her groin to past her knee. Keep this leg in traction, elevated about ten degrees. The next twenty-four hours are critical. Check her vital signs every thirty minutes. Keep me apprised."

"I especially want to know if there is any elevation in her temperature. If she awakens, notify me immediately. Have morphine ready. She'll be in serious pain, and I expect her blood pressure to rise. I'll check on her frequently. If you have a God, I urge you to pray for this woman's recovery."

As his people comply with his instructions and begin cleaning the operating suite, Litvak elevates his voice a little. "Your attention, everyone. Thanks for your excellent professional help today. Our team saved this woman's life. Congratulations." He pauses for a few seconds as the group waits for his next words.

He narrows his eyes and says in a dry, imperious voice, "Listen carefully to what I am going to say next because it is critical to our mission to get to Vladivostok and out of this Godforsaken country. I understand your curiosity. To the depths of your souls, you must understand that what you saw and did today in this operating suite is no longer your concern! It is imperative that you do not speculate about this woman. Do not speak about her to anyone. Start no rumors. Erase from your mind that you were here today." He pauses to survey the room.

"Suffice it to say that this woman is a Russian nurse working with us. She was wounded by Cheka fire in this morning's engagement with the Reds. I will not accept any questions as there are no answers. My words are final. Carry on."

17

Railroad Station, Ekaterinburg, Siberia
20 July 1918

Anastasia is lying unconscious in the ward car of the hospital train. Her right leg is in traction. There is a dextrose solution infusing into a vein in her right hand. Sergeant Gadia, Nurse Botkina, and two corpsmen have alternated a four-hour watch over her since the surgery. Gradually through the night, Anastasia's vital signs have improved. This morning they are almost normal. Most important, there is no elevation in her temperature.

At 0800 hours, Nurse Botkina arrives to relieve Sergeant Gadia. He is exhausted from yesterday's frenetic activities and his long early-morning watch. He takes Anastasia's blood pressure and temperature—all readings are normal. He looks up at Botkina. "Good morning, Tatiana. Our un-named nurse seems to be doing well. Her vital signs are normal. She is breathing smoothly and regularly. About an hour ago, I removed the empty saline bottle and hung a dextrose bottle. When the dextrose infusion is complete, continue with saline. I'm done. You have the watch."

Botkina lifts the sheet from Anastasia and carefully removes the bandages on the surgical sites. She makes a cautious inspection and does not spot anything abnormal or any sign of infection. With her rubber-gloved hand she gently presses the areas around the sites. Responses are normal. She applies more iodine solution to the sites and bandages them. She checks the flow of the intravenous fluid. It is normal.

Within a few minutes, Doctor Litvak arrives. "Good morning, Botkina. How is our patient?"

"All her vital signs are normal. I changed her dressings a few minutes ago. Her color is good. She is improving by the hour."

"Excellent." He picks up her chart and notes the hour-by-hour readings and comments. Satisfied, he removes the sheet from Anastasia and inspects the areas around the wounds. He sees nothing abnormal and notes her much-improved color. "Looks as if she has passed the 'dark hour,'" he suggests. "Any sign that she is regaining consciousness?"

"No, Doctor. Not that I have seen. During my watch last night she did not stir."

"Very well. Call me if you see any change. I'll be in my office."

"Yes, sir."

Satisfied that Anastasia is progressing well and is tended by competent professionals, Doctor Litvak returns to his office to write reports, sign requisitions, and clear the stack of paperwork piled on his desk. He wonders if, even in this war, the weight of the paperwork exceeds the weight of ammunition expended. How does he have time to tend to patients? Fortunately, the ward is empty now. The wounded corporal was discharged this morning.

Shortly before noon, Nurse Botkina notices Anastasia's eyelids twitching slightly. Then, the index finger on her right hand quivers. In a moment, the other fingers move a little. Botkina summons a nearby corpsman. "Our patient may be coming around. Summon Doctor Litvak from his office."

Within a few seconds, Litvak is at Anastasia's bedside checking her heartbeat and pulse. He notes that her cheeks are bright pink. He sees her feeble motions and smiles.

"Amazing," he notes. "Thank God she is young and strong enough to survive the traumas she has experienced." He leans close to her face and whispers, "Good afternoon, Anastasia. Time to wake up." In a slightly louder voice, he says, "Anastasia, it is a beautiful day. Look out the window and see. Wake up, Anastasia." He moves away from her and rubs her right hand gently.

Slowly, both of Anastasia's eyes open narrowly. She stares dully at Litvak. Her face is haggard and without emotion. With bounce in his voice, he says softly, "Welcome to the real world. We are elated that you're awake." He sees a slight flicker across her mouth. Her lips move slowly, but emit no sound. He leans in, bringing his left ear close to her mouth. "What is it, Anastasia? Tell me."

Her eyes seem to brighten a little. She tries to form a word but utters only a feeble noise. "Keep trying, Anastasia," Litvak encourages. "Anastasia, talk to me. How may I help you?"

She pushes her lips together and whispers, almost inaudibly, something that sounds like "water." Litvak smiles broadly. "Anastasia, do you want water?" He places emphasis on the last word. Anastasia closes her eyes for a few seconds, then blinks them opens and makes a slight nod. "I understand," he responds.

Litvak tells Sergeant Gadia to bring a beaker of distilled water with a bent drinking straw. On its arrival, Nurse Botkina raises Anastasia's head slightly and puts the straw in her mouth. Anastasia puckers her cheeks and sips, ever so slowly, a few milliliters of the water. She stops, and Botkina gently lowers her head to the pillow. This minimal exertion exhausts her. She closes her eyes and takes a few shallow breaths. After several seconds she tries to focus on Litvak and, in a feeble undertone, murmurs, "Hurt."

Litvak responds, "I understand. We'll ease your pain." He stands up and turns to face Sergeant Gadia. "Administer fifteen milligrams of morphine to our patient. And continue once every four hours while she is awake." He leans toward Anastasia, "You're going to sleep now. We'll talk when you feel better—perhaps later this evening."

Anastasia sleeps deeply and peacefully. Saline and dextrose solutions continue to infuse into her. Her vital signs remain within normal limits. In the late afternoon, Sergeant Gadia sees that she is awakening. Doctor Litvak is at her bedside quickly.

Her eyes open slowly. They are frightened and suffused with questions. She moves her right hand to touch her taped left arm. She looks drawn and languid.

Litvak speaks in a smooth, soft voice, "Good afternoon, Anastasia. Welcome to our hospital. You are safe. Do you understand?"

After a short moment, she slowly nods her head.

He continues, "A few days ago, you suffered serious injuries. Now you're with friends and in the care of medical professionals. Your prognosis is excellent."

She looks at Litvak with a broad stare. She forms her lips to speak and in a low voice asks, "Who are you? Where am I? Where is my mama—my family?"

Litvak speaks slowly to ensure that he pronounces each word precisely. "Anastasia, I am the doctor who is taking care of you. My staff and I will do all we can to ensure that you recuperate as fast as possible. As you improve over the next few days, I will begin to answer your questions and fill in the details of your odyssey. There is much we need to discuss. For now, I ask that you please trust me."

Without much spirit, she mutters, "Yes." She closes her eyes and sleeps.

18

Railroad Station, Ekaterinburg, Siberia
22 July 1918

Colonel Zak steps out of the command and control car. He surveys the deserted bivouac, the abandoned trenches, and the machine-gun nests around the railroad station. It is dawn, and his men and their equipment are already aboard the four trains. The Czech Legion has been in Ekaterinburg for three days.

Several months before, Legion cryptographers had broken the Reds' Omega code. From electronic intercepts late the previous afternoon, Zak knows that the Reds are reinforced and will launch a major attack at 1500 hours today. A few of the town's citizens huddle around the railroad station. There is fear in their eyes and a few tears. They know that when the Bolsheviks return, Dzerzhinsky's Cheka will wage pitiless retribution upon the townspeople and the Red Terror will descend on Ekaterinburg with a savage vengeance. Zak takes a last look, snaps a salute to the civilians at the station, and swings aboard his car. He enters the radio compartment and tells the operator to transmit his "move out" order to the train commanders.

The trains spew steam and black smoke and send out a clanging din as they slowly make headway, moving east along the Trans-Siberian Railway. The hospital-ward car lurches and sways as its forward motion accelerates.

Anastasia is propped up in bed, sipping potato soup. Her eyes are dark and pensive. She has made steady progress. After her meal, Sergeant Gadia helps her out of bed and holds her as he encourages her to take a few steps with her left leg. She tires easily and quickly, and Gadia helps her back to bed and rigs her right leg back into traction.

She speaks coherently, but her voice is brittle and quick. As Gadia completes the traction, she says wistfully, "I'm troubled. I can't remember. There's a void in my memory."

Gadia pulls a light blanket over her. "Temporary loss of memory is fairly normal considering the serious trauma you've suffered. Your memory will return as you recuperate. For now, focus your mind on healing."

"I can't focus. My mind swirls with dark images. I see myself with my family in the Ipatiev House. For reasons I don't understand, the Bolsheviks took us there and had us in some sort of custody. Were they arranging our passage to England so we could be in exile with our cousins?"

Gadia, with a ready smile, says, "My dear young lady, your progress is amazing. You're recuperating faster than anyone expected. Doctor Litvak and all the medical staff are delighted. But, we're a long way from your complete recovery. Ahead of you are many weeks of healing and many months of physical therapy."

She looks at Gadia with firm resolve and pleading eyes. "You're evading my questions. I must know what became of my family—my mother, my father, my little brother Alexis, and my older sisters. Where are they? Are they in England? Why was I wounded, and why is Mama not taking care of me?" Tears form in her troubled eyes and slowly cascade down her cheeks.

Gadia wipes her tears with a soft towel. "I wish I could tell you about the Czar and the rest of your family, but I don't know where they are," he lies. "News is slow in Siberia. Perhaps as we move east we will have more information. As you continue to improve, Doctor Litvak will respond to your concerns."

"What has happened to Russia? Have the Czar's soldiers defeated Lenin and those Bolshevik revolutionaries?"

"Regrettably, young lady, what we know is that the Bolsheviks have captured Saint Petersburg and have formed a Communist government in Moscow. Their control is spreading throughout Russia. White forces, those loyal to the Czar, and some Western nations are attempting to halt their influence. However, I fear that in a year or two the Reds will dominate all of Russia."

Anastasia props herself up on her right elbow. Whimpering, she laments, "Has God forgotten us? What is his plan for Russia to have these atheists govern it? What has happened to the Metropolitan of our Orthodox Church?" She blankly stares at the ceiling and bobs her head slowly and meditatively as if trying to answer her own questions.

"I'm sorry, but I have no answers," Gadia responds in a dull voice.

"Who does?" Anastasia demands in the most forceful voice she can muster. When Gadia does not answer, she slumps back. She glances at her left hand and realizes that her silver ring is missing. Her mother's instructions snap into focus. She gasps as she realizes the import of this misfortune. "Where is my ring?" she asks in a firm voice. "The ring in the form of Saint Olga's Cross. Do you know where it is? I must have it. It's a gift from my mother, Empress Alexandra, with special significance."

Gadia gives her his ready smile. "Fear not. This question is easy. Nurse Botkina removed that ring when she prepared you for surgery. She is saving it for you. I will ask her to return it."

The conversation regarding the ring becomes a stimulus. Faint images of the past flood into Anastasia's memory. She props herself up on her elbow again and, swaying slightly, says, "I recall sewing ten Maria Theresa gold schillings into my blue dress. It's the last dress I remember wearing. Do you know where my dress and the schillings are?"

Gadia stands and rubs her left shoulder. Flashing that smile again, he says, "That is also easy. Major Klaus, the officer who found you in the maid's hut, has your schillings. Your blue dress has disappeared. I suppose that in a few days the major will visit you and return the schillings. We are keeping him apprised of your progress."

In her weakened voice, she tries to be forceful but without much success. "What hut? What maid? Tell me everything. I don't know where I am or why I'm here on this train. What is this train? Where are we going? I don't know who you are. And who are the soldiers I see? Why do you people avoid my questions?" Exhausted, she falls back on her bed.

Gadia turns to look out the window. In a few moments, he responds, with his eyes focused on the passing forest. "You are safe with the Czech Legion. We are traveling to Vladivostok, where Allied transports will take us home, in central Europe. We will talk later. That's enough for today." He turns and with a hint of a smile says, "You're fretting yourself into a state of exhaustion. You look very tired. I'll alert Doctor Litvak to your concerns. Now, it's time for your pain shot. Please lie down and rest."

Later that evening, Nurse Botkina returns the ring. She slips it on Anastasia's index finger and says, "It's a beautiful ring. What is its special significance? Please tell me."

"Thank you for all you have done for me. And thank you for saving and returning my ring. But I cannot tell you why it's important. It's a secret between my mother and me. Please understand."

"I do, of course." Botkina gently pats Anastasia's hand.

В друго́й ра̌з

It is the fourth day since Anastasia's surgery. This morning, she is sitting up in bed. The traction on her right leg has been lowered so that her leg rests on the bed. Earlier, she had attacked her breakfast with gusto and even asked Nurse Botkina for a second helping of porridge. Now she is reading a tattered novel that someone left in the hospital ward.

On Doctor Litvak's quiet signal, Botkina leaves the ward. Litvak approaches Anastasia and greets her with cheerful laughter in his eyes. "Good morning, young lady. I understand that you pressed Botkina for more porridge this morning." He reads her chart and sees that her vital signs are normal. He checks the dressings on her wounds. Again, all is normal. "A healthy appetite indicates that you are healing."

Litvak checks the tension on her traction, stalling to gather his thoughts and to form his words precisely. "I apologize for not visiting you more often," he says kindly. "I have several wounded soldiers to care for. A few are in very serious condition. Nonetheless, I have been following your recuperation closely. I'm delighted with your progress."

He moves the chair next to her bed so that he faces her directly. He speaks with calculated precision. "This morning, Anastasia, I want to speak with you about the strange events in your life this past week. I'll answer the questions you have posed to my staff over the past few days. You're well enough, mentally and physically, to understand and accept with courage and maturity what I'm going to say."

Anastasia's sharp sensors are alerted. She puts down the book, sits up as best she can, and stares at Litvak with a flushed face and keen eyes. "Already you have frightened me. Is your information so grim?" With a touch of apprehension, she adds, "I'm longing to hear what information you have for me. The black void in my memory and your staff's avoidance of my questions have intensified my distress."

Doctor Litvak leans forward and holds her right hand. "Anastasia, with the utmost sadness in my heart, and with my deepest sympathy, I must tell you that all members of your family are dead. The Bolsheviks murdered them at Ekaterinburg. For reasons we do not know, you escaped with two very serious bullet wounds."

Anastasia stares at Litvak with unbelieving eyes. Slowly his truth suffuses her soul. Her face becomes ghastly pale, and she utters a choking wail that sticks in her throat. She grasps her throat, falls back on the bed, and closes her eyes. After a few seconds, she opens her mouth and screams with surprising power. After another second or two, she recovers and grabs Litvak's hand. Her body is convulsed with wracking sobs. Tears flow down her cheeks without restraint. Through her lament she babbles, "My loving Mama. Little Alexis. My father and my darling sisters—all massacred! I don't understand."

Hearing the scream, Nurse Botkina rushes into the ward. She takes Anastasia in her arms, gently hugs her, and dabs at the girl's tears with a cotton pad while murmuring soothing words. Sergeant Gadia enters, and on a nod from Doctor Litvak, administers a mild sedative.

For the rest of the day, Gadia stands watch over Anastasia. In the late afternoon, she awakens. Her eyes are puffy and crimson. She is weary, and her cheeks are pale. She appears much older than her seventeen years.

Nevertheless, Gadia detects a certain resolve in her mien. She looks at Gadia and manages a tired, faint smile. In a weak voice she asks, "A glass of water, please."

When Gadia hands her the water, she gulps it down. "Thank you, Sergeant. I'm better now." She gazes out the window and watches a flock of Arctic geese in flight. After a few minutes she says, "If Doctor Litvak is available, I should like him to continue his talk."

"I'll fetch him."

In a few minutes, Litvak approaches Anastasia's bed. "Good afternoon, Anastasia. You're feeling better, it appears. Please accept my apologies for being so straightforward this morning about your family."

"Yes, of course. I understand." She tries to sit up but cannot. Litvak lowers the traction rig and places another pillow under her head. "Thank you," she murmurs.

"If you're ready, let us continue our talk," suggests Litvak.

"Yes, but first, please listen to me." In a very disheartened voice, Anastasia says, "The loss of my family is dreadful agony for me to comprehend and to accept, and it is a stinging pain in my heart. But I am resolved to overcome this grief. Now I realize fully the import of what my mother instructed me to do, so many months ago in Saint Petersburg. Her charge is crystal clear. Somehow she knew of the Bolsheviks' plan to assassinate us all, and she decided that it was I who must survive and continue the Romanov legacy. How she accomplished it, I cannot imagine. But she did it. She was so brave and resolute." With vivid intensity in her eyes she continues, "I am now an adult, and I will steel myself to her charge."

She puts her head on the pillow and closes her eyes. Litvak remains silent while he waits for her to relax. Within a few minutes she again is propped up on her right elbow and looking at Litvak. "Please tell me the rest of your account."

Doctor Litvak asks Sergeant Gadia and Nurse Botkina to come closer. "If I miss an important detail, please speak up." He begins. Anastasia interrupts from time to time with questions. After thirty minutes or so he says, "And that is all we know."

No one speaks for several minutes. Then Anastasia shouts, "My hatred for those Bolshevik blackguards is so intense that if I had the means I would kill them all." Her anger subsides quickly. With a calm, strong voice she says, "Doctor Litvak, my mind is eased by your story. Although I don't remember all those events, I do recall some."

Litvak speaks in a clear, authoritative voice. "Anastasia, as the last member of the Romanov royal family, you must know that, outside the protection of the Czech Legion, your life is in acute danger. When the Bolsheviks realize that you escaped the regicide, they will sound an international alarm for your capture and assassination. They cannot afford to have you alive to tell of their brutal chicanery. Motivated by political ideology and, I suspect, a hefty reward, Cheka and Comintern agents will scour the globe to find you. Every party member and Communist sympathizer worldwide will be an informant."

Anastasia's eyes narrow, her mouth hardens. "Yes, Doctor, I understand. My mother told me that our family might be separated, and that I might have to travel to England alone. Although I did not comprehend it at the time, she hinted that I should be prepared for a Communist pursuit. She charged me to travel incognito under an alias. In fact, she gave me the name of Anna Bogrova and ten gold schillings to pay my way."

Litvak leans back in his chair, glances at his staff and, with a fine grin, says, "Welcome to the Czech Legion, Nurse Anna Bogrova."

Другое место

Over the next few months, the Czech trains move into the depths of Siberia. Progress is tediously slow because disparate groups of Red soldiers, Cheka guards, and Bolshevik partisans harass the Legion with ambushes, sniper fire, track blockades, and ripped-up rails. The 7.2-mm machine guns in the armored car spit their staccato *rat-ta-tat-tat* to counter the Red assaults. Legionnaires return fire from the windows in the troop cars.

Occasionally, the 76-millimeter rifle barks with a deafening roar. Colonel Zak tries to keep the trains running through the Red gauntlets. However, when the trains must stop to destroy a blockade or repair a ripped track, Legionnaires debark and engage the Reds in classic firefights. Legion engineers, often under small-arms fire, repair the tracks.

Even though the hospital train has large red crosses painted all over it, it is often hit by small-arms fire. With wounded Legionnaires in the wards, the medical staff struggles to keep all personnel down and away from the windows.

Sometimes the attacking Red forces are large and particularly aggressive. Their usual tactic is to hit hard and then fade back into the forest. When the Reds fall back, Legionnaires sally into the forest to run them down, destroy their bivouac, and inflict as many casualties as possible. Zak has standing orders, "Take no prisoners."

As the Legion advances farther into Siberia, the Reds are fewer and less organized. By late October, an early Siberian winter has engulfed the region. There is almost three feet of snow on the tracks, and some drifts are higher. The Legion trains, battling the snow, finally reach Novosibirsk, about five-hundred miles from Ekaterinburg.

Before entering the town, a patrol from the First Battalion scouts the area and promptly dispatches the few Reds in the area. Colonel Zak's scouts report that the citizens are, for the most part, supportive of the Czechs and Admiral Kolchak's White Army, a regiment of which is camped on the south side of the town. Earlier in the year, Admiral Kolchak had declared himself "Supreme Ruler of All the Russias."

The Legion's meteorologist reckons that the Siberian winter has arrived. There will be no respite until spring. Colonel Zak calls his three battalion commanders to a conference in the command and control car to determine the best course of action. The consensus is to winter over in Novosibirsk. Weather conditions will worsen quickly, and to proceed deeper into Siberia would be folly.

Zak bristles at this inordinate delay in his quest to get the regiment to Vladivostok. Accepting the prudent decision, he instructs the duty radio operator to communicate his orders, "Winter over in Novosibirsk."

19

Oretsky's Russian Teahouse, Peking
21 July 1918

*P*irogov continues his routine, shopping during the day as he thinks of things he will need for his new life in the Russian exiles' village, and hanging out at Oretsky's during the evenings. He actively seeks out conversations with other customers and brings in his search for his mother as a way to elicit information. But, he learns nothing new. Even after he modifies his line of questioning to include the possibility of Russian settlements in the interior of China, the people he questions seem to know nothing more than what Oretsky has already told him.

One evening, a small orchestra of Russian musicians takes over the restaurant, and Pirogov settles in to enjoy the music. The musicians' repertoire extends beyond the traditional folk songs to some graceful waltzes, and soon the audience has pushed tables aside to create a small dance floor. The vodka flows freely, and the room is filled with happy laughter and joyful music. For the first time in many months, Pirogov realizes that he is at ease and content.

"I wonder if I may join you?" A tall, slender woman stands beside his table. "There are no other places available."

"Yes, of course." Pirogov rises and pulls out a chair.

The woman is somewhat older than he, attractive and well-groomed. She sits down gracefully and smiles. "Thank you." Pirogov sees that her face shows lines of weariness, and she wears a little too much makeup in a marginally successful effort to conceal her low spirits. She wears a silk gown in the style of the previous decade, of fine quality but slightly faded. On her ears are heavy pearl earrings, and her thick blonde hair is carefully dressed.

"I've seen you here before," she comments softly as the orchestra pauses between songs. "May I ask, how long have you been in Peking?" She speaks with the accent of a well-educated, patrician Russian.

"A couple of weeks." Pirogov smells her faint perfume. "May I offer you a vodka? I'm about to order another."

She smiles again and nods. "Yes, that would be nice. Thank you."

They sit amiably together. Pirogov invites her to dance a few times and finds that she is a graceful dancer. He is charmed by her delightful mien and well-mannered reserve.

When the orchestra takes a break, he resumes their brief conversation. "And what about you? How long have you been here in Peking?"

"Almost two years," she responds slowly. "I came shortly after my husband was killed on the Eastern Front. He was quite certain that Russia would lose the war and that the revolution would succeed. And he was correct."

"Where did he serve?" This is the first time since he left Saint Petersburg that Pirogov has been in the company of a woman of his own class, and he is enjoying the comfort of easy, polite conversation.

"In Galicia. He was General Sergei Makarenko."

"Oh, I knew of him! A fine leader. His death was a great loss to our army. My condolences, Madam."

"Thank you." Her voice is soft, and the look of sorrow on her worn face touches Pirogov deeply.

"Allow me to introduce myself," he continues. "I am Kirik Antonievich Pirogov. I also served on the Galician Front, before being transferred to service with the Imperial Guard in Saint Petersburg."

"A pleasure to meet you. I am Countess Magdalena Ivanovna Makarenko, formerly of Novgorod." Her smile is faint but warm.

"How did you decide to come to Peking?"

"After my husband died, I was very much alone at our home outside Novgorod. We had no children, and my closest relations were in Moscow.

There were revolutionary riots around the city, and I was frightened. All alone in that big house! And the servants had become unreliable, which made my situation seem even more precarious. A cousin of mine in Moscow wrote to tell me that he and his family had decided to leave Russia and go to the East. He invited me to join them. So I sold everything I could, packed up my jewels and everything else of value that I could carry, and joined them. We traveled by the Trans-Siberian Railway to Vladivostok, then west to Harbin."

Magdalena sips the vodka, smiles faintly, and continues. "There are many Whites in Harbin, but the city was grim and cold, and my relationship with my cousin deteriorated quickly. He expected me to help support him and his large family. Like many people of our class, he has no skills that would help him make a living in this ugly new world we inhabit, and he has always been rather profligate. It was unpleasant to feel myself exploited after having already lost so much, and to see him dissipate my funds almost as quickly as he had lost his own. So I decided to come to Peking. I'm alone here, but at least I feel in control of my own life. And I'm in contact with some other cousins, members of my mother's family, who moved to Canada some years before the war began. They have agreed to help me move there and get settled. So I'm just waiting for the appropriate papers to arrive from Canada. Then I'll be leaving Peking for good."

They sit silently for a few minutes, listening to the music and watching the dancers. Magdalena sips her vodka.

"May I ask how you came to be in Peking?" Her face bears the same gentle smile.

Pirogov realizes that Magdalena might be a useful source of information, but he decides to proceed slowly. "My initial decision was much like yours—Russia had become unsafe for me. The Bolsheviks in Saint Petersburg were hunting down army officers loyal to the Czar, so I retreated to my country estate until the Bolsheviks confiscated it. Then, I realized that it was in my best interest to leave Russia."

"And why did you choose Peking?"

"Actually, I'm looking for my mother, and I hoped she would be here or that someone would know of her. She left Russia when I was still in Saint

Petersburg and left no forwarding information, only that she was going to China. But no one here seems to know her, and I'm beginning to think that she didn't come to Peking."

"What is her name?"

"Maria Pavlovna Pirogov. Have you heard of her?"

"No, I'm sorry I haven't. Where will you search next?"

"I haven't decided. Shanghai would be the logical place, but I have wondered if she might have gone somewhere in the interior. Some of her friends apparently went there, so she may have chosen to join them. But I have no idea where they might be."

Magdalena looks off into the distance. For a moment she is silent, her thoughts apparently elsewhere. Then she turns back to Pirogov. "It's sad that so many families have been separated by this terrible war and now by the revolution." She drinks the last of her vodka and rises to leave. "It's getting late, and I must go. Thank you for the lovely dance and conversation."

Pirogov rises quickly. "Would you allow me to escort you home? I think the streets may not be safe for a woman alone at this time of night."

She nods slowly. "Thank you."

Pirogov pays his bill and escorts Magdalena outside, where he hails a pedicab. She gives the driver an address, and they set off into the dark streets. Even at this hour, Peking bustles, and the streets are crowded with traffic. The sidewalks are still filled with people, many of them tradesmen and porters carrying bundles. Pirogov can see the huddled forms of beggars sleeping in doorways and against the walls of buildings. They ride silently for a few minutes.

"May I be so bold as to ask how you are managing in Peking?" he asks. "It seems to me a very expensive and difficult place to live."

"Oh, it is. I went through my remaining cash very quickly and am now selling the odds and ends of my jewelry. But I also have a job, which helps. I work in a millinery shop. The owner speaks only Chinese and a little English, and because I am fluent in English and French as well as Russian, she finds me useful in helping with European clients. It doesn't pay much, but if I economize, it covers most of my expenses. And when I need something extra, there's always Wuhan's Antik Shop."

"What's that?"

"As you have probably noticed, there are a lot of small jewelers and pawn shops around Peking serving just such people as ourselves, impoverished Russians trying to survive. Wuhan's shop is larger than most, and he also deals in rare antiquities from ancient China. He's unscrupulous, of course, but he pays somewhat better than the others for first-rate pieces. Still, I must be very careful and conserve my resources. I shall need money to buy my boat ticket once the papers come through, and then the rest I must use to establish myself in Vancouver."

Pirogov notices her shivering under her thin shawl, and he pulls off his jacket and drapes it over her shoulders.

"Thank you," she murmurs. "But we have arrived." She points to a small Western-style millinery shop. "I have a room above the shop."

Pirogov helps her down from the pedicab and escorts her to the door. "Thank you for a pleasant evening," he says as she gives him her hand. He bows to kiss it. "Good night."

他唱，

For the next several days, Pirogov meets Magdalena nearly every evening at Oretsky's, and soon they settle into a pattern of eating their evening meal together and talking long into the evening. Pirogov feels strongly attracted to her refined manner, and he relishes their conversations, which range from literature to world events. She also seems to enjoy his company and to relax in his presence.

One evening, Magdalena arrives at Oretsky's with a broad smile on her face. She comes immediately to the table where Pirogov waits and sits down. "My papers arrived today at the Canadian Embassy. At last!"

Pirogov feels a moment of inner conflict, pleased that she soon will succeed in moving to a new and better life, but also sad that he will lose her company. But he masters his emotions and gives her hand a warm squeeze. "I'm very happy for you," he says.

"Thank you," she smiles gratefully. "Tomorrow I make what will be my final visit to Wuhan's. I hope that my favorite pearl earrings will cover the price of my steamboat ticket, but who knows what that old scoundrel will offer me."

They have their dinner as Magdalena chatters happily about her plans for her life in Canada and the tasks she must complete before she leaves Peking. Then, as has become their custom, Pirogov escorts her back to her lodging.

This evening, as Pirogov bows over her hand, Magdalena asks if he would like to come in for a vodka nightcap. He nods and dismisses the pedicab. He follows her through a door next to the shop, up a narrow staircase, and into her room. Her lodging is small and simple—a round Chinese-style table and a few chairs, a settee covered with faded silk brocade, a tiny stove, and a large Coromandel screen behind which he can see the foot of a bed. The worn floor is covered with a once-fine Chinese rug. On the wall is an icon of Czar Nicholas set in a chased silver-gilt frame. The room smells faintly of Magdalena's perfume.

"Please sit down." She pulls a bottle of vodka and a pair of glasses out of a cupboard. "I have no caviar, I'm sorry to say, but these Chinese biscuits go rather well with vodka, I find." Pirogov detects her nervousness as she bustles around preparing their drinks.

She pours the vodka, and they toast each other.

"I shall miss you," Magdalena says. "You've been the only true friend I've found in Peking, and I'll always be grateful to you."

"It has been my pleasure entirely, I assure you, Magdalena. Being with you has brought back the memory of pleasanter days and more civilized times. It is I who am grateful to you."

She looks at her hands, then around the room. Wandering nervously, she straightens a flower in the vase on her table, then replenishes the biscuits on the plate.

Finally, she takes a deep breath and sits on the settee next to Pirogov. Taking both his hands in hers, she speaks. "You're a fine man, Kirik. Interesting and refined. I appreciate that you have always treated me with such respect. And that you've become such a dear friend." She places the fingers of her right hand on his cheek and gently strokes the scar. She stops for a moment, blushing deeply. Then she slips her right arm around his neck, then her left arm, and gently pulls him close to her. She kisses him passionately. In a soft, stumbling voice she whispers, "Kirik, make love to me tonight."

Over the next two weeks, Pirogov spends the early part of each night with Magdalena, leaving long before dawn so she can prepare herself for work and the errands she must complete before her departure. She sells her earrings at Wuhan's for a price sufficient to purchase a third-class steamship ticket from Shanghai to Vancouver on the Pacific and Orient steamship *S.S. Cathay*.

Pirogov feels keenly the imperative for his own departure, but he still has no clues about the location of the Russian village that is his destination. A sense of desperation and frustration weighs heavily on him. He dreads the moment of Magdalena's impending departure, which will leave him alone again, bereft of both friendship and the comfortable passions they share.

Finally, Magdalena announces that she will leave Peking the following day, taking the train to Shanghai, from which she will sail in three days. Her room is now barren of any personal signs of her residence, the icon packed, along with the photographs of her former life which had brought a bit of warmth to the sterile room. Their lovemaking is tender with sadness and resignation. Pirogov realizes how dear she has become to him, and wonders whether, in another time and place, their relationship might have blossomed into something more enduring.

As he is dressing to leave, Magdalena speaks. "I have something I would like to give you." She opens her hand to reveal a heavy gold medal of Saint Andrew on a thick gold chain. "This belonged to my husband, and I could never bear to sell it. It's very dear to me, and I would like you to have it. Perhaps it will protect you and bring you comfort in your future life." She slips the chain over his head. "You will always be in my heart and in my prayers."

Pirogov, moved, embraces her. "As you will be in mine."

Magdalena's slow, soft smile shines on him. "Yes, I understand, my dear Kirik. I am sorry to leave you, too." She embraces him. "There are always so many things left to say, but let's not say them. I know what you have meant to me, and I to you. And I'll never forget you." She embraces him and hands him a slip of paper. "My address in Vancouver. Please write to me from time to time."

"Of course, my dear Magdalena."

"Go with God, my dear friend. You will always be in my prayers."

20

Oretsky's *Russian Teahouse, Peking*
12 August 1918

agdalena is gone, and Pirogov feels lonely and isolated. He sorely misses her, the one trusted friend he had in Peking. To ease his sense of loss, he resumes with renewed vigor his preparations to leave Peking. His one consolation is that he knows that his key to the location of the White Russian community lies in the small desert village dubbed Wu-su, located in the northwestern corner of China.

This evening, he goes to Oretsky's for his evening meal. Tired from a long day and the miles he has walked through Peking's busy streets, he chooses a table in a back corner of the room, wanting only to rest and enjoy some quiet. He orders his meal and a shot of vodka, then settles down to read the evening newspaper and relax.

After several minutes, he becomes aware of someone standing in front of his table. Looking up, he sees an old friend.

"Vladimir!" Pirogov exclaims. He leaps to his feet and embraces his former butler. "My God, man, I'm thrilled to see you. What has happened? What brings you to Peking? When last we spoke in the Moscow railroad station, you were going to join the White Army. Did you? Tell me everything. Please, sit down with me."

Suvorin no longer looks like the suave butler of an aristocratic household. His tall frame is gaunt and his dark hair now streaked with grey, as is the short beard on his lined face. His formerly bright eyes are dull with fatigue and stress. He wears a shabby coat over a badly frayed peasant shirt and threadbare military trousers, and rundown army boots cover his feet.

For a few moments, the two men look at each other as broad smiles cross their faces. Pirogov pulls out a chair for Suvorin, who sinks into it gratefully. Pirogov looks into Suvorin's worn face and sees the faint trace of tears in his eyes. "My dear friend, I'm so delighted to see you, and to know that you're safe." Pirogov returns to his chair. "You need vodka." He waves to Oretsky. Soon both are toasting each other, Mother Russia, China, and Oretsky.

Finally, Pirogov and Suvorin toss down another shot of vodka. "We both have long and interesting stories to tell. How are you here? Please leave out no detail." Pirogov flashes a huge smile and teases Suvorin, "I feared that by now the Bolsheviks would have captured you and made you the *chef de cuisine* in a gulag."

Suvorin stares at the empty vodka glass, looks at Pirogov with tired eyes, and takes a deep breath. His shoulders relax, and his face loses the aspect of stress that it had at first. "A long story, Kirik. I'm sure yours is, too. These are terrible times in our dear old Russia. I'm happy to find you well and looking prosperous."

"Join me for dinner?" Without waiting for an answer, Pirogov signals to Oretsky to bring more vodka and two meals. Then he leans back and gazes contentedly at Suvorin. "Now, tell me what you've done since we parted last year in Moscow."

"Kirik, let me rest for a moment to gather my thoughts. My empty stomach speaks louder than my brain."

Oretsky, recognizing that the two long-lost friends have lots of stories to tell, brings a bottle of vodka and refills their glasses.

For the next few minutes, each relaxes in his chair and says nothing. The vodka starts to bring color and life to Suvorin's face, and his entire affect seems to brighten.

Soon, Oretsky and the waitress bring the first course: salad salted with poached sturgeon and topped with sour cream. Next is steaming hot potato soup. The main course consists of roasted vegetables, plump cabbage rolls, pelmeni dumplings stuffed with ground meat and onions, and a loaf of freshly baked black bread.

Suvorin, still the consummate sophisticate, eats his meal with reserved gusto. During the main course, he recounts his adventures. "After we parted, I took the next train to Omsk and managed to connect with Admiral Kolchak's White Army. I'm too old to be a foot soldier, so with my background they made me the cook for the Admiral and his staff. On reflection, I must admit, I made a witless decision to join the White Army. After a few days, I realized that the Admiral was an evil-tempered old bastard, an incompetent leader, and more interested in building his own glory than in defeating the Reds."

"Led by former czarist line officers, the White Army fought brilliantly and with uncommon valor, despite the incompetent Admiral. We outmaneuvered the Reds and defeated them in almost every battle. Often our machine guns cut down wave after wave after wave of charging Red soldiers. Our artillery diced their cavalry to pieces. By any definition, it was dreadful slaughter. We won the battles, but they were Pyrrhic victories at best. Our losses were staggering, and we didn't have replacements to fill the ranks and man the trenches. We kept falling back because the Reds seemed to have an inexhaustible supply of bodies for the maw of our war machine."

"Then there was an outbreak of typhus. Without proper medical care, our men died by the dozens, day after day. Realizing that I was on the losing side in this no-win civil war, and not wanting to be captured by the Reds, I decided it was time for me to desert and head for China."

Pirogov signals Oretsky to bring more vodka. The old man fills the glasses and retires. "Please continue, my friend."

"I clearly understood that there was no place for me in the new 'people's paradise.' In this take-no-prisoners civil war, the Reds are hunting down and massacring the Whites, and the Whites butcher anyone they suspect is a revolutionary. And, everywhere people are dying of hunger, disease, and despair. Because I knew your mother had gone to China and I suspected, or at least hoped, that you had as well, I decided to follow."

"Early one evening, shortly after dark and with the moon full, I started to hike the twenty miles south to the Red-controlled village of Kalachinsk, a stop on the Trans-Siberian Railway. Surprisingly, despite all the revolutionary chaos engulfing the railroad, it was still functioning most of the time. The Czech Legion trains had passed through the area several weeks earlier. I was fortunate to have a friend in the Whites' cryptography section who prepared forged papers for me as an employee of the railroad." He chuckles and shakes his head. "It's amazing what folks will do for a nice chocolate cake."

He pauses for a moment to savor the pelmeni. "In civilian clothes, with my forged papers and a purloined compass, I avoided the roads to elude Red and White patrols and followed trails in the forest. Two days later, I arrived at Kalachinsk and used some of my remaining funds to buy a third-class ticket to Vladivostok. The Cheka guards accepted my forged papers and let me pass."

Suvorin tosses down his remaining vodka. "Leaving Vladivostok was difficult. The Cheka has the city closed tight. Even foreign sailors are not allowed off their ships except to help load and unload cargo, all under the surveillance of armed Cheka guards. One night, while hiding on the dock among large, outbound, wooden boxes, I found one with the lid not sealed and partly empty. I crawled in. Soon a longshoreman hammered the lid shut, and in due time my box was loaded onto a Panamanian-flagged tramp steamer bound for Tsingtao. Once we were well out to sea, I started making a ruckus. Shortly, a boatswain's mate opened the box and ordered me out. As a stowaway, I was confined to the brig. That afternoon, the cook brought me a meal. I told him of my culinary skills and, by evening, I was the ship's cook. Several days later, we docked in Tsingtao. The captain tried to hire me on as regular crew but, with apologies, I went ashore. Luck was with me again. I saw a truck being loaded with the cargo from my ship. Painted signs on the door in Chinese and English said, "Peking Machine Tools." I jumped in the back of the truck, and here I am in Peking. Now, I'm out of that Soviet hellhole and, God willing, I'll never go back."

Pirogov had leaned forward, absorbed in Suvorin's tale. "An absolutely amazing story! I congratulate you on your skill and verve. Only a man like you could have accomplished it. When did you arrive, and what have you been doing since?"

"I arrived here almost a week ago. I've been looking for you, or at least trying to get some news of you or your mother. But, I realized that finding you two somewhere in China was a nearly hopeless task. Accordingly, I've also been exploring other options. It seems there are excellent jobs here in Peking for a butler of my experience. I've found that many diplomats and European businessmen and their wives appreciate the social cachet of having an Occidental butler, especially one who served an aristocratic Russian family."

Their meal finished, Pirogov orders tea and some of Oretsky's fine Georgian brandy. "How did you manage to find me?"

"Pure luck. I've been checking the various White Russian establishments—hotels and restaurants, places like that—asking after you and your mother. No one knew either of you. I'm staying in a fleabag hostel on the other side of the river, and most of my exploration has been in that part of town. Yesterday, a White told me about Oretsky's Teahouse, where the more affluent Russians congregate. I thought I'd stop in, and here you are."

The two men spend the rest of the evening sipping brandy and telling their adventures in more detail. Having found each other, they are reluctant to part; they leave only when Oretsky reminds them that he wants to close. Even after Oretsky has pulled down the iron grill over his door and turned off the lights inside, the men linger in the street.

"We have more to talk about, Vladimir." Pirogov puts his hand on Suvorin's shoulder. "Will you have breakfast with me tomorrow, here at Oretsky's?"

"I think I can manage to fit it into my busy schedule," Suvorin replies with a wry smile as he embraces Pirogov. "I'll see you here at—when, nine?"

The next morning, the two are seated over strong tea, kippers, and fresh Russian bread spread with butter and peach jam. Both are enlivened by their encounter, and the strain on Suvorin's face has faded.

Pirogov reveals that he has discovered his mother's probable location and that he plans to travel to western China to meet her. "I've been worrying about you, Vladimir, and I'm happy that I can leave here knowing that you're safe. If you need a reference from me in your search for employment, of course I'll be delighted to provide one." After a brief silence, Pirogov continues. "Vladimir, please come with me."

Suvorin nods. "Thank you. But tell me more about this place where you're going. What is it exactly?"

"It's a White Russian settlement in far west China in Sinkiang Province. I heard about this place when I was still in Saint Petersburg, but I didn't know exactly where it was. A lot of Whites who remain loyal to the Czar have gone there by a secret route through Bolotnoye. I understand that it's an agricultural community, like any Russian village, but safe from the Bolsheviks and isolated enough to be largely out of the turmoil that much of China is experiencing. Life there can't be easy, but if my mother is there, I'll be happy." He smiles ironically. "As you recall, I'm no stranger to hard work."

"Yes, I know very well."

"Vladimir, my time here in Peking is short. I plan to leave for Sinkiang Province in few days. Please join me. We'll make a great team." Pirogov stands, withdraws a small chamois pouch from an inner pocket in his trousers, and puts it on the table in front of Suvorin. "First, before I forget, I've been saving these diamonds for an emergency." He empties the pouch on the table. "They are the diamonds you purchased while we were at Beryosha. They're yours. Please take them."

Suvorin stares at the baubles for a few moments without comment. "Thank you, Kirik. You are most kind, but I cannot accept all of them. You must keep some for insurance in these troubled times." Using his knife, he separates the diamond stash into about equal halves and pushes one lot towards Pirogov.

Pirogov looks at the diamonds in front of him, then to Suvorin. "As always, Suvorin, your ideas have singular merit. I should not accept these trinkets, but I will." He slips the diamonds into his watch pocket. After a moment of reflection, he says, "Vladimir, come with me, and let us be Russians again."

Suvorin places the pouch in his pocket. He sips his tea and gazes out the window at the busy street. He puts down his cup and turns back to Pirogov.

"Thank you, Kirik. I'm tempted. But, on reflection, my best option is to stay and work at my trade in Peking for a time. Then I'll emigrate to the West. These diamonds will ensure my well-being here in this city, and later will buy my steamship ticket to the West and perhaps help me establish myself there."

Pirogov, disappointed that his only friend is going his own way, responds, "I understand and respect your decision. I shall miss you. You'll have fine opportunities to use your superb skills and sophisticated manner here in Peking. You'll be a great success. The social elite will vie for your services."

"Thank you, Kirik. Be assured I'll do my best to be the consummate butler for the high-society community of Peking."

"I'm sure you will."

As they get up to leave the café, Pirogov says, "Let's move you to the White Russian Hotel where I'm staying. It's not the Ritz, but it will be more comfortable than your hostel."

"Thank you for the offer, but I'll remain at the hostel. I've made some contacts there that may give me entrée to the culture where I can find employment."

Outside the café they remain silent. Shortly, Suvorin grasps Pirogov's hand in a hearty handshake. "Here is where I leave you, Kirik. I must make my own way."

Pirogov pulls Suvorin to him in a bear hug and kisses him on both cheeks. With tears flowing he says, "May God be with you. Forever you will be in my heart."

Suvorin breaks away and starts to walk down the street. A few paces later, he turns and gives Pirogov a big wave and an even bigger smile.

Pirogov returns the wave, turns around, and walks toward his hotel.

21

Swedish Embassy, Peking
13 August 1918

Once again, Pirogov parts with a dear friend. Without Suvorin, he feels even more isolated in an unfamiliar and treacherous world. Part of him mourns Suvorin's decision to make his own way in China, but he also admires his former butler's integrity and determination to succeed on his own terms. Nonetheless, the heavy feeling of loss weighs on him.

Around noon, Pirogov, dressed in his suit and a black fedora, walks toward the Swedish Embassy. It is a single-story, modern, stone building about ten blocks east of Tiananmen Square. An array of radio antennae sprouts from the roof. Pirogov enters and approaches the receptionist. The lobby is neatly painted in lapis-lazuli blue, spotlessly clean, and furnished with classic birch and teak Scandinavian furniture. The floor is covered with a plush, dark-blue carpet with splashes of gold.

The receptionist projects a stolid, outdoor mien that contrasts with his double-breasted gray suit. The only items on his large desk are the visitors' log and an intercom. On the wall behind him hangs a large Swedish flag—a yellow cross on a bright-blue background—and on the facing wall is a tapestry of the Swedish coat of arms, with its Three Golden Crowns.

The receptionist looks at Pirogov with a stern, quizzical expression. "Your name and your business, sir?"

Pirogov stands at attention and responds in his best military voice, "I am Senior Lieutenant Kirik Pirogov, late of the Palace Guards in the service of Czar Nicholas II, Emperor of All the Russias. Please announce me to your military attaché."

In an equally military voice, the receptionist responds, "Very well, Senior Lieutenant Pirogov, please show me your identification." His right hand slips under the desktop.

Pirogov smiles. "Unfortunately, all my documents were lost in the revolution, and I am in this country without papers. I ask for your understanding."

The receptionist does not immediately respond. His hand remains under the desktop. "I do not understand. You are now in Sweden, not China. Perhaps you should about-face and leave, Senior Lieutenant. We have no business for you here."

Not to be defeated, Pirogov says, "My mission is of critical importance. If you would please tell the attaché that I am here to collect the package that came from your embassy in Saint Petersburg about eighteen months ago, I am confident that he will see me."

With his left hand, the receptionist depresses a lever on the intercom and says, "Colonel, there is a White Russian in the lobby to see you—something about an eighteen-month-old package from Saint Petersburg." Keeping steady eyes on Pirogov, he listens to the response in a small earphone attached to his right ear. "Yes, sir," he says. Looking at Pirogov with curious regard, he says, "An aide will escort you to Colonel Lindstrom."

Shortly thereafter, another man, an apparent duplicate of the receptionist, enters. "Senior Lieutenant Pirogov, before you can enter our embassy, first I must search you."

"Of course."

The escort conducts a thorough search and finds nothing threatening. "Follow me."

They walk down a short hall and stop in front of a solid oak door. The escort knocks sharply three times. From inside they hear "Enter." He opens the door for Pirogov.

"Come in, Senior Lieutenant Kirik Pirogov." Colonel Pare Lindstrom is tall, lean, and fair, and his light blue eyes flash with keen intelligence. His office is similar to the lobby, except that it is somewhat larger and there are no windows. A large, steel, olive-drab safe dominates the adjacent wall. A Swedish flag covers the wall behind Lindstrom's desk.

He rises to shake Pirogov's hand. "Welcome. Please have a chair." He looks at Pirogov with a discerning eye for a few seconds. "So, you are Senior Lieutenant Kirik Pirogov from Saint Petersburg, and without papers? I was beginning to believe that you would never arrive. Sometime, you will have to tell me about your journey. An interesting one, I assume." Before Pirogov can respond, he says, "Let us get to our business."

"Thank you, Colonel. I am here to recover the package I gave to Colonel Carl Gustav Mannerheim in Saint Petersburg on the nineteenth of January 1917."

"Very well. Is there more?"

"Yes, of course. The code phrase is 'Sophie Auguste Frederike von Anhalt-Zerbst, Catherine the Great.'"

Satisfied, Lindstrom says, "Excellent. Please write that phrase on this paper. I want to compare the writing with what's on the package." The colonel goes to the safe, rotates the numbered dial in a precise pattern, swings the locking lever down, and pulls open the heavy door. He withdraws a canvas bag from the rear of the bottom shelf. Opening the bag, he pulls out an envelope and extracts a folded parchment, which he compares to Pirogov's written code phrase. They match. He hands the canvas bag to Pirogov. "Frankly, I'm glad to be rid of this thing. It is not Swedish business."

Pirogov takes the bag, withdraws the box, and carefully inspects the impression on the wax seal. It is his. "Thank you, Colonel Lindstrom." He puts the box back in the bag and rises to leave.

Lindstrom does not rise or attempt to shake Pirogov's hand. He leans forward and puts both of his hands palm down on the desk. In a solemn voice, and with a deep frown, he says, "Senior Lieutenant Pirogov, please remain seated for a few minutes, if you will. I have important information in which I assume you will have keen interest. As a member of the Palace Guard, I assume that you knew the Czar and his family."

Pirogov, somewhat perplexed, returns to his chair. "Yes, I knew all the members of the imperial family. I was particularly close to Empress Alexandra and Grand Duchess Anastasia. What is this information, Colonel?"

Lindstrom, in his official voice, says, "Several weeks ago, I received a Top Secret, coded message from our military intelligence and security service. What I am about to tell you is in strictest confidence until this intelligence becomes public. Do I have your word?"

Intensely apprehensive, Pirogov narrows his eyes and leans slightly forward. "You have my word."

Reassured, Lindstrom continues. "Cryptographers in our security service have decoded a highly classified message from the Presidium of the Union of Soviet Socialist Republics to various high-ranking military officers and apparatchiks, signed by V. I. Lenin. I will read it: 'On my orders, near midnight of 16/17 July, the Cheka terminated Czar Nicholas and all members of his family. The royal family was being detained at the Ipatiev dacha in Ekaterinburg. The Cheka official in charge has confirmed that their bodies, all seven, are buried in hidden graves. The Presidium's official version is that the royal family went on a hunting trip and failed to return; that the three political watchmen whose task it was to protect them are also missing; and that search parties have not found any trace of their party. We have concluded that the royal family has met with a dire misadventure with rogue soldiers or a pack of wolves.'"

Pirogov stares blankly at nothing as Lindstrom's words unfold. As the impact of this horrid tale begins to register, he gasps in horror. "It can't be true. My God! Regicide! All of the family? Anastasia? Even little Alexei?" Leaping from his chair, he cries, "Not even those contemptible Bolsheviks could commit such a ghoulish atrocity. It can't be true. It can't!"

Lindstrom rises, takes Pirogov's elbow, and leads him to a settee. "Senior Lieutenant Pirogov, I assure you, with all the authority of my office, that Lenin ordered this regicide and that the Cheka in Ekaterinburg completed the task with dreadful efficiency. We have incontrovertible authentication from other sources as to the veracity of this intelligence."

Pirogov begins to sob uncontrollably as he realizes the truth of Lindstrom's report—the Empress murdered, Anastasia never to become the magnificent woman she might have been. He puts his right hand over his mouth and drops his chin to his chest; tears tumble down his cheeks.

Lindstrom, struck by Pirogov's severe reaction to his report, says, "My apologies for being the harbinger of such dreadful news." He sits, opens the bottom drawer of his desk, withdraws a bottle of Napoleon brandy, pours a stiff drink into a glass on his desk, and hands it to Pirogov. "Drink up, Lieutenant. This brandy will help you regain your composure."

Clearly overwhelmed, Pirogov responds weakly, "Thank you."

They sit without speaking for several minutes. Gradually, Pirogov's sobs cease and he assumes a steely calm. His feelings, however, are in turmoil. He experiences almost unbearable horror at the killing of people he has known all his life, including two for whom he felt deep affection. He battles seething rage at the despicable cruelty of the Bolsheviks. For an instant, his mind flashes back to the Christmas Ball in January 1917, to Anastasia's glowing face and his own sudden realization that he was falling in love with the smiling girl in his arms. He almost howls with pain, thinking that all her warmth and energy are stilled forever.

Finally, Pirogov stirs himself and stands up to leave. "Thank you for giving me this information, Colonel. And thank you for your kindness. I am grateful for both, as I am for your care of my box." He shakes Lindstrom's hand and picks up the canvas bag. "Good day, sir."

Sick with grief, Pirogov walks out of the embassy into the bright, dusty sun of Peking. The bag hangs loosely in his left hand. Years of military training keep him erect. The agony of this latest loss is so great that only his iron self-discipline keeps him from crumbling to the pavement.

22

City Streets, Peking
13 August 1918

*P*irogov stumbles along the street, away from the Swedish Embassy, now holding tightly to the canvas bag containing the treasure. He is racked with the pain of the deepest sorrow he has ever experienced. His mind is full of imagined images of the massacre of the Romanovs. He cannot concentrate and wanders aimlessly along the streets and alleys of Peking.

After several hours, he is hopelessly lost. He regains some composure as the regicide images begin to fade. He finds that he is in a narrow alley and walking past Wuhan's Antik Shop. A few steps farther down the alley, he spots the universal symbol of a pawn shop, three golden-colored balls hanging on a curved bar. His mind snaps to attention; as the guardian of Russia's most valuable imperial treasures, he ought to have a gun to protect himself and his charge. He enters, walks to the caged counter, and nods to the proprietor. The fellow is worldly-wise and recognizes Pirogov for exactly what he is.

"Good morning, my Russian friend. Welcome to my humble shop. May I introduce myself? I am Lio Chung-k'ai, proprietor. Your distress is obvious. How may I be of service?"

"My apologies, Mister Lio, I just received news that my dearest friends have been murdered. My sorrow has distracted me. Nonetheless, I have tasks to accomplish today. I will need a firearm for protection—a semi-automatic pistol, perhaps. I am going into far western China shortly, and I understand that strife abounds there."

"Indeed! You are correct. There is almost no national government control in many parts of our western provinces." Lio reaches under a counter behind him, withdraws a pistol, and shows it to Pirogov. "Let me recommend this German Lugar, a 9-mm Parabellum—a powerful and dangerous weapon in the hands of a skilled and committed marksman. The seller, a White Russian like you, assured me that he took this pistol off the body of a German major he killed. Its appearance shows that it is battle-worn, as you see. But, it is an excellent weapon when it counts."

Pirogov picks up the Lugar, drops the empty clip, and pulls back the 'ears' to open the breach. It is unloaded. He releases the ears to let the breach close. Pirogov likes its feel. He points the Lugar at the floor and pulls a couple of dry snaps. The trigger is smooth and quick.

"Perhaps you would care to test fire this Lugar? Yes?"

"Yes. But where?"

"I have a firing range in the cellar."

A few minutes later, Pirogov is at the shooter's stand with the canvas bag at his feet. The proprietor has brought a box of fifty rounds. Pirogov deftly loads seven rounds into the clip, slaps it into the Lugar with the heel of his right hand, and charges a round in the chamber. He takes the classic two-handed firing position and, in a few seconds, snaps off all seven rounds at a bull's-eye paper target fifty feet away. Inspection of the target shows that five holes are in the "8" and "9" rings. Two are in the "10" black bull's-eye.

Pirogov eases into a faint smile as he toys with the Lugar. Loaded, the pistol's balance is nearly perfect, and the trigger is velvet-smooth and quick.

"And what is your price for this Lugar and the box of bullets?"

"Only five pounds sterling."

"You have a deal, Mister Lio."

"May I suggest that you consider a shoulder holster so that you can wear this Lugar under your coat and have a quick draw? Only one pound."

"Fine idea. I accept."

Pirogov opens his wallet and gives the proprietor six pounds. He gathers the bag, exits the shop, and hails a rickshaw to take him to his hotel. He shows the coolie a business card from the hotel. Its name and address are printed in Mandarin, Russian, and English.

Later, Pirogov stops at Oretsky's for afternoon tea. He selects a table towards the rear, hangs the straps of his canvas bag on the back of the chair, and orders green tea and cakes. He hails the proprietor. "Oretsky, please sit with me and enjoy this excellent tea. We can reminisce about better days."

Oretsky, with his right eyebrow raised, puts both of his hands on the table palms down, leans toward Pirogov, and responds in his gravelly voice, "Thank you, Kirik Pirogov, for your kind invitation. But, I am loath to talk about the 'good old days' in what was Mother Russia, as they were not 'good' by any measure for the commoners. Now, I exist in this Oriental country as best I am able and do what I can for the Whites who have no hope."

Pirogov, slightly surprised by Oretsky's sullen and emphatic response, recovers and says, "My apologies, my intent was not to open painful memories but rather to engage you in a conversation of some import." Vapors from the tea rise and the pair samples its aromatic bouquet. "Please sit and offer me your sage counsel—if you will."

"Thank you, I shall." Oretsky pulls out a chair, eases into it, and scoots up to the table. He cracks a faint smile as he refills Pirogov's cup and his. He sips. Shortly, he comments, "Clearly, Pirogov, you are not one of the Whites that patronize my teahouse. I have wondered what your stratagem is."

"You are keenly perceptive, proprietor."

"What is this 'import' you mentioned?"

Pirogov realizes that now he must trust someone. "If you would, I need help in planning a trip."

Oretsky retorts, "Go to the American Express office. They are the professionals that plan trips. It is only three blocks away. I will show you." He starts to rise.

"No. Please. I cannot go there." Pirogov's words stumble as he tries to communicate without revealing too much of his secret. "I must arrange my trip *sub rosa*. If I were to have American Express plan my trip, it would be foolhardy." With deep emotion, he details his remark. "The Cheka would have my secret, and many Russians would be massacred—my mother, some of my dearest friends, and many ordinary Russians loyal to the Czar." Calmer, he continues, "I am confounded. What shall I do?"

Oretsky stares at Pirogov with intense black eyes, and strokes his beard in random motions. He whispers, "Perhaps." Patrons begin to file into the teashop. Some greet Oretsky and Pirogov, and the chatter becomes intense. Oretsky finishes his tea, rises, and says, "Follow me to the back room."

Pirogov, reassured by the heft of the Lugar under his left arm, grabs his canvas bag and follows Oretsky.

They enter a small room with no windows, furnished with a small wood table and two chairs. Oretsky snaps the lock firmly closed. Pirogov's senses scream *Cheka snare!*. He grabs for his Lugar.

Before he can withdraw the weapon, Oretsky has his Mauser pointed at Pirogov's heart. "Withdraw an empty hand from your coat, Czarist."

Resigned to the inevitable, Pirogov obeys. His soul cries, *What a fool I am. All is lost. The Cheka have won.*

Oretsky waves his gun toward a chair, and with authority commands, "Sit, Senior Lieutenant Kirik Antonievich Pirogov. Put both of your hands on the table palms down."

"Very well." Pirogov complies. *He knows my middle name. The Cheka has briefed him with the details of my identity. My only option is to have Oretsky kill me. I'll not betray Mother Russia.*

Mysteriously, Oretsky stands a fresh bottle of vodka and two shot glasses on the table. He holsters the Mauser under his jacket. "Now we talk. Relax, my friend. Fill our glasses and let us toast to the assassinated Czar and his lovely family."

Pirogov, bewildered at the unfolding scenario, knows it is best to do what he is told. He remains quiet, and listens. He pours the vodka.

Oretsky raises his nearly overflowing glass. *"Na zdorovje,* Kirik. To our beloved Czar and his family."

Completely befuddled, Pirogov mutters, "*Na zdorovje,*" and swigs deeply. Next, the pair toasts Mother Russia and better times. Not understanding Oretsky's actions, Pirogov remains alert for the opportunity to immobilize the Cheka agent and escape.

Finally, Oretsky says, "Listen carefully, Senior Lieutenant Pirogov." He pauses for another swig of the clear liquid. "I am not a banker. That is my charade." He pauses and watches Pirogov's startled reaction. "Rather, I am Lieutenant General Stanislaw Zinovy Volosenkov, late of the Czar's secret service."

Pirogov stares dumbfounded. Recovering slightly, he mumbles, "The Okhrana."

Volosenkov cracks an amused grin. "Close your mouth, my friend." He fills Pirogov's glass. "Drink."

Pirogov consumes most of the beverage. "My mind whirls with confusion."

Volosenkov's grin fades. "On command of Empress Alexandra, I defected to China to be the conduit for those loyal Russians destined for the secret White compound."

Pirogov imbibes again, and recovers from his astonishment. "Why tell me this secret? I could be a Cheka agent."

"If you were, your body would have gone into the river several days ago."

General Volosenkov tries to stifle a small laugh at his deception, but without success. "Pirogov, I know who you are. I was at the Czar's Christmas Ball in 1917 and saw you dancing with Grand Duchess Anastasia, and you *tête-à-tête* with Colonel Mannerheim." He pauses for Pirogov to assimilate fully the impact of his statements. He continues, "The Empress asked me to be especially watchful for you and to render whatever assistance you might need."

Slightly peeved, Pirogov asks, "General Volosenkov, why wait until now to reveal your amazing secret assignment?"

"For our protection, both of us, my young friend—and for all the loyal Russians to sip tea here in future. You did not need to know until now."

Pirogov reflects for a second. "Indeed, you are correct, General."

With a stern face Volosenkov commands, "I am Oretsky. You have never heard of General Volosenkov. Is that crystal clear?"

Chagrined at his *faux pas*, Pirogov responds with military precision, "Yes, sir."

"To the task at hand." Oretsky points his right index finger at Pirogov. "Make no notes. Write nothing. Say nothing. You must memorize all that I tell you. Do I have your solemn vow?"

"Indeed, sir. My oath as a Russian officer."

"Very well. Your destination is the lamasery at Yumin in northwestern Sinkiang Province—just a few miles from the border of the Soviet Union." He reaches into his coat pocket and withdraws a small packet of printed paper. "Here is your third-class railroad ticket to Urumchi, the train's terminal city. Any questions?"

Pirogov understands "third class," and answers, "None." He fidgets for a beat. "I'll need a map."

"I have one for you with the route highlighted."

"I understand."

"From Urumchi, a local bus goes to Wu-su, about ninety miles north-west. There is no public transportation to Yumin. You will have manage your own way. All clear?"

"Yes."

"The Whites in Yumin keep a post office box in Wu-su. It's number 1894."

Pirogov smiles. "The year of the Czar's accession! How appropriate, and easy to remember."

Oretsky continues in his most professional voice. "Because the various transportation modes are unreliable, your travel time to Wu-su could range between ten days and two weeks—perhaps longer. The local train to Urumchi has no real schedule. This train runs as it can to service the myriad towns and villages along its route to northwestern China. For many, it is the only communication with 'civilization.' Additionally, there are other factors to consider, such as condition of the tracks and bridges, availability of crews, and the weather."

He looks at Pirogov with concern and firmly cautions him, "Understand: The national government has only minimal control over the area along your route. The entire region is fraught with danger—especially for an Occidental. The region is infested with renegade warlords, bandit gangs, bands of military deserters, and Japanese patrols from the Kwangtung Army on reconnaissance missions."

Pirogov reflexively rubs the scar on his left cheek and responds with a touch of bravado, "I survived the Galician campaign, and I will survive this journey—as have many Russians before me."

Oretsky smiles inwardly at his response. "Bravado will not stop a bullet or a bayonet. Lastly, I must caution you to travel inconspicuously and display nothing that hints of value. Without a moment of reflection, thieves would murder you and steal whatever you have."

The hubbub from the teahouse fills the room. Oretsky puts a stack of papers on the table. "I must tend to the Russians. Read, memorize what you need, and leave these documents on the table. Exit my establishment without attracting attention." After he opens the door, he turns and offers, "Saint Christopher will guide you. *Bon voyage.*"

The door is closed before Pirogov can respond. He spreads the material about the tabletop: timetables, maps, handwritten notes from earlier travelers, and copies of pages from publications with information about the passage. Several hours later, the essential intelligence is firmly ensconced in his memory. He faces a tedious and hazardous 2,400-mile journey to Yumin: uncertain railroad travel to Urumchi and, when available, by motor coach to Wu-su, on the edge of the Takla Morku Desert. This village is the last outpost in one of the most remote and unexplored regions of China. Then, it would be by horse-drawn wagon or perhaps by camel to Yumin, when he could arrange it.

In a rickshaw traveling back to his hotel, Pirogov passes a fruit and vegetable market. He recalls an amusement that he and his chums enjoyed as children—using fig skins to stain their hands and faces. He devises a scheme for modifying his appearance and secreting Alexandra's precious coffer. Pirogov commands the driver to stop. He purchases a half-pound of figs and a twenty-pound burlap sack of potatoes. Before leaving the market, he adds a few rotting tomatoes, onions, and cabbage leaves that he finds in the gutter.

Later, in his room, he cuts open some of the figs, sucks out the fruit, and rubs his hands, arms, face, and neck with the inside of the fig peels to darken his skin. After an hour, he notes that his appearance is two or three times darker than before. At a casual glance, with a beard and mustache, he might pass as a tribesman from Central Asia.

Pirogov opens the potato sack and removes most of the potatoes. He places Alexandra's ebony box, in its canvas-carrying bag, deep in the sack. He replaces the potatoes and stuffs the wilted vegetables and the remaining figs on top of the potatoes. The odor of rotting produce surrounds him, but he is counting on the smell being offensive enough to discourage the curious from investigating. He packs his personal items into his well-worn knapsack, and the clothes, boots, and other equipment purchased for his life in western China into a duffle bag.

Sleep escapes him, as a virtual newsreel of regicide plays repeatedly in an endless loop. In the morning, he is haggard and overwrought from the sleepless night. He collects his thoughts and makes firm his resolve for the travel ordeal he faces. He does not shave. *A grizzled chin will enhance the image of poverty and exhaustion that I want to convey.* He picks up his bags, descends to the lobby, and gives his suit and a large gratuity to the hotel clerk. Then he checks out of the hotel.

He hires a rickshaw to take him and his baggage to the railroad station. His mind and eyes are alert to possible danger. The imagined scene of the senseless and vicious murder of the imperial family does not leave his mind. He fights with a feeling of disbelief that people so dear to him have died so horribly.

23

Railroad Station, Peking
20 August 1918

A few minutes before the train's scheduled departure, Pirogov ensures that his duffle bag is loaded safely in the baggage car. Satisfied, he boards the third-class coach of train number 176. Its ultimate destination is Urumchi, almost 2,400 miles to the northwest, and the end of the line. Bits of dark-gray paint hang from the ceiling, and insects crawl on the filthy wooden floor. He chooses a place near the front of the coach and sits on a narrow, straight-backed, hard seat. He stores his knapsack in the overhead rack and the potato sack against the bulkhead under his seat. The sack is not completely out of sight, but it is inconspicuous. Perhaps the pungent odor of rotting vegetables discourages passengers from sitting next to him.

Carrying a fortune in Romanov treasures, his goal is to look as innocuous as possible, perhaps like an overworked farmer. He is dressed in the dirty, heavily worn peasant clothes he purchased the previous day from a street vendor, and he has pulled a grease-and-dirt-stained cloth cap over his long hair. The slight bulge of the Lugar under his left arm is not noticeable beneath the loose-fitting jacket.

The third-class car is jammed with nattering passengers and crying children. Most of Pirogov's fellow travelers appear to be as poor as the image he hopes to convey—weary farmers on their way home from the markets of Peking, provincial peddlers, families on their way to some unknown destination, and several western tribesmen.

Settled in and as prepared as he can be, Pirogov painfully reflects on the slaughter of the Romanov family. A catch in his throat forces him to sit straight and fight the onrushing tears. With resolve, he reasons that what is done is done, and there is nothing he can do about it. *Goodbye, sweet Anastasia, you notorious prankster.* Now, his life's goal is to get the Romanov treasure to Yumin and make a productive life there. The accursed Bolsheviks are in power and will remain indefinitely. His beloved Russia has sunk into the evil, violent Union of Soviet Socialist Republics.

Almost on time in mid-afternoon, the conductor blows his whistle three times and shouts, "All aboard!" in Mandarin, English, and Russian. Then he swings onto the train. The cacophony of the steam engine lurching forward and gaining momentum sends a slight shiver through Pirogov. At last, he is on the final leg of his long journey. The weight of his exhaustion abates slightly as the train begins to move. But it does not accelerate to the normal pace of a departing train. For the next few minutes, the train moves slowly as it passes through an industrial section of the city. Pirogov wonders why. Is there a problem so soon on his first day of travel?

Soon, he sees that the train has switched from the main track to a siding that enters the Wang Poh Arsenal. As soon as the train stops, brakemen uncouple the mail coach. Because his third-class car is only a few cars behind the mail coach, Pirogov sees much of the hectic activities outside. An armored car backs up to the mail coach, and soldiers haul small, heavy sacks from the car into the mail coach. Then there is more huffing and puffing as the engine moves forward. Several freight cars and a flat car are inserted between Pirogov's third-class car and the mail coach. An armored flat car is coupled to the front of the engine.

The hubbub arouses Pirogov's curiosity. He leaves his seat and moves to the front platform for an unobstructed view. On cue, well-armed Chinese regulars board the flat cars and set up sandbag redoubts for their Spandau 7.9-millimeter machine guns. An artillery officer supervises a Skoda 47-millimeter cannon installation on the front of the armored car. Then a senior officer issues a command, and more regulars scramble atop the passenger and freight cars. Clearly, this train is carrying extremely valuable cargo in the mail car. And, it seems that officials must have intelligence of possible serious trouble en route to provide such an extensive defense.

This diversion stirs Pirogov's curiosity and eases the pain of imagining the regicide. Within an hour the train is reassembled, back on the main track, and gaining momentum. He stares out the window, watching as the city vanishes and wondering what adventure lies ahead.

他時，

A week or so earlier, an elderly Chinese man had entered the China National Bank and Trust Company, Ltd., in Peking. He walked with a slight shuffle over the marble tile and used a sturdy cane. In his other hand was a small valise. He was slightly stooped from scoliosis. He wore a gray suit, a dark gray fedora atop his full head of carefully groomed gray hair, and a neatly trimmed gray mustache and beard. His face was hard, and there was menace in his black eyes. At the reception desk, he told the attractive secretary in her tight, green, red-trimmed cheongsam, "Tell Mister Chan Sen-tao, the senior cashier that Colonel Kwei Yung-chin waits to visit with him."

"Yes, Colonel." She flipped a switch on the intercom. "Mister Chan, Colonel Kwei is here to see you. Yes, sir. Right away." She returned the switch to neutral. "Please follow me, Colonel."

Chan rose and made a short bow to greet Colonel Kwei.

Kwei said nothing and, uninvited, took the chair next to Chan's desk. "Well, do you have it?"

Chan was not taken aback by Kwei's abruptness and lack of courtesy. He had dealt with the colonel before. "Of course, Colonel." Chan reached into his top drawer and withdrew a white, letter-size, unaddressed envelope, which he slipped into Kwei's valise. "All the details of the shipment are included."

Kwei picked up his valise and turned to leave.

Chan, in a soft voice, said, "Colonel, may I suggest that you have forgotten something?"

"It is so." From his coat pocket, Kwei withdrew a thick envelope and handed it to Chan. "You will find everything in order."

"Thank you, Colonel, for your deposit."

As soon as Kwei exited the bank, Chan picked up the telephone and dialed a memorized number.

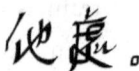

At sunset, the train makes its first stop at Chang-chia-k'ou, a small desert town about forty-five miles northwest of Peking. Some passengers exit, others board, and freight is exchanged. Pirogov watches as armed guards remove several small sacks from the mail car and quickly drive away in an armored car. Slowly, a premonition of disaster creeps into his mind, but he cannot discern its nature.

Soon, a vendor with a steam cart walks the aisle of Pirogov's coach, peddling hot tea, steamed rice, dried fish, and warm buns. He buys his evening meal—nothing like Oretsky's *carte du jour,* but filling nonetheless. As darkness envelops the train, Pirogov slips into sleep, despite his intention to remain watchful.

After a restless night, Pirogov is awakened by sunlight streaming onto his face. He is stiff and sore from bouncing on the hard seat all night.

For breakfast he buys tea and steaming hot congee from the cart vendor. Shortly after he finishes his meal, the train pulls into the station at Chi-ning. With some reservations about leaving the potato sack unattended, Pirogov descends to the boarding platform for some fresh air and a little exercise. Stiffly, he moves up and down the platform, swinging his arms and taking deep breaths of the chill, sooty air. He sees some of the heavy bags being spirited away from the mail coach. Pirogov cannot concoct a reasonable explanation for such bustling activity, except that something valuable is being off-loaded at these small towns. The conductor's boarding whistle interrupts his speculation. Immediately, a sergeant with a fixed bayonet on his rifle approaches Pirogov and forces him back into the coach.

The rest of the day takes him across the dusty expanses of northern China. The train stops frequently at towns along the route, mostly to unload freight, passengers, and a few of the small, heavy bags. The towns are mostly forgettable—dusty collections of wind-worn buildings, dirt streets, and wandering livestock. Pirogov looks forward to each stop as an opportunity to walk about the platform, stretch his cramped muscles, and take a closer look at the area around the station. At the Shih-tsui-shan station, Pirogov buys steamed pork buns and tea from a platform vendor. He sees that the soldiers seem more alert.

The conductor's boarding whistle forces Pirogov to swallow the last of his tea, and he returns to his seat.

The train continues its journey through the long summer day. As it moves westward, more passengers leave than board, and by evening only a few travelers remain in Pirogov's car. There are also fewer stops as the towns become more dispersed. The country is dry, composed of vast, eroded, loess hills. There is nothing green to be seen except for a few irrigated fields in the valleys. *A desolate country*, Pirogov thinks. He wonders if Yumin will look like this, and if his future there will involve the same hardscrabble existence as that of the peasants he observes toiling in their desiccated fields.

He endures another night on the hard seat. At least now the car is quieter because so many passengers have left the train. There are only a few other people in his car—a tribal family, perhaps Uzbek, and a rotund Chinese merchant in an ill-fitting Western-style suit.

Pirogov awakens cold and stiff just as dawn is beginning to color the sky. He walks up and down the car to relieve some of the stiffness in his muscles. The train is passing through a narrow ravine, the track clinging to one side of the defile, with the opposite slope only a few yards away. Suddenly, the train screeches to an abrupt halt; the force is sufficient to throw Pirogov to the floor and send his fellow passengers and their belongings flying around the car.

As he picks himself up from the floor and struggles to return to his seat to make sure the potato sack is safe, he hears gunfire. Despite the ringing echoes that bounce around the ravine walls, his trained ears identify the sound of several weapons—machine guns, rifles, and handguns. Shouts and screams fill the air. He can see nothing from the window, so he assumes the attackers are firing from the walls of the ravine above the train.

He scrambles back to his seat and pulls his Lugar from its holster, loads a round in the chamber, and keeps it in his right hand. From his seat, he can see only the wall of the ravine. Then he notices armed horsemen racing up a rough trail on the side opposite the train, all of them firing toward the Chinese regulars posted near the front of the train around the mail car. The attackers—bandits or a warlord's army—seem well armed, moving with skill under heavy fire.

Suddenly, Pirogov hears a scream inside his car; he, looks around and sees the businessman fall to the floor, hit by a stray shot through a window. Quickly Pirogov rushes to the victim's side. The wound is in his left arm, superficial but bloody. He pulls off the man's jacket and removes a narrow belt from the fellow's trousers. With practiced skill, Pirogov uses the belt as a tourniquet to slow the bleeding, then wraps the jacket against the wound. *Not enough*, he thinks, *and everything is filthy, but for the moment it will have to do.* He pushes the man under a seat where he will be somewhat protected from the firing. Two more bullets crash through the coach's windows and ring throughout the coach. The tribal patriarch herds his family under seats. Before ducking down to join them, he pulls a lethal-looking knife from his coat and displays it to Pirogov, nodding with a menacing smile.

Without thinking, Pirogov has become a soldier again. His Lugar is loaded and ready; he moves quickly to the carriage door and looks out. There are attackers in the rocks above the track on both sides of the train, firing steadily downward. He sees some of the regulars drop to the tracks. For a moment, he is paralyzed by indecision. All his instincts urge him into action, to protect the treasure, to defend the train and his fellow passengers. However, he knows that any action that would draw attention to him endangers his mission. His heart is pounding as he deliberates.

Then the decision is made for him. A slightly wounded, warlord soldier yanks open the rear door. His pistol is at the ready and he shouts a curse in Mandarin. Without reflection, Pirogov snaps off two shots and the man falls dead, spinning backward onto the tracks.

Another approaches the car where Pirogov is standing. A shot between the eyes, and the fellow falls on the platform near Pirogov's feet. Pirogov kneels down to see if the man is wounded or dead. He is dead, but Pirogov is surprised by the sight of his blonde hair and fair skin.

Two bullets whiz by him, and Pirogov does not have time to reflect on how a fellow European became a warlord soldier. "Damn fool," Pirogov mutters. He is now firmly committed to the fight. With abandon he leaps from the coach, races down the tracks, and fires at any target he spots. A horseman flashing his saber races down the tracks toward Pirogov's back. The hoofs pounding on the wooden ties alert Pirogov to turn around. In an instant, the horseman falls to the Luger's bark.

Suddenly, from afar, Pirogov hears a bugle sounding. Hidden in a copse of trees on both sides of the ravine are two battalions of Nationalist cavalry. It's an ambush. Almost before it starts, the battle is over. The corpses and wounded of the warlord's army litter the area. Nationalist soldiers give the *coup de grâce* to the wounded. General Wu Pei-fu and what is left of his army are in full retreat with the Nationalist cavalry in hot pursuit.

Pirogov holsters his Luger and trots down the track toward the regulars. There are many dead and wounded, some hanging from their redoubts, others fallen to the ground. The survivors move efficiently, carrying the wounded into one of the freight cars. Pirogov silently assists with the care of the wounded, helping to carry them to the car now designated as an aid station. He then follows a contingent of soldiers to the head of the train, where he helps remove the barrier of rocks that the attackers constructed to halt the train. He moves automatically, unspeaking, responding only to what he sees needs to be done, and doing it efficiently and silently.

"You are a brave man." Pirogov is so preoccupied with his work that he barely hears the officer addressing him. Someone grasps his arm. "Do you hear me, sir?"

Numbly, Pirogov halts and looks about him. A Chinese major is holding his arm and looking into his face. "Do you hear me?" he asks again.

"Yes." Pirogov is suddenly breathless and exhausted. The major draws him aside to sit on a boulder beside the track.

"I am Major Kwan Soong-chow. I thank you for your help."

Pirogov can only nod.

"Are you injured, sir?"

"No," Pirogov responds. "No, only a little tired, and my ears are ringing."

"Observing your actions today, I would speculate that you are ex-military. You helped saved some of our troops. You are a brave soldier and an excellent shot."

Pirogov has regained some calm. "Perhaps 'reckless' is more appropriate." After a brief pause, Pirogov relaxes a bit. "Please explain, Major, what happened this morning. At first, the warlord army put this train under a severe attack. Obviously, they were after whatever valuables are in the mail car. Then, out of nowhere, pre-positioned Nationalist cavalry ambushed the warlord's army and the battle was over in just a few minutes."

The major responds, "The warlord, General Wu Pei-fu, fell into a Nationalist trap. What his secret agent Colonel Kwei did not know was that Chan, the senior cashier at the China National Bank and Trust, is an undercover agent for the Kuomintang Intelligence Agency. Chan gave the colonel the exact details of this train's schedule and suggested the optimum spot for his attack to steal several hundred kilograms of gold intended for the small banks along this route. The warlord fell into an elaborate ambush planned by Colonel Chiang Kai-shek to kill or capture the wily and powerful Wu Pei-fu, destroy his army, and wrest away Wu's control of this province and much of the others that border it. We went through this elaborate charade because Wu has spies everywhere."

Pirogov nods wearily. He wants only to return to his car and make sure that the potato sack is safe. Finally he asks, "What is it that the warlord was after? What is the treasure in those bags in the mail car?"

"Rocks. Lots of rocks."

Pirogov smiles broadly at the charade so cleverly executed. "Do you have a doctor with your company, Major? A passenger in my car has been shot. He needs medical attention."

"I'll send soldiers to bring him to the aid station." The major pauses. "We both have work to do now, so we'll part. Thank you, my friend, for your help." Before the major leaves, Pirogov says, "The most curious thing happened to me in the firefight. I shot and killed a warlord soldier who seemed to be European. Do you have any idea how a European soldier would end up fighting for a Chinese warlord?"

The major understands Pirogov's bafflement. "After the Treaty of Brest-Litovsk and the collapse of the White Army, many Russian and other European soldiers with no home or family enlisted in the various Chinese warlord armies for the excellent pay."

Pirogov nods in understanding and mutters under his breath, "Fools."

The two shake hands, and Pirogov trudges back to his coach.

The potato sack is intact. In a few minutes, two regulars arrive and carry the wounded businessman away. Pirogov helps the tribal family reassemble their packs and return to their seats. They are clearly shaken, but the man boisterously pounds Pirogov on the back. The two women smile at him shyly.

Then he slumps, exhausted, onto his seat. He looks again at the potato sack and sees that it is undisturbed. And no wonder. The odor of rotting cabbage and fruit is becoming increasingly rank. Quickly, he reloads the Luger and stows it in his holster.

It takes about an hour before the track is cleared and the train resumes its journey. Drained by the attack, Pirogov feels a bitter remorse as he contemplates what might have happened had the attackers been successful, entered the car, and robbed the passengers. He did what was necessary to protect the coffer, he reasons, but he cannot suppress his horror at the risk he took. Had he been killed or seriously wounded, the coffer would have been left unprotected and would never have reached its destination. And, had any of his fellow passengers not been so distracted by the attack, someone might have wondered why a ragged person of unknown origin was carrying a powerful and obviously expensive weapon. Immediately, he scribbles a note: "Please forward the box in this potato sack to post office box 1894 in Wu-su, Sinkiang Province." He stuffs the note deep into the sack, atop Alexandra's box.

Considering the slaughter that afternoon, he wonders, are there any rules of war that apply to warlords and their minions? What a miserable world we live in—death and violence everywhere, with greed and chicanery as the norm.

Shaken by the attack and by his own doubts about his part in it, Pirogov cannot relax. As the train moves through the gathering dusk, he watches the passing countryside of sand, scrub plants, and an occasional oasis with a herd of yaks and sheep munching the sparse grass. A shepherd gives a hearty wave to the train. It is not until midnight that Pirogov's head slumps forward on his chest and he falls into an exhausted sleep, occasionally broken by frightening dreams and the jolting of the coach.

The lumbering train proceeds at its own pace, with long stops here and delays there. The days pass in a blur as the towns slip by: Wu-wei, Chang-yeh, Ho-Hsien, Tutae, and others. Pirogov no longer cares what their names are.

24

Urumchi, Sinkiang Province
29 August 1918

Early in the afternoon, the locomotive blows its steam whistle a dozen times and clangs its bell as it slows while approaching the terminal at Urumchi. As the train stops, the engineer blows volumes of steam into the dry air. The locomotive coughs, and black smoke blows out of the smokestack, obscuring the sky for a few seconds.

The racket arouses Pirogov from the languorous *ennui* induced by nine days of exhausting travel. With slow deliberation, he rises and gathers his knapsack and potato sack. As he begins to exit the coach, his body rebels. All his joints are obstinately stiff, and his muscles are painfully sore. He is physically tired and mentally exhausted. With all the resolve he can muster, he lifts his baggage and takes tentative steps onto the station's boarding platform. No one pays him any attention—not that there are many people about.

The train has stopped in the middle of this two-street town at the beginning of turn-around wyes. Pirogov retrieves his duffle bag from the baggage car and enters the small station. He notes that it is surprisingly clean and well kept. He approaches a skeleton-thin fellow who appears to be associated with the railroad.

"Good evening, sir. Can you help me? I understand that a bus goes to Wu-su from here. Please tell me, what is its schedule and how many hours is the trip?"

Without a blink the stationmaster recites his mantra. "There is no schedule. The bus leaves this station when there are enough passengers and freight to make the trip profitable. The time en route depends on many factors. Mostly it is the coming and going of passengers along the way and loading and unloading of freight. First scheduled stop is Ma-na-su, about forty-five miles from here. Wu-su is about forty miles beyond. Are you going to Wu-su?"

"Yes. What is the fare?"

"Forty-five Chinese dollars."

"How many passengers are going, and how much freight is aboard?"

"Two passengers and about a hundred pounds of cargo. Not enough to make the trip worthwhile."

After his weeks in China, Pirogov is not surprised at Chinese business, in which maximum profit is the tenet of any enterprise. He understands the routine. "How many dollars more do you require for the bus to leave?"

"I do not know exactly, but 3,000 Chinese dollars should cause the bus's motor to start. You want to go now?"

Pirogov opens his wallet and hands the stationmaster 3,000 Chinese dollars. "Let's get moving."

他走。

Later that afternoon, Pirogov is on a London General Omnibus Company double-decker motor coach that is heavily loaded with passengers, freight, mail, and animals. As soon as the bus had pulled up to the station and word circulated that that grungy fellow had paid all their fares, people scrambled aboard with a menagerie of animals: chickens, goats, caged rabbits, and a sow. And somehow several hundred pounds of freight and mail mysteriously appeared and were loaded onto the bus. The driver had carefully helped the passengers board, and ensured that the animals were secured, the freight firmly tied down, and the mail stashed in the space behind his seat. When all seemed to be in order, he had shouted, "All aboard for Ma-na-su, Wu-su, and all points in between."

The desert heat is stifling, and the noise, stench, and lurching and bouncing of the bus over what is euphemistically called "a road" compound Pirogov's misery. Two hours and several unscheduled stops later, the bus arrives in Ma-na-sa, a nondescript desert town of no significance that Pirogov can see. He walks about to loosen his muscles as most of the passengers leave and some of the mail and freight are unloaded. Shortly, the bus driver bellows, "All aboard for Wu-su and points in between!"

Three hours later, after several more unscheduled stops, the bus arrives at Wu-su and stops at the bus station, a small mud-brick and timber building. Pirogov exits and asks the driver, "Is there a hotel or hostel in this town?"

"Yes, of course. I am the bus-stationmaster, telegraph agent, ticket seller, and purveyor of information about Wu-su and the surrounding area," he replies with a hint of irony. "Our bus line operates a hostel. It is that building across the street, the one with the steeply slanted roof. It has four rooms, and they are reasonably clean and comfortable, considering that we are at the end of civilization. No one is staying there now."

"How about a restaurant?"

"No restaurant here. Whan Shu-pe has a noodle shop a few doors down this street."

"Thank you, sir."

The fellow focuses on the potato sack with a curious eye. "Are you so desperately hungry that you must carry your own potatoes?"

"No, I'm playing a joke on someone," Pirogov responds with a forced smile. He is alarmed that someone has noticed his cache and called attention to it.

Pirogov sees a young man loafing by the station and pays him to carry the duffle bag. When they arrive at the hostel, there is no proprietor in attendance, so he signs the register "Kirik Pirogov" and takes a key from the rack, Room 4. The room is small and its furnishings primitive, but it is clean, the bedding freshly washed, and no insects scurry around the floor. The communal water closet is next to his room. He stacks his bundles against the wall and does some exercises to loosen his body. Exhausted, he sits on the bed and ponders what to do with the crown and jewels buried in the large potato sack. He dare not leave the sack in the hostel, and to carry it with him at all times does not make sense and would attract undue attention. He wracks his mind trying to solve this quandary. At last, he reasons that there is no simple solution. He decides to abandon the potato sack and its contents, and carry the box in its canvas bag with him. He can use the straps as a bandolier across his chest, and the box will rest on his hip. Not the best option, but the only one he can devise.

At the noodle shop, Pirogov has a satisfying meal of tea, pork noodle soup, chicken curry, rice, and stir-fried, mixed vegetables from nearby farms. It is the best meal he has had since he left Peking. The proprietor is a jolly, rotund man of middle age and anxious to please his only customer.

In the fading twilight, somewhat refreshed, Pirogov scouts the dusty desert village. He sees no reason for it to exist.

But, circa 1000 A.D., Wu-su was an important and wealthy hub on the Silk Road. Its wells were full of crystal-clear mountain water. Merchants of all types traded and transshipped merchandise to the West and to the East: rugs, camels, silk, jewels, slaves, musk, perfumes, spices, and medicines. Perhaps more important, the Silk Road exchanged technologies and religious and philosophical thought. Such trade brought immense wealth, culture, and scholarship to the town. Around 1050, Buddhist monks established a lamasery and learning center several miles northwest of the town across the Ai-pi range at Yumin. Over the years, the wells had dried and, with the development of more efficient and safer transportation routes between the Orient and the West, the Silk Road waned. Wu-su began its slow decline.

Now, in 1918, Wu-su is an outpost for the national government's presence in northwestern Sinkiang Province and a refuge for occasional travelers: government bureaucrats, prospectors, rug and camel merchants, tribesmen, geologists, traveling mail carriers, and the like. The post and telegraph offices are combined and fly the national government flag. The police station has no officer—the last one was murdered when bandits raided the town several months ago. The pharmacy has a minuscule formulary, consisting mostly of Chinese herbs and a few Western drugs. A small general store has a modest selection of clothing, a few tools, firecrackers, and canned goods. It also sells fresh vegetables, salt pork, eggs, and chickens. The streets are dust in the summer, and mud and ice in the winter. Buildings, such as they are, are made of birch logs and mud bricks.

After a sound sleep in his reasonably comfortable bed and a Spartan breakfast of noodles and tea, Pirogov spots the post office a block down the street. He enters and finds box number 1894. He tries to convince the postmaster to tell him the name of its renter. The postmaster recognizes Pirogov as a Russian, but he is not willing to betray his mailbox renters. To Pirogov's request, he angrily shouts in Russian, *Nyet! Nyet!*

With no other option, Pirogov realizes that he must wait in the post office until someone opens the box. He goes to the noodle shop and arranges to have noodles and tea brought to him at the post office around noon each day. He sits on the lone bench and begins his vigil. For four more days he continues his watch from the post office's opening to closing, 0800 to 1700.

On the fifth day, shortly after the post office opens, a tall Kirgiz enters, goes to box number 1894, inserts a key, and withdraws a stack of mail and several red cards. He puts the mail in his hand-carry pouch.

Pirogov approaches the tribesman from the rear and touches his left arm to get his attention. In an instant, the fellow has a hunting knife against Pirogov's throat, and a trickle of blood flows down his shirt. The tribesman takes a few seconds to appraise this white man impersonating a native. In near-perfect Russian he says, "Who are you to touch me? What is your purpose?"

Pirogov, taken completely by surprise, is speechless. He quickly recovers, pats at the blood with his handkerchief, and says, "I intend you no harm. I am a White Russian seeking sanctuary."

Somewhat reassured, the tribesman withdraws his knife and says, "I am Chen, leader of the Kirgiz, and the representative of the national government in this part of Sinkiang Province. I am the link between the White Russians and the outside world. When I finish my business, I will take you to Yumin, several miles from here. If you are an imposter, you will not see the sunrise tomorrow."

Chen goes to the post office window, hands the red cards to the postmaster, then goes to the caged door that opens to the interior. In a moment, the postmaster opens the door and begins handing the Kirgiz about a dozen large boxes of varying sizes and weights. Chen looks at Pirogov and nods. Pirogov understands and helps Chen load the boxes into his wagon. Chen acknowledges Pirogov's help with a short, "Thank you."

After checking the boxes to ensure that they are secured in the back of his two-horse wagon, Chen motions to Pirogov to wait. Chen stops at the general store and then at the pharmacy. With all packages stored, he tells Pirogov, "Sit next to me on the seat. We should be at Yumin before sunset."

Pirogov does not climb aboard. "Please wait for me. I must go to the hostel to retrieve my belongings."

"Very well," Chen responds. "I'll wait a few minutes."

Soon, Pirogov returns, tosses his duffle bag and knapsack in the cart, climbs aboard, and puts the canvas sack with the crown and jewels between his knees. Chen snaps the reins, and the horses begin to move.

Late in the afternoon, several White Russian farmers are digging an irrigation ditch in the vegetable garden. They wear wide-brimmed straw hats to ward off the scorching sun and light-gray, long-sleeved shirts, loose trousers, and rubber and straw sandals. The sound of the approaching wagon causes them to look up. They see Chen and wonder who their visitor might be.

Pirogov climbs down from the wagon and slings the canvas sack containing the ebony box over his shoulder. He is so weary that he stumbles and catches the side of the wagon to keep from falling. "Good afternoon," he says with as much energy as he can muster. "I am a new recruit to your community. May I see the person in charge?"

A middle-aged woman with a shovel in her hand walks close to him, examines him with a curious eye, and says with a hint of paranoia, "So you say. How do we know that you are not from the Cheka, out to betray us?"

Pirogov responds, "I assure you that I am a loyal Russian, not a Cheka." He pulls the Saint Andrew's medal out of his shirt and shows it to her. "Would a Cheka agent proudly display such a medal?" The woman examines it. "Please, madam, I assure you that I'm not a Bolshevik. I should like to speak with the manager of this community."

"Wait here. We're watching you," she says with a touch of contempt, her shovel held high. Pointing to a farmer standing next to her, she adds, "I'll have Peter fetch the elector of our community. He is Grigori Pavlovich Cherkassky."

"My God!" exclaims Pirogov. "Grigori is my uncle. Yes, I want to see him. And my mother, too, if she's here."

Meanwhile, several farmers have unloaded the village's mail and the various boxes and packages, as well as Pirogov's duffle bag. Chen sees that the Whites have Pirogov under control, and drives away.

Shortly, Grigori Pavlovich arrives. He is a slightly built man in his late sixties, with a firm chin and wide mouth. His eyes sparkle under straight, narrow eyebrows, and his hair is mostly gray. Deep lines etch his sun-browned face, reflecting the weighty responsibility he has for leading and keeping safe this community of White Russian *émigrés*. He says, in a friendly voice, "Good afternoon, friend—or is it my nephew? Tell us who you are and why you are here. I haven't seen my sister's son since he was just a nipper. And I cannot see you well under that straggly hair and unkempt beard."

"I am Kirik Antonievich Pirogov, late of Saint Petersburg and Torzhok, and a former senior lieutenant in the Palace Guards. Tell me, Uncle, is my mother here? Countess Maria Pavlovna Pirogov."

Grigori rubs the scar on his left arm. *Perhaps this fellow is Kirik. His mother will know.* He asks a gardener to fetch Maria.

"Thank you. I haven't seen her in almost two years."

"First, however, I must search you and inspect your knapsack, duffle bag, and the contents of that sack hanging over your shoulder."

Alarmed, Pirogov leans toward his uncle and responds in a whisper. "Please search the sack and the box inside when we're alone. It contains items of great import from Saint Petersburg for safekeeping here."

Grigori, with reservations, replies, "Very well. We'll do as you ask."

Pirogov responds, "Thank you. Also, I'm armed." He withdraws the Luger, ensures that the safety is on, and hands it to Grigori with the grip toward his uncle.

Accepting the Luger, Grigori notes, "I suspected as much. That small bulge under the left arm of your coat is just noticeable."

Grigori begins searching Pirogov's bags. A group of other Russians gather around them. Suddenly from out of the group, a woman cries, "Kirik! Kirik, my son. You're here!"

Maria Pavlovna rushes to the startled Pirogov and grabs him. She hugs him and smothers him with kisses. Through tears of happiness, she says, "I thought you were lost in the revolution. I prayed every night to Saint Christopher to guide you safely here. And my prayers have been answered!"

Pirogov hugs his mother and kisses her on both cheeks. "Mama, dear, I'm so glad to see you and know that you're safe. I've missed you very much. Are you well? Tell me how you came here. Is this a good place? Have the Soviets bothered you?"

"Too many questions. We will talk about me later." Maria moves slightly away from Kirik and looks at him intensely. "My son, what has happened to you? Your skin is so dark. Your hair is straggly, and you haven't shaved in days. What kind of Russian officer are you?" she teases. "And you have filled out your lanky frame." She grabs Kirik again and kisses him. "Thank you, Saint Christopher, for bringing my son to me."

Pirogov puts his head on his mother's shoulder as his tears begin to flow. In a low voice, he says, "Mama, I'm so happy to be with you."

A large crowd has gathered around Pirogov—old friends, former comrades, and others who have heard marvelous tales of Senior Lieutenant Kirik Pirogov's military exploits and his close friendship with the imperial family. He greets some of his old friends and acknowledges others in the crowd.

Maria touches Kirik's arm. "You look exhausted. Let's go inside to have a cup of tea. And you can tell me how you managed to come here."

Kirik looks at his mother thoughtfully. "My odyssey is a long story."

"Son, we will go inside to talk." She beckons to Grigori to follow.

A few minutes later, Pirogov, Maria Pavlovna, and Grigori Pavlovich are seated in Grigori's office, an austere room in the old monastery. The furnishings are simple—a locally made desk, half a dozen chairs, a bookcase filled with well-worn volumes, and a cabinet. A fine icon of the Holy Mother and Child in a bejeweled frame hangs on the wall, the sole touch of color and luxury in the room. A bubbling samovar sits on a small side table.

Pirogov, his mother, and his uncle sit silently sipping tea. They are overcome with the joy and relief of being reunited after so long. Pirogov's face reflects his exhaustion and a kind of bewilderment at finally having reached his destination.

After a few minutes, Grigori asks, "Tell us, what is in that sack that's so important, and emits such a foul odor? I will take it outside." He starts to rise.

Pirogov protests, "Grigori! No! Please leave it."

To ease the tension, Maria, with a faint smile, chides her son. "Did you have to carry your meals and the refuse in that sack?"

"No, Mama."

"My apologies, Uncle. Your forbearance, please. I will explain shortly."

Maria's and Grigori's eyes focus intently on Pirogov.

Pirogov takes a hearty swig of tea. He places his cup on the table and looks first at his mother, then at Grigori. "First, I have terrible news about the imperial family."

Before Pirogov can continue, Grigori interrupts. "Please, if your news is about the regicide, Chen told us about it several hours after the news broke a few weeks ago. We were horrified and were in mourning for seven days. It is impossible for us to comprehend such barbaric behavior."

Pirogov, surprised that Chen would have this information so quickly, nonetheless replies bitterly, "The Bolsheviks are uncivilized brutes. One day, they will suffer retribution."

After a short pause, and with a question in his eyes, Pirogov addresses Grigori. "I don't understand. I was led to believe that this Czarist community is totally isolated and cut off from the world."

"We are isolated, but not totally. The Kirgiz have a powerful shortwave radio and an electric generator. Their radio operator transmits and receives International Morse Code messages from our agent in Peking. Please understand that the Kirgiz are most circumspect about mentioning our community. Otherwise, the Soviet radio intelligence agency would pinpoint our location. Our agent in Peking keeps us informed. Every few weeks, he sends us a stack of newspapers, small supplies, and apothecary goods. The mail and packages Chen brought here today are from our agent and were addressed to 'Urumgi Ygru,' Chen's Kirgiz name."

Pirogov leans back in his chair. "I understand. An excellent scheme." Pirogov closes his eyes. "Excuse me for a moment. I need to clear my mind."

No one speaks for a time. Pirogov finishes his tea and looks at his mother. "Mama, please clear the table, if you will. I must speak with Uncle Grigori in confidence."

After Maria leaves, Pirogov looks at Grigori with stern eyes. "I must have your solemn word that what I tell you and what I will give to you will remain your secret. Commit this to memory—never write it. Should you relinquish your responsibility as elector of this community, you must pass this secret to your successor. If you cannot, I will."

Grigori, responds without hesitation, says, "You have my word."

Pirogov smiles faintly and a small tremor of joy at his success suffuses through him. *Thank you, Saint Andrew, for guiding me to this successful completion of the Empress' mission.* He looks at the sack at his feet, digs deep with both hands, withdraws the ebony box, and places it on the table. Rotted vegetables cling to the box, drop onto the table, and scatter on the floor. The stench is obscene and the sight is loathsome.

Grigori bounds from his chair, exclaiming, "Kirik! What have you got? Pray tell what have you done?"

Smiling faintly, Pirogov rises, brushes some garbage off his jacket, and responds, "I've waged gas warfare to protect that ebony box Empress Alexandra entrusted to me some thirteen months ago."

Grigori dashes to the kitchen to fetch wet towels and a container. Shortly, the pair has cleaned the box and the area, and disposed of refuse.

Grigori stares intently at the box. "Shall I open it?"

Standing next to his uncle, Pirogov says, with precisely enunciated speech, "Please do, Elector. Savor these Russian treasures, and store them where only you and I will know.".

Several minutes later, a matronly woman brings hot tea for the pair. Alexandra's box is secreted. After the teacups are drained, Pirogov withdraws the remaining gold schillings and hands them to Grigori. "Here is the balance of the gold coins Empress Alexandra entrusted to me, and here is the rest of her currency."

With surprise in his eyes, Grigori accepts. "Thank you, Citizen Pirogov. This cache of affluence will enhance our meager treasure substantially."

Pirogov replies, "I'm leaving now to join my mother. Elector, know that I have a loaded Lugar pistol with extra ammunition. With your permission, I will keep it."

"Yes, you keep it."

25

Ekaterinburg
23 July 1918

Colonel Yakov Yurovsky and his Cheka guards return to Ekaterinburg. Yurovsky is a handsome fellow, tall and slender. He is dark, with a pencil-thin mustache, a small aquiline nose, and a hard, straight mouth. His hard blue-green eyes are intimidating. It appears that the Czech Legion has left the town in good order. Nothing seems to be damaged. Yurovsky immediately goes to the graveyard to see if the Czechs discovered the graves of the royal family.

Addressing Ivan Pashich, head of the graves detail, Yurovsky demands, "Have there been any questions about the Romanovs? Did the Czechs inquire about the graves?"

Pashich is a small, dour fellow with moody sadness in his dull black eyes. With trepidation, he responds, "The Romanov graves? No. The Czechs were too busy to bother about anything but their trains." Shrugging, Pashich tells Yurovsky, "We buried the bodies as you directed, Colonel—all six of them."

"Six! There should have been seven bodies. Who did you not bury? Tell me now!"

"I don't know. There were six bodies that we buried."

Pressing hard, Yurovsky demands, "Tell me about those that you did bury. Be absolutely positive about your identifications. If you're not sure, don't guess. I must have the absolute facts. Your fate depends upon your accuracy. Do you understand?"

"Yes, Colonel, I understand. But I'm only a gravedigger. It's not my place to know about the royal family. In the time those people were here, I rarely saw them, and then only from a distance when they were in the garden." He pauses to recall what images he can. He scans the newly dug graves to stimulate his memory. He closes his eyes and after a few moments, he looks at Yurovsky and says, "I am positive that we buried the Czar, his wife, and the little son. And three young females—the daughters."

Yurovsky methodically quizzes Pashich about each of the female bodies, but he's not satisfied with the answers. Nonetheless, from Pashich's responses, he begins to see a pattern. Finally he asks, "Did you bury a teenage girl, about sixteen years old, with long, curly, reddish-brown hair, and somewhat overweight?"

"I'm not sure." Pashich hesitates. "I don't believe so. We could not make positive identification of all the girls. The bodies were so badly mutilated by the multiple bayonet gashes."

On reflection, Yurovsky recalls a couple of significant details about the youngest daughter. He quizzes Pashich more intensely, "Did one of the girls you buried wear a dark blue dress?"

"It's difficult to say. There was so much blood that the clothing on all the bodies was soaked in it. I cannot tell with certainty."

In frustration, Yurovsky grabs Pashich's shirt and pulls him close to his face. "Did one of the girls have a silver ring on the index finger on her left hand—a ring in the shape of the Orthodox cross?"

Pashick closes his eyes as he tries to recall this detail. "Perhaps we did not find a girl as you describe among the corpses." The gravedigger looks down and makes the sign of the cross across his chest.

"Anastasia," snarls Yurovsky. He curses and slams his pistol into Pashich's face, knocking him to the ground with a broken nose and jaw. "Peasant, the socialist state is your god."

Furious, Yurovsky shouts to no one in particular, "Is Anastasia dead? Where is her body? Where is she? She must be hereabouts." Seething, he assembles his Cheka guards. "One of our female prisoners is missing. She is a malignant enemy of the State. When last seen, she was wearing a dark blue dress stained with blood. If not dead, she must be seriously wounded. Find her!"

Quickly, the guards spread into the area surrounding the Ipatiev House. After searching for several minutes, they do not find the missing girl. However, they report finding the cellar stairs, the kitchen floor, and the steps to the outside recently scrubbed clean, although the cellar floor is soaked in blood. Intrigued by this information, Yurovsky recalls the blood-soaked boots and uniforms of the guards as they climbed the stairs out of the cellar after the massacre. With a surge of rage, he realizes that someone has removed Anastasia's body or else helped her escape and tried to cover it up. He orders the guards to expand the search. "Go in all directions for a mile. She must be critically injured with rifle shots and bayonet thrusts. She must be close by. Find her! Or find her body!"

His hasty overconfidence and unbridled zeal have resulted in a grievous blunder that could topple the struggling Soviet state. He realizes that it is untenable for Anastasia, or any member of the Romanov royal family, to be alive. The news of the regicide would spread with celerity worldwide, doing irreparable damage to the socialist government. Anastasia would be the inspiration for a deluge of anti-Soviet propaganda. She would be the symbol that would rally the White forces, the Czech Legion, and the disparate groups waging guerrilla war against the Soviets, and unite them under the heraldic Romanov double eagle. The Western nations would intensify their invasion of Murmansk, Archangel, and the southern Caucasus. The Americans and Japanese would expand their occupation of Vladivostok and Port Arthur. Flush from their victory in 1905, the Japanese would seize Russia's Pacific provinces and threaten Mongolia. The fledgling Soviet Union would be isolated from the world. And if the government could remain in power, it would be years before the USSR would gain worldwide recognition.

At a more personal level, if Lenin and Dzerzhinsky discover that Anastasia has escaped the regicide, Yurovsky knows they will hunt him down and have him killed. He must find Anastasia quickly and exterminate her—and do it quietly. An hour or so later, his Cheka guards report that they have not found a body. No trace of the blue dress. No pool of blood on the streets.

No trace whatsoever.

Surprisingly, Yurovsky reacts calmly to this negative news. His mind is now clear of anxiety and anger. His outward passion abates. His self-confidence has returned, and his mien is that of a professional Cheka officer dedicated to defending the State. Because Anastasia is not lying dead in the street, he reasons that she, or her body, must be nearby. If dead, the muzhiks must have hidden her body—perhaps buried it in an unmarked grave. If alive, she had to have help. For the past few weeks he has noticed little things among the servants. Nothing in particular, but when taken in aggregate, he suspects that most of them were sympathetic to the Czar's family. The maids in particular seemed overly congenial with the daughters. Perhaps one of the servants found Anastasia and has taken her to their hut.

He barks orders to his guards. "Sergeant Major, secure the dacha compound—no one comes in and no one goes out. First Sergeant, assemble the servants from the Ipatiev House—the maids, cooks, gardeners, all of them. Get the husbands, wives, and children. Station them in front of their huts."

With guns drawn and bayonets fixed, the Cheka guards storm the servants' quarters in the dacha compound. In a few minutes, the guards have rousted all family members and forced them to stand in front of their huts. The guards snap to attention as Yurovsky approaches. With military precision, he walks slowly down the line of servants. He looks at each directly in the eye and glances at their family members. If one looks down, he picks up that one's chin so he can look into their eyes. He says nothing. He looks for a sign that he would readily recognize as guilt. He easily discounts the fear expressed in their eyes. He will know the sign of guilt when he sees it.

He completes his first pass, having seen lots of fear and perhaps some guilt. He wonders if perhaps there is a cabal of conspirators among these muzhiks who have helped Anastasia. He discards the notion. They are too stupid and laced with abject fear to organize such a plot.

Then, on reflection, he realizes that what he took for guilt is shame. He announces to the assembled peasants, "I have reason to believe that one of you has committed a grievous crime against the State. I will find this person, one way or another. First, however, I offer amnesty to the guilty party if he or she will step forward."

He waits a couple of minutes, but no one advances. "How foolish for one of you not to admit your offense. Do you not know that confession is good for your soul? Is there no one to step forward?" He waits for a short time to see what effect his words have had. Soon, he has no more patience.

"Now we will find the guilty party the Cheka way. Amnesty is canceled." He walks to the gardener. "Peasant, you have tended the garden well. I admire your skill. I noticed that over these past few weeks you are teaching your son to be a gardener as skillful as you are. Bring him forward. I want to meet him."

The gardener motions to his son to come forward. Just as the boy joins his father, Yurovsky draws his Mauser and shoots the young man in the heart. Then he turns his pistol on the gardener and shoots him in the head.

The gardener's wife and his remaining children scream in disbelief and cry in horror. The second son restrains his mother as she starts to run to her fallen husband and son. The assembled servants emit some whimpers, but they know that it is best to remain silent.

Yurovsky calmly addresses the group, "We can repeat this Cheka process all day. I have an unlimited supply of bullets. Will the guilty one step forward?"

The first sergeant approaches Yurovsky and salutes. "Sir, we have found a blood-soaked mattress in the hut of the maid Khina Demidova."

"Very well, Sergeant." Yurovsky turns to face the servants. "Khina Demidova, come to me. We must have a little chat." With her head down, Demidova approaches and stands in front of Yurovsky.

"Please tell me why your mattress is soaked in blood. Is that blood of your family? Who is hurt? We have an excellent physician here at the dacha to attend to such needs. Or possibly the blood belongs to someone else, is that so?"

Demidova, gripped in fear, keeps looking down. She is afraid to look at Yurovsky. Her guilt will give her away. She does not respond.

Without warning Yurovsky slaps her with all his strength, knocking her to the ground. Her husband comes to her and helps her stand. Yurovsky slaps her again, again, and again. He points his pistol at her husband, "If you do not speak now, your husband will join the gardener and his son."

Demidova breaks. Sobbing, she reveals the details of finding Anastasia. "Several hours after the commotion in the basement, we heard faint cries at the back of the dacha. I went to see and found Anastasia on the steps. She was unconscious and bleeding. My husband and my two sons took her to our home. We did our best to help her, but we had no medicine or medical skills. She was dying. We applied some herbs to the wounds in her shoulder and thigh, and we bandaged them. The bleeding slowed. We could do nothing more." Demidova continues in a halting voice, telling of Anastasia's rescue and escape with the Czech Legion.

Yurovsky's anger builds. He screams at her, "You stupid peasant!" He shoots her in the stomach. "Die in pain, you ignorant muzhik. You traitor to our socialist revolution!" He kicks her body.

"Sergeant Major, form a firing squad and execute Demidova's husband and sons. Arrest all these peasants standing here as counter-revolutionaries and make immediate arrangements to have them sent to the gulag at Strezhevoy. No trial is necessary. Burn their huts and all their possessions." He knows that the fewer witnesses, the better.

His anger not much abated, he roars, "That damn reactionary Czech Legion has her. We'll find her and end this business." This is now his avowed and secret mission in life.

Yurovsky sends out an alarm to all stations along the Trans-Siberian Railway and to all stations with railroad connections. The telegraph wires hum: "An important female *bourgeois* counter-revolutionary has escaped Soviet justice. We suspect that she is on a Czech armored train headed into Siberia. For her capture, the reward is 10,000 Maria Theresa gold schillings."

He does not name Anastasia. That's his secret.

26

Novosibirsk on the Trans-Siberian Railway
14 April 1919

Throughout the winter months, sporadic Red harassment has been more of a nuisance than a serious disruption of the Czechs' winter bivouac. The month before, several units of Admiral Kolchak's White Army and a squadron of Dnieper Cossacks had joined the Czech Legion.

Spring has in a leisurely way warmed Siberia. Colonel Zak has determined that the Legion and its allies can finally leave their winter billet. The trains are ready and the Legion is prepared for its final run to Vladivostok. On his command, all four trains blow their whistles, begin to move, and slowly accelerate.

Anastasia has made slow but steady progress over the winter months. Her wounds are healed, and she has a healthy appetite. She is strong, and her spirit is indomitable. Her hair has grown several inches and Nurse Botkina keeps it neatly trimmed. Anastasia's left arm, now out of the sling, hangs loose. The cast is off her right leg, and she walks with a serious limp and uses a cane. Twice a day, under the stern directions of Nurse Botkina and Sergeant Gadia, she works with determined resolve on physical therapy routines to strengthen her muscles and gain more mobility.

The rest of the time she assists Nurse Botkina in her duties. Anastasia proves to be a quick learner, and staying busy and useful seems to help her cope with the painful memories of her family's murder and her own uncertain fate. She is generally cheerful, although it is clear to her companions that she has spells of overwhelming grief.

However, Doctor Litvak is concerned. Anastasia's progress to full mobility is far too slow. Her arm has limited movement, and the feeling in her hand is minimal. He orders a suite of x-rays for her shoulder and leg.

Based on his assessment, Litvak concludes that the speeding, twisting, expanding bullet that smashed into her shoulder caused massive damage to the muscles, tendons, nerves, and ligaments. There is nothing he can do, and the damage is permanent. Anastasia limps because the compound fracture of her femur did not heal correctly, and there is severe injury to nerves and tendons. With iron fortitude, she accepts his adverse diagnosis. "*C'est la vie*," she responds flippantly. She resolves to work all the harder.

Later that afternoon, Doctor Litvak approaches Anastasia as she works on her physical therapy routines. With an easy smile, he greets her. "Anna, I'm delighted with your dedication. Keep working as diligently as you can." He watches her for a few minutes, then hands her a small leather pouch. "Here are your ten gold schillings that Major Jan Klaus saved for you."

Accepting the pouch, she smiles. "Thank you, Doctor. I was wondering when the major would return them. But I'm curious. Why didn't he bring them to me in person? I'm anxious to meet him and thank him for saving me."

Litvak responds with a tight mouth and grim eyes, "Unfortunately, I must tell you that a Red sniper shot and killed Major Klaus yesterday evening. We found your schillings among his belongings."

Anastasia puts her hand to her mouth to stifle a small cry. "My God!" she exclaims. "Are we all to die at the hands of those Red barbarians? Will our trains ever be safe from them?"

Before Litvak can respond, Colonel Václav Zak enters the car. Captain Litvak and Sergeant Gadia snap to attention and salute.

Zak says, "At ease, men. I'm here to pay my respects to our guest Russian nurse." He approaches Anna as if he is charging a Red trench. "Good afternoon, *Mademoiselle* Anna Bogrova. How is our new Russian nurse progressing?"

Before Anna can answer, Zak says, "Captain Doctor Litvak is keeping me well informed. I am honored that we can be of service to a member of the Romanov royal family. Understand that as long as you are in our protection en route to Vladivostok we will keep your identity secret. And beyond, I will add. Now, please excuse me. We are approaching Bolotnoye. I must return to the command and control car. We may have some trouble from the Reds. Good day, *Mademoiselle* Anna Bogrova." He does a sharp about-face and dashes out.

An advanced Legion patrol enters Boltonoye. Mounted Cossacks scout the surrounding area with orders to conduct hit-and-run tactics. Amazingly, they discover that most of the Reds have evacuated the town. The Cossacks mop up the few stragglers.

Colonel Zak is not surprised at the Reds' sudden departure. His cryptographers have decoded radio intercepts that tell Zak the Reds are grouping around the Lake Baikal tunnels several hundred miles to the east. This intelligence reveals that the Reds are determined to make a stubborn resistance to thwart the Czechs' progress eastward. They have set dynamite in some of the tunnels that cut through the Hamar-Daban mountain range on the south shore of Lake Baikal.

Zak orders a reinforced company of Cossacks to conduct a long-range reconnaissance of the area between Bolotnoye and the tunnels, and to reconnoiter the Red deployment around the tunnels. "Communicate *en clair* on your shortwave radio, using frequency 3950 kilocycles, at 2200 each evening."

Болотное, Сіберіа
14 Июлъ 1919

When the trains stop at Bolotnoye to pick up their advance patrol, Anna enters Litvak's office, where he is completing a report. She is wearing the standard nurse's uniform—long gray skirt, full gray blouse with a large red cross embroidered over the left breast, gray cap with the red cross, black hose, and black shoes. Her once-curly hair is now worn in a short bob and is a glossy black. She has a small haversack hanging loosely from her right shoulder containing a few personal items, the schillings, and forged documents prepared by a corporal in the Intelligence Division. She says, "Good afternoon, Doctor."

"Hello to you, Nurse Anna Bogrova." Litvak notices her changed appearance and raises his eyebrows. "It looks as if you're ready to work with the wounded in the wards. I see that you even have your medical kit. I'm impressed. How is your leg?"

"My leg is as well as it's ever going to be," she says with finality. She sits down and holds her cane with her right hand. Then she pauses as she forms her words carefully. She stares at Doctor Litvak for several seconds with sorrow forming in her eyes. In a soft voice, almost a whisper, she says, "With deep sadness and my undying gratitude and love, I must tell you that Bolotnoye is where I must leave you. My mother charged me to make my way south from here and join an expatriate White settlement in China."

Litvak is dumbfounded. He stares at Anna for several moments with narrow, questioning eyes. Neither speaks for a long while. Shaking his head slowly, he responds in a choking voice, "I don't understand, Anna. Your treatment is not complete. You have no experience in the world outside of the Palace and this train. How will you manage? I admit that we did not discuss your future, but we assumed that you would stay with us to Vladivostok, and perhaps travel on to a Western country. Please reconsider and stay with us."

Anastasia smiles gently, but shakes her head. "I must leave. This is what I promised my mother I would do."

"But Anna," Litvak continues, "we must assume that the Reds have discovered by now that you were not murdered in the regicide. They'll be watching for you everywhere, and no doubt there is a generous reward waiting for anyone who finds you. It will be best if you stay with us until we are safely out of the Soviet Union."

She smiles again. "But I no longer look like my old self, do I? Nurse Botkina cut my hair into a very modern style, and she found some mustache dye to color it. Also, I'm wearing a nurse's uniform and carrying a medical kit. And look!" She reaches into her medical kit and pulls out a pair of dark glasses. "Nurse Botkina gave these to me. She told me they were worn by a soldier whose eyes had an extreme sensitivity to light." She puts them on. "Now, tell me, would you recognize me as the girl you found in Ekaterinburg?"

Litvak looks at her. He realizes that the somewhat chubby girl he rescued in Ekaterinburg has matured into a slender, almost fragile-looking young woman. Her formerly round cheeks have interesting hollows, and her blue eyes seem enormous in her thin face. Her face reflects the grief and physical pain she has suffered over the past year, and her eyes are those of a much older woman, one who has seen far too much of the ugliness and cruelty of the world. Litvak realizes there is nothing in Anna's current appearance to link her to the pampered aristocrat she once was.

Litvak shakes his head. "You're very brave, Anna. The disguise will be of some help, I'm sure. But still, you would be safe with us."

Standing and leaning on her cane she says, "I'm eighteen years old—a full-grown woman with adult responsibilities. I must execute them to the best of my ability." She is silent as small tears trickle down her cheeks. In a choking voice she stumbles, "With all my heart, I thank you and your staff for all that you have done for me. You saved my life and made me as whole as I can be. I shall always remember you. God keep you and your wonderful people and get you safely home. Earlier, I said goodbye to Nurse Botkina, my surrogate mother, and Sergeant Gadia, my older brother. I love both of them with all my heart." She leans forward and hugs Doctor Litvak, then kisses him on both cheeks. She steps back and says, "Goodbye, my caring father. Now, if you would be so kind, please help me down the steps of this railroad car."

27

Railroad Station, Bolotnoye, Siberia
14 April 1919

Nurse Anna Bogrova walks slowly across the wooden planking of the railroad station platform, using her cane to help take the weight off her right leg. It is a bright, sunny afternoon, and wildflowers paint the land in a potpourri of vivid colors. A scattering of high clouds break the patina of the deep-blue sky. The boreal forest surrounding the town is thick and bright green.

At one time, the station was painted white. Now, with its flaking gray paint, it looks dilapidated. The windows are coated with dirt and several have broken panes. Trash is scattered everywhere. Today, a few of the town's inhabitants have come to gawk at the Czech armored trains.

Using her cane as support, Anna shuffles to the telegraph office, which has an outside window with a small shelf facing the platform. On the shelf are blank telegraph forms and a variety of pencils. She softly taps the shelf with her right hand to attract the agent's attention. The clerk, Vaslav Nikolsky, approaches the window and says, "Good morning, Nurse. How may I help you?"

Anna wonders if this man is her contact. "Good afternoon," she says as she places her right hand on the shelf at the bottom of the window. Her Saint Olga's ring is obvious, but Nikolsky seems not to notice. "Please tell me when is the next train to Duzhba? And how far is that town?"

"Good afternoon to you, Nurse. It's curious that you should get off that Czech hospital train at Bolotnoye. Are you going to help a sick person in Duzhba? That godforsaken town is about five hundred miles south of here, almost in China, where it ought to be."

"Yes. A party apparatchik with a fever," she lies. "But first, I am to meet a colleague here. Then we are to travel together to Duzhba."

"A Czech nurse to help a Communist?" He stares at Anna.

"I am Russian, not Czech, and I have no politics," Anna retorts with passion. "Out of compassion, the Czechs let me ride on their train from Novosibirsk to here."

"No matter. There is no train to Duzhba until tomorrow morning, if then. If it's on time, it will leave this station sometime around nine o'clock—that is, if the Bolshevik engineer and his fireman are sober and have the inclination to fire up that relic of an engine and go. The trip will take at least thirty hours, maybe more. It depends on how many passengers there are, how much freight there is, and how many intermediate stops the engineer makes."

"In this glorious socialist state, I also am the stationmaster and the ticket agent. Ten rubles for the ticket, Nurse."

Anna pulls a gold schilling from her knapsack and slides it to him under a telegraph form. "I will have one ticket, please." After the transaction is completed, she leans close to Nikolsky and asks in a low voice, "Do you know my colleague, a young man whose name is Anton Andreev, who might have come here looking for me?"

Nikolsky slips the coin in his pocket and leans back. Squinting at her, he says sarcastically, "How can I know this fellow Andreev? I don't even know your name."

Anna leans on the window sill to take the weight off her right leg. "I am Anna Bogrova from Novosibirsk. Do you remember him?"

Nikolsky withdraws slightly back into the telegraph office and puts his hand on the shelf. "Perhaps I might, but at my age, my memory is not as sharp as it ought to be."

Anna begins to see his pattern. "Maybe it needs a slight stimulus."

"Perhaps it does."

"Perhaps I may help." Anna pulls another gold schilling from her sack. She rubs her thumb back and forth over it. After a time, she places the schilling close to her right eye and pretends to make a comprehensive inspection. As she slowly turns the coin about, it reflects the sunlight in a sweeping arc across Nikolsky and the telegraph office.

The stationmaster, nearly mesmerized by the gold light, turns his palm up and whispers, "Perhaps my memory is coming around."

"Make sure that it does, and is accurate," Anna says as she places the schilling in his palm.

He quickly closes his palm and pockets the coin. He leans toward her and says in as soft a voice as he can manage, "I know of your Andreev. He came here on the Trans-Siberian Railway about a year ago and asked about you. I told him that I did not know you and assured him that you had not been here. He asked me to tell you that he is going to Peking and that he plans to meet you in China sometime within a year or so. He boarded the train and left Bolotnoye. What is peculiar about this fellow is that he was in a Communist Party commissar's uniform, not a medical outfit."

Anna is perplexed and disheartened by this news. She stares sharply at Nikolsky and says, "Do you know why Andreev went to Peking? Was he in good health?" Silently, she sends a prayer to Saint Olga to keep him safe.

With some impatience Nikolsky responds, "I don't know. He didn't confide his secrets or the state of his health to me."

"That is indeed unfortunate," Anna says as she discreetly puts her right hand on the shelf. "I will need his assistance in treating my patient in Duzhba."

Nikolsky takes Anna's hand and looks at her ring carefully. "That is an interesting ring," he comments. He stares at Anna for a long time, wondering if indeed this is Anna Bogrova. Over two years ago, an Okhrana agent instructed him to help a young woman with the credentials that this woman has offered. The ring is correct, as is the gold coin. But she could also be an agent-provocateur working with the Cheka. With his eyes narrowed, in a cautious voice, he says, "Such a religious symbol is unorthodox in today's socialist atheistic utopia. I would suggest that you remove it. There are a couple of

Cheka agents in this town, and they are watching for a young woman about your age. A counter-revolutionary, we are told."

"That is an excellent suggestion." Anna removes the ring and slips it into her knapsack. "Thank you, Comrade—I'm sorry, I don't know your name."

"My wife calls me Vaslav Nikolsky, the grouch."

"Again, thank you, Comrade Nikolsky." Anna pauses. "I'm stranded here until the train arrives tomorrow. I don't know anyone in this town. Will you help me?" Speaking with some force, she says, "Those gold schillings ought to buy me some assistance."

Recognizing her plight, Nikolsky says reluctantly, "You may stay in my home tonight with my wife and me. Sit on one of the benches in the station until my shift ends in about three hours." Having seen Anna hobbling and relying on her cane for support, he asks, "How far can you walk? My home is about a mile from here."

"I don't know. Not far, I expect. Certainly not a mile." From her exercise routines, she knows that overexertion causes searing pain.

"I'll bring my cart here to take you to my home."

"Thank you. You're very kind."

The gawkers have left, and the station is deserted. Nikolsky is now convinced that the nurse is Anna Bogrova. He speaks in the softest manner his hoarse voice allows. "Do you have papers? By now, I'm sure, the Cheka agents know of your arrival from the Czech train. People gossip carelessly in this town. Surely the Cheka will soon be here to question you."

Anna pats her knapsack and says with a touch of smugness, "I have an internal passport issued by the Party Secretariat for the Sixth District of Novosibirsk. The commissar for internal travel stamped my passport with a visa for me to visit Duzhba on a medical mission, and it is valid for two months. Also, I have a copy of my medical license."

With one eye cocked and in a mocking tone, Nikolsky says, "Indeed, I am impressed. I didn't realize that the Czechs had such gifted artisans."

In an instant, Anna realizes the subtle meaning in his comment. She blushes and puts her hand to her mouth. She takes a deep breath and relaxes as her tension fades. Now she is confident that Nikolsky is the contact of whom her mother spoke. She flashes a warm smile.

Nikolsky does not return her smile and says in a hushed voice, "Do as I say. Look the Cheka agents straight in their eyes. Have your papers ready. Answer their questions forcefully and do not elaborate. Act annoyed that they would question you, someone on a mission of mercy sanctioned by the Party Secretariat for the Sixth District of Novosibirsk."

"I accept your advice wholeheartedly."

"Make sure that you do. Over the past three years, I have helped many of your friends emigrate south—so far without incident. I suspect that your real destination is Yumin. Is that not so?" Before Anna can answer he says, "Duzhba is about three miles from the Chinese border, and Yumin is five miles further."

Without comment, Anna turns away and limps into the station. She clears off a ramshackle bench near a window with a shattered glass pane. Sunlight streams through the broken window and highlights the dirt and dust around her. A single, bare light bulb hangs from the ceiling, flickering as the power fluctuates. Occasionally, it goes dark altogether. She sits carefully, relieved as the pain in her right leg begins to subside. She sets her knapsack by her right side. Once settled, she retrieves her book and begins reading. The dark glasses protect her eyes from the sun's glare on the pages. Behind them, she feels protected, almost hidden from the world.

Nikolsky was correct. Within thirty minutes, two men approach Anna. They stand on either side of her. One is tall, the other taller. Both wear rumpled, ill-fitting, light gray suits. Their fedoras are dark gray with a crimson band. The eyes of the tall one are dark and without expression. He is heavy and wide with a square jaw, straight mouth, and a razor-thin mustache. His black hair has a touch of gray at the temples. The taller one has cool gray eyes with a hint of mirth. His jaw is slack and chinless, and his large mouth reveals a hint of inept dental work. He appears to be bald.

The tall one demands, "What is your name, Nurse?"

Anna stares at him with cool, narrow eyes while framing her response. With an imperious voice she says, "Who are you to ask?"

Slightly taken aback, the tall one spouts, "Cheka agents do not have suspects question them. We are agents of the State Security Agency, and we ask the questions, Nurse."

"Anyone can say they are Cheka. Show me your papers."

Flabbergasted at this cheeky nurse, the tall one demands, "What is your name?"

"Show me your authority to question me and I will answer your question."

Frustrated, the tall one loudly exclaims, "We can arrest you now for your impertinence."

Anna counters, "Do it and the party chairman in Duzhba will most likely die. I am here at the direction of the Party Secretariat for the Sixth District of Novosibirsk. You will answer to them."

The tall one's visage turns obstinate and harsh. His eyes are stone cold. With fury, he blurts, "We do not answer to every party apparatchik in the Soviet Union. We answer only to Comrade Felix Dzerzhinsky, the People's Commissar for Internal Affairs. Is that clear?"

With her eyes fixed on the tall one, Anna smiles whimsically and responds, "I'm impressed. Show me your credentials and I will answer your questions."

Calming down, the tall agent realizes that this nurse might have some serious party connections and could really be on a commission for the State Secretariat. He nods to his cohort and both draw their Cheka badges and identification cards. The agents hold them in front of Anna's face.

"Thank you, gentlemen. My name is Anna Bogrova, and I live in Novosibirsk."

The tall one demands, "Why did you come to Bolotnoye on that Czech train? A Russian fraternizing with the Czechs is most suspicious."

"My mission is urgent, and because of the bitter war that rages all around us, that Czech train was the only transportation available. Those fellows were kind enough to let me ride with them. At no charge, I might add."

"Who is your father? Where is he?"

Anna's eyes narrow and her mouth opens slightly. "My father was Sergeant Ivan Rodionovich Bogrov, late of our victorious Red Army. He lies in a grave at Omsk, shot dead by a czarist soldier." She searches her knapsack and withdraws two carefully folded papers, which she hands to the tall agent. "Here is a copy of my father's army record and a certificate of his death."

"So, your father died defending the State from the czarists. Nonetheless, we must confirm your identity. Show me your internal passport and travel visa."

"Very well." Anna complies with a quick, hard smile. She draws her passport, visa, and medical documents from her knapsack and hands them to the Cheka agent.

He peruses the documents. Satisfied, he hands them back to her. "Your documents are in order." Ready to leave, the taller one points to her cane, and says, "I see that you use a cane and that you do not use your left arm. Tell us why."

"I am not ashamed of my deformities. I was born this way. My mother was malnourished during the hard winter of 1900. The Kolchak landowner would not increase her meager bread and potato ration. There was no milk, no meat. She died giving me life," Anna replies with solemn certitude. She says a silent prayer to Saint Olga that the Cheka do not ask for proof of her malformed body. The massive red scars would give her away.

"Thank you for your service to our socialist State, Nurse Bogrova. We questioned you because you fit the profile of a renegade enemy of the State. We are looking for a young woman about your age who may be wounded. She is wanted for counter-revolutionary activities that are inimical to the State. Go about your business."

28

Railroad Station, Bolotnoye, Siberia
15 April 1919

The scream of the steam whistle tells Bolotnoye that the local train is departing and headed for Duzhba, last scheduled stop in the Union of Soviet Socialist Republics and end of the line. It is shortly after ten in the morning. From this rail spur, the train is departing almost on time. It consists of an Iron Duke-class steam locomotive with a coal tender, three aging passenger cars, and a freight car.

Vaslav Nikolsky and his wife Katya bring Anna to the station in their wagon, pulled by a tired gray horse. Anna wears her nurse's uniform, and her knapsack is slung over her right shoulder. As the group approaches the train, Nikolsky pulls Anna aside and whispers, "Ask the stationmaster in Duzhba, Ivan Vachot, 'When is the next train to Bolotnoye?' He'll respond, 'Not today, perhaps in a few days.' Vachot is a short, husky man with black eyes. He's almost completely bald and has a bushy beard."

Anna responds, "Very well."

Nikolsky continues. "When this train leaves, I'll send a telegram telling Vachot what time it left the station, and that Nurse Anna Bogrova is among the passengers. He is to assist you in any manner to help you tend to that sick Party official. He'll understand the unsaid message."

Katya hands Anna a basket containing three bottles of water, black bread, strawberry jam, sausage, and fruit. Nikolsky explains, "There is no food service on these local trains. This will help tide you over."

Katya adds in a trembling voice as tears form on her cheeks, "God speed you in this godless nation."

Anna shakes Nikolsky's hand and kisses Katya on both cheeks. "Thank you for your hospitality and courage. I am forever in your debt, and I will pray to Saint Olga for your safety."

She glances around the station and sees that the two Cheka agents are watching her. She forces a smile and waves to them. Somewhat shocked that a former suspect would offer them such a courtesy, the taller agent acknowledges her with a slight nod.

Nikolsky helps Anna climb the two worn, steel steps to reach the interior of the coach. On entering, she turns, offers a big smile, and waves goodbye to her paladins.

The car is worn and battered. There are still traces of former grandeur, but the car should have been retired twenty years earlier. Most of the windows are smashed, cracked, or missing, and the car is filthy and littered with trash. Some of the seats are missing, too, and the upholstery of those that remain is dirty and often torn. Anna spots one that appears to be nearly whole. She wipes it as clean as she can, and sits cautiously.

The few other passengers scatter around the car, taking whichever seats offer the best chance of a somewhat comfortable ride. As Anna has already noticed in her brief time in Bolotnoye, people in the new Russia are less open to strangers than formerly, and they tend to avoid contact when possible.

Another shrill whistle and the engine's wheels spin, straining to gain traction. The train lurches forward in its first gasp of purchase. It screeches, clangs, and bangs in a cacophony of ear-splitting clamor. After several miles, the ride smoothes into a syncopated sway and the noise abates moderately.

Anna retrieves her book and tries to read. Black soot from the coal-burning engine swirls into the car and precipitates a coughing spasm. She uses her handkerchief to cover her nose and mouth, and protects her eyes with the dark glasses. Reading is impossible. She steels herself for the long journey to Duzhba. Looking at the passing scene, she notices the landscape change quickly from forest to savanna to desert. To pass the time, she recalls the events of the past two years: the heartbreaks, compassion, horrors, love, vengeance, professionalism, war, and her inherited responsibilities. And she wonders why God saved her from the regicide at Ekaterinburg, and what His design is for her.

Другое место

It is late afternoon of the following day. The train arrives in Duzhba only three hours late. It had stopped several times at settlements along the route to unload and load passengers, freight, and mail, and for the engineer and fireman to chat and sip vodka with the locals. Anna has passed an uncomfortable night curled up on her lumpy coach seat, shivering in the draft blowing through the broken windows. She almost sobs with relief as the train slows to its final stop. She is the only remaining passenger.

The Duzhba station is even more dilapidated and grimy than the one in Bolotnoye. Waiting at the station are a man who fits Nikolsky's description of Ivan Vachot, and a porter. No one else is there. From what Anna can see, Duzhba looks less like a town than a miserable outpost entirely forsaken by civilization. A harsh wind stirs up dust from the streets and, except for a scrawny dog lounging in the shade of a dilapidated building across the way, there is no sign of life. The porter climbs into the freight car and unloads a small crate and an equally small mail sack.

Anna's face and uniform are smudged with soot, and she tries to wipe it off with her hands. All she accomplishes is to spread the soot around, grind it into her uniform, and blacken her hands. Vachot enters the passenger car and greets her. "Good afternoon. I am the stationmaster. You must be Nurse Anna Bogrova. Correct?"

Anna, tired, sore, and dirty, responds, "Yes, I am Anna Bogrova—behind all this grime." As she trudges to the door, using her cane for support, she asks, "Would you be so kind as to help me off this train? I cannot manage by myself."

"Yes, of course." Without ado, he picks her up in his stout arms and carries her to the station platform. Setting her down, he says with a sly twinkle in his deep black eyes, "Always glad to assist female passengers on my line."

Somewhat taken aback by Vachot's impetuous and much too familiar approach, she squeaks, "Do you have a place where I can wash? I am filthy with soot."

Vachot cracks a faint smile at Anna's plight. "No. There's no place here to wash. Nikolsky's telegram tells me that you're here to treat a sick Party apparatchik. Correct?"

With a touch of anger in her voice, Anna says, "Yes, correct. As there is no place to wash, let us not waste time chatting. Please take me to him so that I can begin my nursing duties." She searches within her knapsack and withdraws a small writing tablet and a pencil. "Before we go, I need to plan my return. Please tell me when is the next train to Bolotnoye."

Vachot squints with his chin outthrust and stares at her with a mischievous glint in his eyes. Then he roars with laughter, slaps his thighs, and stomps his feet, raising a cloud of dust from the platform floor. Gasping for breath, he manages to utter, "And I'm supposed to say, 'Not today, perhaps in a few days.' Yes, that's it. Correct? My dear young lady, I've been running this underground passage to China for too many years to deal with secret messages identifying those who are loyal to Mother Russia. Everyone comes through here—czarists, Whites, Kolchaks, Czechs. And those who just want to escape Felix Dzerzhinsky's Red Terror—Ukrainians, Poles, Finns, Mensheviks, army deserters, highwaymen, smugglers, and everybody in between. Don't be concerned, I can smell a Bolshevik from a mile away—a putrid odor that lingers far too long."

"You amaze me, Mister Vachot, with your cavalier approach to security. Surely the Cheka will soon arrest you. They're not stupid, you know. And the ones that I have met smell only of unwashed bodies and dirty clothes."

"It's not their bodies I smell, it's their souls."

"That is profound, Mister Vachot. I pray that your nose keeps you out of Dzerzhinsky's gulags."

"Not 'Mister,' please. Use the title 'Comrade,' Nurse Bogrova. Such a title blends better with the correct political atmosphere."

"Very well. Let us disregard my charade as a nurse and get to the business at hand. I understand that you are to take me into China and to the town of Yumin. Is that correct?"

"That is correct. I've made the arrangements. If you are prepared, we can leave now. But first, may I suggest that there is the matter of a Maria Theresa gold schilling to compensate me for my services."

With a sense of frustration and mockery, Anna says, "Yes, Comrade Vachot, that is correct." She withdraws a schilling from her knapsack and places it in the palm of his outstretched right hand. He inspects it carefully, concludes that it is genuine, and puts it in a small leather purse attached to his belt.

Vachot manages a crooked smile and points to his wagon, hitched to two gray and white horses at the side of the station. "I'll bring the wagon here and lift you onto the seat."

"It is not necessary to move the wagon. With my cane, I can walk there. Being cramped in that railroad car for so many hours, I need the exercise. You may help by taking my knapsack."

"Easy enough, my dear lady," he says, returning her mocking tone.

When they arrive at the wagon, Vachot lifts Anna onto the wagon's hard wooden seat. He climbs on, and with a snap of the reins the horses begin to move. "This isn't much of a road. It's rutted and rough, so hold on tight to that hand grip." After a minute or so, he says, "It's about three miles to the Chinese border, and then another five miles to Yumin. We'll be there before sundown. There's nothing much at Yumin—some abandoned huts and the once-deserted lamasery where your compatriots live."

Anna holds tight as the wagon bounces along the dusty trail. The sun beats down in a dancing heat. She takes one of the water bottles Katya gave her and drinks. After a few minutes she asks Vachot, "How will we know when we cross the border? And what about Cheka guards?"

He responds, "Many years ago, there used to be a triple-strand wire fence along the border, but peasants from both sides have torn it down for the wire and posts. There are no guards. In the years I've been making this trip, I haven't seen one. The Russians never cared much about this godforsaken desert, and apparently neither do the Soviets."

"Pray tell," asks Anna, "why have the White Russians chosen this miserable desert to settle in? I'm at a loss to understand."

After a brief pause, Vachot responds. "Despite its inhospitable surroundings, Yumin sits in a sheltered valley blessed with a crystal-clear mountain stream, green grass, wildlife, and fertile soil. And the abandoned buildings are still habitable. Also, it's very remote, with no Chinese authorities close by. It makes an ideal place for you Russian expatriates to assemble and settle."

After fifty minutes or so, Vachot pulls up the wagon, scans the desert ahead and the blue sky above them, and says, "We're in China now. Do you smell the sweet air of liberation?"

"No, Comrade Vachot. My nose is not as sensitive as yours. All I can smell are the desert dust, the horses' rear ends, and you."

Vachot manages an arch smile, cracks the reins, and the wagon continues its plodding pace. A couple of hours later, the wagon tops a small hill. To the northeast is the snowcapped Altai mountain range. Below is a small, verdant valley. In the distance is the lamasery—a large, one-story central building with a group of smaller stone buildings behind it. People are working in a large field planted with vegetables. Beyond them lie fields of ripening wheat.

Anna whispers a silent prayer, "Thank you, Saint Olga, for my deliverance to freedom."

The wagon stops in front of the central building. Several denizens approach. One man, who seems to have authority, says, "Welcome to our White Russian community in China. I am Grigori Pavlovich Cherkassky, elector of this community. Please tell us who you are and why you are here."

Anna manages a wistful smile through her tired, dirty face. "Someone help me down, please." Grigori takes her hand and then her waist and lifts her to the ground. Vachot, seeing that his passenger is in safe hands, hands her the knapsack, turns his wagon around, and moves to return home. Anna leans on her cane. She removes her dark glasses, and says in a firm voice, "I am Nurse Anna Bogrova, formerly of Novosibirsk. I am here to escape the Red Terror. My father was a czarist, murdered last year by the Bolsheviks. I am seeking sanctuary."

"We welcome you, Anna Bogrova. We need a person with your medical training. But before we admit you to our community, we must ensure that you are who you say you are—that you're not a Cheka secret agent." More people have gathered around. "May we see your papers?"

"Of course." She retrieves her forged identification documents and hands them to Grigori.

He accepts them. "Thank you, Nurse Bogrova." He begins to study the papers.

One man in the crowd moves closer to Anna. There is a puzzled look on his face, as if he's trying to place the new arrival. The better to focus, he squints his eyes, and extends his right hand over his eyebrows to shield his eyes from the late sun. He muses, *This woman looks vaguely familiar. But I can't place her. I don't recall any slender, crippled woman with bobbed black hair. But I know those impudent blue eyes. I don't know any nurses, and certainly I don't know any czarist families from Novosibirsk. Perhaps we danced at some cotillion?*

The word "danced" triggers a flash of comprehension. He knows. "My God! It's Anastasia!" he shouts with exultant joy. "She is Anastasia! This woman is Grand Duchess Anastasia Romanov!" He rushes through the crowd, takes Anna in his arms, and kisses her cheeks, mouth, and eyes, and kisses them again. He pulls away from the startled newcomer and holds both her hands in his. "Anastasia," he says softly, his voice cracking with emotion. "Anastasia, you're alive!"

Grigori stops reading and looks quizzically at the pair. The crowd is silent with bewilderment.

Anastasia's blue eyes widen and tears flood her cheeks. She tries to regain her composure, but cannot. Neither says anything as they focus on each other. Then, she says through her tears, in her most imperious voice, "Senior Lieutenant Kirik Antonievich Pirogov, please control yourself. You embarrass me in front of these Russians." She reaches for Kirik with her right arm and pulls him close to her. She puts her head on his shoulder and weeps openly. Through her tears she murmurs, "God love you, Kirik. You are my family now."

Grigori studies Anna for a long minute. The crowd, now much larger, begins to murmur, "Anastasia? Can it really be the Grand Duchess Anastasia?"

Grigori looks at Pirogov and demands, "You are positive that this woman is Grand Duchess Anastasia Romanov?"

Pirogov, smiling from ear to ear, "Of course I'm sure. I've known her for most of her life. She called me by my name and military rank. I don't know how she survived the regicide. The horror of it has changed her countenance, but those blue eyes haven't changed. She is Anastasia Romanov."

Grigori turns to Anna, "Is this true? You are Grand Duchess Anastasia Romanov?"

Before she can answer, an older woman rushes to Anna and pulls her into a motherly hug. It is Maria Pavlovna, Kirik's mother. "My dear child, it's a miracle! You're alive and have come to us. Anastasia, we heard that the Bolsheviks murdered you, along with your family, at Ekaterinburg. Thank God, thank God." She drops into a deep curtsy.

Tears still tumbling, Anastasia hugs Maria. She cries, "How I have missed you, Maria Pavlovna. I'm so happy that you escaped the Soviet Union."

By now Grigori and the crowd are convinced that the new arrival is indeed Grand Duchess Anastasia. Most of the women curtsy and the men bow deeply. Anastasia, now somewhat composed, says in as loud a voice as she can muster, "Everyone, please listen to me. What I am about to say is critical to our safety. Grand Duchess Anastasia Romanov is dead. She died in Ekaterinburg with her family in the Ipatiev House on 17 July 1918. I am Anna Bogrova, a nurse from Novosibirsk. From this moment on, I beg you to speak of me and treat me as such."

29

Yumin, Sinkiang Province, China
30 September 1919

A small mountain stream meanders down the Yumin Valley. Remnants of last winter's snow cling to the towering Altai range that straddles the border between China and the USSR and forms the valley's northern boundary. The sun is low in the sky and casts long shadows in this early autumn afternoon. Gray skies are approaching, and the bitter northern Chinese winter will soon follow. The grass is brown in the pastures, the sheep and goats have been brought down from their summer grazing in the mountains, and formations of ducks and geese fly south.

This quiet, bucolic scene is deceiving. The community is abuzz with harvest activities: reaping wheat, bundling hay, canning fruit from the extensive orchards and vegetables from the sprawling gardens, and drying mushrooms picked in the forests above the village. A cool, stone springhouse is full of butter and cheeses, and the smokehouse is well stocked with hanging pork, beef, chicken, and lamb.

At first glance, Yumin appears much like a typical agricultural village in Russia. Peasants work the fields, herd livestock, prepare irrigation conduits, and do all the chores required of a large farming community. But, the reality of Yumin is far more complex. The "peasants" of Yumin include a mixture of about one hundred twenty-two people: titled aristocrats, kulaks, former soldiers, skilled craftsmen, professionals such as engineers, an artist or two, several university professors, a medical doctor, and an Orthodox priest—all working in harmony to build and maintain their new home.

Yumin, isolated from the chaos in the USSR and the turmoil in China, is thriving due in large measure to Grigori Cherkassky's firm but enlightened leadership. The government of the community consists of Grigori, the village's founder and now its elector, and eleven villagers elected at large who serve as an administrative council.

One of Cherkassky's first tasks when he established Yumin as a refuge for White Russians was to befriend the community's nearest neighbors, the Kirgiz community located about five miles south of Yumin along the same mountain stream that waters Yumin's fields. The Kirgiz seemed pleased to have Europeans and their Western skills nearby. A handshake agreement was made quickly. In exchange for fresh victuals, especially fruit and vegetables, and an assurance that the Russians would maintain the flow of the stream, the Kirgiz act as the community's secret conduit to the outside world.

Yumin's land, buildings, and whatever is of value are held in common. The rationale is that large-scale communal efforts are more efficient and productive than individual enterprise. Perhaps without intending to, they have formed a Soviet-style commune, but with one important difference—in the Soviet Union's collectivism, the state owns the commune and confiscates 80 to 90 percent of its production; in Yumin, the denizens own the commune and benefit wholly from their labors.

The old lamasery is a large, well-built stone building with a high dome over its central area. A cluster of smaller stone structures stand beside and behind it. The Russians have converted the open area under the dome into the community's general meeting room. A small room nearby serves as an office for the elector and his administrative aide.

The lamasery's former prayer room has been converted into a chapel. Craftsmen have built a modest altar and an iconostasis. Precious icons that some of the villagers brought with them from their former homes glow on the iconostasis and the faded plaster walls. On Sundays, a single flickering candle casts a soft glow in the chapel. The community rings with the sweet sound of ancient hymns and the drone of the priest's chants.

Down the hall a few paces is the infirmary. It has only three beds, the most basic equipment, and a modest formulary. The physician has a small adjoining room for his office and living quarters.

The monastery's former library is now a schoolroom. The professors do their best to give the children a modest education—Russian grammar, world history, geography, mathematics, and basic science. Some of the Kirgiz children have joined the classes, and the young Russians are quickly mastering the language of their Kirgiz playmates.

The former refectory serves as the communal dining room, and meals are prepared in the kitchen next door. The chief cook was formerly *chef de cuisine* in the palace of a wealthy prince in Moscow. Under his direction, the cooks prepare appetizing meals from the bounty of their fields, gardens, orchards, and pastures.

Out of respect for the Buddhist monks who built, worshiped, and lived in this lamasery, Grigori Pavlovich has decreed that the monks' small inner sanctuary and all its accouterments would remain unchanged. In the center of the sanctuary, a three-foot-high carved bust of the Buddha rests on a massive teakwood stand intricately carved with the tale of the Buddha's travels from India to China.

The remaining rooms in the lamasery are used as living spaces. The rooms are small and clean, sparsely furnished with items constructed by village carpenters. To accommodate all the residents, craftsmen have been converting the outlying buildings into living quarters similar to those in the lamasery where some of the family groups live.

The administrative council gave Pirogov a room in the bachelors' quarters in one of the outlying buildings. His assignment is to work on the irrigation detail that builds and maintains the freshwater transport for the community and the Kirgiz community downstream. Its current project is building a large reservoir in the foothills behind the village to capture and store winter run-off water from the mountains. A manually operated dam made of stout birch logs ensures a steady supply of water year-round. After the reservoir is completed, the villagers plan to stock it with brown trout and pikeperch to provide an additional source of food.

Unused to hard labor for over a year, Pirogov was, at first, only marginally effective in shoveling dirt and hauling rocks. At each day's end his hands were blistered and all his muscles screamed in pain. But, after a few weeks, he regained the robust physical condition he had developed in Beryosha, and now he shovels dirt with the best of his coworkers.

Anna's arrival created a murmuring stir. Because of her continued and forceful insistence that she was no longer the Grand Duchess Anastasia Romanov but Anna Bogrova from Novosibirsk and now one of the ordinary citizens of Yumin, the hubbub quickly died. She has melted quietly and quickly into the routine of the community. Because of her impairment, Elector Grigori Cherkassky assigned Anna to a private room next to the infirmary.

When he learned of her experience assisting Nurse Botkina on the Czech train, the Elector charged Anna with assisting Doctor Vladimir Markov, once a colonel in the Russian army's medical corps. The doctor is of medium height and build, about fifty-five years old, with small, pale eyes, and bushy eyebrows. He is almost bald, with patches of thin gray hair at his temples. Today, he wears a white smock over dark-blue striped coveralls.

Doctor Markov is pleased with Anna's modest nursing skills and her desire to learn. He considers her his apprentice and teaches her advanced hands-on patient care. She is a quick learner, and Markov assigns her more and more responsibility with the patients.

When there are no patients in the infirmary and all other chores are completed, Elector Cherkassky tasks Anna with reporting to Maxim Fedosov, the administrative assistant to the elector and the bookkeeper for the commune. Her job is to take care of the petty details that are burdening Fedosov, and her long-term goal is to learn his trade. She wonders how effectively she will function as an administrative clerk.

Fedosov proves to be an excellent mentor and works diligently with Anna to ensure her progress. His striking appearance belies his sedentary profession. He is thirty years old, slightly over six feet tall, weighs two hundred pounds, and has a muscular physique; his erect shoulders carry his large head high. He has a dark complexion; his jet-black eyes shine with a hint of menace, and his short, black hair is peppered with a few hints of gray. His jaw is square, lips are thin, and his eyebrows arch brazenly. He walks with a long and forceful stride, seemingly always on an urgent mission.

Before the Revolution, Fedosov was an accountant at the House of Fabergé in Saint Petersburg. In January 1918, he and his family attempted a daring escape from the horrors of the Bolshevik Revolution in a horse-drawn sled. A Cheka patrol spotted them a few miles out of town. Fedosov did not stop at their command to "Halt!" In the ensuing gunfire, his wife and two children were killed and he was wounded. But, he pressed on, and eventually evaded the Cheka. Two days later, a White patrol found him slumped in the sled and near death. The patrol leader, Corporal Boreslav Tsigler, a former telephone operator at the Fabergé workshops, recognized him and knew him to be staunchly anti-Red. In the following weeks, with expert medical care, Fedosov recovered, joined Admiral Denkin's White Army, and fought with them in their retreat through Siberia. At some point, he deserted and made his way to Yumin. One summer day in 1918, he walked into the White Russian compound—a little thin, a little ragged, and limping slightly from his wound. After a comprehensive briefing, the elector admitted Fedosov as a member of the community, and because of the new arrival's profession, assigned him to handle the administrative details of the commune and to be its bookkeeper. Occasionally, he lapses into melancholy at the loss of his family, and Anna does her best to be sympathetic and supportive.

Working with Maxim Fedosov, Anna becomes immersed in the administrative details that keep the commune running smoothly. Over time, she learns how to post debits and credits, prepare profit and loss, balance the checking account, and manage the budget and cost accounting. Anna is pleased that she is contributing to the welfare of the community and, for the first time in her life, earning her own way. She quietly wins the respect and affection of the villagers by her assiduous care for their ill and her willingness to engage fully in the labor of her assignments.

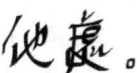

Anna's grief fades only marginally. Sometimes, when she is alone in her room, she breaks into wrenching sobs. The pain of the loss of her family and her crippling wounds, she knows, will never leave her. But, on the surface, as she goes about her daily tasks and interacts with her fellow villagers, Anna is serene. At times, and more and more frequently, she realizes that she is actually happy in her new life and looks forward to the future.

Maria Pavlovna and Anna quickly form a loving bond. Maria's affection for Alexandra is transferred to her friend's sole surviving child, and Anna finds a surrogate mother to comfort and guide her in her new life.

Maria's adaptation to the rigors of her work as a cook is an example and inspiration to Anna, and the older woman's tender affection helps ease the pain of her grief. As winter grips the village, the daylight grows short and howling snowstorms sweep down from the mountains. Anna spends most of her evenings in Maria's room. While the two women tend to the endless work of mending worn work clothes and darning socks, they talk about the happenings in the community, their work, and often their memories of people and events in the past.

During these long winter evenings, Pirogov frequently visits his mother and Anna. Sometimes he joins the conversation, other times he reads aloud to them, delighted to be with the two people he loves. What they all enjoy most are challenging card games and friendly banter. As time passes, Pirogov notices that he and Anna speak less of the past and more about their life in Yumin. He understands with peaceful satisfaction that each of them realizes that Yumin is now their life and their home. He is proud of Anna for her willingness to adapt to the realities of her new life and for her contributions to the community.

The attraction between the two young people, first realized at the Christmas Ball in 1917, has survived the traumas of the Revolution and their travails. The two resume the easy teasing that passed between them so long ago at Tsarskoe Selo. In the cold winter months in this isolated valley in China, something much deeper grows slowly and incessantly.

Pirogov had realized years earlier that he loved Grand Duchess Anastasia Romanov. Were their ranks not so vastly different, he would have sought to marry her. But now he is at a loss as to how to court a deposed princess in hiding. So he remains silent, being with her when he can.

As winter melts into spring, life returns to Yumin. The orchards come into bloom, the trees are covered with pink and white blossoms. The air is thick with the buzz of bees, and a lark sings somewhere in a fallow field.

The villagers begin tilling and planting the fields and tending to new-born livestock. Conversation at meals focuses on the farm tasks accomplished and those to be done: resumption of work on the reservoir, building additional irrigation ditches, where to clear land for new fields, and when to send the sheep and goats into the mountains for summer forage. The elector and advisory council debate how much food to preserve for the coming winter, how much to send to the Kirgiz, and how much to sell for cash in the market at Urumchi, about one hundred forty miles to the southeast, or to barter in the general store in Wu-su.

One Sunday afternoon toward the end of May, Pirogov plans to inspect an irrigation ditch that is under construction. It runs near the central compound, then into fields that lie fallow about three thousand feet away. Impulsively, he invites Anna to join him. He is delighted when she gleefully accepts.

Anna, with her stout cane, walks slowly but confidently. Nonetheless, Kirik takes her arm, and she leans on him for extra support as they stroll toward the nearby ditch. His mind is less focused on the scenery than on the small, slender woman next to him, with her faint scent of soap and sun-dried linen. The pleasure he felt holding her in his arms as they danced at that long-ago Christmas Ball floods back, more poignant than ever. He gives a deep sigh of satisfaction.

Pirogov explains that the council wants to clear a new field for barley and create a small pond where they can raise ducks and geese. The fowl will help control insects in the orchards and barley fields, and they will supply the village with eggs and meat.

Anna smiles. "I'm fascinated by how everything we do is interlocked and works in harmony."

"We're building a thriving community."

Anna's smile broadens. "Yes. We're all invested in what we've made."

They begin the short return to the compound. The warm sun induces calm in the duo; each is deep in thought.

"Kirik," Anna begins at last, "when I arrived here last spring, I thought I'd never feel safe or happy again. I was in such pain, in my body and in my mind. I frequently had nightmares about the execution of my family and about the Bolsheviks finding me." She falls into silence and leans against his arm.

"You and your mother have been so good to me. You've helped me fit in and learn the ways of Yumin, but even more you've given me a new family. I'm not eloquent enough to tell you fully how grateful I am, or how much I love you both."

Pirogov doesn't know how to respond. Instead, his arm tightens around her, and he basks in the warmth of her small body against his and in the comfort of her words.

As the summer wanes, Anna and Pirogov spend more and more time together. In the evenings, they often join Maria on the terrace behind the lamasery to enjoy the sun setting behind the mountains. There is an easy warmth in their companionship, and an underlying emotion that is unfulfilled.

Late one Sunday afternoon, Kirik and Anna walk along the stream toward the foothills of the mountains. Anna does amazingly well with her cane. Near the end of the trail is a bench where people can rest and enjoy the panoramic tableau of the valley. They sit silently, enjoying the view and being with each other. A gentle breeze carries a slight chill from the snow-capped mountains.

Pirogov takes Anna's hand. "Are you getting cold?"

"I'm fine, thank you, Kirik."

After a few minutes, he clears his throat nervously. "Anna ...," he begins. Then he takes a deep breath and begins again. "Anna, I'm not a poet, so please forgive me for speaking plainly." Awkwardly, he clears his throat again and says in a rush, "I love you. Please be my wife."

Anna, taken aback by Kirik's unexpected proposal, recovers quickly. She smiles easily, but behind her eyes there is a hint of pain.

Before she can respond, Kirik continues, "We are no longer in Saint Petersburg, confined by the strictures of court protocol. Now we're just farmers, exiles in constant fear of the Bolsheviks. We must make the best of it. The old court rules no longer apply to us. I love you with all my heart. Let me be with you for the rest of my life, to care for you and protect you."

Anna's hand tightens reflexively in his. She is silent for a long time, so long that Pirogov begins to wonder if he has offended her.

"Kirik, I have loved you for as long as I can remember, ever since you were my playmate and big brother at Tsarskoe Selo. I shall always love you." She rises, takes a few steps toward the stream, and turns toward him with tears sliding down her cheeks. "Kirik, I cannot marry you." She looks at the gently flowing stream. With resolve, she continues, "I cannot marry anyone, ever."

Kirik rises and approaches Anna. "My dear Anna, I'm confused. You love me, so why do you refuse me?"

She extends her hand to him. "I have fulfilled half of my mother's charge by emigrating to Yumin and finding you with the imperial treasures. But I cannot comply with her entreaty that I continue the Romanov line. It would not be moral or responsible of me."

With cold precision she continues. "I have resigned myself to denying marriage forever. Sooner or later, the Bolsheviks will find me and kill me, either here in Yumin or somewhere else on this planet. They cannot afford to leave me alive, or to risk that I might carry on the Romanov direct line of succession. I can accept that, but I cannot put anyone else in danger. The Reds took us into that cellar in Ekaterinburg and murdered my family, and nearly me, without reason or mercy. Everyone I loved was taken from me in an instant. I could not live with myself if my presence damned you to the same fate."

"And have you thought of the children we might have if we married? Would you want your children to be hunted down and exterminated like vermin, as my family was? Because that is what the Bolsheviks will do. Could you live with that? And what if our sons had hemophilia? I learned more about this disease when I was with the Czech doctor on the train. It's hereditary, passed from mother to son. Daughters inherit only the capacity to disseminate it to their sons. Little Alexis suffered horribly all his life. He endured the most agonizing pain, and every moment he was in danger of dying from a tiny bump or cut that a healthy person wouldn't even notice. Would you want that for your sons and grandsons?"

Kirik tries to think of some compelling reason to refute her logic. "Your reasoning is sound. But your heart betrays you."

"Kirik, I've thought about marrying you since I was a child. God, I want to marry you and have your children. But I will not. The consequences are too dire. My dear Kirik, please know that you have my heart forever."

Pirogov knows Anna is right. Marriage would place on her a grievous burden of fear and guilt. He comes to terms with the fact that his love for her must be deep enough and his character strong enough to leave her free.

The twilight begins to fade. His heart broken, Pirogov responds, "I understand what you say, my darling Anna, but my heart doesn't accept your rationale. I won't cause you more anguish by trying to persuade you to change your mind. I realize that you've thought about your decision for a long time, but it will take more time for my heart to accept it. We shall say no more about this." He lifts her hand and kisses it tenderly.

Anna takes Kirik's other hand and looks lovingly into his brown eyes. "I love you, Kirik. Know to the depths of your soul that I love you and shall for the rest of my life."

϶Ø

Saint Elizabeth's Academy for Young Ladies, Peking
10 March 1917

Yen Hei-lan slaps the little girl hard in the face, knocking her to the ground. A large red welt begins to form on the girl's cheek. Yen, with her legs spread apart and arms akimbo, stands over the crying girl, demanding that she take back the ethnic slur she spat out in a playground quarrel. Yen proclaims in an imperious voice, "Madeleine, get this through your malignant French soul, I am Chinese! Not a 'Chink.' I am not a 'slope-eyed Chink.' Especially, I am not a French colonial vassal. It is you, the pale-skinned round-eye, who are the alien."

Yen glares at the sobbing child. Occidental imperialism fuels her rage to the point where she has no voice. Screaming in her brain are the Western rapes of her China: Unequal treaties forced on China at gunpoint. Trade concessions stifling the coastal cities. Western gunboats patrolling the Yellow and Yangtze rivers. Christian missionaries prostituting her ancient Confucian religion. Opium despoiling an ancient traditional society. Gasping for breath, Yen continues in a near shout, "We were a great civilization while your ancestors lived in trees. Get out of my country. My China! Get out now!"

Yen Hei-lan is thirteen years old and enrolled in the exclusive Saint Elizabeth's Academy for Young Ladies. She is a beautiful woman-child with large black eyes that seem too wise for her age. Already her tall feminine body is nearly fully developed. Learned and capable far beyond her years, she is fluent in Mandarin, English, Russian, French, and Japanese.

Her classmates are children who come predominantly from the Western embassies and legations. They regard Yen Hei-lan as a loner, selfish, aggressive, and unscrupulous. Nonetheless, she is the champion athlete of the Academy—an outstanding field hockey player and captain of the tennis team. Her only friend is an attractive, sixteen-year-old Persian. The rumor among her classmates is that the Persian and Yen have a relationship that is something more intimate than that of just friends.

Several years ago in Shensi Province, Yen's parents were killed in the crossfire of a battle between the troops of warlord Marshal Chang Hsueh-liang and Colonel Chiang Kai-shek's Nationalist soldiers. Colonel Chiang had just launched his Northwest Campaign to rout out warlordism in China. Now, Yen is the ward of her uncle, Wuhan Wei-kuo, the premier antiques dealer in Peking.

Sister Mary Beatrice O'Hara, of the Order of the Sisters of Charity of Saint Elizabeth, rushes to the aid of the fallen child. O'Hara is short and dumpy, but she moves with speed and grace. Her rosy cheeks, deep blue eyes, and heavy brogue signal her Irish heritage. Her white habit flaps in the wind and her long skirt swishes loudly. She helps the fallen child to her feet, wipes her tears, and consoles her with sympathetic assurances and an old-fashioned hug. She tells Madeleine, "Go to the bathroom and clean yourself. Then go to the kitchen and make an ice pack for your cheek. I will visit with you shortly."

She turns to Yen. "Mistress Yen, your conduct is unacceptable. I'm appalled at your behavior. Young ladies of Saint Elizabeth's do not strike anyone, no matter the provocation. We do not harangue our fellow students. We do not engage in politics. Here, we are all equally committed to academic scholarship, the social graces, and chivalrous sportsmanship. Have not these three tenets been the hallmark of your education at Saint Elizabeth's?"

Yen recovers quickly from her outrage. She knows that she must appear contrite because to be expelled would bring shame on her uncle and herself, and would ruin this singular and expensive opportunity for an education *nonpareil*. She feigns humility and remorse to answer Sister O'Hara's reproof.

"You are correct, Sister. I am shamed by my ill-advised conduct. May I suggest, however, Sister Mary Beatrice, that I was deeply wounded by the racist slur 'slope-eyed Chink,' spoken by a person who, just a few decades ago, my ancestors would have considered a barbarian."

"Mistress Yen, be quiet. You have done enough and said enough. I empathize with your hurt. Madeleine's insult is appalling and not in keeping with our protocols. I shall speak to her—quite sternly. Yet no matter the provocation, our young ladies always maintain their self-control. We assiduously practice the etiquette of polite, genteel society, no matter the circumstances. At all times we gracefully maintain the conventions expected of us as students and graduates of Saint Elizabeth's. Every semester, is that not what we have taught and demanded of you, and all our young ladies?"

Seething inside yet under complete external control, Yen responds, "Yes, Sister. You are correct. I have failed in my obligations to you and this esteemed school. May I beg your forgiveness?"

In a more conciliatory tone, Sister Mary Beatrice says, "My dear Mistress Yen, I do not have the power to forgive. Only a priest in the confessional, through Christ, can forgive. But I must say that I am bitterly disappointed at your behavior today. You are the brightest student in our school. You are a champion athlete, a natural leader, and mature far beyond your years. Please understand, Yen, that your moral and corporal destiny will be decided by your forbearance of others, those who offend you, and those who are not as accomplished as you in intelligence, industry, comeliness, and position. Compassion must be your counsel. Lock these prescriptions in your heart and follow them always. Is that unequivocally clear?"

"Yes, Sister. I understand and, in future, I will uphold the highest time-honored conventions of Saint Elizabeth's."

"Very well, Yen. I accept your assurances. But there must be atonement to ease my disappointment, to make amends to Madeleine, and to reaffirm your commitment to our ideals. In keeping with this school's commitment to scholarship and propriety, as your punishment for today's misconduct, you must write a letter of apology to the wounded child, and write it in French. I will review it, and if it is satisfactory, I will return it to you so you can deliver it personally to Madeleine and make appropriate verbal apologies. Additionally, next Monday you will hand me a five-thousand-word essay, written in Russian, that discusses the border dispute in Inner Mongolia between the Union of Soviet Socialist Republics and the Republic of China. Include such themes as the Trans-Siberian Railway, Japanese influence in Manchuria, and warlordism in the northwestern provinces."

"Yes, Sister. Such an assignment is appropriate for my wanton misconduct. You will have both documents Monday morning, as you require." Her thoughts, however, rage with controlled anger. Hei-lan does not capitulate to officious Occidentals. *These barbarians underestimate me,* she muses.

His Royal Britannic Majesty's Embassy, Peking
15 July, 1917

The military *attaché*, Brigadier Sir Malcolm Stanford-Brownsworth, VC, GBE, hero of the Battle of the Somme, peruses *The Times,* Hong Kong edition. In the obituary column, he reads that "Mother Superior Sister Mary Beatrice O'Hara, Order of the Sisters of Charity of Saint Elizabeth, and Rector of Saint Elizabeth's Academy in Peking, has died of a mysterious illness. The physicians at Saint Alphonse's Catholic Infirmary could not diagnose the infection or explain the rapid progression of the disease. Sister O'Hara expired within two days after complaining of severe headaches. An autopsy is pending."

Indeed unfortunate, he muses. His youngest daughter, Marbella, attends Saint Elizabeth's Academy and speaks highly of Sister O'Hara. On page seven there is a small item that notes, "Madeleine de Boise, the eleven-year-old daughter of the French *chargé d'affaires,* is missing. Chief Inspector Malcolm Bernard-Smythe, lead homicide detective of the International Police Force, says that there are no clues regarding her disappearance. However, he suspects foul play. Enquiries are continuing."

31

Yumin, Sinkiang Province, China
6 July 1933

It is early summer in this remote mountain valley. There is a gentle breeze from the north, and lazy cumulus clouds drift slowly southward bringing the smell of rain.

The White Russians who live in this valley have lost hope for Mother Russia. Fifteen years ago, the Bolsheviks had brutally murdered the royal family: Czar Nicholas II, Emperor of All the Russias, the Empress Alexandra, and four of their children. Their country is now the Union of Soviet Socialist Republics, and Josef Stalin, Premier and First Secretary of the Communist Party, rules with an iron fist of imperious tyranny through his gangster cadres, the Communist International (Comintern), and the secret police, known as the People's Commissariat for Internal Affairs or NKVD.

The White armies of General Denikin and Admiral Kolchak are defeated. The Western allies have withdrawn their expeditionary forces from Murmansk, Vladivostok, and the Caucasus. However, Japan still poses a direct threat to the Soviet Union. It maintains control of Sakhalin Island and Nomanhan in western Mongolia and has begun the occupation of Manchuria, a Chinese province with a long, contiguous border with the Soviet Union.

Imperial Russia is but a memory. The White Russians in Yumin want only to be left alone. They are apprehensive because the Bolsheviks control the nearby-unguarded border, making them ominously vulnerable. The Chinese National Government has no presence here. Several years ago, there was a solitary military policeman stationed in Wu-su, the nearest town, several miles away. He was killed trying to repel a bandit raid. There has been no replacement.

Today, several dozen people hoe, plant, and water the vegetable gardens. The wide fields are bright with the tender green of young plants. A thirty-two-year-old woman with a pronounced limp works in the onion patch. She wears simple, white, cotton trousers, a long-sleeved blouse, and a wide-brimmed straw hat.

From the entrance of the lamasery's main building, Nikolai Danilov calls, "Anna!" He waves a beckoning arm. "Please come here. We need you in the infirmary." His white laboratory coat flaps in the slight breeze.

Anna Bogrova turns and responds, "I'll be right there." Her countenance is that of a much older woman. Her face is lined with the horror of the Revolution, the loss of her beloved family, and the rigors of the community's agrarian life. Dark shadows underlie blue eyes that no longer sparkle. Her hair is cut short in a no-nonsense bob. She retrieves her stout wood cane and walks slowly to the entrance of the lamasery. She winces in pain as her right foot stumbles on a rock.

She and Danilov enter the infirmary. Danilov is a tall, thin man with a weak chin, bright brown eyes, a full head of salt-and-pepper hair, and an amiable manner. He is the first son of a prominent family in Kazan and a former corpsman in the Imperial Russian army. Now he puts his considerable medical skills to use as an assistant in the infirmary.

The pair enters the infirmary and greets Doctor Vladimir Markov.

Immediately, Anna sees Grigori Pavlovich Cherkassky, the community's elector, lying in one of the beds with his eyes closed and his cheeks pale. A sheet is pulled up to his chin. Maria Pavlovna is sitting beside the bed, sobbing, and holding her brother's hand. Doctor Markov stands next to Maria. He acknowledges Anna's arrival with a slight nod.

With grave apprehension, Anna asks Markov, "What has happened to Grigori?"

Markov, in a soft, consoling voice, responds, "Grigori died sometime after breakfast. For the past several years I've been treating him for atrial fibrillation. I cautioned him to relax and delegate some of his responsibilities, but he ignored my advice and seemed to work all the harder in a race to beat the Grim Reaper. Danilov found him slumped over his desk, after he didn't respond to a knock on the door."

Anna gasps and puts her hand to her mouth. She turns to Maria and embraces her. "My dear friend, my darling mother, I'm heartbroken with you. I share your grief. Grigori was a great man. With his inspiration and leadership, we built this community. His tireless perseverance kept it functioning, and kept us safe. He was respected by all of us. We will miss him sorely."

Danilov pulls up the sheet to cover fully Grigori. "I'll make the arrangements for the funeral service and burial."

Several days later, the administrative council meets *in camera* to nominate candidates for the community's elector. Maxim Fedosov is the chairman of the council because of his administrative position. He calls the meeting to order, stands, and says, "It is clear to me, and I suspect to most of you, that Anna Bogrova is the logical choice. She has excelled in all her tasks. She tackles them with industry, intelligence, and integrity. Her comity and community service have endeared her to all of us." He returns to his chair. Pavel Shubin, the priest, seconds the motion. With only minimal debate and by unanimous vote, the council nominates Anna Bogrova to be their next elector.

That evening in the community meeting room, Fedosov calls the meeting to order. "Good evening, White Russians, citizens of Yumin. Our business this evening is to select an elector to guide us in the coming years— years that may well be challenging and perhaps dangerous. Our neighbor to the north is consolidating its power and becoming internationally aggressive. We need a strong, wise, and just leader. This morning the council nominated Anna Bogrova to be our next elector."

Instantly, a roar of applause fills the room. The citizens stand and chant, "Anna! Anna! Anna!"

Fedosov bangs his gavel. As the hubbub dies down, he speaks, "We have decided. Let us welcome Anna Bogrova as our new elector."

Caught completely by surprise, Anna slips low in her chair and murmurs to Kirik, sitting next to her, "No, no, it cannot be. I can't do it. I'm too young. I have no experience. Choose Doctor Markov. He's much more qualified than I."

Fedosov walks to where Anna is sitting. "Come with me, Elector Anna, and address the citizens of Yumin."

"I can't do it. I'm not qualified. I'm a cripple. Choose Doctor Markov."

Markov, sitting a few chairs away, rises. "Citizens, let us welcome our new elector, Anna Bogrova."

All stand and applaud. Anna slumps deeper in her chair. Kirik, realizing that the decision has been made, looks at her and takes her arm. "The die is cast. Stand next to me, dear Anna. I'll escort you to the front of the room to greet the council and take the oath."

地震。

It has now been several weeks since Anna became the elector of the Yumin community. Although she accepted the position reluctantly, with her usual rugged determination she has accomplished her tasks exceptionally well. She has earned the respect of all.

Today she sits at the elector's desk with stacks of paper scattered around her. Hanging on the far wall is a portrait of Czar Nicholas and Empress Alexandra. Behind her hangs the flag of Imperial Russia. She leans back in her chair and stares at the ceiling. A lone fly buzzes about, distracting her from intense thought. A deep frown crosses her face, not about the fly but about the severe problems facing the community. She has no ready or easy solutions.

Soon after being elected, Anna had realized that the community's plight was dire and getting worse by the day. The primary problem is that the community's population is growing rapidly. Soon, the valley's limited resources will not support the community's needs or the water ration for their Kirgiz neighbors. The reservoir has been instrumental in ensuring ample water for all, but now, a decade after its construction, the water resources will soon be dangerously inadequate. The founders, mostly concerned with safety, did not plan for such growth. The viability of the community is fading fast.

Will our community implode in chaos? Anna wonders. *Or, can I ease the transition in some orderly manner? How do I prepare for the end?* She has fretted over these questions for weeks, but she is no closer to answers than when she was first elected.

Her other major concern is that their presence cannot be kept secret much longer. Although there has been no indication that the Soviet secret police are aware of their existence, she reasons that sooner or later the Soviets will find them and attack. *The Bolsheviks' ardent passion must be to assassinate me*, she sighs to herself. *We are defenseless.*

The only options she can fathom are to move the community into the interior of China or disband it and let the inhabitants move elsewhere and fend for themselves. Neither option seems palatable.

She walks into the community room and spots a caretaker sweeping the floor. "A favor, please, Vasily. Find Kirik Pirogov and ask him to meet me in my office. He's probably working at the reservoir. After Pirogov enters my office, ask Fedosov to come here."

"Yes, Elector Bogrova."

An hour later, Pirogov knocks on Anna's office door. He hears a faint "Come in," and enters. His coveralls are smeared with mud, as are his face, arms, and hands. "Please excuse my appearance, Anna. We're putting the last touches on that new ditch. We made a trial run with the newly configured dam to see how the water flows and to find leaks. It is working very well indeed. Because you summoned me from my work, I assume your need is important. I will wash later."

"Thank you for coming, Kirik, my dear friend. Please sit down and make yourself comfortable." As Kirik settles into a chair, Fedosov knocks and enters. He greets Anna and Pirogov, and then sits. He sees the concern in Anna's face. "What's troubling you, Elector?"

Anna leans forward and speaks in a grave voice, "Kirik, Maxim, I need to ask your advice about our community. This past year your support and counsel have been the pillars of my administration. Now we must face our community's upcoming crises and devise a solution."

"Frankly, Anna, I've been anticipating this meeting for several months," Fedosov comments. "We're overextended, and we can't meet the needs of our people. Our citizens complain about scarcities. For many of them, the isolation and secrecy are stifling. They feel that the world is passing them by."

Pirogov contributes, "I've heard the grumbling too. Anna, it's getting serious. We must quickly devise a solution to address these issues."

Anna looks at Kirik and then at Maxim. "You're correct on all accounts. But there's much more. The children and young people need a better education than we can provide to ensure they have a future in the real world. We're not equipped to provide modern medical care for our aging population. Many of our older citizens need to retire to an easier life. We have no facilities for such people."

Anna continues, "I also hear the grumbling about the isolation, autocracy, and repetitive routines of farming. Many people long for another life in a more open society. Our governance and facilities are inadequate to handle their needs. Something has to give. I'm at a loss."

Fedosov leans forward in his chair and offers, "Well said, Anna. Your analysis is cogent and accurate. I can add no more."

Anna speaks, now with more conviction. "I have considered the options: either move or disband. Neither has much appeal, and remaining here is untenable. The Soviet threat increases daily. We're perilously vulnerable. What are we to do? Kirik? Maxim?"

Kirik leans forward and flashes his most encouraging smile. "Anna, you have synthesized our circumstances precisely. Let's discuss these two options. There are no others."

He leans back in his chair. "To move this entire community into central or eastern China would be a monumental task, expensive, and time-consuming. And many of our people, especially the original settlers, may well experience severe distress in abandoning so much of what they've built over the years. Also, our younger residents, those who came here as babies and small children, are now in their late teens and would not be content to live in yet another isolated community. They want and need true freedom. Lastly, we couldn't conceal such a move. Within days of our attempt to relocate, it probably would become worldwide news. And soon we could expect a visit from the Soviet's NKVD."

Fedosov interrupts with resolution in his voice, "Anna, we have to disperse: Set our people free and encourage them to fend for themselves in an open-market economy. It's the only solution."

Anna turns and looks at the Russian flag. After a time, she responds in a cautious voice. "There is no other option. We must disband. But how? The dislocation and dispersal of so many people would be a monumental task. There are two hundred twenty-six people living here. Consider the intricate logistics needed to move so many people to who knows where—perhaps China or somewhere abroad. And what would the Chinese government say? They have tolerated us benignly in this remote part of China because we have been good neighbors. But I wonder at their reaction to this many Russians moving into the more prosperous provinces of their country."

Pirogov reflects, "The Chinese government may not be much of a problem. The chaos that engulfs most of this country has the Nationalists fully occupied."

Anna comments, "Yes, that makes sense."

Pirogov continues, "And what of our neighbors, the Kirgiz? We are tied as one group. Should we abandon them?" He falls silent for a time as he ponders his own question. "In time, I reckon that they would take over our facilities and fend again for themselves."

Anna remains silent for a time as she carefully forms her next thought. "The Kirgiz lived without us for years. Over time, they will function very well without us." She puts her elbows on the table and rests her head in her palms. "God, please give us inspiration." For a minute or so, the room is quiet. She looks at her two visitors and speaks dejectedly. "Most important, we don't have the funds to finance such an undertaking as the relocation of our entire community." She looks at the pair pensively. "We'd be obligated to give everyone a generous stipend that would allow them to establish new lives for themselves. How can we afford such a move? It's hopeless!" she utters in despair.

Fedosov responds, "Anna, hopeless it is. Considering all of our liquid assets, we have an equivalent of about one thousand British pounds sterling."

Anna frowns sullenly. "Those funds are just about enough to move about twenty families into central China." She shuffles some papers and stacks several others into random piles. "I don't know of any outside source that would help us."

Kirik looks at Fedosov and then settles deep into his chair. Silence again permeates the room. After several minutes, the annoying buzz of the fly snaps Kirik out of his musings. "Anna, please consider one way to raise a lot of funds quickly."

Anna looks at Kirik with incredulity. She jabs teasingly at him, "Shall we rob the bank in Ko-er-mu? Ask the Kirgiz for a loan? Sell the reservoir to the Chinese? Or become a bandit gang and pillage this worthless countryside? What have you in mind, Mister Know-It-All Kirik Antonievich Pirogov?"

"Sell some pieces of the Romanov jewelry."

Stunned at this outrageous suggestion, Anna leans forward with her eyes focused intently, and points her right index finger at Kirik, ready to dismiss his suggestion as nonsense. "Kirik, what are you ...." Instantly she understands. She leans back in her chair and cracks a crooked smile. "Capital, Kirik. Capital!"

Later that evening, Fedosov and Pirogov meet in Anna's office. She opens a chamois bag and withdraws the emerald necklace that Queen Victoria gave to her mother as a wedding present. Holding it against the light, she gazes at it sadly. "Mama let me wear this beautiful necklace at our Christmas Ball, do you remember, Kirik? I felt so pretty and grown-up that evening. It never occurred to me then that everything would end so quickly, or that one day I'd have to sell it." Then, pulling her shoulders back and raising her head proudly, she says, "I've decided that Maxim is to travel to Peking and sell this bauble."

Pirogov responds quickly and perhaps too loudly, "I should be the one to go to Peking. I've been there, and I'm a former soldier. Choose me, Anna."

"Kirik, I need you here to help me. Until Maxim returns, you are going to be my assistant. Maxim has keen knowledge regarding financial matters and his experience at Fabergé augurs well for a profitable deal. Please understand, Kirik. And brief Maxim as best you can about Peking."

"Of course, Anna."

Anna stands and lets the necklace slip slowly into Fedosov's outstretched palm. With a sigh of regret, she murmurs, "This necklace probably is the most valuable piece in the collection. I have no concept of its worth. It must be several thousand British pounds." Then, she hands him seven thousand Chinese dollars and two hundred British pounds sterling. "Traveling money—not for vodka or loose women in the fleshpots of Peking," she teases Maxim gently to ease her angst.

Fedosov places the necklace and cash in a trouser pocket. He smiles mockingly, "Perhaps I shall obey your command, Elector Anna Bogrova." He leans forward and kisses her on both cheeks. "Elector, I'll send a telegram weekly to keep you informed. I should return in two months—three at the most."

She can no longer hold back her emotions. Tears tumble down her cheeks. She grabs Fedosov in a tight embrace. "Maxim, my dear friend and mentor, Godspeed."

32

Wuhan's Antiks Shop, Peking
21 August 1933

With trepidation, Maxim Fedosov turns into Tsingtao Street a few blocks south of Tiananmen Square. The dark, narrow passage is more an alley than a street. Overhead, placards stretch across the alley between multistory buildings and nearly obscure the late afternoon sunshine. The alley is lined with a *mélange* of establishments that offer sundry wares for sale or barter: herbs from gentle palliatives to deadly poisons; antiques and knickknacks; and jewelry, from junk to priceless gems. Apothecaries offer drugs from aspirin to laudanum. A live animal shop sells everything from hares to cobras. Other vendors hawk vegetables, butchered meat, French pastries, apparel from workers' garments to *haute-couture* ensembles, a pipe of opium, and women of easy virtue.

Fedosov is now forty-four years old, but his manner is that of a man much older. His pace is slower and his stride is shorter. His hair is thinner, with patches of white, and his face reflects the years of sorrow at the loss of his beloved wife and two darling children. His suit, the work of a former Moscow tailor's assistant, is respectable but far from the professional clothes he once wore, and it is slightly rumpled from its long trip in Fedosov's valise. Yet, there is still the shadow of a more sophisticated and affluent past.

Several blocks down the alley, Fedosov spots his objective—Wuhan's antique shop. The sign over the door reads simply, "Antiks." As Fedosov enters, a small bell attached to the door tinkles softly. The shop is jammed with bric-a-brac and tourist souvenirs, with barely enough room for anyone to move about. These items belie the true nature of this place. The proprietor, Wuhan Wei-ku, emerges from behind a black, beaded curtain at the back of the shop. He is of indeterminate age and short of stature. Today, he is dressed in a black gown and a skullcap with a long red tassel covers his short black hair. His penetrating black eyes dominate his lean, expressionless face. His alert manner projects the air of a shrewd entrepreneur.

Wuhan is the premier dealer of valuable antiques in Peking. For steep fees, he represents foreigners at auctions and in clandestine private sales of valuable antiques. Lacking scruples, and having superior knowledge of antiques, archeological artifacts, and the black market for such items, he negotiates all deals to his own pecuniary advantage. He is not above skirting the legalities of the Antiquities Department in order to foster a lucrative deal.

Fedosov greets Wuhan in Russian. Wuhan bows in greeting, turns to part the beaded curtain behind him, and speaks softly in Mandarin to his niece, Yen Hei-lan, who is in the office in the back.

Yen Hei-lan glides into the customer area of the shop and greets Fedosov in fluent Russian. "My uncle and I welcome you, sir, to our humble establishment." She wears a red, skintight cheongsam, slit to the upper thigh. A golden dragon embroidered on the cheongsam wraps its way sinuously around her bewitching body. Yen is no longer the budding teenager of Saint Elizabeth's Academy. Now she is a startlingly beautiful, sensuous woman with long, shapely legs and large almond eyes that sparkle with wicked sin. She has a wide, full-lipped mouth; high cheekbones; glowing, pale-olive skin; and long, black hair cascading over her shoulders. Her wasp-thin waist enhances her near-perfect figure. As she speaks, she looks boldly at Fedosov with a provocative smile.

Fedosov stares at her, awestruck by her exotic beauty and her coquettish mien. Somewhat awkwardly, he nods and gives a short bow. Trying to recoup his composure, he mutters, "Thank you. I am Maxim Fedosov, formerly of the House of Fabergé in Saint Petersburg."

Yen responds with a small bow and expands her smile. "We are much pleased that you have come to visit us—possibly to do some small business?

Perhaps we can be of service." Notwithstanding Fedosov's outward appearance, she takes his measure as a man of faded *savoir-faire*, someone who once enjoyed a degree of importance and still commands respect. She purrs, "You have come far, I suspect. Please sit at our table and let me offer you a cup of tea to relieve your fatigue. It is more pleasant to do business when one is comfortable." Beneath her calm exterior, Yen is experiencing a shiver of curiosity and excitement. *Whatever could a former employee of one of the world's greatest jewelers be doing in our shop?*

She escorts Fedosov to a softly lit lounge behind the jumbled shop. It is furnished with soft leather chairs, a large teak and ebony coffee table, and thick silk carpets. An *étagère* holds a collection of exquisite Sung celadons, and hanging on the paneled wall is a magnificent brush painting of a karst mountain landscape from the sixteenth century. As Yen moves to the table, the clinging cheongsam enhances her every curve. Her provocative movements intensify Fedosov's discomfort. He slides uneasily into a high-backed chair covered with bright green silk.

The diminutive Wuhan takes an adjoining chair. Yen sits across from Fedosov, focusing on his eyes. "My name is Yen Hei-lan, but please call me Black Orchid. That is what my name means in your language."

On Wuhan's subtle signal, a young female servant brings tea and cakes. Black Orchid pours tea and passes the cakes. After a polite pause and a sip or two, Black Orchid asks coaxingly, "How may we be of service?"

Fedosov clears his throat. "I'm not quite sure how to begin. I'm here on delicate business that requires scrupulous discretion."

In her most soothing voice, Black Orchid says, "We understand. We are experienced in such circumstances. Please be relaxed and tell us about this delicate business. We will listen carefully and do what we can to be of assistance."

Fedosov, somewhat reassured, says, "Friends have recommended Wuhan's Antiks Shop for a fair deal and few questions."

She smiles, "I have heard such rumors. Please, do continue."

Not sure how to proceed in this alien environment, Fedosov replies in a soft, tentative voice, almost a whisper, "I have a necklace for sale. A rare jeweled necklace." As he speaks, he gains more confidence and his words have more authority. "The owner is an old friend who wants to remain anonymous. This person needs funds and has asked me to act as her intermediary."

"Indeed, you have intrigued us. Do you have this necklace with you now?"

"Yes, I have it."

"Excellent. Perhaps it would be best to let us inspect it."

Fedosov withdraws a chamois pouch from his coat's inner pocket and removes the heavy emerald-and-diamond necklace. He hands it to Black Orchid.

"Thank you, Mister Fedosov," she says with a large smile and fluttering eyelashes. "This necklace is indeed beautiful. My uncle is the expert with such items." She carefully hands the necklace to Wuhan.

Wuhan draws a jeweler's loupe from an inner pocket of his black gown. Under the loupe's ten-power magnification, he carefully inspects the magnificent piece. He spots the Romanovs' double-eagle, royal crest and "Alexandra" engraved on the back of the catch. On reflection, he is convinced that this necklace is part of the missing Romanov collection from the Soviet Union. As he examines each gem and the intricate platinum setting, he wonders if the necklace is a solo item or whether it comes from a cache of the other missing jewelry. If so, then perhaps the also-missing, legendary Saint Catherine's Crown is with these treasures. There are no clues as to how the crown or the Romanov family jewels vanished, where they are, or who was responsible for their disappearance. Wuhan is intrigued. He muses to himself, *How does this shabby Russian come to have this rare royal treasure? Who is his patron who owns this necklace? And why is this treasure for sale?*

Wuhan turns to Fedosov. Speaking through Black Orchid, he continues, "This necklace appears to be from the missing Romanov collection. May I ask how your 'old friend' came to own it?"

Cautiously, Fedosov responds, "That is a matter I may not discuss."

"Very well," Wuhan responds. He turns and whispers instructions to Black Orchid in Mandarin.

Black Orchid flashes a smile and asks, "May I ask what amount you are asking for this necklace? And, should we conclude a propitious bargain, in what currency you would prefer payment? Or would you prefer gold, valued in United States dollars at yesterday's closing price on the Chicago Board of Trade?"

"No, I do not want to deal in gold, and I do not want American dollars, which are too weak on the international market. The American Depression has severely devalued the dollar." After brief reflection, he says, "I would prefer payment in British pounds sterling. I understand that this is the only currency that is stable and has worldwide acceptance. Do you approve?"

"Of course," she responds. "And your price?"

Fedosov recalls Anna's comments regarding the inordinate amount of funds needed to move the citizens of Yumin, and he tries to recall some of the transactions he witnessed at *Fabergé*. Hesitantly he responds, "Seventy-five thousand British pounds sterling. A most reasonable price for this rare and valuable necklace."

"Thank you, Mister Fedosov." She glances at Wuhan for his signal, then nods with understanding. "Please know that because of the notoriety surrounding this necklace that once belonged to Empress Alexandra, we must be absolutely discreet if we purchase it. Should the Soviet government discover our involvement, we would become prime targets for NKVD justice."

"Be assured that only my principal and I know of my visit. We have no desire for this transaction to be made public."

Black Orchid nods and looks for a signal from her uncle. She makes a counteroffer of thirty-five thousand pounds. Fedosov refuses with a forceful negative headshake. They continue dickering for the next several minutes, interrupted with sips of tea while each bargainer evaluates the other's strategy. Black Orchid relays Wuhan's offers and Fedosov's counteroffers. Eventually, they agree on fifty-five thousand pounds.

Wuhan shows no emotion. However, inwardly he is exceedingly pleased with this surprisingly lucrative bargain. He knows that this Romanov necklace will fetch upwards of two hundred thousand British pounds sterling, perhaps much more, from the black-market collectors with whom he deals.

"Congratulations, Maxim Fedosov. You have bargained astutely. Let us conclude this business. To what name shall we make our check payable?"

Fedosov responds somewhat sharply, "Mistress Yen. I would prefer cash, if you please."

Somewhat taken aback by the sharpness of his response, Black Orchid says, "Please excuse me if I have offended you. Regrettably, it is not possible to pay in cash. We do not keep such funds here in our shop. It would be foolish to invite burglars to rob us. We will pay by a check written on the China National Bank and Trust Company, Limited, here in Peking. My uncle will telephone the bank's senior cashier, Mister Chan Sen-tao, to confirm that our check will clear with your identification and endorsement." She catches Fedosov's eyes and in the same even, relaxed way asks, "In what name shall we make our check payable?"

Black Orchid's question catches Fedosov off guard. He leans back in his chair and looks away at a curved ivory tusk in the shop's interior as he carefully forms his reply. "I'm embarrassed to admit that I would be in an awkward predicament trying to cash a check. I have no papers. No passport. No form of identification. I'm in China, as you might say, 'unauthorized.' Legally, I am a nonperson. With the chaos consuming your country, no one has bothered me, especially because I am an Occidental."

Black Orchid replies with feigned sympathy, "It is as we suspected. Your predicament is familiar to us. Over the past several years we have dealt with many White Russians in similar circumstances. All with mutual satisfaction, I might add."

Fedosov says, "If you can make satisfactory arrangements, then please make the check payable to bearer."

Black Orchid counters in a smooth, indifferent voice, "That is not possible. We cannot write our check as you ask. That would be careless business, especially for this amount of money. We would be courting danger for you and for us in these troubled times. Besides, Mister Chan will demand identification and a signature."

"Are we then at an impasse?" asks Fedosov dejectedly.

"Not at all. Perhaps there is a way. We have an associate who might be of service. He can produce an authentic-looking passport for you that will satisfy the closest inspection. If this opportunity is satisfactory, tell us of which country you want to be a citizen. And what name will you use?"

Intrigued by Black Orchid's offer, Fedosov replies, "What is this man's fee for such a service? At the moment, I am short of funds. I have just enough pounds to pay my hotel bill and return to my home."

Black Orchid sees a critical opening on his inadvertent *faux-pas*. Should she press the issue to find out where he came from, or should she wait? On short reflection, she says, "His fee is nominal, and we will cover it. This is part of our service for treasured clients."

Fedosov responds quickly. "Because of my accent and upbringing, I suspect that the country ought to be a Slavic nation. Can this associate of yours make a Polish passport? "

She smiles, "Yes, of course. Any country is possible."

Thinking quickly as Black Orchid responds, he recalls the late manager of Fabergé. "Use the name Zinovy Annikov. He was a friend of mine, a former colleague who died in the Revolution."

"My sympathies for your loss. Please be patient. Such detailed work will take several hours, and our associate will need your photograph. Come with me to the back of our shop and I will take your photograph with our new Graflex camera. In the meantime, my uncle will telephone our associate, Mister Lin Ping-shu, to tell him about your needs." She hands Fedosov a business card. "Here is Mister Lin's address. It is three doors down the street. His sign says, "Draftsman." Take your photograph to him and wait while he completes your documents."

While the process of taking and developing Fedosov's photograph proceeds, Wuhan writes the check on a special account. He telephones Mister Chan Sen-tao at the China National Trust Company Bank, and Chan acknowledges that he will honor the check with proper identification and signature.

Fedosov and Black Orchid return to the table and engage in a desultory conversation. She flirts provocatively. Shortly, the female servant enters and looks closely at Fedosov as she hands him his photograph. The ever-stoic Wuhan hands his check to Fedosov, who inspects it and finds it in order. He puts it in his jacket pocket, stands, makes a short bow, smiles, and thanks his hosts.

Black Orchid responds, "It is our pleasure, I assure you." As Fedosov turns to leave, Black Orchid touches his arm and says in a low voice, "In the Celestial Kingdom, our custom is to conclude a successful business transaction with tea to have good feelings."

Wuhan gives a knowing glance to Black Orchid. She understands exactly what to do. In her most soothing voice says, "I will prepare the tea for us. We have a rare and very special oolong from Fujian that we reserve for only the most important occasions."

Fedosov, his eyes narrowing thoughtfully as he regards Black Orchid's exotic form, replies, "Yes, please." He returns to his chair and watches her cheongsam swirl as she exits the office. His pulse is several beats faster than usual.

In the back of the shop, Black Orchid concocts her special tea. She spikes Fedosov's cup with a libido-enhancing herb and a small drop of hashish to confuse his mind. Returning to the lounge, she serves the tea and they toast each other. Soon the tea ritual is concluded. Fedosov is pleased with the propitious bargain he has concluded. He flashes a broad smile and gives a short bow to Black Orchid and Wuhan.

It is twilight as Fedosov leaves the shop and steps into the alley. He is proud of himself for the way he has outfoxed Wuhan—settling for a price far more than he had imagined. He hails the rickshaw conveniently positioned just a few feet from the entrance. As he climbs into the cab, Black Orchid exits Wuhan's shop. Her long stride exposes her left leg provocatively. "Will you so kind to give me a lift to my apartment? It is close by," she purrs.

Somewhat euphoric from the drugged tea and dazzled by her sensuous beauty, Fedosov nods agreement. "It is my pleasure."

33

Black Orchid's Penthouse, Peking
22 August 1933

Black Orchid's penthouse overlooks the Forbidden City. She has furnished it with fine art-deco pieces. Hanging on the walls is an array of paintings by Impressionist masters—Cézanne, Monet, Degas, and Gauguin. She also has several pieces by Piet Mondrian—excellent forgeries of which hang in various museums and private collections around the world.

In the early morning, wearing a filmy black negligee, Black Orchid searches Fedosov's jacket pockets as he sleeps from a frenzied night of rowdy sex, rich hashish, and rare Dom Pérignon Reserve. She slips her uncle's check from his jacket. Then she finds the instructions from Anna Bogrova confirming that Fedosov is to deposit the proceeds from the sale of the necklace into the commune's coded account in Barclay's Bank in Peking, and to communicate with her in an encrypted telegram using their RCA code.

Black Orchid is intrigued by yesterday's events. *Who is this Anna Bogrova? If she owned that necklace or has the authority to sell it, could she be a member of the Romanov family? But who? Surely she is not one of the grand duchesses. They were all murdered in 1918. Then who is she?*

She quickly realizes that here is an astonishing opportunity for profit and power. Fedosov probably knows the location of the rest of the missing pieces of the Romanov jewelry, and possibly even of Saint Catherine's Crown.

Smiling pleasantly to herself, Black Orchid opens her negligee and gazes at her image in the mirror of a fine, shagreen-covered, art -deco, French vanity. Admiring her voluptuous body, she shivers slightly, evoking the exquisite pleasure she luxuriated in last evening. A smirk creeps over her face as she recalls what the nuns at Saint Elizabeth's Academy for Young Ladies taught her about the virtues of chastity. She wonders how many essays the departed Sister Mary Beatrice O'Hara would demand of her if she could have witnessed her seduction of Fedosov and her delicious enjoyment of their carnal gratification.

Ever so slowly she turns around to change her image in the mirror. With brazen affirmation she utters, "I am a whore, an especially beautiful and skillful whore. A whore who enjoys her work. And I am proud of it."

Her life was not always so. With searing pain, she remembers how her uncle first brought her to his bed. She was a terrified ten-year-old, bewildered at what he was doing to her, and then overcome by excruciating agony as he stole her virginity. The rapes continued until she was fourteen and pregnant. A torturous abortion by a maladroit midwife was her reward for all those years of subjugation and humiliation. Afterward, Wuhan took his pleasure from a series of housemaids.

Wuhan then demanded that Black Orchid use her exquisite beauty and exceptional erotic skills to induce his clients into profitable deals. After a time, she began to derive intense sexual pleasure from these trysts. Unknown to her uncle, she has enhanced her personal wealth by accepting valuable gifts from her 'guests.' She has learned that Wuhan easily accepts most of her lies, or else he cares little about losing small treasures while he focuses on much larger gains.

"Yes, I am a whore," she congratulates herself. "And if my deductions are correct regarding the Romanov jewels and Saint Catherine's Crown, I'll be a fabulously wealthy whore, and free from my heinous uncle. I can be whoever I choose—Catherine the Great reincarnated, the Queen of Sheba personified, or perhaps an international adventuress with many influential men sniffing after my favors." She sighs with the satisfaction of the completely surfeited.

Driven by the fantastic possibilities for incredible riches, Black Orchid turns toward Fedosov, lying naked on the bed in a drug-induced stupor. She smiles to herself. *Now I shall learn precisely who Anna Bogrova is, where she is, and whether she has the Romanov jewelry.*

She binds Fedosov's hands and feet spread-eagle to the bedposts with thin leather straps, and then straddles him at the waist to keep him from thrashing. She rouses him from his stupor with a vial of ammonia.

Fedosov coughs several times, and opens his eyes. He tries to move but cannot. He realizes that Black Orchid has lashed him to the bed and that she has him pinned down. "Bitch, what are you doing?"

"Such invective from a 'respectable' Russian. I blush. Nonetheless, welcome to my party, Maxim. You are my guest, and you are going to tell me some secrets—some dark secrets."

"I have no secrets. And if I did, I'd not tell them to you."

"My dear Maxim, did you not enjoy our night of debauchery? Have you no love for Black Orchid this morning?"

"None. Last night was an aberration—to my regret. Release me!"

"Not yet. Perhaps after you have told me your secrets."

"Possibly you did not hear or understand me. I have no secrets."

"We'll see. Maxim, please notice my syringe." She waves it slowly in front of his face. "It's filled with belladonna, a deadly poison, and it induces excruciating pain."

Fedosov begins to understand his desperate predicament. His eyes narrow, his pulse quickens, lips tighten, and perspiration covers his brow.

"Maxim, tell me, who is Anna Bogrova, and where is she? Are there more pieces of the missing Romanov jewelry? How many? What are they? Is Saint Catherine's Crown with them?" The dripping needle is dangerously close to Fedosov's cheek.

Fedosov mutters, "No. I don't know."

"Fool!" She pricks his cheek with the needle. Fiery pain explodes in his face, and he screams in agony. He gasps for breath.

Black Orchid waits patiently for him to recover partially. "Tell me truly what I ask. I have all day to play with you."

He tries to focus his eyes on her. Slurring his words under his pain, he says, "I am a bookkeeper, that's all. I am not a jeweler."

"Maxim, you take me for a fool. You sold a fabulous Romanov necklace to me yesterday. A child could see through your perfidy. Enough!" She jams the syringe deep into his other cheek.

He emits strange guttural sounds as the pain overwhelms his being. He thrashes violently—anything to ease the agony. The leather straps hold tight, cutting deep into his ankles and wrists, and his oozing blood stains the sheets. He shrieks barbarically and falls into semi-consciousness.

Black Orchid coldly assesses Fedosov. Several minutes later, he calms somewhat. She squeezes the ammonia vial under his nose.

Maxim coughs several times, and a dim light returns to his eyes.

Black Orchid smiles mischievously. "Welcome back to my party, Maxim." She shifts her position so that her face is closer to his. After a few minutes, she says coyly, "Look here, Maxim. I have another syringe. This one is filled with morphine." She sticks the needle in his arm and squeezes a few drops of the opiate into him. There is not enough of the palliative to ease his intense, lingering pain.

In a soft, friendly voice, she says, "Answer my questions and I'll give you enough of this narcotic to ease your suffering and send you to paradise." She lets Fedosov consider her proposition. "If you tell me truthfully, I'll let you go." She waits a few seconds for his answer.

He shakes his head negatively.

With a stern voice she demands, "Listen to me carefully, Maxim Fedosov. If you do not answer all my questions, I will jam this syringe full of belladonna into your eye and you will die in the agony of the damned."

Through the fog of pain, his mind still confused by the residue of last night's drugs, he mumbles, "You strumpet, you talk nonsense. There is no jewelry at Yumin." Instantly, he realizes that he's made an egregious blunder.

Black Orchid smiles sardonically. "Thank you, Maxim. I knew we would reach an accommodation."

Fedosov now realizes that he no longer has an option. *If she kills me, the mission to move the Russians out of Yumin is lost, and the successful completion of my mission is imperative.*

Black Orchard leans over him, her face just inches from his, "Who is Anna Bogrova? Tell me and I'll let you go."

"How can I trust you?"

"You have no choice."

Fedosov knows that she is right. *I have no choice. Any information I tell Black Orchid has time-limited value. Once I return to Yumin, the community, Anna, and I will disperse and vanish.*

With his hands tied, Fedosov cannot rub his face to ease the pain. "All right, I'll tell you what I know," he sputters. "Anna Bogrova is Grand Duchess Anastasia Romanov."

Black Orchid gasps at this astonishing statement. "What!" She glares at him. "You're lying to me, Fedosov. Do you believe that I am stupid? Uninformed? Anastasia is dead. The Bolsheviks murdered her, and her family, in 1918." She moves the syringe needle on the skin just under his right eye. Fedosov feels it and tightens his body. "Continue with this fabrication, and I will blind you." She moves the needle menacingly. "Tell me the truth!"

"It is true! Anastasia survived. Somehow, her mother saved her from execution; however, two bullets wounded her. Now she is a cripple."

Black Orchid wonders, *Perhaps there might be a thread of truth in his story.* Impatient for details, she demands, "Tell me, Maxim Fedosov, just where is this Yumin where Grand Duchess Anastasia Romanov of Imperial Russia resides?" Then more forcefully, "In China? Japan? Cochin China? Manchukuo? Does she have the Romanov jewels? Is Saint Catherine's Crown with them? Shall I prick you again with my needle? Tell me quickly and truthfully, where is she?"

Fedosov's mind is clouded with searing pain and fear for his mission. He responds between coughs and grasps of air, "Anastasia and some White Russian expatriates live in a commune in an abandoned lamasery in Yumin in northwestern Sinkiang Province."

"Very good." Black Orchid sits back for a moment and smiles. "Now, the jewelry! Tell me about the Romanov jewelry and Saint Catherine's Crown. Are they in Yumin?" she demands.

Struggling at his impossible situation, nearly paralyzed with pain and fear, and resolved to save himself, Fedosov answers weakly, "Yes." He closes his eyes and weeps internally at his betrayal and loss of honor.

Invigorated at Fedosov's positive response, Black Orchid slaps him hard. His head snaps and he moans. "More! I need the details. Make sure your answer is correct. If I sense deception, I'll jab my needle in your eye."

With fatalistic resignation, he speaks in a low voice, almost a whisper. "There is a large cache of Romanov jewelry at Yumin, and yes, Saint Catherine's Crown also is there."

At this news, Black Orchid's eyes open wide, and her whole body tenses in anticipation. "Describe the jewelry. How many pieces? What are they, and what are the rare stones?" She grabs the back of his head and pulls it close to her. "I am impatient for the truth. No more stalling, Fedosov. Quickly."

Continuing softly, he says, "I've not seen this cache, but I know it's there because Anastasia gave me its inventory as part of my duties." Fedosov continues for the next several minutes to tell her what he can remember.

Black Orchid absorbs all the details of the cache. Satisfied, she relaxes, and smiles at her good fortune. Wanting more information, she demands, "How did the cache and the Crown get out of Imperial Russia? "

"At Empress Alexandra's command, her godson, Kirik Pirogov, smuggled the Romanov jewelry and Saint Catherine's Crown out of Saint Petersburg and into China. Anastasia has hidden the jewelry someplace in the lamasery. She has not told me where."

"Fedosov, you are a stupid liar." Black Orchid leans over his face and forces a drop of belladonna under the skin beneath his right eye.

He screams. His eye swells closed. As the pain begins to ease, he whispers, "It is the truth, I swear."

Staring at him, she snaps, "Save yourself. Where are the jewels and the Crown?"

Semi-dazed by the excruciating pain, Fedosov sputters, "I don't know. She handed me the emerald necklace when we met in her office."

Black Orchid moves the syringe menacingly close to his left eye. "You are absolutely telling me the truth?" she demands.

"Yes. Yes, of course."

With the amount of pain she has inflicted on Fedosov, she is convinced that the naïve fellow no longer has the strength or courage to dissemble. Black Orchid has one last item to resolve—blackmail. "Will Grand Duchess Anastasia be proud of you when she sees the photographs of our carnal ecstasy last evening? My associate worked the Graflex camera admirably. Endorse my uncle's check or Anastasia will see your debauchery. Then you may go back to your grand duchess—if you dare."

Trapped, Fedosov, summoning what resolve he has left, spouts, "You harlot, I damn you!"

"What strong words you have for a libertine," Black Orchid snaps mockingly.

After a short pause, he says, "Hand me the check."

As she unties his right hand, she says, "If you are so pure of soul, relay our evening of sinful pleasure to your Anastasia. Omit no detail. Will she trust you all the more?"

Fedosov closes his eyes in complete defeat. Clumsily, he makes the endorsement. She grabs the endorsed check—a nice addition to her personal account.

As Fedosov struggles to free his left hand, he mutters, "Morphine. Give me the morphine."

"Yes. Yes, of course," Black Orchid energetically replies. She jams the belladonna syringe into Fedosov's carotid artery. In convulsive agony, he expires. Smiling at her extraordinary success, she summons two of Wuhan's goons to get rid of the body. "The Sanggan River will do for this White Russian."

34

Wuhan's Antik Shop, Peking
22 August 1933

lack Orchid, having visited the China National Bank earlier, enters the shop. Reflecting the pride she feels for her accomplishments this morning, her head is upright, shoulders straight, stride long and forceful. As she enters the office where Wuhan is working on accounts, Black Orchid has a smirk on her face.

Wuhan's well-ordered, spacious office is in marked contrast to the jumble of merchandise seemingly stuffed at random on shelves along the narrow aisles in the shop. The office is brightly lit with a bank of art-deco fixtures. Cloud-silk brocade tapestries from the Yuan and Ming dynasties hang on the pearl-luster walls. Wuhan acquired these tapestries from clients who traded them for other valuable antiquities. The floor is covered with a large antique Chinese rug. Wuhan's teak desk is an old-fashioned roll-top, trimmed in ebony and rosewood. Hidden in the desk is a small, durable, steel safe with a four-tumbler lock. There are no windows or rear entrance. At the back of the room, a narrow, circular stairway leads to Wuhan's apartment on the top floor.

Today, Black Orchid is wearing a powder-blue shamfou trimmed with gold ribbing. The pants are full cut, and the jacket is cut on the bias. Wuhan looks up as she parts the beaded curtain. With her arms akimbo and with a faint smile, she pronounces, "I have news, venerable uncle."

"I sincerely hope that your news is favorable, my most treasured niece."

"Indeed it is," she responds with alacrity. "Under the influence of my gracious hospitality and with only minor chicanery, the Czarist Fedosov relayed an extraordinary tale about a coterie of White Russians living in Sinkiang Province. They have renovated an abandoned lamasery, in a place called Yumin, as their home in exile. He was unable to tell me any more before he left. Astonishingly, their leader is none other than Grand Duchess Anastasia, the fourth daughter of Czar Nicholas Romanov." She pauses for a moment for dramatic effect. "The striking news is that she has the Romanov jewels and Saint Catherine's Crown!"

With a quizzical look, Wuhan blurts, "Such a story must be a fairy tale. I suspect that you are playing a joke on me. Please do not do so. I am in no mood for funny business. I have serious concerns about this necklace."

"Uncle, I am sincere. Please let me continue." Without waiting for permission, Black Orchid says, "A close associate of the imperial family smuggled these baubles out of Saint Petersburg and eventually delivered them to Anastasia in Yumin. Fedosov knows that she has sequestered the stash somewhere in the lamasery, but he does not know where. He believes that only Anastasia knows their hiding place."

Startled, Wuhan looks at his niece. Indeed, she is beautiful. He wistfully recalls how he satisfied his passion with her young, helpless body. He closes his eyes to assess her report. After a few moments, he rises and grabs her arm. "My niece, you bring amazing news. But I am skeptical. How can I evaluate its authenticity? Why should I trust Fedosov to tell you the truth? I admit that there is some credibility to his story because it explains how he had possession of the Romanov necklace. But he could have stolen it. Indeed, this is a puzzle."

Black Orchid pulls her arm away and, with a scowl, retorts, "Uncle, I assure you that my report is fully accurate. At my inducements, Fedosov was anxious to tell me the details of these White Russians. I am absolute certain that his tale is authentic."

Somewhat mollified, because he understands her inducements, Wuhan returns to his chair. "Very well, please continue. I am interested to hear more."

"Through some stratagem of Empress Alexandra's, Anastasia survived the Bolshevik regicide of 1918, though she was seriously wounded. How she got to Yumin, I do not know. Now, to conceal her true identity, she goes by the name Anna Bogrova."

With a faint smile, Wuhan says, "You have done well, my niece. Indeed, this is a most amazing story. I need to reflect upon it. Perhaps there is an opportunity here for Wuhan's Antik Shop. Tell me, did Fedosov discuss other pieces in this collection? How many are there? What kind? Any descriptions whatsoever?"

A slow smirk creeps onto Black Orchid's face. "Complying with my encouragements, the Czarist revealed that Grand Duchess Anastasia has stashed a large component of the Romanov jewelry collection someplace in the lamasery. Even Saint Catherine's Crown! With additional coaxing, Fedosov divulged a comprehensive inventory of the collection." She pauses for Wuhan to comprehend fully the scope of this extraordinary intelligence. Proud of her coup, she continues, "As soon as the fellow departed, I record-ed the details in my diary." With a dramatic flourish, she withdraws the diary from her dress and with much ado drops it on Wuhan's desk.

Perhaps more interested in the jewelry than her brazen conduct, he picks up her diary and scans the inventory. He returns the diary to Yen and stares at her. With a touch of praise, he comments, "Interesting. Interesting, indeed, niece. What details about the individual pieces did he give?"

Realizing that her bravado has violated protocol, she says with humili-ty, "He departed shortly after I had the immediate intelligence. Perhaps I was too intent on focusing on the inventory rather than on the particulars of the collection. On reflection, I should have prolonged our morning's experience."

Wuhan stares into space. He considers the causative factors involved in Fedosov's story and what is known about the Romanov jewelry. Of prime consideration is calculating the risk involved versus the potential reward. After a minute or so, he says, "Indeed unfortunate. Such information would have helped me assess the approximate value of the jewelry. But no matter. The value will certainly be in the millions of pounds. I suspect that Anastasia has the Romanov's personal jewelry, which the Soviets claim is missing. Yes, my niece, I see the potential for some profit. Nonetheless, singular caution must be our counsel. The Soviet government has possession of the formal collection, and the NKVD is looking for the missing personal articles and the crown. I do not wish for these blackguards to visit Wuhan's Antik Shop."

With a hint of impatience, Black Orchid responds, "Do you not consider it prudent that we make arrangements to relieve Anastasia of these trinkets?"

"Your comment is appropriate, and I shall reflect on it. First, I must concoct a scheme that will ensure immense profit with minimal risk. With such enticements as we can muster, we need to inveigle a collector to finance the journey from Peking to Yumin. The trek is long and dangerous. Much of the area is controlled by warlords and bandits who will murder at the least excuse. Accordingly, we must keep our own confidence. Also, we must ensure that this Fedosov does not interfere."

Black Orchid moves to the back of the shop and begins to make tea. "You may rest assured, Uncle, that Fedosov is no longer involved. I escorted him to the Bank of China, where Anastasia has an account. After he deposited your check, we had dinner in my apartment. This morning he complained of chest pains. Before I could summon medical assistance, he expired. To avoid any notoriety, I reasoned that it would be expedient if your assistants disposed of his body. I am led to believe they deposited it in the river. There should be no inquiries. He was unknown to the authorities and there is no one here to report him missing, as I understand."

Wuhan is not deceived by Black Orchid's fabricated yarn, but he cares little about her lies or actions since Fedosov is no longer a factor. However, suspecting chicanery about the check, he says with a quizzical voice, "It is unfortunate that you could not recover my check. It is of minor consequence in the broad scheme I will develop to relieve the Russians of their jewels and Saint Catherine's Crown. I will ask Mister Chan Sen-tao at the bank to put a stop payment order on this check. I suffer no loss. Please tend to the shop while I consider what is to be done."

Black Orchid seethes inside at Wuhan's intuitive perception and finesse at parrying her thievery. *Surely, Mister Chan will tell uncle that I have cashed this check and will show him my countersign signature.* She knows that Wuhan's style is not to confront her now, but rather to implement vengeance unexpectedly. *I shall take appropriate measures when the circumstances are propitious.* The tinkling bell over the door pulls Black Orchid from her black mood and she enters the shop to attend to a visitor.

Wuhan realizes that he must sell the Romanov necklace as soon as possible. He is not absolutely positive that Fedosov did not confide in another White Russian in Peking about his visit to his shop, or the sale of the necklace. If he did, then Fedosov's disappearance could start rumors or concerns and bring detectives from the International Constabulary and eventually the Soviet secret police to his shop.

Wuhan, a high-stakes gambler, calculates that the odds of such an occurrence are extremely low. Even if it were the case, it would be several months before trouble would appear—perhaps as much as a year, probably more. By then, he would have disappeared into one of the innumerable overseas Chinese communities with a treasure of incalculable wealth.

He realizes that his best option is to sell the necklace privately to one of the several wealthy collectors to whom he has sold China's treasured artifacts in the past. An auction among them would garner maximum profit. And to further entice spirited bidding, he will hint at fabulous riches yet to be had.

Wuhan drafts a cablegram, encoded in his specially designed RCA cipher, to be sent to eight of the wealthiest and most avid collectors. All command vast financial resources and have revealed that they are willing to overlook certain official protocols if the prize warrants. It reads:

PLEASE BE INFORMED THAT I HAVE ACQUIRED A MAGNIFICENT PIECE OF JEWELRY, MISSING THESE MANY YEARS AND WHOSE HISTORY IS WRITTEN IN BLOOD STOP BECAUSE OF THE SINGULAR NATURE OF THIS OBJECT, I AM UNABLE TO ADD MORE DETAILS STOP IT IS AN ITEM THAT WILL ADD IMMEASURABLE PRESTIGE AND VALUE TO YOUR COLLECTION STOP MAY I SUGGEST THAT WITHIN THE NEXT FORTY-FIVE DAYS YOU APPEAR IN MY SHOP TO INSPECT AND BID ON THIS

ITEM STOP THE OPENING BID IS 250,000 BRITISH POUNDS STERLING STOP ADDITIONALLY, I SUGGEST THAT FOR THE SUCCESSFUL BIDDER THERE IS AN OPPORTUNITY TO AC-QUIRE THE REMAINDER OF A VAST PRIVATE COLLECTION AND ANOTHER ITEM OF IMMENSE WORTH AND HISTORICAL VALUE STOP MY FEE FOR THIS ONCE IN A LIFETIME, GOLDEN OPPORTUNITY IS 25 PERCENT STOP BECAUSE OF POTENTIAL NEGATIVE RAMIFICATIONS SHOULD INFORMATION ABOUT THIS OFFER BECOME KNOWN TO CERTAIN INTELLIGENCE AGENCIES I URGE YOU TO BE DISCREET STOP REPLY SOON-EST STOP WUHAN.

The addresses are:

Colonel Guenther von Hemholtz, SW Salvage Company, Windhoek, Southwest Africa;

Samuel Marlowe, c/o Composite Press Service, New York, U.S.A.; Gaspar van de Hoff, General Delivery, The International City, Tangier;

Hasim Erdogan, Erdogan Enterprises, Limited, Constantinople;

Chormondely Fanshaw-Chadwick, Government House, Pretoria, South Africa;

Lorenzo Socrates, Goa, Portuguese India;

Comandante **Pedro Sánchez-Navarro,** c/o *Guardia Civil,* Ceuta, Spanish Morocco;

Mordecai Jacomides, Celestial Empire Explorations, #2 San Lazaro Walk, Macao.

Finally, he hands his encoded text and the list of potential bidders to his shop girl to deliver to the RCA cable office. With a slight smile on his face, he gives a deep sigh of satisfaction. He always enjoys these auctions of rare and valuable items. The fierce acquisitiveness of his clients amuses him, and the prospect of an enormous addition to his personal wealth satisfies his own greed. This day, he concludes, is beginning in a most propitious adventure.

A week later, responses to Wuhan's cablegram begin to arrive. Chormondely Fanshaw-Chadwick of South Africa responds that he is unable to attend the auction because he is going to Basutoland to hunt for the lost Luzamba Diamond Mine. The following day, Gaspar van de Hoff's cable says that it is best that he remain in Tangier incognito because Interpol is investigating his "activities" regarding certain arms transactions related to the Italian incursion into Ethiopia. The same day, Wuhan receives notice that Hasim Erdogan's cable was undeliverable, "Addressee Unknown." The next day, *Comandante* Sánchez-Navarro sends his regrets. His regiment has been mobilized to counter a Rifi uprising.

Two days after that, Lorenzo Socrates responds that he is unable to attend because he is on a hunt for the tomb of the fifteenth-century Mogul emperor Tamerlane. Later that day, Wuhan receives a response from Colonel von Hemholtz, who sends his regrets because he is recovering "cargo" from the sunken tramp steamer *Golden Prussia* of the Deutsch Orient Line. Mordecai Jacomides sends his thanks for the invitation; however, he declines to attend—the roulette wheel has been unkind.

By the end of the week, Wuhan is concerned that his scheme to recover the Romanov jewelry and Saint Catherine's Crown is collapsing. He fidgets with his accounts, but does not accomplish much. His mind is focused on Sinkiang Province and the treasures hidden there. So far, seven of his potential bidders have declined his invitation. His stratagem to sell the emerald necklace and find a collector to finance a trip to Yumin is fading rapidly. He understands: wars and threats of wars, rising fascism, the Comintern spreading Bolshevism worldwide, the League of Nations meddling in international commerce, and the worldwide depression have all undermined his lucrative trade in the illegal sales of art treasures. Nonetheless, he knows other wealthy international buyers who would pay handsomely to own the Romanov necklace. It is Saint Catherine's Crown and the remainder of the Russian collection that he covets for himself.

By late that afternoon, only a few customers have entered the shop. Their total purchases would not pay the electric bill for the day. Although Wuhan does not depend on walk-in traffic for his income, these casual visitors are important for appearances.

Near closing time, the tinkle of the doorbell rouses him from work at his desk. He tells Black Orchid to respond to what he expects is just another tourist. An RCA messenger boy, dressed in his brown-green uniform and overseas cap, enters the shop. Black Orchid snaps, "Boy, give me that cablegram." He promptly hands it to her and waits with his hand outstretched for the tip that does not come. "You may leave," she says dismissively. "Your business here is done."

Black Orchid slowly scans the envelope. It is addressed to Wuhan, in care of his Antik Shop, and it is from Shanghai. She dares not open the envelope, but she will know its contents shortly. Strolling lazily to the back of the shop, she parts the beads and states matter-of-factly, "Another cablegram for you, Uncle. Probably another collector sending his regrets." She tosses the cablegram on the table and returns to the shop to prepare for closing.

Wuhan frowns at her insolence, picks up the cablegram, and slices open the envelope. He sees that it is from Samuel Marlowe—one of his most reckless and spendthrift collectors. The cablegram reads:

WUHAN WEI-KUO STOP C/O ANTIK SHOP STOP PEKING STOP MY NY OFFICE FORWARDED YOUR CABLEGRAM TO ME AT MY HOTEL IN SHANGHAI STOP YOUR DESCRIPTION MOST INTRIGUING STOP WILL CATCH THE 1900 BLUE EXPRESS TO PEKING THIS EVENING STOP MEET ME TOMORROW, FRIDAY 01 SEPTEMBER, AT 2030 IN MY SUITE AT THE HOTEL DE LA CHINE STOP BRING THE ITEM STOP MARLOWE.

At last, Wuhan speculates, he may well have nabbed a sponsor. He knows well the impulsive Marlowe and his singular drive to get what he wants, no matter the cost, danger, or consequences. With Marlowe, finesse is not necessary. All the American needs are the particulars—the details of the treasure and how to get it. All else fades to insignificance.

Yes, tomorrow I will enthrall Marlowe with the lure of the prize of the century.

35

Hôtel de la Chine, Peking
1 September 1933

Trevor Pryce enters the Cygne Blanc Lounge at the cocktail hour, spots an empty stool at the bar, and settles in. He places a camera bag containing his 35-mm Leica camera kit on the bar and his Australian Jacaru hat on the seat next to him. The lounge is decorated in art-deco style—chrome trim, etched glass, and leather chairs. On the wall are autographed photographs of famous motion-picture stars, politicians, and tycoons. In the far corner, a five-musician combo plays a medley of American show tunes. An attractive Eurasian chanteuse in a bright-green strapless gown and matching elbow-length gloves sings romantic lyrics in a throaty, sensuous voice. On the microscopic dance floor, a few well-dressed couples sway to the music.

Pryce wears long, khaki trousers, a short-sleeved bush jacket, a loose-hanging, tan scarf, and ankle-high boots. His clothes are wrinkled and soiled. His hair is untidy, and he has a three-day beard.

The barman, Dah Tung-lu, is fluent in the banter of Westerners. "Welcome home, Mister Pryce. I am pleased to see that you are in good health. Your trip to Kansu Province was productive?"

Pryce responds, "Yes, very much so. Dodged a few bullets. Damn near got bitten by a cobra. Taken prisoner for a few days by a Japanese patrol of the Kwangtung Army. And General Wu, the warlord of Kansu Province, almost impaled me with his saber. Nonetheless, got a great story and dozens of rolls of dynamic photos of Wu's raid on a Buddhist monastery to steal rare antique porcelains dating from the Chin dynasty. I'll have a gin and bitters. Double the gin. I'm exhausted."

Pryce is in his early thirties, square-jawed, tall, well-built, with blue-green eyes and short-cropped, brown hair. His mien reflects his British upper-class upbringing and his Cambridge education. With a working knowledge of Mandarin, he covers China as a successful freelance photojournalist for several international news media. He left England quietly after the *Times* broke a scandal regarding his indiscretions with a married peeress of the realm. Currently, he has no girlfriend, but he's known to cavort with Occidental women of the international community. His social life mostly consists of palling around with other expatriates in various pubs in the Foreign Concessions.

Working on his second gin and bitters, he hears a husky female voice say, "Please remove your hat, or whatever that thing is, from this stool." She taps him on the shoulder. "This is the only stool left at the bar, and I need a place to park and get a drink."

"Of course," Pryce responds. He turns and sees a rather striking, well-dressed blonde. He picks up his hat and places it over his camera bag. "My apologies. Please sit down."

She sits and gives Pryce an appraising perusal. She likes what she sees. She orders a double rye whiskey from the barman, "Straight." On delivery, she takes a healthy swallow, leans back on the stool, offers her right hand to Pryce, and says, "Hi." She gives him a high-wattage smile. "I see you're a photographer. Any good?" Before he can answer she continues, "My name is Alexandra Marlowe—Alex for short. I'm from New York in the good ol' U. S. of A." She wears a mid-calf-length, pleated, white skirt; a white blouse with a collar trimmed in blue; a long, open, periwinkle-blue weskit; circular blue hat with a narrow white brim, and white and blue, T-strap, heeled sandals.

Pryce takes her hand and looks into her blue eyes. "My pleasure. I'm Trevor Pryce of Peking, China—the center of the universe. And, yes, I'm a talented photographer. I make an exceptional living as a photojournalist. In fact, if you're Alex Marlowe, executive editor of Composite Press Service, you frequently publish my photo-articles. And your checks are prompt and they always clear. In fact, my photo-article on warlordism in northwest China, which was published two years ago in your magazine *Copy*, earned the Mollenhoff Award for Investigative Reporting."

Alex, taken aback by her *faux-pas* at missing Pryce's name, smiles with embarrassment and says, "Of course! My apologies for not recognizing your name right off. Your long English vowels should have been my first clue. My treat for the next round."

Alexandra Marlowe is the daughter and only child of Samuel Marlowe. She is proudly handsome in her early thirties, tall, and with long, shapely legs, a fair complexion, short, shiny blonde hair, a wide, sensual mouth that smiles easily, and a decent figure. Her indigo-blue eyes are vibrant and coquettish, and her husky voice has an easygoing resonance. Alex earned an MBA from Columbia University and currently is the chief operations manager and the brains behind her father's business empire.

The combo begins to play Cole Porter's "Night and Day" in a slow Latin beat. Alex takes Trevor's arm, slips off the bar stool, and says, "Let's dance. This is my favorite song."

"Alex, I'm not presentable. I have a three-day-old beard, my clothes are filthy, and I'm exhausted."

"Don't be a fuddy-duddy. Dance with me." It is clear from her manner that she is accustomed to getting her way.

He bows clownishly and responds mockingly, "Yes, my lady. As you command."

They glide smoothly to the rhythm of the music. The combo segues into Porter's "Love for Sale." After a brief musical introduction, the chanteuse moans the lyrics, "Love that's fresh and still unspoiled. Love that's only slightly soiled. Love for sale."

Alex moves closer to Trevor, and with a faint, wistful smile says softly, "Once more, please." She flutters her eyelashes at him. As they gently sway to the erotic music, she puts her cheek on his shoulder. Trevor draws her a little closer and senses a simmering passion in her.

As the music fades, they return to the bar, with the pulse of each beating a little faster. Alex says with a miniature smile, "Come up to my suite."

After a brief pause for its erotic implications, she says, "I want Dad to meet you. Have dinner with us. We're working on an enterprise that ought to pique your interest as a photojournalist. If it develops, as we suspect it might, then you'll have a fantastic story of great historical import. Composite Press Service will cover your expenses, and will pay handsomely for your photographs and text. In return, you will let us publish the story exclusively."

Preparing to leave, Trevor picks up his camera bag, puts on his hat, and says, "You've stirred my curiosity. Tell me more."

She replies in a cool, businesslike voice, "Can't. Not until you make a firm commitment."

Trevor, slightly puzzled at the sudden transformation of Alex's demeanor, says, "Fair enough. I'm going to my flat to get this grime off, change into clean clothes, and in general make myself presentable. Deal?"

"Deal. It's Suite 412. We'll expect you about seven. Please don't dress for dinner. We're not that formal." She tosses down the last of her whiskey and in a mocking English accent says, "Cheers. Here's to good times. Toodle-oo and all that, ol' chap."

A couple of hours later, Alex answers Trevor's knock on the door. Trevor flashes a large smile. "Good evening." He wears a tan sport jacket and white linen trousers. His crisp white shirt is set off by a subdued red tie with a neat Windsor knot.

Alex opens the door wide, stands aside, and says, "Please come in. Nice to see you again. I want you to meet my father." She is dressed in an ankle-length, coral-colored dress with a full flaring skirt and short sleeves. Her only jewelry is a pair of discreet pearl earrings, small but obviously of the highest quality.

The Marlowe suite is large and sumptuously decorated in subdued colors. The furniture is in the ubiquitous art-deco style seen in most modern public buildings in Peking. There are vases of fresh roses scattered around the room. A few excellent Chinese paintings hang on the walls.

Trevor and Alex approach Marlowe. "Dad, I'd like you to meet Trevor Pryce. Trevor, this is my father, Samuel Marlowe. However, everyone calls him Marlowe."

"My pleasure, sir," says Trevor.

Marlowe does not offer his hand. "Sit down, young fellow. Have a bourbon with me. So you're the man Alex has been babbling about. And we publish your work. I'm impressed."

Marlowe is fifty-seven years old, a large, tall man with a harsh face, curly, brown hair with white-tinged sideburns, and sharp, blue eyes. A self-made multimillionaire, he owns a vast empire of corporations that include gold mining, heavy-duty manufacturing, telecommunications, petroleum, and publishing. This evening, he wears a dark-blue, double-breasted sport coat and plain white trousers with a knife-sharp crease. "I understand that you're here to find out about the deal that inveigled me to Peking, and to decide if you want to get involved. Do I have this correct?"

Trevor settles comfortably in a tan, leather armchair and responds in a friendly tone, "Yes, sir, that's correct."

Alex pours three stiff bourbon drinks in tall, thin, crystal glasses. "Ice or soda, anyone?"

Trevor responds, "Soda, please."

Marlowe grunts, "Straight." He leans toward Trevor, looks him square in the eyes, and says "It's fine with me if you tag along. I suspect that there's one hell of a story buried in the mumbo-jumbo I've gotten so far." He takes a long drink of his whisky. "Here's the deal, Pryce. If you get involved, the terms Alex mentioned earlier apply. If you bow out, what you hear and see here tonight is strictly confidential. Do I have your word?"

Trevor has been evaluating Marlowe and what he has learned so far is tempting. Satisfied, he says, "You have my word."

A faint smile flickers across Marlowe's face. "Understand, my avocation is the acquisition of rare, and usually expensive, Oriental artifacts. And I have the resources to pay for them. Yesterday, for instance, we were in Shanghai to inspect a Tang Dynasty jade figurine collection called 'The Songs of the Emperor.' It was too stunning to resist." On the coffee table is an open teak box. Inside, couched in soft velvet, are twenty-four statuettes from the eighth-century court of Emperor Li Longji. "He picks up one of the pieces, looks at it carefully, and then shows it to Pryce. "The delicate carving on this jade highlights intricate details not seen on most figurines of this period.

Notice that each face is unique. It's a beautiful collection that I'm proud to own." He returns the figurine to the teak box.

Alex interrupts, "A refill, Dad?"

"Of course." He takes a long swallow of his newly poured drink. "Pryce, let's get down to business. At eight thirty an antiques dealer named Wuhan Wei-kuo will be here with a piece of jewelry that he says is 'a magnificent work of art whose history is written in blood.' He has devised some elaborate story connected with this item, and he implies there are several more pieces from the same source in a collection somewhere in China. None of this is defined yet, but getting to it apparently involves some travel. A few years back, I purchased a beautiful Song Dynasty tapestry from Wuhan. I had it authenticated by two experts. I must admit that he projects a mien that does not engender confidence. Do you know this fellow?"

Trevor sips his bourbon, leans back, gives a quick side look at Alex, and says, "I've worked with Wuhan on two photographic projects. He paid my fee on the spot with genuine coin of the realm. Nonetheless, I would suggest that you ought to be cautious. I'm not sure he's totally trustworthy. His reputation in the trade is slightly shady."

Alex, concerned, entreats Trevor, "Why? What do you know about this fellow? What are the details?"

"Rumor has it that he's been involved in several 'irregular' sales of valuable ancient Chinese artifacts. I've heard that he was having serious trouble with the Antiquities Department for dealing in contraband. What is he hawking this evening?"

Marlowe frowns, "I don't know. He's not saying. He'll have the jewel with him. Meanwhile, let's eat. I've ordered porterhouse steak dinners, rare, with all the trimmings."

彼時,

At eight thirty sharp, there is a soft rap on the door. Alex opens it and says to the Chinese man standing there, "Good evening. You must be Mister Wuhan. Please come in. We're expecting you."

Wuhan gives a bow, "It is so. Thank you." His smile has a hint of mendacity. He is dressed in a white, doubled-breasted, Western suit, with a white, silk shirt, a cream tie, and white shoes. He has a white Panama hat in his hand.

Alex escorts Wuhan to a divan. "Mister Wuhan, you know my father." Wuhan bows and says, "Good evening, Mister Marlowe." He quickly surveys the suite with furtive eyes.

Gesturing to Trevor, Alex says, "I understand that you and Trevor Pryce have worked on photograph assignments."

Wuhan casts a wary look at Pryce. *Why is that photographer here? No doubt to interfere with my plans.* "Yes, indeed. I have had the pleasure to work with Mister Pryce on several successful projects."

Price acknowledges Wuhan with a slight nod.

Wuhan returns it with a shallow bow and, without invitation, sits on the divan.

Alex asks, "Mister Wuhan, would you care for some tea?"

Wuhan smiles softly and says, "That would be most kind."

Alex brings a tea service from the suite's kitchen and pours the tea into a thin, white, porcelain cup decorated with a black dragon, then places it in the accompanying saucer.

"Thank you, Mistress Marlowe." Wuhan takes a gentle sip.

Marlowe, anxious to find out what Wuhan has for sale, rises, goes to the divan, stands in front of him, and says, "Enough of this polite chatter. Let's get down to the business. Let's see this 'art work,' or whatever you've got."

"As you wish, Mister Marlowe."

Placing his cup carefully in its saucer on the coffee table, Wuhan reaches into his inside coat pocket and withdraws a chamois pouch. He holds it in his right hand for a few seconds for effect. Six eyes are focused intently on the pouch. With deliberate care and showmanship, he withdraws the Romanov necklace and extends it to full length. The bright light from the standing lamp beside the divan hits the jewels and is reflected throughout the room.

The room is silent. Finally Marlowe says, "That's a beauty. What is it?"

Wuhan, with deliberate articulation, says, "This necklace is the wedding gift that Queen Victoria sent to her favorite granddaughter, Princess

Alexandra of Hesse-Darmstadt, when she married Czar Nicholas II, Autocrat of All the Russias." He pauses for dramatic emphasis. "This necklace is from the missing Romanov collection."

A wary silence suffuses throughout the suite. Shortly, Marlowe exclaims, "Well, I'll be damned!"

Alex, in her most contemptuous voice, demands, "Mister Wuhan, that is a most incredible claim. What proof have you?"

"Mistress Marlowe, I offer my professional expertise, and the well-know fact that this necklace belonged to Empress Alexandra." He withdraws a folded photograph from his inside coat pocket and hands it to Alex. "My assistant copied the original image from a Russian publication with her Graflex camera."

Alex reviews the photograph. "Indeed, the Empress is wearing this necklace."

Marlowe stares at Wuhan. "How do we know it's genuine and that your story is true? 'Fess up, Wuhan. Any deal we might make is in the balance. If you try to hoodwink me, I'll wring your yellow neck. Are we clear?"

"I understand quite well, Mister Marlowe. I have learned from an unimpeachable source that indeed this necklace belonged to Empress Alexandra and that it was her wedding present from Queen Victoria."

"What unimpeachable source? Where did you get this bauble?"

"I am reticent to reveal confidential information about my business. I am sure you understand."

Alex leans forward, puts her elbows on her knees, rests her chin in her palms, and with keen perception evaluates the sparring between her father and Wuhan.

"I don't understand one damn bit," growls Marlowe. "Where did you get it, and from whom? If you can't answer forthrightly, we will have no more dealings. Am I clear?"

Wuhan, faced with Marlowe's ultimatum, decides to prostitute his principles for the greater profit. "Very well. A few days ago, an impoverished White Russian offered to sell this necklace to me. Based on my informed inspection, and review of several photographs of this piece in Russian Treasury publications, I vouch for the authenticity of this necklace." Wuhan sips tea to gather his thoughts and form his following response carefully while not revealing too much of his secret.

Alex interrupts, "Get on with it."

"For reasons I do not understand, the Russian had firsthand knowledge of the necklace's provenance. He convinced me that he was acting as an agent for the rightful owner, and that there are more jewels from the Romanov collection here in China. We completed the transaction, and that's the last I saw of him."

Marlowe is silent. He looks at Alex, who does not respond.

Breaking the silence, Wuhan continues, "I assure you that your interest will be well served by purchasing this necklace. Our previous transaction has been beneficial for you, is that not so? May I suggest that you inspect the inscription on the clasp?" He hands Marlowe the necklace and a ten-power loupe.

Marlowe goes to the standing lamp, puts the loupe to his right eye, and scrutinizes the clasp. After a few seconds he says, "I don't understand what I'm seeing. It's gobbledygook." He hands the necklace and the loupe to his daughter. "Alex, take a look. What do you see?"

Alex examines the clasp. "I see the hallmark of Rundell, Bridge & Company, the London jeweler who made most of the jewelry for Queen Victoria. There is also the Russian double-eagle, royal crest and an inscription. I make it out to read 'Alexandra.'" She looks closely at the emeralds and diamonds. "The gems are genuine, and very fine." She hands the loupe to Wuhan and the necklace to her father. "I suspect that this necklace is authentic."

Marlowe says gravely, "Wuhan, who else knows about this necklace?"

"Only one person on my staff, and she is sworn to secrecy."

"You're sure?"

"Absolutely, Mister Marlowe."

"Make damn sure."

Marlowe returns to his chair. While making up his mind, he stares at the necklace, and feels the surface of the jewels and the platinum setting. He turns it over several times. Wuhan has seduced him. Marlowe takes a healthy swallow of his whisky and glares at Wuhan with a deep frown and narrowed eyes. He looks to Alex, then returns his gaze to Wuhan. He extends his right hand with his index finger pointed to the antiques dealer and growls, "What's your price?"

Wuhan, not intimidated, flashes his thin, professional smile. "I offer this queen's ransom to you for only 250,000 pounds sterling."

A stunned silence permeates the suite. Then, almost in unison, there are incredulous gasps from Alex and Trevor. Marlowe, unflinching, continues staring at Wuhan. His eyes narrow slightly. For a few seconds, Alex sits silently, coldly rigid, with a stony face and flashing eyes. Then she leaps out of her chair, puts her hands on her hips, and cries, "Dad, that's almost a million dollars. That's ludicrous!"

She addresses Wuhan sharply, "Mister Wuhan, you cannot be serious." She turns to Marlowe. "Dad, this is nonsense. Return the necklace to Mister Wuhan, tell him goodbye, and let's go home. I'm sick of China and all these dealings of yours. I want to get back to my office and my job. I want to see the Yankees play the Dodgers at Ebbets Field, to eat a hot dog covered with mustard and dripping with relish. I want to sleep in my own bed. It's time we quit this collecting compulsion of yours and return to our business back home."

With her adrenalin surging, she returns to her chair and finishes her drink with a couple of deep swallows. She covers her face with her hands and rocks her head back and forth, hoping to clear her anger and frustration.

Marlowe remains stoic and silent, still fondling the necklace. He does not look at Alex.

Wuhan is somewhat taken aback by Alex's outburst. "Mistress Marlowe, I assure you that I am quite serious. What I ask for this spectacular necklace is far below market value. And please recall that the buyer of this necklace will have the opportunity to purchase the remainder of a truly fabulous and historically significant collection of Romanov jewelry."

Before Alex can respond, Marlowe growls in his last-and-best-offer voice, "One hundred fifty thousand pounds sterling. Either accept my offer or get out."

Wuhan sits quietly while he calculates his profit and the odds that Marlowe's offer is in fact firm. He sips some tea, then carefully places the cup back on its saucer. His mind whirls; there is a large profit to be had when

Marlowe purchases the jewelry at Yumin. He realizes that he has no other potential buyers ready, and that if he accepts Marlowe's offer, his profit will be 95,000 pounds—not what he expected, but handsome nonetheless. He looks at Marlowe with his faint, professional smile and says, "I accept."

Suddenly, the tension in the suite evaporates. Alex slumps in her chair, mentally spent. Trevor gulps down his bourbon and makes mental notes of tonight's proceeding.

Marlowe whips out his checkbook, quickly writes a check, and signs it with a bold flourish. He hands it to Wuhan and says, "My check is drawn on the China National Bank and Trust Company, Limited. It will clear on your presentation."

"Thank you, Mister Marlowe. You drive a hard bargain. I am confident that there will be no problem with your check. The bank's senior cashier, Mister Chan Sen-tao, is an old friend."

Marlowe, satisfied that he has made a propitious bargain, lets the necklace slip into the chamois pouch, and stuffs it into his coat pocket. He turns to his daughter. "Please refresh our drinks, and make them potent. I need a boost."

"Dad, you're an idiot! Our country is in a deep depression. We could have used those funds to expand our business, add machine tools, help the economy, and create jobs," Alex exclaims as she refills the glasses.

"Don't worry about it. We have plenty more in accounts and investments all over the world."

He tosses down a large gulp of whisky and says to Wuhan, "What's the deal with the remainder of this Romanov collection? How many pieces are there? Who has them? And where are they? I need straight answers, Wuhan."

Wuhan calmly sips his tea. Then, he sits forward on the divan and replies, "Your questions are relevant. Unfortunately, I do not have answers to all. Here is what I do know. Again, I assure you that my source is totally reliable. I am led to believe that this Romanov jewelry collection is extensive. And it is in the possession of a community of expatriate White Russians living in a distant province of China. As I understand, the owner needs funds and the Romanov jewels are for sale at a very reasonable price." He inches forward in his chair and takes a sip of tea.

"There is more." Wuhan pauses and, for dramatic effect, flashes an intriguing glance at each person in the room. Then, he focuses with intensity on Marlowe. "The major piece in the collection is the fabled and missing Saint Catherine's Crown!"

This startling revelation causes Alex and Trevor to snap to alert. Alex sings out, "Saint Catherine's Crown? It can't be! The Bolshevik government has buried it in one of their vaults. It's been missing since Saint Petersburg fell in 1917."

Marlowe, with his interest seriously piqued, says to Wuhan, "Alex is right. No one has seen or heard of Saint Catherine's Crown since the Bolshevik Revolution. How can you be sure the Whites have it? How and why is the crown in China?"

"I am confident that my source's information is true. He came from the place where the crown is held, and he was close to the custodian." He pauses to let his audience absorb the import of this revelation. "I assure you, Mister Marlowe, that the crown is in China, and it is in the possession of the White Russians. It is a mystery how it came to be with them. My source did not reveal its history," he lies. "Even under some special inducements, he would not say. Unfortunately, he expired of a heart attack before we could continue. Nonetheless, my reputation stands on, and much of my resources are committed to, the veracity of my statements."

Marlowe grumbles, "Perhaps. What're the logistics and your take?"

Wuhan responds, "First, may I suggest that we form a mutually profitable scheme to recover the Romanov jewels and Saint Catherine's Crown? I will make all travel arrangements and pay all upfront expenses. Accordingly, my finder's fee is twenty-five percent of the purchase price. Naturally, you will reimburse all my expenses with an added fifteen percent handling fee."

Marlowe simmers for a time, then bellows, "Twenty-five percent is outrageous. The usual finder's fee is twenty percent. What's got into you for such thievery?"

Wuhan responds patiently. "My fee is higher than normal because the potential of this deal is extraordinarily high—much higher than our usual transactions. Naturally, I will accompany you as your guide, and to protect my own interest, as it were. Also, I am taking considerable fiscal and physical risk."

Marlowe takes another swallow and growls, "I need more information before I agree to your terms. No more games, Wuhan. Out with it!"

Wuhan, in an uncharacteristic response, says, "Mister Marlowe, we must be courteous and trusting if we are to conclude an auspicious arrangement."

Marlowe grunts, "Very well."

Wuhan continues. "Required is a trek into an interior province some considerable distance from Peking. At the moment, I am not at liberty to say exactly where the cache is located. However, I will reveal its exact location after we confirm this deal, and when we are within a day's travel from the Russians. You understand that I must protect my own position."

With an incredulous expression, Alex interrupts Wuhan's spiel. "Dad, Wuhan is spinning fairy tales. Don't fall for it. Let's go home."

"Alex, do you realize the fiscal gain and dynamic political impact if we were to recover Saint Catherine's Crown and the Romanov jewels? It would be the coup of the century." Marlowe addresses Wuhan, "Before I decide to accept your scheme, I must at least know in what province this cache is hidden. Otherwise we have no deal."

"Very well, Mister Marlowe. The Russians are in Sinkiang Province, close to the Soviet border. I will reveal exactly where in due time."

"Sinkiang! That's over two-thousand miles to the northwest," Alex, rising, proclaims with blazing eyes and flaring nostrils. "It's in one of the hottest, driest, largest deserts on our planet. Warlords, bandits, and renegade soldiers control most of the area between Peking and Sinkiang. There are Japanese patrols in the area. And there's no controlling Chinese government anywhere near there. So far as I know, there's no reliable transportation to Sinkiang Province. This scheme is foolhardy."

Wuhan responds, "Mistress Marlowe is correct. However, I will make arrangements that will ensure a strong measure of safety."

Marlowe does not move for several seconds. His face is devoid of expression. His eyes narrow as he slowly and carefully evaluates Alex's concerns, the potential rewards, and the intoxicating thrill of the adventure. He gets up from his chair, wanders to a window, and gazes down at the activities in Tiananmen Square. He drinks his whisky with deliberate, small sips, and scratches where it does not itch.

After a few minutes, Marlowe returns to his chair, sits on the edge, and tells Wuhan, "All right. Let's go. Should you attempt any type of fraud, I'll personally send you to your ancestors—head first."

Alex, resigned, says in a cool, collected voice, "Dad, this is a huge mistake. But if you're determined to go, I'll do what I can to support you—this one last time." She adds with a forced smile, "I mean it."

Trevor remains silent as he observes the drama unfolding before him. He wonders what kind of adventure he has agreed to join. *Is Marlowe wacko? But Alex is enticing. What's the real story behind Wuhan's narrative? Is it a lark? Or is it the story of the century?*

Wuhan rises and goes to Marlowe to shake his hand to conclude the deal. "You have made the correct decision, Mister Marlowe."

Marlowe does not rise nor does he shake Wuhan's extended hand. "My word is my bond. You know that."

"Very well. Because of the hazards Mistress Marlowe has detailed, it would be prudent to charter an aeroplane to take us to Sinkiang. I suspect that it will take me a week to ten days to complete all the details."

"Naturally," murmurs Marlowe. In a more positive tone, he tells Alex, "Please show Wuhan to the door. We have concluded our business."

There is a restful quiet in the suite after Wuhan leaves. In a minute or two, Alex picks up the glasses and the tea tray and returns them to the kitchen.

Marlowe finally speaks. "Another whisky, please. I have lots to think about." After Alex returns with his drink, he gulps it down. He points his index finger at Pryce and demands, "Are you with us, Pryce?"

"Absolutely! This caper has the potential for the scoop of the year."

Satisfied, and in an exuberant voice, Marlowe tells Trevor, "What the hell. The night is early. And you two young people ought to be out having fun, not moping around with me. Trevor, get out of here and show Alex a good time!"

36

Sun Yat-sen Aerodrome, Peking
10 September 1933

On the parking ramp at the China National Aviation Corporation terminal, a Ford Trimotor's right engine ticks over slowly. Two experienced CNAC pilots are in the cockpit. It is not yet dawn, but the eastern horizon shows a dim line of light. A low fog obscures the ground. Standing near the open door of the aeroplane are Marlowe, Alex, and Trevor. They are restless, obviously waiting for someone.

The Trimotor was Ford Motor Company's first venture into the aviation business. It entered commercial service in 1926. Cruising speed is about a hundred miles per hour. Range is 1,500 miles. A typical crew on a scheduled airline flight consists of pilot, copilot, and nurse-stewardess. The Trimotor's payload is twelve passengers with forty pounds of luggage each. On today's charter flight, there is no stewardess. Passengers sit on wicker seats covered with down-stuffed pillows, aligned along either side of a narrow aisle. There are no amenities en route: no meals, no heating, no cooling, and only minimal soundproofing. On board are four dozen bottles of water, a few snacks—canned and dried meat, canned peaches, and soda crackers, and five light blankets.

Marlowe fidgets aimlessly with a notepad. He wears grey knickers, a light tan jacket, and a golf cap. Finally, his frustration overcomes him. Standing with his legs apart and his hands akimbo, he frowns and barks to no one in particular, "Where the hell is that damn Wuhan! He's late. Over an hour." He slaps his legs in frustration and looks into the fog, hoping to see Wuhan's automobile approach. "How the hell can we find that crown and those Romanov jewels if we don't know where we're going? Why do we have to wait until we're airborne and close to the Russians? That Chinaman is playing his hand far too close for my liking. If he tries to double-cross me I'll wring his swindler's neck." After a brief pause, he mumbles, "Perhaps I was too hasty to agree to his scheme." He paces back and forth beside the aeroplane and considers canceling the trip. On reflection, he growls, "But damn, I want that crown! No matter what, I must have it."

Alex takes Marlowe's right hand, looks encouragingly into her father's eyes, and says, "Calm down, Dad. Wuhan wouldn't miss this opportunity for such a large profit and a chance to recover his expenses. I suspect that he's playing a game with us, to stoke your passion for the treasures in Sinkiang." She wears sharply tailored, loose-fitting, khaki trousers and a long-sleeved, white, silk shirt under a khaki jacket. A white, monogrammed, silk scarf hangs loosely around her neck. There is a sand-colored beret cocked on the right side of her head.

Marlowe, calmed by Alex's assurances, responds, "You're right, darling daughter. My acquisitiveness all too often overwhelms my good sense—what there is of it."

Alex looks at him with wide eyes and a reserved brightness at this unprecedented admission of one of his character shortcomings.

As the wait extends, Alex and Trevor engage in meaningless banter. In the two weeks since they met, they have become close friends, and then passionate lovers.

Alex appreciates Trevor's dedication to his work and his stable, sensible approach to life. He is fiercely independent, and she has found his word to be steadfast. After a lifetime of coping with her mercurial father, and years of managing his business interests while he pursues his obsession for elusive treasures, she feels enormous comfort in the company and arms of a man who is not only gentle and affectionate but completely trustworthy.

The previous men in her life came mostly from the business and social worlds into which she was born. There was about them a stolid, self-satisfied sameness that quickly bored her. Trevor's ambition and intense curiosity intrigue her. His manners are polished. And he exudes a compelling physical strength, sharp mental acuity, and sexual energy that arouses her latent passion. She knows that a large part of her feeling for him is based on inordinate lust. But she also feels a deepening emotion that might be love. Even as she jokes with him in the Peking dawn, she wonders, *Is Trevor the man with whom I will spend the rest of my life?*

At first, Trevor was attracted by Alex's sophisticated allure, polished beauty, and unbridled passion, but soon he found her keen intelligence challenging. And he discerned that beneath her air of competent strength, there was a vulnerability that touches him deeply. He had no intention of getting serious with Alex or abandoning his carefree, bachelor life. In the International Community, there are attractive females aplenty who seek his company, but with Alex he finds more than the casual satisfaction of his sexual desire. He senses a growing bond between them that both troubles him and gives him a sense of peace that he has never experienced before. Their joking appears casual and meaningless, but their eyes reveal a growing connection that transcends their passion.

Trevor is dressed in moleskin riding breeches and calf-length, laced boots. His Jacaru hat is cocked at a jaunty angle, and his bush jacket is draped over his shoulders. His camera bag rests by his travel bag on the ground by the aeroplane's door. He withdraws the Leica and snaps photographs of the Trimotor and his two traveling companions. The faint glow of the early sunrise and the low ground fog that engulfs his companions and parts of the aeroplane present a delicate tableau made for an award-winning photograph.

"Alex," Trevor says as he takes several close shots of her, "as I mull over the dynamics of this treasure hunt, the key questions are, who brought the Romanov jewelry and Saint Catherine's Crown to China? Why? And how did these treasures get to Sinkiang Province?"

He returns his Leica to the camera bag. "The last I knew, Saint Catherine's Crown was on display in the Hermitage Museum in Saint Petersburg, and it had been there for over a hundred years. After the

Revolution, I assumed that the Bolsheviks had confiscated it. Now we hear that the crown is in China, and may be for sale. This is a mystery of singular import. There's an explosive story here."

"And that's why you're going with us. True? Or do you have more tawdry reasons?" Alex teases him flirtatiously. She continues in a serious tone, "Naturally, you'll file your photo-story with the Composite Press Service, as we agreed."

"Naturally," says Trevor with a touch of irony in his voice. "But it'll cost you plenty."

She responds coyly, "I have plenty."

"I'm counting on it," he murmurs with a lecherous grin.

Time passes without Wuhan. The eastern sky brightens. Alex looks at Marlowe and then at Trevor. "Trevor, let's go for a walk," she says. "I need to move around. This waiting for the unknown is spooking me."

"Right. Let's walk." He takes her arm and they stroll casually down the parking ramp behind the Trimotor churning the low-lying fog.

After a hundred strides or so, she says warily, "Even though I agreed to support Dad on this odyssey, I have reservations. This entire scheme doesn't smell right." She turns to Trevor, her face tight with anxiety. "We've committed to this trip based on Wuhan's story and nothing else. And he's a dubious source at best. As you said, he frequently makes shady deals, and he's under investigation by the Antiquities Department. I just don't trust him."

Trevor stops and takes both her hands. With deep empathy he says, "Alex, I understand your concerns. I have some myself. We're gambling on another man's game. Discretion dictates that we call off this flapdoodle, return to the hotel, have a healthy shot of whiskey, and retire to my flat." He pauses to reestablish his believability. "So far the stakes are minimal."

He begins to lead Alex back to the Trimotor. He continues with a brighter voice, "On reflection, however, consider the munificent reward and the return on your investment if this deal is legitimate. Wuhan may be shady, but he's no fool."

"All that's true. It's a noble goal. Your story has Pulitzer Prize potential and will boost our circulation manyfold." They continue to walk without speaking. Just before they reach the aeroplane, she says, "But I don't like to gamble when I don't know the rules of the game."

Alex approaches Marlowe, who is still fuming at the tardy Wuhan. With appealing eyes, she says, "Dad, I'm having second thoughts. Let's reconsider going on this wild goose chase. It's based on unsubstantiated information from a Chinaman of dubious character."

Marlowe stops pacing. He looks at Alex with a questioning frown. "What's got into you?"

She stands in front of Marlowe with her feet firmly planted and her eyes intense. "Dad, this trip is nonsense. Let's go home. We're both apprehensive about Wuhan. I don't trust him. He's too secretive. Too equivocal. And, I suspect, duplicitous. We don't know where we're going in Sinkiang, or what conditions we'll meet en route, or what we're going to find when we get there. There are too many unknowns. It's dangerous and foolhardy. God forbid that we should wander into Soviet airspace. Dad, give it up."

Marlowe responds emphatically, "I hear you. You're correct on all points. Nonetheless, we're going—if Wuhan ever gets here. I'm after that crown so I can stuff it up Gaspar Wickham's bulbous nose. With all his international clout, he's bested me all too often and I want satisfaction. Wuhan be damned!"

Defeated, Alex retreats to Trevor, conveys Marlowe's response, sits on her luggage, and runs her hands over her face to ease her tension. Trevor rubs her shoulders in understanding and support.

A few minutes later, a limousine appears through the fog and slows to a stop close to the aeroplane. Wuhan Wei-kuo steps out, a leather briefcase tucked tightly under his left arm. With short, precise steps, he walks past Marlowe without any acknowledgement. He wears a dark brown, double-breasted, Western suit, and atop his head is a well-worn, gray fedora.

Marlowe snaps, "You're late. You're over an hour late. I don't cotton to tardiness. No more, do you understand?"

Unperturbed, Wuhan merely glances at Marlowe as he climbs aboard the aeroplane. He steps into the cockpit and hands the pilot a note with the destination for the day—the aerodrome at Lan-chow in Kansu Province. It is some 730 miles west—about nine hours in the air. Then he turns to leave the cockpit, without speaking.

The pilot calls after Wuhan in Mandarin, "Wait! I need more information about this flight." He is clearly perturbed. "All I know is that our final destination is somewhere in the far western interior of China. Giving us only the destination for today is not satisfactory. For safe and proper planning, I must have the complete schedule for this trip."

Wuhan stops and turns to face the pilot. He gazes at the man impassively, but says nothing.

The pilot gestures with his right hand and upturned palm toward Wuhan and continues, "I must fly by Visual Flight Rules for our entire trip. There are no navigation aids in central and western China. What weather reports we can get are unreliable. We will have to navigate over uncharted terrain. Without more information, this entire flight is in serious jeopardy."

Wuhan's stare is faintly amused and disinterested. "You have been well paid—in gold. We will take off shortly." He turns and leaves the aeroplane and returns to the limousine.

He opens the door and assists Black Orchid out of the vehicle. She takes Wuhan's right arm and they walk toward Marlowe's party. She is dressed in *derrière*-tight jodhpurs; a low-cut, form-fitting blouse; an unbuttoned leather jacket; highly polished leather boots; and a wide-brimmed, Australian-style, bush hat. Her long, black hair flows around her shoulders. Her only makeup is a small blush of lip rouge. She walks as if her strides were erotic ballet moves.

Marlowe and Trevor gape in awe. Alex turns blistering red. Now she is certain that this trip does not smell right. She blurts, "Who is that?"

Trevor mumbles appreciatively without taking his eyes from Black Orchid, "An Oriental female, I reckon."

Alex elbows him in his ribs and hisses, "Close your mouth, you lecher."

Recovering, Marlowe quizzes Wuhan, "Who is this woman? What's she doing here?"

Wuhan responds, nonplused, "This is Yen Hei-lan, 'Black Orchid' in your language. She is my niece, the daughter of my sister. She is my ward and my assistant."

Black Orchid smiles politely at the travelers. As she climbs into the Trimotor, she takes quick notice of Trevor. Inwardly, she vows to have her way with him.

Wuhan continues, "Black Orchid will travel with us because she will help protect my interests. And she has exceptional language skills. Most important, it is she who discovered the location of Saint Catherine's Crown— very propitiously, I might add. To restate, I will keep the location of the Romanov jewels and the Crown private until it is appropriate to inform you."

Marlowe, flustered by the checkmate, wags his index finger at Wuhan and cracks, "Damn you! You'll get your twenty-five percent and that's all." He turns and points to the door of the Trimotor. "That woman is not part of our deal. You Chinamen always have tricks up your sleeves. I don't like it one bit. I want to know where we're going. You've chartered this flight, but I've paid for it in gold. I have the letters of credit, not you. I'm in charge. Understand?"

Wuhan, entering the Trimotor, turns to Marlowe and says quietly, "It is so. Shall we depart?" Wuhan takes the starboard front seat, behind the copilot.

With Wuhan winning the opening gambit, the other travelers silently climb aboard and take seats at random. The crack of the other two engines starting, and the thunder of all three engines catching full throttle, preclude any conversation. On the copilot's hand signal, the passengers buckle their safety belts.

Shortly after the tension of the takeoff abates, Wuhan mentally reviews his scheme to exploit for himself the Romanov jewelry and Saint Catherine's Crown. These treasures will be his booty, and his alone. *After landing at Wu-su, the pilots will service the Trimotor and wait for the passengers to return later that day or the next.*

We will travel in the automobile I have hired for the trip to Yumin. I will return solo with the treasures, and tell the pilots that the other passengers are returning via the Soviet Union. He pats his briefcase and feels the persuader— a small Mauser 9-mm semi-automatic.

About halfway through their return from the lamasery, he will shoot the driver and Black Orchid. At gunpoint, he will abandon Marlowe, Alex, and Trevor in the Takla Morku Desert.

At Peking, he will empty his safe, store the Russian treasures and his valuable inventory in a knapsack, and catch the train for the port of Tanggu. He will board the Panamanian-flagged tramp steamer bound for Portuguese Goa on the Indian subcontinent, where he will disappear into its large Chinese community.

37

Ordos Desert, Shansi Province, China
10 September 1933

The Ford Trimotor drones over the Ordos Desert in central China. The engines' roar is loud, with a synchronous, numbing rhythm. Cold air wails through the leaky compartment. It's a 730-mile flight to Lan-chow, about nine hours flying time. Several hours outbound, the passengers are quiet, sprawled uncomfortably in their wicker seats, lost in their own thoughts. Shortly after takeoff, Trevor had distributed the blankets, and most of the travelers are wrapped in them.

Marlowe is in a funk. He does not lose gracefully, especially to Chinamen. He's puffed up and slouched down in his seat with his arms across his chest. Wuhan is tranquilly asleep. Black Orchid is reading the poems of the seventh-century Tang poet Ts'ui Tun-li. In the last seat on the port side, Trevor is preparing the historical introduction for his story about Saint Catherine's Crown.

Across from Trevor, Alex is studying a Composite Press Service financial report. Occasionally, she steals furtive glances at Black Orchid. Alex wonders about this obvious *femme fatale's* real purpose. She has an eerie feeling that Black Orchid is gravely dangerous and poses an intrinsic hazard to the entire expedition, but she shakes off this feeling and returns to her reports. Soon her wariness gets the better of her, and she silently vows to scratch out Black Orchid's seductive eyes if she gets anywhere near Trevor.

Alex looks across the aisle at Trevor. He is engrossed in his writing. Alex leans over and taps him on the shoulder. She whispers into his ear, "What're your thoughts about our Oriental female traveler? Skip the beauty and sexy manner. I can see that all too clearly."

Trevor sticks his pen in his shirt pocket, "So can I. The Orient in all its splendor."

Alex realizes that he is teasing her. She forces a carefree smile and lightly punches him on the shoulder. "Shut up, you degenerate libertine!"

Trevor laughs at her snappy riposte. "Say again your question, please."

"I heard what Wuhan said about Black Orchid, but I'm skeptical. She's clearly out of place on this trek, and from my perspective not needed. Is there something I'm missing? Is her presence here part of the game's rules that we don't know or understand?"

Trevor does not respond immediately. After some mental consideration, he says, "You ask cogent questions, but I don't know the answers. However, I reckon that Wuhan's explanation is accurate, and I don't suspect anything else. She is his assistant. I believe it's that simple. The fact that she's erotically beautiful is incidental. Wuhan should have had her tone it down a bit for this trek to the outback of China. But he didn't, and we have to live with it."

"Trevor, you are naïve to a crippling fault when trying to understand and deal with women. I suspect that your silk-stocking upbringing in merry ol' England has skewed your perspective. But no matter. I'll guide you." Alex stares at him with flashing eyes. "My first guideline is, stay away from that woman or I'll stab you in your unfaithful heart and elsewhere. Get it?"

Responding mockingly, Trevor says, "Yes, my lady." He grins. "But she is a knockout."

Alex punches him again. "Damn you. Get serious and try to understand my concern. I have really dreadful feelings about her."

"I understand. There's nothing more I can add." There is a long pause as Trevor tries to change the topic. "I'm working on the introduction to my article regarding the crown. May I read what I've written so far?"

Alex sighs with resignation. "Sure, let's hear what you have." She slumps down and stares at the back of the seat in front of her. She doesn't believe that Black Orchid's presence is benign, but she understands that the woman's exquisite beauty is distracting both her father and her lover. And certainly she's jealous. In the days and nights she and Trevor have spent together, she has developed a deep emotional bond with him. Perhaps she is falling in love with him. She considers this possibility. Yes, she reckons, Trevor is someone she could spend her life with. And until she knows for certain, she doesn't want to see him stolen away from her by a conniving seductress.

Trevor starts his story about the crown and the events of the times. "In June 1762, Catherine Friederike Auguste, Princess of Anhalt-Zerbst, in concert with officers of the Royal Court, staged a coup to overthrow her enfeebled husband, Czar Peter III Romanov. Court lackeys assassinated Peter in a staged brawl, orchestrated at Catherine's behest. On 28 June 1762, the archbishop of Saint Petersburg crowned her Czarina Catherine II. As befitting the ruler of all the Russias, then the largest empire in Europe, Catherine ordered that a crown of immense beauty be designed for her. After her death on 17 November 1796, the nobles of her court dubbed her 'Saint' because of the sweeping social and economic reforms she had introduced. She modernized Russian society and made Russia an important force in world affairs." Trevor concludes, "That's it so far."

"That's wonderful," mutters Alex. "I'm sure you'll have a great story." She's still miffed that Trevor is so cavalier about Black Orchid and does not share her concerns. However, she's a shrewd enough woman to realize that jealousy is a poor weapon in trying to keep a man's loyalty, and that most men pay little heed to a woman's intuition. She resolves to keep her own counsel and remain vigilant about their guide and his voluptuous niece. She turns to Trevor and favors him with a brilliant smile.

As the Trimotor drones on, Trevor takes a break from his work. He retrieves his Leica and takes a few photographs of the passengers in whatever state they are in. Alex gives him a deep frown, then a wide smile for several snaps. He focuses on Black Orchid.

Seeing that Trevor is photographing her, she removes her blanket and flashes her most enticing smile. He snaps a dozen photos of her as she changes expressions and position. He gives her a wave of thanks. Alex notices this subtle interplay. *Or is it foreplay?* she wonders.

Trevor returns to his seat and secures his camera. He too wonders about Black Orchid's role in this adventure. Although he has assured Alex that he is not concerned about the obvious *femme fatale*, he does have reservations about her. Black Orchid's beauty and sexuality seem too intentionally flaunted, for what reason he does not yet understand. And her sudden, unannounced addition to their company hints at some nefarious ploy of Wuhan's. Her presence makes him uneasy, not because he is tempted by her erotic allure, but because she adds yet another element of danger to an expedition already fraught with risk. He reasons that his best chance to discover her role in this trek is to play along and see what happens.

Black Orchid had noticed that Trevor responded to her playful poses with several extra photographs. She definitely likes what she sees in Trevor and wonders if she has successfully contrived the first step in her planned seduction. She flashes him a coquettish smile to entice a conversation. Moving to her side, Trevor tells Black Orchid about the story he's writing and what a great journalistic coup it will be. She listens quietly, nodding occasionally. When he finishes, she responds with a charming smile. "I am confident that you will write a prize-winning story."

The touchdown at Lan-chow is smooth and uneventful. After the passengers have deplaned and their luggage has been unloaded, the pilots take advantage of the overnight layover to do mandatory maintenance on the plane—checking oil levels and adding several quarts, straining the petrol, and filling the tanks. They examine the hydraulic lines and control cables, then wipe the propeller blades with thin, oily rags to spot and feel for nicks and cracks. Finally, to ensure that the Trimotor is airworthy for tomorrow's flight, they complete a comprehensive "walk around."

Meanwhile, across the dirt road from the hangar, the travelers are ensconced in a hostel—a shabby excuse for lodging compared to the elegant Hôtel de la Chine in Peking. The rooms are small, with nondescript, time-worn furniture. Ripped wallpaper hangs from the thin walls. A squeaking ceiling fan rotates slowly. The communal commode is down the hall. There are no facilities for bathing, except for an empty rain barrel with a ladle, outside the back door.

After picking at a tasteless meal in the shabby dining room, Marlowe invites Alex and Trevor to his room to share a bottle of bourbon. Too exhausted to talk much, they drink the whiskey straight and quickly, while they reflect on today's flight and wonder what Wuhan has planned for tomorrow. There is nothing to do but wait and see, and stay alert.

Alex and Trevor return to their respective rooms and say goodnight dispassionately. She is still somewhat annoyed at Trevor for his attentions to Black Orchid.

Before Trevor can undress, he hears faints taps on his door. It's Black Orchid, in red, satin pajamas and a white, gossamer-thin, embroidered, silk peignoir. She asks, "Please come into my room across the hall and help me adjust the bed. It does not feel right. Perhaps the head ought to be raised."

Trevor enters her room and fiddles awkwardly with the bed. Black Orchid leans over to assist him and he can smell her perfume, a sultry, deeply erotic scent. She takes his palm and slowly moves her cupped fingers across it.

"I'm in your debt," she purrs. "Thank you so much. Goodnight." She sees him to her door.

Through the thin walls, Alex hears most of the interplay in Black Orchid's room. Because it is over so quickly, she knows that nothing serious has happened. However, Black Orchid's flirting is not so subtle. *Did Trevor catch the Chinese woman's sexual innuendos? Will her female wiles ensnare him? Probably,* she figures. She wonders how Trevor could be so stupid and feckless. "Men!" she snorts.

地震。

The Trimotor hums along over a low mountain range in the Tsaidam Desert. Today's destination is Ko-erh-mu in Tsinghai Province, a flight of about 500 miles—a seven-hour flight with a strong headwind. The aeroplane drones on and on. The desert below stretches endlessly, a monotonous expanse of dun-colored earth broken only by low hills, scrub brush, and scattered small villages in the rare savannahs.

The passengers sit dully, weary after a nearly sleepless night in the bug-infested hostel. At breakfast over tea and rice gruel, Black Orchid had tried a few enticing smiles on an unresponsive Trevor.

After boarding the Trimotor, the passengers stolidly resume the seats they had occupied the day before. Wuhan settles comfortably into a deep slumber, apparently unperturbed by the discomfort of the previous night or the rigors of the journey.

Marlowe frets restlessly, torn between boredom and eagerness to reach the end of this trying journey. His efforts at breakfast to elicit information from Wuhan about their destination were met with only a thin smile. Now he fidgets, looks out the window, and mutters to himself, "Damn Chinaman, full of secrets. Leading us into who knows what." He tries to read a book about the history of the Romanovs but quickly abandons it. *Damn desert. Who the hell would live in this godforsaken place? Damn it all. What does that crown look like? What's it worth in the good ol' U.S.A.?*

Trevor picks up his notebook and continues drafting the introduction to his intended article on the recovery of the Romanov jewels. His eyes are dull with fatigue. Work for him has always been a comforting distraction, a way to escape boredom. Soon after the Trimotor is airborne, he is engrossed fully in his writing.

Alex had slept restlessly, bothered by the bugs, the heat, and the hard cot. Her mood is foul, but she's far too wise to reveal her annoyance or her continuing concerns about Wuhan and Black Orchid. While tossing on her hostel cot, she had decided that further discussion of her worries about this trip would be pointless. Not only were her father and Trevor dismissive of her suspicions, she decided that she might learn more about the intentions of their Chinese companions by remaining silent and watchful. As for Trevor, his apparent disinterest in Black Orchid's attempts at flirtation over breakfast had reassured Alex, for now. But how long will he be able to resist? There is no doubt that Black Orchid is powerfully enticing. After glancing at Trevor, hard at work, Alex resumes her study of the corporation's financial reports.

As the cool air whips through the aeroplane, Black Orchid wonders just how serious Trevor's affection for Alex is. On reflection, she concludes that their relationship is just so much animal passion. *I am going to have that man no matter what, she vows. He will become mine and Alex will fade into nothingness, even if I have to facilitate it.* She slumps into her seat to devise a strategy.

Alex, ever watchful and keenly attuned, drops her reports and stares at Black Orchid. Perhaps through some sixth sense, she seems to understand the other woman's scheme for Trevor, and she pledges to thwart Black Orchid's prurient plan. Her affection for Trevor may not yet be real love, but it is powerful and has captured her soul. *Trevor isn't the greatest man with whom I've kept company, but damn, he's got something that has me entranced. I can't compete with Black Orchid's beauty and her exotic mien, but I can offer Trevor sincerity and true affection. My love is not for sale. It's true love that's only slightly soiled.*

Trevor, now asleep, is blindly oblivious to the dynamics between Black Orchid and Alex.

The Trimotor drones on into the western sky.

卫

Yumin, Sinkiang Province, China
11 September 1933

I t is early evening. The sun has slipped below the horizon, and the autumnal twilight is quickly fading. Maria Pavlovna staggers into the infirmary, grabs for a chair, misses, and collapses unconscious to the floor. Nikolai Danilov picks her up and places her on a bed. He feels her forehead. It is burning hot and her skin is clammy. He calls to Doctor Markov, who is working in his office next door. "Doctor, I need you in the infirmary. Maria Pavlovna is here and is seriously ill." Danilov takes her vital signs—blood pressure is seriously low and temperature high at 103.8 degrees.

Markov enters, notes Maria's vital signs, and performs a physical assessment. He sees a few red spots on her face and chest. Markov has seen these symptoms in the army, and his preliminary diagnosis is typhoid fever. He frowns deeply. Turning to Danilov, he says, "I suspect that she's infected with typhoid. Start an intravenous solution of dextrose in saline. Lay a cool compress on her forehead. I'm going to fetch our elector."

Anna is in her office focusing on accounts and a pile of administrative details—skills she learned long ago working for Maxim Fedosov. Markov enters her room without knocking and without greetings. "Anna, we have a serious medical problem. Come with me to the infirmary. Maria Pavlovna Pirogov is gravely ill."

Anna rises quickly. "I'm coming." She reaches for her cane and follows Markov. Maria is covered with a thin, wool blanket, yet she shivers, and her body is soaked with perspiration. Danilov raises her head with his left hand and tries to get her to sip water from a glass in his right hand. She is semi-conscious, weak, and unable to drink. He returns her head to the pillow and replaces the cold compress on her forehead.

Markov speaks in a low voice, "Anna, I must emphasize how serious this situation is. I suspect that Maria has typhoid fever. Her temperature is very high, and there are bright, rose-colored spots on her chest. Her other symptoms also indicate typhoid." Markov removes the stethoscope from around his neck and makes another assessment of Maria. "Anna, I am not certain that Maria is suffering from typhoid. I would need a medical laboratory staffed with competent technicians to confirm it. Nonetheless, we must treat this disease as if it were."

Danilov interrupts, "I've checked our pharmacology book. We need the medicine chlorophenol to treat this disease. We have none here, and without it there is no hope."

Anna bends down to look at Maria and feels her heated forehead. She straightens and looks fearfully at Markov. It is apparent that Maria is dying, and there is little that they can do to help her except to ease her suffering with cold compresses.

Markov pauses to form his next comment. "Anna, this medical event is much more complicated. Our entire community is at risk. We face a typhoid epidemic. This disease is caused by bacteria in our water or food. We must have chlorophenol to protect everyone in the community, and we must find and isolate the source of the disease. Otherwise, our community probably is doomed."

After a short pause, he continues in an urgent voice, "We must notify Chen of this danger and tell him the protocols to prevent this disease from spreading—boil all drinking and cooking

Anna finds a chair, carefully lowers herself into it, and hangs her cane on its right arm. "Markov, your counsel is well taken. I will send a rider to the Kirgiz immediately. Nikolai, attend to it and call a general meeting. We need to ensure that all our citizens know Markov's instructions."

"Right away, Elector."

Anna's eyes gaze on Maria. *How shrunken she seems.* She wonders how Maria, who has always been such a bastion of strength, can now be so racked by this terrible illness. Anna takes several deep breaths to calm herself, and to mentally reviews the seriousness of their plight. In a minute or so, she asks, "What are our options?"

"There's only one option," Markov replies. "We must get the medication, or Maria dies."

Pained to hear Markov's words, Anna massages her withered left arm to ease her angst. Slight pain shoots through her left shoulder. Eventually she replies, "But where do we find this medicine? Wu-su? Are there other pharmacies in this dreadful desert that would have it?"

Danilov responds quickly and with clarity, "When I was in Wu-su two weeks ago to purchase medical supplies, there was no chlorophenol in the general store's formulary. In fact, there was not much medicine of any kind in stock. Aspirin, iodine, castor oil, and laudanum were all that I could purchase. Unfortunately, the proprietor does not expect any supplies for several months. My educated guess is that there are no towns within Sinkiang Province where we might find chlorophenol."

Anna reflects on an alternative. "Let's have Chen send a shortwave message to ...." She pauses as she realizes that they do not know where to send such a message. The only surety lies in Peking, and even if the radio transmission is successful, it will take far too long for the chlorophenol to arrive.

Anna looks at Danilov dispiritedly. "Where then? Do we have to go to Ko-erh-mu in Tsinghai Province eight hundred miles to the southeast? That's too far. Without reliable transportation it might take a month or more for the round trip. That's not reasonable. We need the medicine now."

Markov quickly checks on Maria. Her temperature is rising dangerously. He knows that soon it will increase to the point that it will cause brain damage, dehydration, heat prostration, and finally death. He turns to face Anna. "The only possible nearby source of chlorophenol is in the dispensary in Duzhba, in the Union of Soviet Socialist Republics, only eight miles away. If not there, we're lost."

Anna sits back in her chair, stunned that the only viable option she has lies in the Bolsheviks' Soviet Union. After weighing the alternatives, Anna cautiously says, "I'm fearful of the dangers involved in sending one of our people on a trek into the Soviet Union. A couple of years ago, I heard through dissidents that the NKVD had arrested and executed our contacts and their families in Duzhba and Bolotnoye. We won't have any support across the border." As she tries to reason through her dilemma, her conversation with Ivan Vachot, the stationmaster in Duzhba, pops into her mind. His Bolshevik-detecting nose finally failed him.

Anna asks Danilov to fetch Pirogov. *Kirik needs to know about his mother's illness*, she reasons. *And I cannot make this critical decision by myself.*

In a couple of moments, Pirogov rushes into the infirmary. "My God! Is it true, Anna? My mother is dying from typhoid?" He goes to Maria, and feels her brow. Instinctively, he quickly pulls his hand away. "Oh, Mother," he whispers. His face is stiff with shock and sorrow.

"Yes, Kirik," Anna responds gently. "It's true. We have typhoid in Yumin." Anna is nearly overcome by the terrible possibility that she will lose her beloved second mother, and that her dearest friend will lose all that remains of his own family. Struggling to control her tears, she briefs Kirik on the unfolding scenario. Then she says, "We need the chlorophenol now. The only source within reason is in Duzhba in the USSR."

Her thoughts continue, now aloud, "If we send a courier and he is captured, our entire community will be compromised. The NKVD will be ruthless in extracting information from him. On the positive side, the desert border in this outback of the planet is long and unguarded, and it's a fair gamble that there is no NKVD presence in Duzhba." She pauses as she evaluates the risks. "Kirik, what choice is there? We must have that chlorophenol, or else Maria and Yumin are doomed."

"No decision really. Of course I'll go. I'll risk anything to save my mother."

Anna gazes at Kirik's distraught face. Her dear, brave friend has never lost his courage or fierce determination to survive and protect those he loves. But in her heart she knows that Kirik is one more loss that she—and Yumin—cannot afford.

"Thanks for your offer, but I need you here." She places a gentle hand on his arm. "Stay with me."

Danilov volunteers, "Anna, I'll go to Duzhba, with your permission. I have medical experience and can communicate with the pharmacist."

Anna reasons to herself. *After sixteen years in exile and an arduous, toil-filled existence, we have shed most of our sophisticated manners. Now we look and act like everyday farmers scratching for a hardscrabble living. However, our language is still more polished in pronunciation and usage than the average Soviet peasant or the rough-and-tumble, Godless Bolsheviks. Nonetheless, I have no choice.*

With trepidation, Anna says, "Very well, Nikolai Danilov. You go. We are depending on you." With tension in her voice, Anna continues, "Your mission is critical, prudence is your guide." Then, in a somewhat lighter tone to boost his resolve, Anna says, "We will never recognize that villainous Bolshevik government and that odious abomination, the Union of Soviet Socialist Republics." She nods briskly. "It's too late today for you to leave. Start your trip tomorrow at daybreak. Return by nightfall. We will pray to Saint Nicolai for your success and safe return." She rises. "Come with me to my office. You will need rubles."

३९

Yumin, Sinkiang Province, China
12 September 1933

I t is a beautiful, late summer day. In the Yumin Valley, the altocumulus clouds are thicker than the day before, and the temperature has dropped two degrees. Riding one of the village's few saddle horses, Danilov begins his trek over the mountain pass. Today, he wears dark trousers, a white shirt, tan cap, and black boots. He carries a tan jacket and a two-pint canteen of water. He has safely buttoned his forged papers inside his shirt. As he exits the Yumin Valley and descends into the Takla Morku Desert, the ambient temperature rises appreciably. After two hours, he estimates that he has covered about five miles and has crossed the unattended border into the Soviet Union.

He spots a large rock outcropping overlying a shallow gully. Leaving his horse and climbing to the top of the rock, he scans the landscape to the west and south looking for any sign of border guards. There are none in sight. In fact, the area looks as deserted and desolate as the desert he has just traveled. He rests his horse in the shade of the outcropping and takes three or four deep swallows of water to recharge his body. In twenty minutes or so he resumes his ride, slowing his horse's pace to conserve energy for traversing the three miles to Duzhba village.

Entering Duzhba, he is amazed to see that it is a ghost town, not the village of several hundred souls that it was when he passed through seventeen years ago en route to Yumin. There is no attendant at the train station. No guards. No one. He wonders, *Does the train still service this worn-out burg?* He looks at the rails. They are shining, so he guesses that there must still be some train service to keep them from rusting. He wanders around and finally spots an old man sitting on the porch of a ramshackle, stone house.

"Good afternoon, Comrade," Danilov says with a broad smile. "What has happened to this town? Where has everyone gone? Who lives here?"

"That's a lot of questions for a stranger. Who are you? Where do you come from?" the old man asks.

Danilov is caught off guard with this quick riposte. He replies, after a second of reflection, "I'm on a survey for the People's Commissar for Agriculture and Husbandry. We're looking for suitable sites to establish collective farms."

The old man looks at Danilov quizzically and smiles. He knows Danilov is lying and is probably one of the White Russians he has heard rumors about. He does not care. With a snort, he says, "There's no place around here for farms, collective or any other kind. It's all dried up, the topsoil blown away, and the wells gone dry."

"What are you doing here? Are you the only occupant of this ghost town?" Danilov queries.

"I'm no occupant. I came down here a few days ago to visit my old home and retrieve a few personal treasures." The old man stands and pulls a portrait of a middle-aged woman from his kit. He shows it proudly to Danilov. "My wife for forty-two years. She died last year of typhoid. Can you believe it? Typhoid! In this modern Soviet state." He looks at the portrait for a few moments, looks up, and says, "I'm waiting for the train to take me back to Bolotnoye."

"My sympathies," says Danilov as he looks carefully at the portrait. "A fine-looking woman." He points to the abandoned train station. "So, you're saying that the Bolotnoye train still services Duzhba?"

"That's correct—if that drunken old Bolshevik engineer can actually get the train here. If he's not too inebriated, the train ought to be here most any time. After twenty years operating this train with his brain soaked in vodka, I wonder how he and that dilapidated train survive."

Danilov realizes that his only choice is go to Bolotnoye to get the chlorophenol. With sorrow in his heart, he knows that Maria will die that evening or the next day. He also knows that the welfare of the entire Yumin community depends on his success. He wonders how he will endure the five-hundred-mile train trip and whatever dangers lie ahead for him in the Soviet Union. No matter. There is no decision. No debate. He must go.

The pair starts walking to the station. Danilov says quizzically, "I don't understand. If there are no passengers or freight, why does the train make the round trip to this ghost town?"

They find a rickety bench in the crumbling station and sit. The old man looks at Danilov with waggish eyes and responds, "In our glorious socialist state, the People's Commissar for Transportation in Moscow has decreed that all trains will maintain pre-Revolution schedules."

Leery of criticizing the state, Danilov responds, "That's interesting."

Knowing that he must abandon his horse, Danilov rides it back to the edge of town where they entered. He pours his remaining water into his cap and lets the horse drink. Then, he turns its head toward the direction they came from, and slaps it on the rear. The horse gallops headed for home.

Later that evening, the Bolotnoye train passes the station. The engineer gives a perfunctory wave and takes the one-coach train about a mile farther down the tracks to enter the wye switch and reverse its direction.

Danilov asks the old man, "Where is the stationmaster, and what is the cost of a ticket?"

"No cost. There's no one here to sell tickets. Just get on and go. Your first question is more complicated. You're asking about Ivan Vachot, are you not? He got himself in lots of trouble. A couple of years ago, he tried to buy some equipment at the People's Community Store in Bolotnoye, and tried to pay for it with a foreign gold coin—something he ought not to have had in this glorious socialist state. The manager signaled to the NKVD guard at the entrance. Vachot bolted before the guard could make the arrest, and the guard cut him down with a blast from his submachine gun. No one knows where he got the gold coin."

Danilov makes a deep sigh and says nothing. He knows that the secret of their community is safe for now.

The train pulls into the station and comes to a screeching halt. The men rise and board. Conditions in the coach are worse than they were seventeen years before. There is no place to sit, so they squat among the rubbish on the filthy wooden floor.

The old man continues. "A few days after that incident with Vachot, the NKVD swept into Duzhba determined to find the source of that gold coin. They didn't find anything. But as a precaution to protect this glorious socialist state, the NKVD arrested everyone in town and sent them to a gulag somewhere in Siberia."

The train lurches to a start with spinning wheels, sparks flying, a couple of toots from the steam whistle, and the ringing of the bell. Danilov, jerked back, does not ask the obvious question.

His companion continues, "That day, I was out in the foothills hunting rabbits and missed the action."

They remain silent as the train lurches along to Bolotnoye.

Two days later, a weary, hungry Danilov approaches the entrance to the Stalin People's Hospital in Bolotnoye. Above the double doors of the entrance is an enormous color portrait of Josef Stalin with his extended right arm pointing to the hammer and sickle ensign on a dark-red background. As Danilov attempts to open the door, an NKVD guard approaches him.

"Your papers," he demands. The guard wears a dark-tan uniform and a pointed budenovka cap with a large red star centered on the front. He has the NKVD insignia sewn on his left sleeve near the shoulder. Danilov reaches into his shirt pocket and hands him the forged documents. The guard is a semi-literate peasant and cannot read all the text. But the photograph resembles the man he has challenged. To compensate for his inability to read Danilov's documents, he asks with hostile authority, "What is your name? Where do you live? Why are you here?"

Danilov answers the guard's questions with the fiction his documents support. His tone is curt and forthright. Assuming that this will end the matter, he asks directions to the pharmacy.

The guard is not completely satisfied and asks, "Who is your father? Did you join us in overthrowing the czarists? Where did you serve?"

Danilov is surprised and unprepared for these additional questions. He stumbles a bit and fakes plausible answers. The guard's suspicions are aroused by the way this man speaks—he is too polished for this area, and his demeanor smacks of the *bourgeoisie*. To alleviate his concerns, the guard sends the standby messenger to fetch his sergeant.

He tells Danilov, "Stay here. The sergeant will confirm your identity and your business."

In a few minutes, Sergeant Elena Vavilova arrives and the guard briefs her about Danilov. Upset by this summons from her administrative duties, Vavilova reckons that this is just another erroneous alarm from the dimwit private. The sergeant is a tall, husky woman with stony dark eyes that betray her Oriental heritage. To solve this contretemps, she asks Danilov a barrage of questions. "Why are you here? Where did you come from? What is your trade? What ministry do you work for? Where were you born? Who is your father? Are you a revolutionary? Did you serve in our glorious Red Army? What campaigns?"

Danilov does not have ready answers, and he is not skilled in subterfuge. He stumbles as he tries to make up plausible stories. Moreover, his language and mien seem too affected for these uncultured peasants. The sergeant is not a particularly bright woman, but she is a committed revolutionary and she is not satisfied with Danilov's answers. They are plausible, but his manner of delivery does not engender her confidence. True, he looks like a farmer. His hands are rough from field work, and his face is tanned from long exposure to the sun. But something about him does not ring true. She decides that she ought to take him to the barracks for the captain to interrogate.

Danilov has become ensnared in Stalin's omnipresent security apparatus. Since Lenin's death and Dzerzhinsky's untimely demise, Stalin has dissolved the Cheka and formed the Commissariat for Internal Affairs (NKVD). He has appointed Genrikh Yagoda its leader. Using the NKVD as his strong arm, Stalin focuses on purging his old Bolshevik comrades and the senior officers of the Red Army, fearful that someone might arise to challenge his leadership. Through an extensive network of informers and enforcers, Stalin has tight control over the everyday life of the proletariat.

Sergeant Vavilova brings Danilov to the office of Captain Leonid Prokoviev, the senior NKVD agent in this area. She briefs him about her suspicions. Prokoviev's office is lined with file cabinets, and his desk is littered with stacks of paper and file folders. There are portraits of Lenin, Stalin, and Genrikh Yagoda on the wall, and behind him is a large Soviet flag. The floor has not been swept in weeks.

Prokoviev is tall and slim, and his manner has a hint of savagery. He is a smart, dedicated revolutionary, and keenly upset at his posting in this desolate outpost in Siberia, and his failure to be promoted to major. He feels he deserves much better. In a battle with the Czech Legion near Vladivostok, a ricocheted *fléchette* ripped out his left eye, and others tore into his arms and torso. He was hospitalized for months and needed massive injections of morphine to ease his agonizing pain. Now he wears a black patch over his missing eye. And he is a morphine addict.

Prokoviev carefully peruses Danilov's documents and sees nothing to make him suspect that they are forged. Nonetheless, he has a faint, uneasy feeling about this fellow. He slowly walks around Danilov, looking him over. He is not sure what to make of this rough farmer—his papers are in order, his dress is appropriate, and his responses are reasonable but awkward. But something about Danilov triggers concern. At last Prokoviev commands the sergeant, "Search this fellow and let's see what we can find." The sergeant quickly finds the large stash of rubles taped to Danilov's chest. Prokoviev's suspicions are heightened. He interrogates Danilov with rapid-fire questions. "Who are you? Where did you come from? Why do you have so many rubles? Why are they hidden? Why are you going to the hospital? Are you ill? Under our socialist system all medical treatment is provided by the state. There is nothing to buy here in Bolotnoye. Perhaps a train ticket? To where?"

Danilov begins to stumble, and his answers become even more awkward. He contradicts himself and cannot look Prokoviev in the eye. He is intensely frightened and not sure that he can cope with this untenable and dangerous predicament. There is so much at risk. Danilov knows that he is not a brave man, but he resolves that he will do what he can to protect the security of his community at Yumin.

Prokoviev soon realizes that Danilov is a fraud and arrests him. He wonders if this fellow is a White Russian. He has heard rumors that there is a White Russian settlement in China somewhere across the border.

"Find out who the fellow is," he orders Sergeant Vavilova.

"Yes, sir," she snaps. The sergeant smashes Danilov in the nose with her fist wrapped in a thick cloth. He staggers against the opposite wall and falls down. Blood spurts out. The sergeant picks him up and delivers two quick, hard jabs to Danilov's stomach. He bends over and collapses on the floor. A stiff uppercut to his jaw snaps his head back.

The sergeant yanks Danilov to his feet. "Who are you? Why are you here?" A stiff right-cross to Danilov's right eye knocks him to the floor. Blood oozes from the damaged eye and it swells shut. The intense questioning continues with repeated blows to the eyes, chin, and stomach. Danilov does not answer. The sergeant holds Danilov upright and jams her knee into his testicles. He collapses and screams in intense pain.

"Why are you going to the hospital? Tell the truth! We know who you are."

Danilov remains mute.

Prokoviev decides to try a different approach. He goes to his desk, opens the top drawer, takes out a small box, and withdraws a syringe filled with six milligrams of morphine, his afternoon dose. Prokoviev picks up Danilov's chin so he can look into his eye. "The pain is intense, is it not? I can ease your pain and send you to paradise for several hours." He shows Danilov the syringe. "In this syringe are six milligrams of morphine. It's all yours. Just tell us what we ask. It's that simple." He instructs the sergeant to open Danilov's mouth and squeezes a drop of the bitter narcotic on his tongue. "Isn't that better?"

With the enticement of the morphine and under such intense physical and psychological pressure, a bloody, semiconscious Danilov cracks and mumbles through his distorted mouth what he knows about Yumin, including that Grand Duchess Anastasia is the elector of the community and goes by the name of Anna Bogrova.

Prokoviev smiles broadly and says, "Thank you. I'm sure that you feel better unburdening your soul to us. Am I not correct?"

Removing his jacket and pulling up his shirt sleeve, Prokoviev sticks the syringe needle into a vein in his own right arm and empties the narcotic into it. He smiles and says, "I feel better already. How about you?"

Sergeant Vavilova, with a hard, satisfied grin, picks up Danilov and slams him into a chair. She turns to Prokoviev, "Captain, clearly this fellow is one of those White Russians we've heard about."

"Excellent, Sergeant. No doubt. Shackle his legs in irons and put him in solitary confinement in the brig."

"Yes, sir." The sergeant leads a couple of privates as they haul Danilov to the brig, a small, nondescript, block building formerly used as a granary. They toss his limp body into the empty cell. The solid steel door has a small, iron-barred window. There is no furniture or toilet.

Prokoviev is astonished at his good fortune in capturing Danilov and the startling intelligence he has gained from the prisoner. This means that his long-delayed promotion is assured, and he knows that the 10,000 gold schilling reward is still viable. Smiling broadly, he telephones his superior, Colonel General Yakov Yurovsky.

40

NKVD Headquarters, Vladivostok, Siberia
12 September 1933

Colonel General Yakov Yurovsky, executioner of the Romanovs, is now the senior executive of all twenty-one NKVD battalions in Siberia. It has been fifteen years since his murderous rampage against the Czar and his family in Ekaterinburg in 1918. Yurovsky has no regrets about completing this extraordinary service for his socialist state. He retains his slim figure with daily exercise. Behind his bifocal glasses, his eyes have a remote and bitter look. His thinning, dark-brown hair has streaks of grey, and he wears a neatly trimmed mustache. Today he wears his summer casual uniform. The NKVD red and silver badge is sewn on his shirt over his left breast.

His office is a two-room suite. A teak desk and rosewood credenza occupy a large square room whose floor is covered with a Persian carpet. The walls and ceiling are painted pastel blue with dark blue trim. A row of metal filing cabinets stands against one wall, each containing mostly classified information and secured by a four-tumbler combination lock. The rest of the room is decorated in leather and chrome modern furniture and accessories. The Soviet hammer and cycle flag hangs limp on a stand behind the desk. The second room serves as Yurovsky's private quarters, with a sofa, bed, armoire, nightstands, and a full bathroom.

These days, Yurovsky attends to the stacks of paperwork on his desk. He shuffles massive piles of directives, reports of arrests and executions, requisitions for supplies, personnel transfers, and promotions—all duties about which he cares little. Frequently, he wonders if this is the reward for his long and faithful service to the Soviet state. He often longs for his free-ranging days as a junior officer, when there was action in the field hunting down enemies of the state. He fondly remembers feeling the warm metal of his pistol as it spoke, and the fierce fighting against Admiral Kolchak's White Army, the Czechs and their trains, and the Japanese at Nomonhan in Mongolia. The left side of his shirt is festooned with row upon row of heroic awards and campaign ribbons, including a gold star on his Hero of the Soviet Union medal, and the Order of Lenin badge. Age, the campaigns, and four battle wounds have honed his socialist zeal and intense devotion to the Communist Party.

Notwithstanding Yurovsky's success and rapid promotions, his overarching aspiration is someday to find Anastasia and bring her to Soviet justice. His failure to execute her at the House of Special Purpose in 1918 gnaws at his soul and, in his mind, is the one black mark on his otherwise sterling record. Comintern operatives, military *attachés*, and other secret agents are searching for her all worldwide, but she has disappeared without a trace. He wonders, *Did she die from her wounds? Could she be plotting to restore the Romanov Dynasty? Was she captured by the Japanese? Is she hiding in some Western nation trying to rally support against the Soviet government?* He quickly rejects this last option because the massive Soviet intelligence apparatus would know about it.

The telephone rings on his private line to field commanders and snaps him out of his brooding. He answers, "This is General Yakov Yurovsky."

The voice on the line is faint. "Yes, Captain Prokoviev. I can hear you. Slow down and stop rambling. Speak coherently, get to the point, and stop wasting my time." He muses that Prokoviev sounds as if he has just had his afternoon morphine fix. Yurovsky is tempted to terminate this vapid call, close his office, and head for the officers' club for some tension-relieving libations and a substantial venison dinner. And perhaps chat with that tantalizing new barmaid with her daring green eyes and voluptuous body. His hand is in mid-air, poised to return the phone to its hook. "What? Say that again!" He sits up straight, alert now, and paying close attention to his caller. "And say it slowly and coherently. Start at the beginning and skip no details. Make no mistake, Prokoviev." As he listens, his blue-green eyes open wide. His eyebrows arch. A large grin of satisfaction slowly creeps over his face. He moves to the edge of his chair and leans forward, as if he were ready to propel himself out the office door.

"You are convinced that the White is telling you the truth? Congratulations. You're positive that the White said that Anastasia is in Yumin? Grand Duchess Anastasia Romanov! Anastasia in China close to our border in Sinkiang Province? Amazing! Excellent, Prokoviev. I want to question this czarist myself." He pauses for a moment to collect his thoughts. "I'm leaving this evening on my train. We should be under way shortly. I'll be in Bolotnoye in two days. Keep our guest healthy and well entertained. As soon as I arrive in Bolotnoye, have my train switched to the feeder line to Duzhba, and have that line cleared of all traffic."

He buzzes his aide on the intercom squawk box. "Major Rodek, come here."

"Yes, sir," the major responds. In a few seconds he enters Yurovsky's office, walks to the desk, stands at attention, and gives a snappy salute. "Sir?"

Yurovsky stands. Exercising his unchallenged, despotic authority, he commands, "Major, call the railroad station and alert the NKVD officer in charge that I want my train ready to roll in three hours. I'm going to Bolotnoye, then onward to clean out a nest of czarists plotting to overthrow our socialist government." He has decided that, for the moment, he will conceal that his real motive is to arrest Anastasia. "Tell the stationmaster to clear all traffic on the Trans-Siberian Railway from here to Bolotnoye, and beyond if necessary. I want a clear track for my high-priority train."

Yurovsky does not have any intelligence on the Whites' order-of-battle. He rises and pounds the desk in frustration. "That addict Prokoviev has failed to extract from his prisoner any important military information. How many Whites are at Yumin? How well-trained and armed are they? What is their defensive deployment? What is their will to fight? That idiot! I must assume that the Whites are well-prepared and will fight. And what Chinese military forces are in the area?" He pauses for a few seconds. "If there are any Chinese, they probably are just border guards that are ill-equipped and poorly trained. Nonetheless, they could be a nuisance. I'll have my force equipped for a maximum effort to counter stiff resistance."

He snaps at the major. "Alert our battalion's duty officer and tell him that I want the duty-section company ready to move out in two hours. They are to have full kit—rifles with one hundred rounds and rations for seven days. I want five Pulemyat 7.7-mm machine guns with five belts each, and five 76-mm mortars with fifty rounds each. We'll need two coaches for the troops, three freight cars for our supplies, and three flatcars for our vehicles. And I want my executive coach fully provisioned—well-stocked bar, fresh linen, spotlessly clean. And staffed with my cook, steward, and my personal attendant."

He pauses briefly in his rant and continues in a softer tone. "What's her name? That barmaid with the green eyes and that amazing figure? See that she's aboard to help my staff."

Recalling himself to his mission, he returns to the business at hand. "No questions, Major? Excellent. Execute!"

41

Takla Morku Desert, Sinkiang Province
12 September 1933

By noon of the third day of flight, the Trimotor is high over the Takla Morku Desert. This is the final day of the long, energy-sapping trip. The previous day's flight was exhausting, and last night's hostel was even worse than the one at Lan-chow.

The aeroplane's destination today is the small dirt airstrip at Wu-su, about eight hundred miles northwest of Ko-erh-mu. Only Wuhan, the pilots, and Black Orchid know that Wu-su is today's destination and the termination of the flight section of their trip. Wuhan keeps this information to himself to ensure that Marlowe will not double-cross him. The farther they venture into the interior, the more confident Wuhan is that he has control of the expedition.

The Trimotor bores on in its twelve-hour flight of mind-numbing tedium. The roar of the three Wright R-975, 300-horsepower engines is deafening. Hot air, laden with fine sand grains, whistles through the leaky aeroplane, stinging uncovered skin and eyes. In defense, the passengers have wrapped handkerchiefs over their faces and donned sunshades to protect their eyes. Occasionally, irregular air currents jostle the aeroplane. The travelers are too exhausted and bored to do much except doze and gaze at the burning desert below them. The terrain varies from scrub savanna to barren hills, and from tall sand dunes to snow-tipped mountains.

Late in the afternoon, Wuhan makes his way toward the back of the aeroplane. He leans toward Marlowe, taps him on the shoulder, and says in a soft voice, "Excuse me, Mister Marlowe, for disturbing you. I should like to speak with you."

Marlowe, roused from a fretful sleep, opens his eyes, sits upright, and rubs his face to stimulate circulation. He grumbles, "What is it?"

"We are nearing our next landing place. Now I am prepared to reveal our destination."

Marlowe perks up and growls, "It's about time. Get on with it."

"Wu-su is our last stop in this tin monstrosity. We shall be in northwestern Sinkiang Province, close to the Soviet Union."

"God, is that where the jewels and crown are?"

Wuhan, with a faint smile at Marlowe's sudden eagerness, responds, "No. Please understand that Wu-su is not our ultimate destination. We shall spend the night in a hostel in this village."

Marlowe, now fully awake, interrupts, "Another night in a purgatory?"

Wuhan ignores the question and continues, "I have arranged for a luxurious automobile and chauffeur to be shipped by railroad to Wu-su. I am confident that you and your party will be satisfied. Tomorrow we will ride in it for the twenty-mile trip to Yumin."

Fatigued and impatient, Marlowe growls, "Where are those Russian treasures, you scoundrel?" He pauses, and then bursts out, "There, in Yumin?"

Wuhan, now immune from the barbarian Marlowe's intemperate outbursts, says, "Yes." He continues in a patronizing voice. "The treasures are there— in a long-abandoned lamasery."

Now on a keen edge, Marlowe snaps, "What lamasery?"

"It is a Buddhist lamasery that once prospered on the Silk Road. Now it is a thriving commune for White Russian expatriates who are hiding from the Soviet secret police." Wuhan moves closer to Marlowe's ear. "That is where Saint Catherine's Crown and the Romanov jewelry are hidden—somewhere in that White Russian lamasery."

Over the deafening roar of the engines, Alex hears only snippets of the conversation. Not knowing the details, she uses discretion and does not interfere.

Trevor, vitally interested, nonetheless reckons it's best to listen and learn.

Now that Marlowe knows the key details of his quest, he sits back in his wicker seat, and a faint smile tries to surface. It fails. "That's some tale, Wuhan. I'm counting on it being true in all aspects. Else, you may greet your ancestors sooner than you could imagine. Clear?"

"I shall answer all your questions forthrightly. Also, Mister Marlowe, I would suggest that the surprise of the century awaits you."

"No more intrigue, Wuhan. I don't like surprises. I want the crown first, then the Romanov jewelry. I want to get back to Peking. And be rid of you and all your surprises and intrigue."

Wuhan stoically responds, "I assure you, Mister Marlowe, I have no intrigue. The surprise of which I speak is truly astonishing. It is also to Mistress Alexandra's and Mister Pryce's strategic advantage, I would say."

Alex overhears. "What are you saying, Wuhan? What advantage?"

"Enough said for now. Soon you will see." Wuhan slips back to his own seat.

Marlowe and Alex realize that Wuhan will say no more and wonder why he has teased them. Surprises are not part of his twenty-five percent. Alex spouts, "What tomfoolery is afoot?"

Black Orchid catches snippets of the conversations and smiles inwardly. She knows of Wuhan's surprise and his planned perfidy.

The Ford Trimotor hits turbulent air over the Tien Shan Mountains. A strong crosswind embraces the aeroplane. The copilot motions to the passengers to fasten their seat belts—there is rough flying ahead. The wind velocity increases as sand from an intense windstorm swirls upward and lashes the Trimotor. Visibility is near zero. The Trimotor violently bounces up, down, and sideways in a wind gone mad. The pilots fight the manual controls to right the aeroplane as strong winds blow the Trimotor far off course.

Suddenly, the right engine sputters. The pilots try to adjust the fuel flow and the carburetor's air mixture, but to no avail. The engine coughs and dies. Sand has overwhelmed the filter and clogged the carburetor. The windmilling, two-bladed propeller creates intense drag, pulling the airplane abruptly to the right. The Trimotor does not have variable-pitch propellers to feather to decrease the drag. The pilots try unsuccessfully to straighten the plane to get it back on course and regain lost altitude.

Alarm spreads among the passengers. Marlow shouts, "What's happening? Can't these Chinese fellows fly this thing?"

Without warning, the center engine quits. The Trimotor noses down and pulls more strongly to the right. Below are the mountains and desert. The pilots cut the sputtering left engine to even the drag. After the incessant cacophony of the three roaring engines, the silence is deafening. Alarming! The only sound is the howling of wind through the porous fuselage.

Fear engulfs the travelers. Wuhan is hysterically terrified. He cries that his ancestors are casting devils at him. Black Orchid murmurs a silent curse— her ensemble is ruffled. Trevor and Alex squeeze each other's hands. Marlowe bellows, "We're going down!"

Trevor calls to the others, "We're crashing! Put your head between your knees."

"Oh, God!" shouts Alex.

Attempting a dead-stick landing, the pilots put the Trimotor in a shallow, nose-down attitude. However, with the flight characteristics of a flat rock, the aeroplane loses altitude too rapidly. The desert looms as the Trimotor gains velocity in its descent. The pilots, in a concerted effort to decrease the aeroplane's rapid rate of descent, pull back the control columns to raise the nose and make a belly landing on the open desert. They cut all electrical power to prevent fire.

The Trimotor hits the desert hard, knocking off the wheels and skidding violently out of control along the desert floor. The passengers scream, shout, and cry. Suddenly, the Trimotor plows nose-down into a narrow, dry wash with steep walls. The center engine smashes into the cockpit, killing both pilots instantly. The sudden jolt loosens the bolts holding Wuhan's seat, and he is flung into the cockpit and engine. Seat belts prevent the other passengers from being thrown around, but flying debris hurtles around the passenger compartment, some smashing into the travelers.

The wind suddenly stills as the storm moves to the south. As the aeroplane settles and debris falls to the floor, the passengers sit up and look about.

"Where's Dad?" cries Alex.

"Curse this desert!" is Marlowe's response.

Trevor calls out, "Does anyone need help?"

Black Orchid's softly accented voice, seductive even in peril, floats through the dust. "Take my hand and help me." Then weakly, "I'm all right."

Not hearing from Wuhan, Trevor slides forward to see how he and the pilots are doing. He sees the carnage and realizes that both pilots are crushed to death. Wuhan is unconscious and has a long, deep gash in his forehead. Blood oozes out of the wound. From the position of Wuhan's body, Trevor realizes that he must have several broken bones and internal injuries. Feeling the vein in Wuhan's neck, Trevor finds a weak pulse, and notices that his breathing is very shallow. Wuhan is alive, but there is nothing Trevor can do for him now.

The passengers negotiate the uphill tilt of the aeroplane to reach the rear door. Trevor pops the door opens and Alex spills out, a short drop to the desert floor. She's bruised and cut superficially, but not seriously hurt.

Black Orchid scrambles out behind her, bruised and disheveled, no longer the fashion plate and sex kitten.

Marlowe drops to the desert floor and emits a small cry as his right foot hits the desert at an awkward angle.

Last out is Trevor, bruised and cut. He moves quickly around the wrecked Trimotor to see if there is any danger of fire from spilled petrol and oil. There is none.

Trevor tells Marlowe, "Wuhan's seriously hurt. I need help to get him out of this wreck."

Marlowe has a turned ankle and can barely walk. "Can't. Not with this ankle."

Trevor turns to Black Orchid. "Let's get your uncle out of this smash-up."

She brushes the dust off her jacket as she looks at Trevor. Softly she says, "I will attend to my uncle." Black Orchid climbs into the passenger compartment and goes to Wuhan. She sees the gaping wound in his head. He is barely conscious and looks at her blankly. Her toxic hatred of her uncle simmers as she stares at the wounded rapist.

After a slight pause and with deliberate resolve, she takes off the slim leather belt on her jodhpurs and slips it around her uncle's neck. As she slowly chokes him with this improvised garrote, she whispers, "My revenge for those rapes when I was a child, for making me the whore of your clients, for the torture of my mind as your slave. For the life you denied me."

As she gives the final twist to the garrote, she whispers, "And for planning to abandon me and steal the Romanov treasures and the crown for yourself. I have known about your treachery from the time you left the forger's shop. Under persuasion, and the promise of a large bribe, that fellow told me of the documents he made for you. Unfortunately, he died too easily. The cobra struck too quickly and too deeply." Wuhan eyes' glaze with death and his breathing stops.

Black Orchid takes the forged travel documents from Wuhan's pocket and stuffs them into her jacket, then pulls her belt from around his neck and reinserts it into her pant loops. Rifling his briefcase, she removes the small Mauser and holster, and slips the pair into her valise. She stares at Wuhan's body. "Tell your honorable ancestors that Yen Hei-lan sends her reverent regards."

She makes her way to the door and jumps to the desert floor. Feigning sorrow and shock, she softly announces, "My uncle has expired."

Trevor looks at her in surprise. The old man was severely injured, he knew, but Trevor doesn't think he would have died so quickly. Puzzled, he climbs back into the aeroplane and sees that Wuhan is indeed dead. He examines the red marks around the old man's neck. Frowning and somewhat uneasy, he returns to the others.

The desert sun beats down. Marlowe, still disoriented, asks no one in particular, "Where are we? How do we get out of here?"

Alex responds, "From the beginning, I've had doubts about this trip. Dad, your ridiculous fixation on Oriental treasures to best Gaspar Wickham got us into this mess."

Trevor takes charge. "Hold on. No time or need for recriminations. Let's work as a team and do our best to survive in this God-awful place." He surveys the bleak terrain around them. "I reckon we're somewhere in the northern sector of the Takla Morku Desert. If so, Wu-su is in the general area, but I don't know in which direction or how far it is. Let's get organized. We should get our luggage out of the aeroplane and salvage anything that will be of help."

Within a few minutes, the travelers recover the useful items—their luggage, Trevor's camera kit, a tool box, blankets, tarpaulin, the water and snacks, and the wicker seats.

Trevor picks up his kit. Turning to the others, he says, "Pick up what you can and follow me. We'll make a camp in the wash under the aeroplane's wing."

Black Orchid seems oblivious to the seriousness of their desperate situation. She rearranges her clothes. Adjusts her hat. Sits on the desert floor, and waits for the others to decide on a survival strategy.

Alex asks, "Shouldn't we bury the pilots and Wuhan?"

Trevor says, "No. Folks, understand that we're in a grave survival situation. We can't waste the energy. Nature will take care of them. From this point on, we need to conserve all the energy we can. We have only eight quarts of water, our most important survival item. We'll ration it—one pint per day for each one of us." *Not nearly enough water. With this scorching heat, one person needs three or four quarts a day. We'll see.*

Marlowe spouts, "Let's get out of here. We'll get our directions from the sun. With some help, I can make it."

Trevor responds sharply, "That's nonsense. We have no clue where we are or in what direction to go. With our limited water supply, we'd not last three days in this blistering desert. Our best chance is stay here in the shade, be still and quiet, and hope that someone will find us. If not ...."

Gradually, the others begin to grasp the direness of their predicament. Moving slowly under the searing sun, they prepare their camp in the dry wash. To make a shade over the camp, Trevor instructs Alex and Black Orchid to help him rig the tarpaulin over the wash and attach it to the left wing of the aeroplane.

42

Yumin, Sinkiang Province, China
13 September 1933

Night engulfs the community. Anna tends to Maria Pavlovna as best she can with cool, damp towels on her forehead and cheeks. A few minutes ago, the community's priest performed the last rites for Maria. Anna wonders what has happened to Danilov. *He should have returned yesterday with the chlorophenol. What is keeping him?*

Doctor Markov takes Maria's temperature. It continues to climb. Soon she lapses into coma. A few hours later, Maria expires. Anna carefully closes her eyes and pulls the blanket up to cover her face.

Deep shadows of sorrow swell in Anna's eyes as she cries, heartbroken at losing her old and faithful friend. Woodenly, Pirogov takes Anna in his arms to comfort her and himself. Then his embrace tightens as he realizes that Anna is all that remains of his past and his family. In a few minutes, Anna recovers her composure and asks an aide to find a carpenter.

He arrives shortly. At first glance, he sees and understands the scenario. "Anna, I will build a coffin, and arrange for the burial detail to take care of Maria and put her to rest in the cemetery. I will craft carefully a Russian Orthodox cross for her gravesite."

"Thank you." Anna dabs her swollen eyes with a handkerchief. She is overwhelmed by these misfortunes. Nikolai Fedosov's long silence bodes ill because she knows he would never desert the community. Maria's death is extraordinarily painful. And why has Danilov failed to communicate or to return from what was expected to be a simple mission in Peking? Where is her mother's bracelet or the funds from the sale? These adversities and the pressure of leading this collapsing community torture her soul.

She addresses Markov. "I haven't heard from Nikolai. He's so responsible. I fear the worst. I expected him to return with the chlorophenol yesterday. If he does not return by tomorrow afternoon, we must conclude that he has fallen into trouble with the Reds. And if that is so, we're probably compromised and in danger from a Bolshevik raid. I have had such a foreboding for many weeks."

Markov exclaims with intensity, "Your grim analysis is correct. However, we have a more immediate concern. We must find out how Maria contracted typhoid. The only logical conclusion is that our water or some of our food is contaminated. But which? And how? We have no means to conduct tests to find out. More of us will likely fall ill with this disease if we don't take corrective measures now."

Anna slowly walks to the window and stares into the night, mulling her options. She struggles to breathe under the weight of her fear and sorrow. After a minute or two, she turns to look at Markov and Pirogov. With painful resignation, she says, "Our situation here in Yumin is untenable: typhoid, overpopulation, lack of adequate resources, isolation. Our society is eroding under these pressures. There is only one solution. We must disperse."

Markov sits at his desk, "Your reasoning is correct, and I concur. I've had the same thoughts for sometime."

Anna returns to her chair. Picking up her cane and tapping it lightly on the floor, she carefully forms her next thoughts. "I'm the one the Bolsheviks want. I should not endanger this entire community. I'll make arrangements to leave."

Pirogov immediately snaps out of his stony grief. "No, Anna!"

Markov understands her reasoning, but has serious concerns about her decision. With firm conviction, "Anna, you're too hasty. At this critical moment, we need your leadership. To abandon Yumin and send our people out into the world after so many years in the depths of China requires planning and work. Otherwise, it would be a disaster. Please reconsider."

Anna does not respond immediately. She closes her eyes and continues tapping her cane.

Markov does not intrude. From long experience he knows that Anna is developing a well-reasoned answer. Pirogov too is silent, his eyes focused intently on her.

After several minutes of silence, Anna opens her eyes and speaks. "I'm in a quandary. No matter what my decision is, I put our community in jeopardy. I'll decide later."

"You can count on my assistance."

Anna picks up her cane and paces across the room several times. Finally she says, "Doctor Markov, we've been associates and friends for many years. May I have your word that what I am going to tell you will be kept secret until I release you or you know that I am dead?"

"How grim, my dear Anna." After a short pause, "You have my word of honor."

It does not take Anna long to reveal the secret of the treasure, its ultimate destination in the Smithsonian Museum, and Pirogov's mission. "Doctor Markov, it's imperative that you and Kirik take charge of this community if I am gone, and oversee the dispersal of the population."

Without comment on Anna's charge, Markov says, "Please excuse me, Anna. I must scrub the infirmary with disinfectant."

"Yes, of course. Also, I suggest that you maintain confidentiality about my musings about dispersal. There's no need to frighten people more than they already are."

"I understand."

Supported by Pirogov, Anna returns to her small, spare room. It is furnished with a simple bed, a wooden nightstand, a desk, and a chair. Pinned to the wall over her desk is a photograph of her family that she clipped from a magazine. Worried to exhaustion, she sits at her desk and puts her head in her hands to ponder the fragility of this community. Her leadership role is a responsibility she did not seek but which was thrust upon her. Two of her closest friends have expired, and the community lies under multiple threats.

She raises her head to look at Pirogov, who stands stolidly in the doorway, tearless and cold, his eyes focused far away. For an instant, she feels a surge of sympathy and warmth for the person she trusts most. *He has lost as much as I have—his family, his home, his position, his career.* Her own pain almost suffocates her. *How much more loss can we bear?*

Intensifying Anna's disquietude is the lack of communication from Fedosov. For nine weeks after he left in June, his weekly telegrams arrived regularly at the Post and Telegraph Office in Wu-su. Then nothing. His report about his well-being and the sale of her necklace is long overdue. His last message said only that he had arrived in Peking and through contacts in the White community had decided on a strategy to sell the necklace. There were no details.

She cries out loud, "Maxim, where are you? Come home. We need you desperately."

43

Takla Morku Desert, Sinkiang Provence, China
13/14 September 1933

idnight, and bitter cold envelops the survivors' camp. It is their second night in the Takla Morku Desert. The sky is crystal clear, the wind is quiet, and the moon is full and high on the horizon. The survivors are asleep, wrapped in their light blankets, and huddled next to each other for warmth. There is no more bickering or recriminations. They are resigned to the seriousness of their plight, and even Marlowe has stopped grumbling and is helping where he can. What conversation there is focuses on their desperate circumstances. Under Trevor's guidance, they have rationed their meager water and food. Only Black Orchid still seems to be above it all.

A soft female hand covers Trevor's mouth. Black Orchid whispers, "Trevor, be quiet. Come with me. It is important."

Trevor awakes and mumbles, "What?"

Black Orchid withdraws her hand. "Quiet. Follow me. I have some pressing information for you."

Trevor crawls out of his blanket and says, "Why can't it wait until tomorrow? This is nuts."

Without answering, Black Orchid starts to walk down the dry wash, looks back at the perplexed Trevor, and beckons him with her arm.

Shrugging, the reluctant Trevor follows Black Orchid. She artfully swings her *derrière* in her tight jodhpurs. About a hundred yards from the camp, she rounds a bend, stops, and looks back at Trevor who is closing rapidly. She sits on the desert floor and leans back against the side of the wash, digging the heels of her boots into the desert sand. Trevor stands nearby. A full moon lights the scene. Black Orchid stares at Trevor. She has a burning desire for what she sees. Neither speaks for a time.

As the silence becomes awkward, Trevor says, "What is it you have to say that's so damned important?"

Black Orchid smiles provocatively and says, "Have a cigarette with me as we discuss how to save ourselves."

"I don't smoke. Get on with it."

"I normally don't smoke either, but these are special." From her jacket pocket she withdraws a gold-plated cigarette case. She withdraws a cigarette and offers another to Trevor.

"No, thanks. What's going on?"

Black Orchid lights the hashish cigarette and inhales several deep draws. Coquettishly, she blows smoke in Trevor's face. She rises just enough to take Trevor's hand and says, "Sit with me. I am cold."

Trevor shakes off her hand. "Say what you have to say and let's return to camp."

"Why are you afraid of me? I am not going to eat you. Let us be friends." She begins to unbutton her blouse. "If we are going to meet our ancestors, let's meet them with *élan*."

Trevor is no fool. He tells her, "Button up. We need all our energy to survive. I'm not playing your fool's game."

Rebuffed, she pouts, "Why do you spurn my invitation? Am I not beautiful? Desirable?"

"That you are, Black Orchid. You're the most beautiful, desirable woman I've ever seen. You're also the most dangerous and duplicitous woman I've ever met. I want nothing to do with you. But I'll work with you until we complete this journey—if we do. And then I'm done with you. Forever!"

Smarting from Trevor's rebuff and realizing that her overtures have been rejected with finality, she suspects that Alex is her problem. She muses that she can easily remove that obstacle. She wants Trevor for herself and will have him, one way or the other.

Trevor begins to walk back to the camp. "Wait, Trevor." She calls to him softly. "Treachery you do not know about infects this journey. I must have your oath not to reveal what I say. Do you agree?"

Trevor, caught off guard, responds, "What treachery? The only treachery I see is you. Wuhan was alive when I saw him. He might have made it if we'd gotten him out of the aeroplane. When I went back into the Trimotor, I saw those belt marks around his neck. I don't trust you and I won't agree to anything you propose. You're just weaving another of your schemes. For what end, I don't know, or care." Trevor walks away, not realizing what a dangerous enemy he has made. Black Orchid is not used to being refused.

Returning to camp in a rage, Trevor stumbles over a strut from the aeroplane. The racket awakes Alex. In the bright moonlight, she sees Trevor and Black Orchid coming into the camp. Black Orchid has not buttoned her blouse. Alex surmises that at last Black Orchid has had her way with Trevor. She is wounded that Trevor is so easily bewitched.

他時，

It's now three days after the crash. The sun is high in the sky and the heat is oppressive. The survivors sprawl haphazardly under the shade from the tarpaulin. The heat and a dry wind suck their mental and physical energy. They are thirsty, weak, and losing hope as dehydration symptoms increase alarmingly—disorientation, headaches, and dizziness. After a while, and without warning, the hot desert wind dies.

Trevor realizes that drastic action is needed if they are to have any chance to survive. They have only a day or two before they succumb. Now may be their only chance. Marshaling what energy he has left, he speaks hoarsely.

"Folks, our situation is desperate. With no more water, we'll last only one or two more days. Now that the wind has died, our only option is to burn the aeroplane. Perhaps someone will see the plume of black smoke and investigate. And it will be a fitting end for Wuhan and the pilots."

Marlowe mumbles, "You're going to destroy our camp?"

Trevor ignores Marlowe's comment. "Muster all the strength you have and let's get moving while the wind is down."

The survivors haul their gear out of the wash and away from the aeroplane. Trevor and Alex retrieve screwdrivers from the aeroplane's tool kit. With all their remaining energy, they jam the screwdrivers into the left wing. Eventually, they puncture a fuel tank. Petrol spills onto the desert.

"Get clear, everybody," Trevor warns. Backing off, he tosses a lighted match into the petrol, which ignites with a loud *whoosh*. An intense fire quickly erupts, engulfing the wrecked Trimotor—a funeral pyre for Wuhan and the pilots. Black smoke billows high into the still air. The survivors watch in awe and hope.

44

NKVD Headquarters, Bolotnoye, Siberia
15 September 1933

Colonel General Yakov Yurovsky slaps Nikolai Danilov's battered face. Danilov stumbles under the stinging blow. "Tell me your name again. Your real name! How many Whites are at Yumin? What weapons do they have? What are their defenses?" Yurovsky shouts. His eyes are narrow and flashing with rage. He slaps Danilov again, this time with all his strength. Danilov is knocked against the far wall and slips to the floor. Sergeant Elena Vavilova yanks him upright and stands him in front of Yurovsky.

The questioning continues. "Are you positive that Anastasia is there? Tell me about her, and you may return to your cell. I will order Captain Prokoviev to have a sumptuous meal for you and all the water you can drink."

This evening, Yurovsky is in his service dress uniform, a six-button tunic with collar tabs. On each tab are three five-pointed stars on a zigzag gold background with red piping all around.

Danilov, bruised, confused, and in intense pain, mumbles incoherently from his swollen mouth. Yurovsky nods to Captain Prokoviev, who takes the lit cigarette from his mouth and jams it into Danilov's cheek. Danilov utters a muffled scream and tries to free his arms from Sergeant Vavilova's vise-like grip.

Yurovsky puts his face a few inches from Danilov and whispers, "Tell me about the bitch Anastasia. She is in charge of the Whites at Yumin? Is she well? Married? How many children? Does she remember me?"

Danilov swings his head from side to side in what small defiance he can muster. Yurovsky ignores his negative response and continues, "I'm eagerly waiting to meet her again. I'm confident that she'll be delighted to see me now, as Colonel General Yurovsky of the NKVD. Perhaps she will give me a kiss." He roars, laughing at his own joke. Prokoviev and Vavilova give perfunctory chuckles.

Yurovsky demands, "Tell me about Anastasia, Danilov, and save yourself." He nods to Prokoviev.

Prokoviev holds the burning cigarette threateningly close to Danilov's left eye. Unable to resist the psychological and physical torture any longer, Danilov mutters that Anastasia is the elector of Yumin and now uses the name Anna Bogrova.

Yurovsky smiles sardonically as he hears Danilov's confession. He demands, "How did Anastasia survive my midnight party at Ekaterinburg?"

Danilov sputters, "We don't know. She has not discussed the regicide with any of us, and we have not asked."

Yurovsky recalls that July midnight in 1918 at Ekaterinburg—the highlight of his career, but as yet unfinished. Over the years, he has heard rumors and read unconfirmed reports of a White Russian commune in Sinkiang Province. But its exact location was unknown, and the rumors were too vague to justify any action that would violate Chinese sovereignty. Satisfied that he has all the information his prisoner can provide, Yurovsky draws his Tokaver 9-mm pistol and shoots Danilov twice in the stomach to let him die slowly and painfully. Yurovsky commands Sergeant Vavilova, "Get rid of this counter-revolutionary garbage."

Yurovsky sits on top of Prokoviev's desk and says, "Do you remember that there is a reward of ten thousand Maria Theresa gold schillings outstanding? It is yours if this White is telling the truth and I find Anastasia. As a rich capitalist, will you forget your socialist commitments?"

"No, sir. Absolutely not."

"Perhaps you will donate the reward to the Fund for Wounded Veterans of the Revolution? Eh, Captain Prokoviev?"

Prokoviev, caught off guard, responds with a stumbling answer.

"Yes, of course. You have made an excellent suggestion."

Satisfied, Yurovsky commands Prokoviev, "You and Sergeant Vavilova will prepare to join my company of NKVD soldiers. We are going to China. And Anastasia is mine."

Prokoviev objects, "Comrade General, we cannot go into China and kill and arrest people, some of whom will be Chinese citizens. It will ignite an international incident. Comrade Stalin is courting the West for aid and recognition. Such a sortie into China could well thwart his efforts. Even now, we're having clashes with the Chinese along our Mongolian border."

Yurovsky jams his pistol into Prokoviev's face. "Do you want to see tomorrow?"

45

Takla Morku Desert, Sinkiang Province, China
16 September 1933

I t's another feverish, scorching day without a cloud in the sky. The wind remains still. The aeroplane is a smoldering metal frame, and its ashes simmer. The survivors' camp, now set up farther down the dry wash, is covered with the tarpaulin as protection from the blistering sun and fallen ash. The forlorn travelers are hunkered down in the dry wash, heads down. Hope of rescue is fading fast. They exhausted their water supply yesterday morning. Now, none of them has the energy or will to talk, move, or hope.

On the far horizon, dust is kicked up from the desert. A troop of Kirgiz tribesmen gallop on their Takhi Mongolian horses toward the remnants of the still-smoldering aeroplane. The Kirgiz trace their origins to Indo-Iranian and Mongol ancestors, and they speak an Altaic language. The men's jet-black hair is long and tied in a bun at the back of their heads. They are Muslims, excellent horsemen, and herders of camels, goats, and sheep. They are complacent about peaceful outsiders but are quick to defend against any threat to their way of life.

In 1925, the struggling Chinese Republican government was trying to rule this vast and unorganized country. In large measure, remote Sinkiang Province was beyond their control. General Chang Kai-Shek, Commander of the Republican Expeditionary Army, sent an emissary into the province to negotiate a treaty with the Kirgiz. In return for the Kirgiz protecting the province, the government gave the tribe several thousand surplus German Mauser Model 98 rifles, ammunition, and other military equipment from World War I. Chen's father signed the treaty and pledged allegiance to the Republican government.

The noise of the tribesmen's arrival rouses Trevor. He slowly climbs out of the dry wash and is flabbergasted to see the troop of riders. He is overjoyed, yet apprehensive because they could be hostile. They are well armed with military rifles, and each has a bandolier of ammunition across his chest.

His throat is so dry that he can barely speak. On his knees, he waves with his open hand and smiles broadly.

The obvious leader approaches, dismounts, and bows slightly. Seeing that Trevor is an Occidental, he extends his hand for a handshake. Bewildered, Trevor, with all the energy he has remaining, rises, and extends his hand. After the handshake, he falls back down on his knees.

The leader helps Trevor stand and speaks a few words of greeting in his native Altaic language. Trevor shakes his head, "I don't understand." The rest of the ragtag survivors manage to crawl out of the dry wash. They stare at the tribesmen in wonderment and apprehension. Alex cries happily. Black Orchid smiles faintly. Marlowe remains silent as he surveys the scene.

The leader speaks to Trevor in Mandarin. "My name is Urumgi Ygur. I am a Kirgiz. My Chinese name is Chen Tu-hsiu, or simply Chen. My father sent me to the Autonomous Technical University in Chunking, where I earned my degree in mechanical engineering and learned the Mandarin language." Chen is a medium-sized man with very wide shoulders and intense black eyes. He wears khaki trousers and shirt, and a high-crowned straw hat with a very wide brim.

Trevor introduces himself and the others in Mandarin, and tells Chen the details of their situation.

On Chen's instructions, several horsemen dismount and offer the travelers water. Chen advises Trevor, "Tell your companions to sip slowly. They must wait to let the body accommodate the sipped water before taking their fill."

He continues, "Yesterday, we saw the smoke and wondered what was burning so fiercely. We do not see such fires in the Takla Morku."

As the survivors begin to revive, Chen's men offer them goatskin sacks of water. Later, the survivors gobble delicious victuals of unknown origin.

Trevor, somewhat refreshed, says, "We are most grateful to you, Chen. We would not have lasted another day. You saved our lives. We're in your debt."

"Say no more," Chen replies. "It is the hospitality of the Takla Morku."

"Where are we? We were supposed to land at the aerodrome at Wu-su. How far is Wu-su?"

Chen smiles faintly. "There is no aerodrome at Wu-su. It is a dirt strip cut into the desert." He continues, "We are about sixteen miles northwest of Wu-su, very near the Soviet border."

Trevor is not surprised that the strong wind pushed them so far off course. "We were going to Yumin to do some trading with the White Russians living there. Will you help us?"

Chen reflects that this must be serious trading to bring these white people so far from Peking. He does not see that they have anything to trade. Nonetheless, he agrees to take them to Yumin. He knows the White Russians well. Over the years, Anna and he have forged a trusted friendship. He trades hard goods and other supplies for their vegetables and wool, and brings them mail and telegrams from Wu-su.

The survivors recover essential items, while Trevor snaps a few photographs with his Leica. The bedraggled travelers, not skilled equestrians, mount spare horses, and bounce awkwardly as the troop trots away.

46

Yumin, Sinkiang Province, China
16 September 1933

Doctor Markov knocks on Anna's door. After hearing her faint response, he enters, and with a faint smile says, "We may have positive developments. Within the last three days, we have not had a single case of typhoid." Before Anna can respond, he continues. "And Chen reports that there is no typhoid in their village."

Anna forces a smile and responds, "At last, there is a parcel of good news in this province." She shuffles papers on her desk as her mind whirls. "I don't understand. Why has the disease not suffused throughout our community?"

"I have no definitive answer. Partly, I suspect, it's because of the precautions we've taken. Or, because of some aberration with the organism that I cannot fathom."

"Whatever the reason, Doctor, our people will continue the safeguards until we are positive that the disease is no longer a threat."

"Excellent advice, Elector. I will see to it."

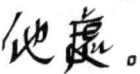

The travelers and the Kirgiz riders approach the village. Some of the White Russians are working in the vegetable gardens while others tend to the sheep and hogs. Chen greets the priest, Pavel Shubin, who is working in the orchard, and tells him that he has Occidental visitors for Lady Anna.

"Are these white men Soviets?" Shubin asks. "Are they spies for the Bolsheviks? Who are they?"

Chen responds, "No. Not spies. Survivors from an aeroplane crash in the Takla Morku—an Englander, two Americans, and a Chinese woman. They are from Peking and are here to visit with Lady Anna to do some kind of business."

Shubin and the other Russians realize that the visitors probably are not dangerous because of Chen's assurances and their Kirgiz escort. Moreover, the newcomers are too gaunt and ragged to present any serious threat.

On Shubin's invitation, the travelers dismount. Trevor thanks Chen, and Alex offers him her fountain pen. He refuses her gift. Trevor snaps several photographs, including a close-up of Chen on his horse and a long shot of his troop. On Chen's signal, the Kirgiz horsemen turn and gallop south, headed for their village, about five miles away at the southern edge of the valley.

Father Shubin studies the travelers for a few seconds and then approaches Trevor to shake his hand. "We don't have many visitors. You are welcome to stay until you have regained your strength and we arrange for your return to Peking. If you would follow me, I'll find the elector of our community and ask her to meet you."

He escorts the travelers into the lamasery and leads them to the village council meeting room. It is Spartan—a few handmade chairs and a plain wooden table. He excuses himself, and in a few minutes an elderly woman brings tea. She does not speak as she sets out the cups and saucers and pours the steaming liquid. The weary survivors sip the hot beverage gratefully. Too exhausted and saddle-sore to speak, they settle in their chairs and wait.

The travelers are beginning to feel somewhat restored when Shubin escorts Anna Bogrova and Kirik Pirogov into the room. Trevor and Marlowe rise to greet them.

"Please be seated, gentlemen. I am Anna Bogrova, the elector of this community. And this is Kirik Pirogov, my assistant. Welcome to what's left of Mother Russia."

Shubin moves to the back of the room.

The men resume their places as Anna examines her guests. Other than her fellow settlers, they are the first Europeans she has encountered for seventeen years. Her emotions waver between acute curiosity and intense wariness. Ever present is her fear that the Bolsheviks will discover and murder her and the White Russians in Yumin. She wonders if these filthy, bedraggled visitors, despite their appearance, might still bring danger into her fragile community.

Pirogov remains quiet and takes the measure of these uninvited visitors. His scrutiny lingers on the Chinese woman. Black Orchid notices and smiles gently.

Anna takes a vacant chair and rests the cane on her knee. Pirogov remains standing as if on guard. "Father Shubin tells me that you survived an aeroplane crash in the Takla Morku, and that our friend Chen rescued you and brought you to us." Anna is obviously fluent in English but speaks haltingly, searching for words long unused.

She shuffles to ease the strain on her right leg. "Father Shubin also said that you are from Peking and have come to see me to do some business. Correct? May I ask what sort of business brings you to this remote place with so many difficulties?"

Alex responds for the group, "First, permit me to introduce us. This is Samuel Marlowe, my father. He is the owner of the Composite Press Service, among other ventures." She gestures toward Marlowe, who is sitting silently. He still has not recovered fully from the effects of the crash, his twisted ankle, and their ordeal in the desert. "This is Trevor Pryce, a photojournalist for the Composite Press Service." Trevor bows slightly. "And I am Alex Marlowe, the general manager of my father's properties."

"Unfortunately," she continues, "our primary contact, Mister Wuhan Wei-kuo, the proprietor of Wuhan's Antik shop in Peking, was killed in the crash. His niece, Mistress Yen Hei-lan, represents his interests. When dealing with Occidentals, she prefers to be called 'Black Orchid,' which approximates her name in English."

Anna nods to acknowledge the introductions. "May I pour more tea? Some honey to sweeten it?"

Alex scans her group. "No, thank you. We much appreciate your hospitality. As you can see, we've had a difficult time surviving in the desert. Chen quite literally saved our lives."

Anna carefully looks at each of this motley crew. She is troubled by their unexpected visit and uncertain about their intentions. Instinctively, she gazes at Black Orchid and sees her exotic beauty under the grime. Black Orchid has remained silent, but her demeanor projects a cold and dangerous ambience.

Black Orchid sees that Anna is focusing on her and decides that this is the time to unmask this woman. She looks directly into Anna's eyes. "Mistress Bogrova, may we confirm that, in fact, you are Grand Duchess Anastasia Romanov?" Before Anna can answer, Black Orchid continues, "I have indisputable information that Anna Bogrova is your alias and that you are the fourth daughter of Czar Nicholas the Second. Am I not correct?"

Anna recoils in shock, and with her eyes open wide and mouth agape, she throws her hands to her face and gasps in startling dismay. Tears roll down her cheeks. She shakes her head back and forth in a negative response. "No. No. I am Anna Bogrova from Novosibirsk." Through her sobs, she faintly utters, "Kirik."

Pirogov, standing behind Anna, takes her shoulders in his hands and holds them affectionately. His eyes flash at Black Orchid with indignant scorn. He leans forward and whispers in Anna's ear, "This Chinese woman is trouble. Be cautious."

Anna, through her tears, addresses Black Orchid, "Mistress Yen, your questions are provocative and without foundation." She recovers her composure somewhat and wipes the tears from her cheeks.

The Occidentals look in shock at Black Orchid for her imprudent and brutal questions. Then they focus on Anna in wondering silence. Can it be that Anna truly is the Grand Duchess Anastasia Romanov? An intense atmosphere of disquiet suffuses the room. In a moment, the Occidentals suspect that Black Orchid is correct. Anna's heartbreaking reaction gave her away.

Anna turns to Kirik, whom she fears is about to assault the Chinese woman, and whispers, "Kirik, be calm." To ease his anger, she adds, "I sense that Black Orchid is no more than an impudent vamp."

Kirik nods silently, but remains watchful.

Alex, knowing the anguish Anna is suffering, rises and goes to her. Kneeling at the side of her chair, Alex takes her hands and says, "Anna, your secret is safe with us. You have my word that you can trust us. We may be crude, but we have sterling integrity." She turns and stares at Black Orchid with threatening eyes.

Black Orchid smiles faintly and turns her head away.

Anna smiles weakly through her disquiet at Alex. "Thank you for your compassion." Anna understands that her secret is exposed and she must accept it. With resignation and her head high, she says proudly, "Yes, Mistress Yen is correct. I am Anastasia Romanov." She pauses for a moment. "My secret had to be uncovered sooner or later, and I am pleased it is with an Occidental reporter and not the Soviet secret police, who have searched worldwide for me and have failed." With a slight gasp she continues, "So far." She stifles the urge to bolt to her room. Tenderly, she asks, "Please keep my identity confidential. Perhaps in a few months, Mister Pryce, I will release you from your pledge and you can write your story."

Alex speaks, "We will maintain your secret for as long as you want. You have my word."

Trevor muses, *My God! Anna Bogrova truly is Grand Duchess Anastasia Romanov. We have uncovered the scoop of the century. What a sensational story! And I have to suppress it—at least for now.*

Marlowe narrows his eyes as he stares at Anastasia in stoic silence.

Black Orchid, in a patronizing voice, says, "Anastasia is the mystery at which my uncle hinted."

The Occidentals are shocked at Anastasia's appearance. The merry little princess they knew from newsreels and old photographs of the royal family has vanished. Now they see a woman with lines of horror etched in her face, a crippled right leg, and a nearly useless left arm. The long, curly, brown hair of her teenage years is streaked with gray and cut in a short bob. She wears simple khaki trousers and shirt, and black sandals. Nonetheless, she carries herself with the erect posture of someone raised to wear a crown. Even in rough clothing and in these humble surroundings, she projects the *élan* of her earlier life.

Trevor, consumed with the moment, says to Alex, "Think of the potential if we could convince Anastasia to return to the West with us. The worldwide political explosion probably could lead to the overthrow of the Bolshevik government and generate any number of prize-winning stories."

Alex commands, "Slow down, Trevor. I've given my word."

"And mine also. However, I must document this fleeting and historical moment." Trevor pulls out his Leica and snaps a quick series of photographs of Anastasia, a couple of Pirogov, and several of their surroundings. The word *Pulitzer* pops into his mind.

Pirogov rushes to Trevor and demands the film, but Anna motions Kirik away. "It is too late. Pryce will need these photographs when he publishes his story. Come stand by my side. Be my strength."

Anna addresses Pryce directly, "Remember that I have your promise to protect my identity. The survival of this entire community depends on your discretion."

Without hesitation, Pryce responds, "On my honor, Mistress Bogrova."

Anna addresses the group, "First, I must ask how you came to know of my secret and our White Russian community at Yumin? We have avoided any publicity, and we keep to ourselves. Except for Chen, we do not communicate directly with the outside world." Anna again shifts her position to ease the strain on her leg. Suspecting that it was through Maxim that these people know about her and Yumin, she asks cautiously, "Perhaps you know of my associate, Maxim Fedosov? Two months ago, I sent him to Peking to negotiate some business for us."

Black Orchid addresses Anastasia with a pensive face and a solemn voice. "I knew Mister Fedosov. A few weeks past, he came to my uncle's antique shop to sell an emerald and diamond necklace. We authenticated this necklace as part of the missing Romanov jewelry. My uncle and Fedosov agreed on a price of 55,000 British pounds sterling. My uncle paid him by a check written on the China National Bank and Trust Company, and he contacted the head teller, Mister Chan Sen-tao, to ensure that Fedosov could cash it. My uncle also agreed to get Mister Fedosov a forged passport that would provide sufficient identification to allow him to cash the check."

Anna leans forward in her chair and says, "Yes, that was my mother's necklace, a gift from Queen Victoria to her granddaughter. But I haven't heard from Maxim in many weeks. He was to send me a telegram confirming the sale. May I ask when this transaction was completed?"

"It was about a month ago, around the fifteenth of August," Black Orchid responds confidently.

Anna, now anxious, gravely asks, "Possibly, Mistress Yen, you may know of his whereabouts?"

Black Orchid, with her most somber face, says, "It is my heartsick duty to tell you that brigands killed Mister Fedosov in a holdup in an alley near my uncle's shop."

Anna gasps at the appalling news. She cries inwardly at the loss of her friend and associate. Through her grief she says, "Maxim was a close associate and a trusted administrator. His demise is a critical loss for our community."

Pirogov stares in bewildered surprise. He kneels and hugs Anna tightly.

Trevor, knowing that Black Orchid is lying, frowns but keeps his peace. His duty is to Marlowe, and he sees no reason to interfere with Marlowe's plans.

After a minute or so, Anastasia recovers. "Thank you, Mistress Yen. Maxim was on a critical mission for our community's well-being. Please tell me all that you know, and where is your uncle's check?" Her voice is clear, but shaky.

Black Orchid responds with counterfeit sincerity, "My deepest sympathies." She pauses for effect and then continues, "I found Maxim Fedosov to be a gentleman. I would have liked to know him better."

Pirogov interrupts her. "Yes, Maxim was a fine gentleman and a driving force in this community."

Black Orchid stares at Pirogov, and instantly knows he is her enemy and that she must be wary of him. His devotion to Anastasia is patently apparent. She continues with a straight face, "It was dark when I left the shop for the day. I found Mister Fedosov dying in the alley. With his last breath, he told me your secret. Regrettably, the brigands stole my uncle's check. Before we could stop payment, the check was forged and cashed."

Pirogov asks, "Is there any chance to recoup the funds from the check?"

Black Orchid speaks with perfidious distress, "I am afraid not." She continues her lies. "I made the check payable to 'Bearer.' The payment is lost."

"Then you will return the necklace to us?"

"That I cannot do. We made an honest bargain with Maxim Fedosov, your agent. His loss must be yours, not mine."

Anastasia pauses to absorb the import of this second reversal. Without the money from the sale of the necklace, her plan to disperse their community is negated. With a choke in her voice she responds, "Indeed unfortunate. We need those funds for the future of the community." Struggling to accept the enormity of what Black Orchid has said, she asks, "Where is Maxim now? Who made the arrangements for his interment?"

"My uncle, Wuhan, took full responsibility and had him buried with full Orthodox ceremony in the International Settlement's cemetery."

Anna slumps in her chair, mentally and emotionally drained.

Black Orchid continues, "Perhaps you should know that Chief Inspector Thomas MacTavish from the International Police Force is in charge of this murder investigation. He has determined that Fedosov tried to resist the ruffians but was overwhelmed. The inspector questioned my uncle and me extensively. Afterward, he affirmed that enquiries would continue until the ruffians are apprehended."

Anna tries to control her painful distress and to put on a brave face. After a long silence, she turns to the other guests. "Mister Marlowe, again I ask, please tell me why you have come here." Her question is rhetorical because she has already surmised the reason—to possess Saint Catherine's Crown and the Romanov jewelry.

The tea and rest have revived Marlowe. He responds, "Our sympathies for your loss, Your Highness."

"Thank you kindly, Mister Marlowe. But please just call me Anna. Grand Duchess Anastasia Romanov is a relic of the past. She no longer exists. I am Anna Bogrova from Novosibirsk."

"As you wish, Anna." In an effort to set the stage for the real business at hand, he continues, "Under these dire circumstances, you've done exceedingly well in organizing this community and keeping it functioning all these years. Congratulations."

"I am but a small part of this White Russian community. I thank you for all of us."

"But from what I can see, it appears that you cannot continue here indefinitely. You're too close to the Soviet border. Resources must be meager. And I suspect that after so many years your people have tired of this austere place and want to venture into the real world. They must realize that the Russia you knew will never exist again. You can't return."

"Mister Marlowe, I regret to say that you've analyzed our situation with absolute clarity. I must confess that each day our plight grows a little worse. How much longer we can remain, I cannot tell."

"Perhaps I can help. I am a collector of Asian antiques. I have a large collection in my private museum in New York. Black Orchid's uncle told us about your cache of Romanov jewelry and Saint Catherine's Crown. I am prepared to make an offer for the jewelry and the crown. And to help you and your people migrate to the West if this is what you would prefer. I will make all the arrangements—passports, visas, and transportation—to any Western country you wish. I have important contacts in Washington who will facilitate approval of any plan we develop."

Anna smiles weakly and responds, "Thank you for your most generous offer."

Marlowe continues, "Payment can be in British pounds sterling, Austrian Maria Theresa gold schillings, United States dollars, Mexican silver pesos—any currency or any precious metal you select. I'll make the deposit in any bank you choose. All you need to do is allow me to inspect the cache, agree on the price, and shake hands to conclude the deal."

Anna reflects. "Saint Catherine's Crown is not for sale. It is the last remaining Romanov icon not in the Bolsheviks' murderous hands. Eventually, I want to donate the crown to the Smithsonian Institution. I would consider selling the remaining Romanov jewelry, if your offer is appropriate."

Pirogov interrupts, "How can we trust you? You are unknown to us and have no references that we know."

"Kirik Pirogov, is it? Yes, that's your name. You make a valid point, Pirogov. Do you have a way to check quickly with my bank, Barclay's, in Peking? If you do, I'll put the payment in trust for your people as soon as we conclude the deal."

"Fortunately, we do have such a way. Our Kirgiz friends have a powerful industrial radio, and we can encode and send messages in Morse code to Peking. It probably will take a few days for a round-trip confirmation."

"Splendid. Let's do it. Here is my account number." Marlowe scribbles a series of numbers and a few letters on a scrap of paper and hands it to Pirogov. "I suggest that you send your message for the attention of Mister Reginald Smyth-Lancaster, the bank's first vice president."

"I will take care of it shortly."

Anna comments, "Our bank is the China National Bank and Trust in Peking, and Mister Chan Sen-tao, senior cashier, handles our account. Kirik, please keep me informed."

"Of course."

Alex senses that Marlowe wants to press the deal. "Dad, Anna has just received two doses of soul-searing information. We'll talk tomorrow."

Anastasia responds, "Thank you, Mistress Marlowe. If you would please excuse me, I have much to do this afternoon. I need to reflect on these dreadful and momentous events, and to consider your business offer. Too much has happened too quickly."

Pirogov helps Anastasia to her feet. Leaning on her cane, she comments, "Please let me offer you the hospitality of our home. Our facilities are humble, I'm afraid, but I hope they will be adequate. The housekeeper will provide you with fresh clothes and water for bathing. Let us plan to meet again at dinner, which is at seven o'clock. Father Shubin will show you to your rooms."

Trevor says, "Thank you. We're tired and appreciate your generosity."

Anna smiles at Trevor, then she and Pirogov leave.

Alex is determined to keep Black Orchid away from Trevor. On the way to their rooms, she trails the group. When Father Shubin pauses to show Marlowe his room, she tugs at the priest's sleeve. In hushed tones, she requests, "Put Mister Pryce next to my room. The Chinese woman should go at the end of the hall."

Black Orchid, attuned to intrigue, overhears Alex. She smiles inwardly. She has no further use for Trevor. She has another scheme in mind.

Later, the travelers sit around a table in the lamasery's dining room. After a modest dinner of peas, onions, boiled potatoes, and small slices of roast lamb, they are refreshed and satiated. Trevor asks Anna for permission to take more photographs.

Resigned that her secluded life and that of her friends in Yumin is finished, Anna says, "Very well. Please be discreet."

Trevor draws his Leica from his bag and snaps photographs of the scene, his colleagues at the table, and some of the villagers. He scribbles notes for his story. Marlowe is lost in his plan to conclude the deal. Alex makes small talk with Anna and Pirogov.

Black Orchid smiles when addressed but only murmurs pointless nothings in return. She has been analyzing the dynamics of the meetings and the characters of Anastasia and Pirogov. *Tonight, I will seduce that handsome Pirogov.* She quickly discards this notion—she has a more important task set for this evening.

When the conversation stalls, Marlowe addresses Anna, "We are indebted to you for your generous hospitality. And I must say, I'm eagerly looking forward to seeing the Romanov jewelry and Saint Catherine's Crown."

Anastasia responds, "Mister Marlowe, tomorrow morning when we all feel better and can think more clearly, I will show you the jewelry, except for one piece that I want to keep. It's a sapphire brooch my mother gave me for my fifteenth birthday. It is all I have left of her." She pauses, rises carefully, retrieves her cane, and glances briefly at her guests. "This has been a stressful day. Tonight I have work to complete and I must review the day's events."

Anna takes a few steps toward the door, turns, and forces a smile. "Good evening, everyone. We shall meet again in the morning to discuss terms."

Pirogov rises and escorts Anna to her room. They engage in a short conversation, and then he leaves for his own quarters.

The weary travelers walk silently to their assigned quarters.

Black Orchid hesitates for a moment outside Pirogov's room, looks at the knob, and moves to her room. Inside, she withdraws the small Mauser 9-mm pistol and its holster from the valise, lifts the donated full, short skirt, and straps the holstered weapon on the inner thigh of her left leg. She muses, This pistol *is my passport out of this miserable place at the end of the world.* Satisfied, she reviews her forged transit papers for transit through the Soviet Union to Peking.

47

Yumin, Sinkiang Province, China
16 September 1933

In the early morning hours, Black Orchid slips silently into Anastasia's room and cautiously moves to rouse the sleeping woman. She clamps her left hand over Anastasia's mouth and whispers in her ear, "It is Black Orchid. I am here to solve your plight." As Anastasia tries to sit up, Black Orchid loops her belt around Anastasia's neck and gives it a hard twist. "It is to your advantage to tell me where you have hidden Saint Catherine's Crown and the Romanov jewels. Take me to them. Now!"

Anastasia refuses to speak and struggles to get free. Her hands go to her neck to loosen the garrote, but she's no match for the strength of the tenacious Black Orchid. Anastasia gags. Black Orchid tightens her grip. Anastasia gags again. She can hardly speak. Blackness engulfs her eyes. "Where are the jewels?" Black Orchid demands in Anastasia's ear.

Anastasia manages to gurgle, "No."

"Damn you! Tell me where they are!"

Anastasia cannot speak, but she feebly shakes her head negatively. Now in a frenzy of frustration, Black Orchid tightens the garrote. Anastasia can no longer gag and begins to lose consciousness. Her frustration increasing, Black Orchid tightens the loop again. "Tell me and I will loosen this garrote." Anastasia slumps unconscious. Enraged and without reason, Black Orchid continues to tighten the garrote. In a few seconds, Anastasia convulses and emits the death gurgle.

In ignominious defeat, and only partly aware of what she has done, Black Orchid cries out, "No! The crown and the jewels are mine. I shall not be denied." She shakes Anastasia's lifeless body. "You are not dead. Get up. Get up! Where are they?" Finally, Black Orchid lets Anastasia's limp body slump onto the bed. Her open eyes stare blankly. Black Orchid slips to the floor on her knees and repeatedly blows deeply into Anastasia's mouth in a desperate attempt to invigorate her dead body. She lets the garrote slip to the floor.

Doctor Markov is in the infirmary next door, working on patient records. The ruckus alarms him. He grabs his revolver and bolts into Anastasia's room. In a fleeting second, the horrible scene is clear. He levels his pistol at Black Orchid. "Stop! My God! What have you done?" He moves to the bed, but Anastasia's dead eyes do not see him. "Anna, Anna!" he cries. He spots the bloody red welt around Anna's neck, and the stained garrote on the floor. He points his revolver at the kneeling Black Orchid's head. Trembling in body and voice, he murmurs, "Murderess, you have slain a holy woman." Overcome with inconsolable grief, loss of reason, and compulsion for justice, he cocks the revolver. He shouts, "I damn your malignant soul to eternal perdition!" His index finger begins to squeeze the trigger. His mind clears, and he comprehends the evil he is about to do. He relaxes, and withdraws his revolver from Black Orchid's head. "Get up."

Black Orchid rises and looks at him coyly. "Surely we can reach an accommodation," she purrs. Other Russians now enter the room and see what has happened. Markov shouts, "Anastasia is dead! Murdered by this Chinese woman." Some of the Russians scream, some yell, and some sob. Several grab Black Orchid and hit her repeatedly in a crazed fury. The others stand immobile with shock and disbelief.

Markov yells at them, "Stop! Stop! Secure this wolfish assassin with ropes. Put her in the potato cellar. In the morning, we'll decide what to do with her."

Two men grab Black Orchid, bind her with thin ropes, and gag her with a hand towel. They start down the hall with their prisoner.

Markov grabs a weeping woman, "Get Kirik Pirogov. Rush."

Passionate sorrow grips the White Russians as the news of Anastasia's death spreads through the community.

Pirogov fights his way through the people crowding Anna's room. In an instant, he sees the dead eyes of his beloved Anastasia. He howls in excruciating agony. Sobbing uncontrollably, he drops to the floor, grabs Anastasia's body in his arms, and rocks her back and forth. He murmurs in her ear, "My dearest love. My love. My love."

Markov leaves Pirogov to mourn in private.

The commotion awakens Trevor, Alex, and Marlowe. Trevor and Alex enter the hall and see the Russians escorting the bound and gagged Black Orchid down the hall. Trevor snaps a few frames with his Leica. He enters Anastasia's room and gasps at the death scene. He is stunned with grief that this courageous woman has met such an ignoble and unnecessary death. Nonetheless, he recognizes his journalistic responsibility and snaps several more frames.

Alex enters and looks at Trevor. "My God, what has that harlot done?"

Trevor turns Alex away and says in a low, sad voice, "Black Orchid murdered Anastasia."

Alex gasps, slowly sobs, then whispers, "Butchered in this godforsaken place by that scheming harlot. I knew Black Orchid was deceitful, but I didn't conceive of her as a murderess. It's beyond my comprehension that Anastasia is dead by that strumpet's hand. She had suffered so much and had overcome so many hardships. Surely, Anastasia is a saint."

"Please, Alex, return to your room. I'll tell you more later. For now, I want to help, if I can, and to document this unfolding scenario with my Leica." Gently, Trevor turns Alex and pushes her toward her room.

Marlowe stumbles, half awake, into the hall.

Alex snaps, "Dad, return to your room. It's all over." He complies without question.

Pirogov, with a face expressing absolute horror, rushes down the hall after Black Orchid. Enraged, he screams, "I am going to kill you, you viperous murderer! You have destroyed my love! I'm going to kill you."

The bindings on Black Orchid's hands, tied by grief-stricken villagers, are slipshod. With minimal effort, she sheds the thin ropes and whirls around, throwing off her captors, then grabs the small pistol on her thigh and snap fires

at the charging Pirogov, emptying the magazine. Several rounds have knock
Pirogov down. One of Black Orchid's guards smashes a chair on her head and
knocks her unconscious.

Chaos reigns.

Markov shouts in his commanding voice, "All of you! Return to your
rooms. Now! Tomorrow I will explain." The Russians straggle away, whispering
to each other. Markov grabs two husky Russian men. "Stay with me."

Father Pavel Shubin arrives. "I have heard." He looks into Anna's room.
"I will minister to her."

"Please do, Father. That Chinese woman shot Pirogov and I need to
attend to him. Come with me, you two."

Father Shubin enters and, with loving care, closes Anastasia's eyes and
covers her with a white sheet. He places his crucifix on her chest and kneels to
pray. "Dear merciful God, please accept the soul of this humble martyr. She
was pure of mind and body." He continues with the ritual prayers for the dead.

Markov reaches Pirogov, lying on the hall floor. He is awake and in
serious pain. Markov makes his assessment and sees that a bullet has grazed
the left side of Pirogov's head and the wound is bleeding profusely. Another
bullet has ripped into his right leg. Another is lodged high in his left chest
near his shoulder.

Markov strips off Pirogov's shirt and uses it to bind his head to slow
the bleeding. He nods to the two men with him, "Help me get Pirogov to
the dispensary."

Trevor continues working with his Leica until the group disappears
behind the closed doors of the dispensary.

He returns to Alex's room and finds her sitting on the bed and sobbing
softly. She stands and hugs Trevor, and he kisses her gently. "Alex, the drama
is over for tonight. We'll know Pirogov's condition in the morning. Doctor
Markov appears to be an excellent professional."

Alex, weak with sorrow, wipes her face. "Really? This place is so primitive." She hugs Pryce tight. "Can we endure yet another crisis on this damned
expedition? Anastasia is dead. How horrible. In the few hours that we were
together, I was deeply impressed by her sterling character and dauntless

courage. I am distressed that I'll not become friends with her." She begins to sob softly again. Recovering shortly, she changes the subject. "In the hall, you hinted that you were suspicious of Black Orchid's homicidal bent. How? What made you think so?"

Trevor releases her and both sit on the bed. "From the beginning of this odyssey, I saw Black Orchid was an enigma. She was too perfect, too overt, too something I didn't understand."

Alex acknowledges Trevor's assessment and cracks a crooked smile. "You men are really dumb. Her overt sexuality had you mesmerized. From my perspective, she was a trollop and not to be trusted."

Trevor looks at Alex with narrowed eyes. "Perhaps, but we digress." He pauses to organize his thoughts. "Wuhan was still alive when I first saw him after the crash. When I returned he was dead, and I saw garrote marks on his neck. There is no doubt that Black Orchid murdered him. For what reason, I can only guess. From the evidence, I reckon that she had planned from the beginning to double-cross him and the rest of us."

"Murder, intrigue, double-crosses, shootings—it's too much. Let's go home. I can't stand any more of this mayhem." She kisses him passionately. "Stay with me tonight, Trevor. I'm distraught and I need your love and strength."

In his room, Marlowe sits on his bed, and reflects on the turmoil around him. *That Anastasia woman was a charming lady. She impressed me with her determined spirit. In the short time we had, she earned my profound respect. Too damn bad that the Chinese bitch murdered her. Surely, the Russians will administer swift and sure justice. I'd help if I were able.* He paces, trying to determine a plan of how to deal with the Russians. "I need Alex," he says aloud. "Tomorrow, when things have calmed down, she and I will work on a strategy."

地震。

Father Shubin joins Doctor Markov in the dispensary. Shubin strips Pirogov and covers him with a white sheet. Pirogov lies on a stout oak table, a substitute for an operating table. His eyes are etched in pain.

Markov hands Pirogov a small glass filled with a milky liquid. "Swallow this bromide quickly."

Pirogov takes the glass, looks at the liquid, and forcing a small smile, murmurs, "What devil's nostrum have you concocted for me?"

Markov lifts Pirogov's head. "Drink, and shortly you will be euphoric and then you'll experience paradise in a deep sleep."

Pirogov complies, then coughs and sputters, "Damn. What was that foul-tasting stuff?" The glass tumbles to the floor.

"Laudanum—an opiate to render you senseless. Now be quiet. I have work to do."

Pirogov's pain begins to ease. "Tell me, what of that murderess? Is she dead?"

"No. Black Orchid is bound tightly and locked in the potato cellar. Be quiet. Go to sleep."

48

Altai Mountain Range, Sinkiang Province, China
17 September 1933

The high-powered rifle cracks, and the stag drops to the ground. Chen and his two younger brothers are hunting deer in the southern foothills of the Altai Range. The men dismount, and Chen gives the *coup de grace* with his powerful German Luger. They begin dressing the deer. Chen glances at the White Russian compound two miles away in the valley below.

His thoughts briefly turn to his friend and trading partner, Anna Bogrova, and to the group of foreigners that he escorted to the compound. He knows that she is distressed at not having heard from Fedosov. Smiling slightly, he thinks about the delightful surprise he has for her. She and her compatriots will soon eat their fill of venison. And his people will enjoy fresh potatoes, beans, and onions from the Whites' gardens.

He shifts his gaze to the Soviet border and sends a short prayer of thanks to his God that his tribe lives outside that evil place. Just as he is about to return to the work at hand, his attention is caught by a fast-moving cloud of dust headed southeast toward Yumin. Retrieving binoculars from his saddlebags, he focuses on the moving cloud and is alarmed by what he sees. A military truck convoy, which he identifies immediately as Soviet by the red star ensigns, has crossed the Chinese border and is headed full speed toward the White Russian compound. He knows full well the calamity that will shortly befall the Whites. Anna and her compatriots have always been apprehensive that one day the Soviets would invade their compound, arrest Anna, and take her back into the Soviet Union. Her fate there would be one of torture to extract a confession of "crimes against the state," then a trial based on trumped-up charges, followed by a quick execution. As for Anna's companions, they undoubtedly would be cut down by machine-gun fire.

"Stop!" he shouts to his brothers. "We must return to camp. Now."

४९

Yumin, Sinkiang Province, China
17 September 1933

Eight trucks, each containing a NKVD platoon of twelve soldiers, roar into the White Russian compound at Yumin. Flying defiantly from each truck is the dreaded red hammer-and-sickle ensign of the Union of Socialist Soviet Republics, and emblazoned on each truck door is a large, vividly red star outlined with a black stripe. Colonel General Yurovsky directs the operations from his command vehicle. Riding with him are Captain Leonid Prokoviev and Sergeant Elena Vavilova.

As the trucks screech to a stop, sergeant platoon leaders shout orders to the soldiers to surround the compound. "On the double!" Not sure what resistance to expect from the Whites, the first sergeant commands, "Weapons loaded and at the ready! Shoot any White who tries to escape."

The terrified villagers attempt to scatter to the safety of the mountains, but the soldiers quickly have them encircled and held at bay with fixed bayonets.

General Yurovsky commands, "Tighten our circle of control." He orders the third platoon, "Cut off these field hands from the lamasery. Form a skirmish line in front of the steps. No one enters or leaves that building." He takes a quick survey of the operation and spots the outlying buildings. "Second platoon, marshal all Whites in those lodges and put them with this group."

An hour earlier, General Yurovsky had ordered a reinforced platoon to scout the area and report on the Whites' defensive positions—machine-gun nests, artillery and mortar emplacements, and sentries. The lieutenant in charge returned and reported that he could not see any military activity, only some farmers harvesting corn in a field, and a few working in a vegetable garden. Yurovsky is puzzled. Surely, he believes, the Whites must know that the NKVD would arrive one day. Are they not prepared? Or have the years, the desert sun, and their isolation sapped their resolve? On reflection, he reasons that they probably have no will to fight. Accordingly, he orders Captain Prokoviev to keep the heavy arms in the trucks. There is no need to expose these expensive weapons to the elements. His force can occupy the community with rifles and pistols only.

Yurovsky leaps out of the lead truck, grabs a field worker, and demands, "Where is Anastasia?"

The worker responds fearfully, "There is no Anastasia here. You need to speak with Doctor Markov. He's in charge now."

Puzzled, expecting that Anastasia would be in the village and easy to find, Yurovsky points his pistol at the trembling farmer and orders, "Bring this Doctor Markov to me." Not knowing what possible threats might be inside the lamasery, Yurovsky tactically decides to force Markov to come out into the NKVD's area of control.

Yurovsky climbs the steps of the lamasery and meets Markov as he walks out of the building. He announces, "I am Colonel General Yakov Yurovsky. I represent the People's Commissariat for Internal Affairs of the Union of Soviet Socialist Republics. I am here to arrest Anastasia Romanov for crimes against the state. Take me to her."

"General, you have no jurisdiction here. We are in China. Your authority ended at the Russian border, some five miles away." With false bravado, Markov continues, "Go away. Leave us alone. We bother nobody."

Yurovsky, not accustomed to back talk, points his pistol at Markov's heart. "You're going to have your White army or the Chinese militia force us to leave? I see no Chinese authority and no White army, you imbecile. The NKVD's authority is worldwide. Take me to Anastasia now, or else I'll terminate every last czarist in this place."

Realizing that he has no other option, and totally despondent at Anna's death, Markov loses his resolve. He knows that this invasion is the end of their community. "Come inside, General. I will explain."

Sergeant Elena Vavilova and several soldiers hold Marlowe, Alex, and Trevor at gunpoint in the meeting room. Vavilova sees that these three are Westerners. She grabs Marlowe by his shirt and demands in Russian, "Who are you? Where are your papers? Why are you here? Are you agents for the czarist Whites?"

Marlowe, not understanding her, tries to shrug off her hand. "Who are you people?" he demands. "What's happening? Release us immediately!"

Unaccustomed to this kind of resistance to her bullying, Vavilova slaps him hard and sticks her pistol in his face. "We will find out," she bellows. Marlowe, reeling from the blow, realizes that his usual bluster will not help him. He falls silent.

Alex attempts to reach her father, but a guard points his bayonet at her stomach, halting her forward movement.

Yurovsky and Markov enter the meeting room. The general gives a cursory glance at the three travelers. He'll attend to them later.

"Where is Anastasia?" he demands.

Markov, frightened, is reluctant to answer the NKVD general. He drops his eyes to the floor and mutters something unintelligible.

"Damn you, you stupid *mudak.*" He aims his pistol at Markov's privates. "Tell me now. Else, you will die in agony far away from your lost Czarist Russia."

Realizing that it is vain to resist, Markov looks down the hall. In a soft voice he says, "She is there. In her room."

"Bring that royal bitch to me."

"I cannot. It's impossible."

"You refuse a general officer of the NKVD?"

"No, General. I cannot because …." He stumbles at the horror of her murder. Revived, he speaks in a clear, strong voice. "Grand Duchess Anastasia Romanov is dead."

Startled speechless, Yurovsky narrows his eyes, and raises his pistol to Markov's head. Time becomes motionless as his disbelief melds into 'perhaps.' Shortly, the general recovers and returns his pistol to its holster. "How?"

Markov speaks firmly. "General, I am distressed to tell you that Anastasia was murdered early this morning by a Chinese woman—one of our newly arrived guests; she arrived with the Westerners. We are at a loss to know why. The murderess is our prisoner—now confined in our potato cellar."

Yurovsky bursts into a rage. He is furious that someone has cheated him out of his destiny to bring Grand Duchess Anastasia Romanov to Soviet justice. Shortly, he controls his passion and demands, "Take me to Anastasia's body." *I must confirm with absolute certainty that she is dead. I cannot fail a second time.* He knows that Stalin's jurisprudence is swift and merciless.

Markov leads Yurovsky and two NKVD soldiers to Anastasia's room. Yurovsky sees the white sheet covering a body. He yanks it off, spots Shubin's cross on the woman's breast, and sweeps it to the floor.

He is shocked to see the incredible change in Anastasia. Can this worn-looking, middle-aged woman really be the pretty little grand duchess he remembers from the Ipatiev House just seventeen years ago? Stripping away her gown, he examines the wound scars in her shoulder and thigh. Opens her eyelids and stares into her dead blue eyes. He feels the bones in her face. She is a Romanov, without doubt. Anastasia is indeed dead.

Yurovsky's anger and frustration erupt into fury. "It is Anastasia. Murdered. I have been cheated!"

Yurovsky commands Markov, "Bring the Chinese woman to me. Now!" A few minutes later, a guard shoves a disheveled Black Orchid into the dispensary. Her hands are tied securely behind her back, and there is a rope around her neck, held tightly by one of the White Russians. Yurovsky stares at her intensely and says nothing. After a time, he asks in a deceptively gentle voice, "Did you kill Anastasia?"

Black Orchid looks at Yurovsky coyly, makes a faint smile, and says, "So it is rumored."

No fool, Yurovsky yells, "Why?"

Black Orchid looks away and cocks her head as if devising a response. She turns to Yurovsky and extends her most seductive smile.

Yurovsky stands in stunned silence. He invaded China to arrest Grand Duchess Anastasia Romanov and to bring her to Soviet justice NKVD-style. He glares at Black Orchid in angry dismay as he realizes this Chinese woman has deprived him of his compelling obsession to complete the task left undone at Ekaterinburg.

Yurovsky snarls at her, "You simpleton!" He draws his pistol and points it at Black Orchid's forehead. Her face turns ashen as she understands the full reality that her schemes have failed and for once her charms cannot save her. She opens her mouth to protest as Yurovsky fires. The impact of the bullet snaps her head back and slams her body to the floor. His rage not satiated, he stands over her and empties the pistol's magazine into her lifeless body. He flashes a lightning-quick grin at the enabling feeling of the kicking, warm pistol in his hand.

In the dispensary, Pirogov hears the shots and the hubbub and tries to raise himself off his bed on an elbow. He falls back, still weak from loss of blood and woozy from heavy doses of laudanum. He calls out weakly, but no one responds.

Several minutes later, Sergeant Bogdan Yezhov and two of his men enter the dispensary. They are inspecting rooms in this wing of the lamasery. The sergeant goes to Pirogov's bed and sees the heavy bandages on his head and his leg in traction. The sergeant is a seasoned combat veteran and has sympathy for the wounded of any stripe. He says in a firm but empathetic voice, "I am Sergeant Yezhov of the NKVD, and we have captured this czarist refuge. Who are you? What happened to you?"

Pirogov comprehends the enormity of this NKVD invasion and winces in distress. Finally, he realizes, *The Soviets have found us, and I have no ability to resist.* He murmurs softly, "Pirogov, Kirik Pirogov, administrative assistant."

"Tell me, what happened to you?"

Knowing that all is lost and there is no need to antagonize the NKVD, he whispers, "Come closer. I am very weak and hazy from opium." The sergeant leans toward Pirogov. "The Chinese woman who murdered our elector shot me while she was trying to escape. Yesterday, it was."

The sergeant, not knowing the details of the shooting and suspecting that Pirogov is an important member of this White Russian community, decides that he will report to one of the officers.

With a snappy salute, the sergeant makes his report to Captain Prokoviev. He dismisses Yezhov curtly. "General Yurovsky has no interest in wounded czarists. Return to your duties."

"Yes, sir."

The Occidentals hear the gunshots and, gripped in fear, they wonder what has happened. Later, a White orderly under escort of a NKVD guard enters the room. "General Yurovsky has shot and killed the Chinese woman in retaliation for her murder of Anastasia. The general will be here in a few minutes to interrogate you."

They are aghast at Yurovsky's brutality and the menacing NKVD. *What have we gotten ourselves into?* Alex wonders to herself. She is now convinced that she was absolutely correct—this journey is a disaster.

"Dad, say nothing," she commands her blustering father. "Do you hear me and understand? These Soviet Communists don't give a damn who you are or how much money you have. Be quiet!"

Marlowe, under Vavilova's watchful eye, clearly understands Alex's message.

Yurovsky's anger subsides as his adrenalin rush abates. Shaken that his mission to kill Anastasia has been foiled, he regains his composure. Nonetheless, his revenge on Black Orchid does little to alleviate his keen disappointment.

He goes to the meeting room and looks over the three Occidentals. Finally, he commands in broken English, "Who are you? What are you doing here? This is no place for Westerners."

Alex knows how unscrupulous the Bolsheviks are. The shots she heard and the report that Yurovsky murdered Black Orchid have confirmed her fears. The NKVD doesn't care who it kills or where. Now, desperately concerned for the safety of her party, and gripped in fear, Alex responds respectfully, but with a quiver in her voice, "General, my father and I are citizens of the United States of America. Mister Pryce is a British subject." Waiting for a response, her heart races and faint perspiration appears on her forehead.

Yurovsky does not reply. He carefully inspects the three of them. While he evaluates his options, he absently pats the pistol on his hip.

Chilling dread seizes Alex's soul, and without thinking she blurts out, "We came here in good faith to purchase the Romanov jewelry and Saint Catherine's Crown."

Startled at this revelation, Yurovsky's eyes narrow in a questioning stare. He cocks his head slightly to one side and leans toward Alex.

In an instant, Alex realizes that she has made a monumental blunder. Obviously, Colonel General Yurovsky was unaware that the Russian treasures are here. Trevor turns away to avoid showing his angst. Marlowe's mouth drops open in shock—Alex does not make such gaffes. To recover from her mistake, and to distract Yurovsky, she stumbles, "We had no part in Anastasia's murder and deplore what Black Orchid did."

Yurovsky grabs Alex's arms and pulls her to within a few inches of his face. His eyes, in a narrow squint, stare into hers. In his most official voice, Yurovsky demands, "Tell me more. Tell me all you know about the Romanov jewelry and Saint Catherine's Crown." He pushes Alex away from him. In a more relaxed voice, he demands, "I have all afternoon to hear your tale." He pauses for effect and looks first at Marlowe, then at Pryce. He loads a fresh magazine in his pistol. "Your answer must be accurate. If not, I will shoot your father. Then Mister Pryce. Then you in the stomach. And I'll find these baubles with or without your help. Am I clear? Do you understand?" He raises his voice a little to emphasize his threatening intent.

Alex murmurs in a soft voice, "Yes, General, I understand."

Marlowe, understanding Yurovsky's dire threat, intervenes. "General, please understand that we mean no disrespect to you or the Union of Soviet Socialist Republics. We have no political agenda. I am a collector of rare Oriental *objets d'art*. We learned about the Russian treasures hidden in this community from an antiques dealer in Peking. Black Orchid was his niece and our guide. We are here on legitimate business to negotiate a sale."

Yurovsky is not much interested in these stupid capitalists and does not want to increase the already serious contretemps he has started. "Nonsense. Even in your capitalist country it is criminal to traffic in ill-gotten merchandise. What gives you the right to pirate the Soviet Union's treasures?"

Without waiting for an answer, Yurovsky turns to Markov. "Bring the Romanov jewels and Saint Catherine's Crown here." Yurovsky correctly assumes that, as the person in charge, Markov knows their hiding place.

With a slight hesitation, Markov says, "Yes, General. I'll fetch them and return shortly. They're hidden in a room some distance from where we are."

Yurovsky commands Sergeant Vavilova, "Go with him. Make sure he complies with my order precisely and quickly. If he does not, shoot him."

"Yes, sir, General." She draws her pistol and sticks it in Markov's back. "Move."

Markov walks quickly to the lamasery's sanctuary with Vavilova trailing close behind him. They approach the Buddha statue. He manipulates two of the carved figures in the teak stand, and a secret door snaps open. He withdraws the ebony coffer and looks at it with sorrow, knowing that this final relic of his motherland's imperial greatness will now be in Bolshevik hands. Then, he retrieves the large leather pouch containing the remaining personal jewelry of the Romanovs.

The pair returns to the meeting room with the treasures. Markov places the box on a table, opens it carefully, and gently lifts Saint Catherine's Crown in its ermine wrap out of the box. He spreads the ermine on the table and sets the crown on it. Sun beaming through a window hits the enormous, blood-red, four-hundred-carat ruby atop the Crown. Blazing red light is reflected throughout the room. There is a subtle murmur from the group. The diamond-encrusted platinum crown sparkles in all its dazzling beauty—hundreds of faceted diamonds, all perfect in color and cut, sized and arranged to create an object of breathtaking magnificence. Beside them, enormous South Sea pearls gleam as though lit by an inner fire. Everyone in the room gazes in amazement. No one attempts to touch the crown. A few gasp, even Yurovsky, but no one speaks.

Markov empties the leather pouch and spills the dazzling jewelry on the table. There are ruby-encrusted brooches, diamond rings, sapphire-mounted platinum bracelets, giant strings of perfectly matched pearls in silk pouches, a dazzling, green emerald bracelet, and a brilliant sapphire brooch whose clasp is engraved with "QV" and Saint George's Crown—a king's ransom and then some. The jewels sparkle and glisten in the wandering sunbeams.

Yurovsky recovers. He picks up the crown and brings it close to see it more clearly. He adjusts his glasses and turns the crown slowly. "So these are the Romanov baubles—the decadent harvest of the labor and lives of thousands and thousands of serfs. Did the Romanovs understand its value in human life?"

Alex wonders at this out-of-character comment from the butcher of Ekaterinburg.

Carefully, General Yurovsky wraps the crown in its ermine wrap and puts it back into the coffer. He returns the jewels to the pouch. Handing these two items to Captain Prokoviev, he orders, "Store these Soviet treasures in your truck securely and carefully. Guard them with your life—which depends on their safe return to our motherland."

Marlowe, seeing his prize about to be lost, makes a feeble attempt to bribe Yurovsky. "I will deposit in any bank, in any country you choose, more Maria Theresa gold schillings than you can imagine. Leave us the crown and the jewels. You have had your revenge."

"Be careful what you say, capitalist. Be quiet, or else I will charge your party with conspiracy, theft, and counter-revolutionary activities. I will arrest you and send you to a gulag. No trial will be necessary. You will disappear into the Siberian snow."

Marlowe is struck mute.

Alex quickly intervenes. "My apologies, General. Sometimes my father is imprudent. We mean no disrespect to you or to the Soviet Union." After a slight pause, as her apology registers, she asks, "Will you help us return to Peking?"

"Enough, woman."

Yurovsky is somewhat mollified that he has recovered Saint Catherine's Crown and the Romanov jewelry. It is small recompense for his failure to execute Anastasia, but at least he can tell Comrade Secretary Stalin and Director Genrikh Yagoda that Anastasia is dead, and he has recovered these long-lost, great treasures of his country.

He realizes that the Westerners are no threat to the Soviet Union. It's best to tread cautiously with them, especially because he has violated Chinese sovereignty and murdered a Chinese citizen. Besides, Comrade Molotov is traveling in the United Kingdom and United States attempting to gain recognition for the government of the USSR. It would be impolitic to jeopardize Molotov's efforts by harming citizens of these two capitalistic countries.

Satisfied that he has full command of the situation, Yurovsky exclaims, with his voice ringing triumphantly, "These treasures will be displayed in the State Hermitage Museum in Leningrad—ironically, in Catherine II's palace. And it was she who established this museum. The proletariat will see how the czarist aristocrats exploited their labor for these trinkets."

Turning to Markov, he snaps contemptuously, "You and your Whites are a pathetic excuse for Russians. Remain here in China and continue your hardscrabble existence. Die here in your squalor. It's your destiny. Your czarist Russia no longer exists, and it never will. Today and for all time, my country is the Union of Soviet Socialist Republics."

Yurovsky turns to leave. He stops and looks at the stranded travelers. "I have no quarrel with you. You may ride with us to Bolotnoye. There you can board the Trans-Siberian Railway to Vladivostok. I will provide you with transit and exit papers."

Pryce, speaking for the group, responds, "We thank you, General, for your forbearance." As General Yurovsky moves away to organize the NKVD's return to the Soviet Union, Pryce retrieves his Leica, which is hidden under a discarded tablecloth on the floor, and snaps several frames.

Marlowe quickly whispers to Markov as the doctor turns to leave the room, "Have faith. I'll be in touch."

Yurovsky, satisfied that their return preparations are proceeding apace, returns, and cautions the Westerners, "You will say or write nothing whatsoever about the events of today." After a slight pause he continues, "If ever there is any revelation of my foray into China, my agents will 'entertain' you, no matter where in the world you might be. Remember, the NKVD, through the Comintern, has tentacles worldwide."

50

Kirgiz Camp, Sinkiang Province, China
17 September 1933

I t is midmorning as Chen gallops to the center of his tribe's camp. He shouts repeatedly as he turns his horse around and around. "The Soviets are invading Sinkiang! The Soviets are invading our home! The Soviets are after Anna and the Whites. Gather your weapons. Follow me!"

Within a few minutes, several hundred Kirgiz men, women, and youths are armed, mounted, and headed at a gallop for Yumin. Within a few hundred yards of the compound, the riders quietly dismount and, using whatever cover they find, split into two groups. The first, led by Chen, quickly encircles the Soviets gathered at their trucks. They then slowly advance to tighten the loop. The second group, led by one of Chen's younger brothers, moves across the lamasery's steps to encircle it in a tight loop that effectively isolates the two NKVD components. At some points, the Kirgiz are two riflemen deep. Their rifles are at port arms, indicating readiness rather than imminent action.

The NKVD's first sergeant, a veteran of the White and Czech campaigns, not knowing the intentions of these advancing tribesmen, rallies his NKVD guards, regular soldiers, and truck drivers into a defensive position around the trucks. Their arms are at the ready, but no shots are fired. The Kirgiz circle continues to tighten.

Chen, unarmed, advances to the group around the trucks.

The Soviet first sergeant, not wanting to start an armed conflict with the Chinese without orders, demands, "Who are you? What are you doing here with these armed men? Leave before we gun you down."

Chen continues his advance and is soon facing the sergeant. "Welcome to Sinkiang Province in the Republic of China. My name is Chen, and I am the leader of the Kirgiz people of Sinkiang Province. We wish to ensure that you have a pleasant visit and that you have no untoward experiences while you are here."

The hardened NKVD sergeant growls, "Get out of here. We're on the people's business and want no interference from locals. You are treading on dangerous ground when you interfere with the NKVD of the Union of Soviet Socialist Republics."

The front rank of several hundred Kirgiz closes the loop even tighter.

Chen calmly looks at his watch and responds in a firm, but friendly voice, "I sincerely hope that you are enjoying your stay in China. Unfortunately, I see that your leave is about to expire. I suggest that you return to the Soviet Union now, only five miles away, before you are missed by your superiors. We would not want you to have troubles when you return. Some of my troops will escort you to the Chinese border to ensure your safe passage."

The sergeant puts his hand on his holstered pistol. "Are you insane? I do not take orders from a Chinaman. I am a noncommissioned officer of the People's Commissariat for Internal Affairs and only take orders from my superior officers. Now go away and leave us alone. I have no more patience with you."

"Pardon me, Sergeant, but I am not a Chinaman. I am Kirgiz, and we control this province by a warrant from the Republican government." On Chen's signal, the Kirgiz troops fix bayonets and close the loop even tighter. "Allow us to make sure that you have an uneventful journey to the border." Several hundred Kirgiz now stand within a few feet of the NKVD soldiers.

Chen, the tone of his voice hardening, says, "It is your choice, of course. You can leave now or remain forever here in the Celestial Kingdom. Leave your weapons and the trucks. It is but a relatively short hike to the border. Be sure to carry some water."

The sergeant, quickly assessing the untenable situation of his troops, surrounded by the mass of well-armed, disciplined Kirgiz warriors, realizes that he has no options. He reluctantly orders his men, "Drop your weapons. Fall in."

Chen, with a faint smile, says, "There is no need for a military march. Walk at a normal pace, and enjoy this fine day and the beautiful scenery. My brother and his friends will guide you. We wish you a pleasant journey home."

The commotion outside has piqued Sergeant Vavilova's interest. As she exits the lamasery she is surrounded by the second Kirgiz troop. Chen advances on this group. "Your pistol, please, Sergeant." Vavilova raises her pistol to shoot him. Chen's youngest brother gives her a quick chop to the neck from behind, knocking her to the ground unconscious.

Chen nods to his brother in thanks as he enters the lamasery, followed by a dozen of his people. Others enter through the rear doors. Soon the Kirgiz have complete control of the lamasery. On Chen's command, the Whites and the travelers lie face down on the floor. General Yurovsky, Captain Prokoviev, and the remaining NKVD soldiers are surrounded.

Yurovsky bellows, "Who the hell are you people? What are you doing here? Get out. Now!" He tries to retrieve his pistol, but a husky Kirgiz knocks the general's right hand away with the butt of his rifle.

Engulfed in pain, Yurovsky uses his good hand to pull his broken right hand across his chest. He exclaims in a blazing fury, "You stupid peasant! How dare you strike a general officer of the People's Commissariat for Internal Affairs! You and your whole tribe are as good as dead. Do you hear me?"

Chen stands in front of Yurovsky. "Good morning, General. We hope you have had an agreeable visit here in China. It is our custom to greet our visitors warmly and wish them a safe stay. I am Chen, a member of the Kirgiz people, and leader of this welcoming committee in Sinkiang, a province in the Republic of China." After a brief pause while he surveys the area, he continues, "It would be fortuitous if you and your people would allow us to take care of your weapons while you are here. If you would be so kind?"

For once in his life, Yuorvsky is checkmated—and by a tribal peasant at that. Frustrated, angry, and embarrassed, he surrenders his pistol. The others follow his lead.

"Thank you, General. I must assume that you are here to visit with Anna Bogrova and the Whites in this community. Yes?"

"I have no comment for the likes of you, the scum of the proletariat."

Chen smiles mildly. "Yes, I am a tribesman, yet I have honor and true friends. See that you respect our hospitality while I learn more about your visit to our Chinese sovereign territory."

Chen asks the Russians and the travelers to rise and tell him what has happened. He does not see Anna or Black Orchid. "Where is Anna? And the Chinese woman?"

Marlowe advances and vigorously shakes Chen's hand. "Thank you, Chen, and your people, for saving us—once again, I might add. We can never repay your outstanding service. Whatever I can do for you, anything, I will do it."

"Do not fret. It is my responsibility to ensure that our guests have a safe and pleasant visit in our province."

Trevor says, "Thank you, Chen. We again are in your debt." He begins to document the scene with his Leica.

Alex, with tears trickling down her cheek, murmurs brokenly, "Thank you." She seems to grope for more, but can only repeat, "Thank you."

Marlowe explains, "General Yurovsky, while in an uncontrolled rage, shot and killed Black Orchid."

"Why would he kill the Chinese woman? She was not a White Russian."

"Unfortunately, I must tell you that Anna, the Grand Duchess Anastasia Romanov, is dead."

Before Marlowe can continue, Chen grabs Marlowe's shoulder and with shock in his voice asks, "How did this happen? She was well just a few days ago when I saw and talked with her."

"It's a nasty business." Marlowe pauses as he forms his next words and his eyes narrow. "Black Orchid killed Anna last evening with a garrote. She was apparently trying to force Anastasia to reveal the hiding place of some

Russian jewelry that's supposed to be hidden in this lamasery. We reckon that she was planning to double-cross us. She had a concealed pistol under her skirt and some travel documents in her bag. I think she planned to take the treasures for herself and escape alone through the Soviet Union."

Without comment, Chen turns to Yurovsky. "Your visa for this visit to China has expired. And I suspect that we will never issue you another. It is time for you to return to the Soviet Union, where you belong, among the godless people."

He motions to his guards to escort the prisoners out of the lamasery.

Doctor Markov approaches, "General, your crippled hand needs attention. Let me put a splint on it." He attempts to take the general's hand.

Yurovsky abruptly snaps his hand away and spouts, "No maladroit czarist fakir touches me."

On the lamasery steps, Chen tells Yurovsky, "We will escort you to the Chinese border to ensure your safety. It is our fond hope that you will have good feelings about your short visit to China."

Yurovsky sees that his soldiers are gone and their weapons lie on the ground. "What have you done with my soldiers?"

"They grew tired of China and went home. To fully enjoy this delightful weather, they decided to walk. The trucks appeared to be a burden of some sort."

"You stupid fool. You had better kill me now because I plan to return with a division force and wipe out every last Kirgiz, White Russian, and Chinaman in this province. Prisoners, if any, will die slowly in my gulags."

"You speak foolishness for an uninvited guest without resources. Please understand, we have commandeered your trucks, your weapons, and all your supplies." Chen smiles knowingly. "They will be useful to us should you attempt to visit us again."

Chen tells his brother to organize their group and escort the general and his soldiers to the border. "At a slow walk, in deference to the general's age."

He addresses Yurovsky in a mocking voice, "I am sure, General, that you will have a fine reception in the Soviet Union on your return—naked, as it were. Should I send a telegram to the Director of the NKVD, Genrikh Yagoda, to announce your return?"

51

Yumin, Sinkiang Province
19 September 1933

Markov, as acting head of the White Russian community, realizes the impracticality of keeping Saint Catherine's Crown and the Romanov jewelry in Yumin. As the Occidentals gather to make their farewells, the doctor approaches Marlowe and, remembering Anna's instructions, asks him to take these treasures to the Smithsonian Institution. "They are to be held in confidential security for one hundred years. Then they are to be displayed in a Romanov exhibit that tells the story of the regicide, Anastasia's heroism, the Czech Legion's indomitable spirit, the Kirgiz' faithful courage, and the NKVD's duplicity."

Without hesitation, Marlowe agrees to Markov's request, and the two men conclude the deal with a hearty handshake. Marlowe, smiling, says, "You have my word." He takes the ebony box that holds Saint Catherine's Crown, and the chamois pouch with the Romanov jewelry, and tucks them into his knapsack.

Markov notes, "You've had an unexpected and dangerous visit with us. For that, I extend my sincere regrets." He shakes hands with the three visitors. "Before you leave, Kirik Pirogov asked me to thank you, Alex, for your empathy toward Anastasia."

Alex responds, "May I see him? Is he well enough for a visit?"

"He is heavily sedated, but come with me to the dispensary and let's see how coherent he is this morning."

They enter the dispensary quietly and Alex approaches Pirogov. He manages a weak smile. "Hello, Mistress Marlowe. Thank you for coming."

"Doctor Markov tells me that you're recovering and that you'll be completely healed in a couple of months."

"So I've heard." He looks away for several seconds, then an expression of pain crosses his face. "Let us not discuss the horrors of last evening. I do not have the strength to review it."

"Of course." She smiles. "We are leaving in a few minutes and we wish you good times. Do you have plans?"

Pirogov does not respond on cue. Alex smiles and takes his hand. He says, "After we have successfully moved our people to safety and have provided funds for them to start a new life, perhaps I will emigrate to Canada. I have a friend in Vancouver."

Alex kisses him on the cheek, "God love you and your brave Russians."

She joins her father and Trevor. The Occidentals ought to be happy that they are about to board one of Chen's captured trucks to travel to safety, but they are strangely silent. Yurovsky's threat of deadly retaliation by the Soviet secret police fills them with apprehension.

Increasing their angst are the memories of the horrible events of these past few days—the aeroplane crash, their struggle for survival, their rescue, the murders, the sterling courage of Anastasia, the determination of the White Russians, and the loyalty of the Kirgiz.

Just before they board the truck, Marlowe says to Markov, "In a few weeks, may I suggest that you check the commune's bank account. I assume you are a cosignatory." On his return to Peking, Marlowe plans to deposit one million pounds into this account. Over the last hours, he has reflected on the events of these past few days. He realized that he and his cronies are seriously lacking in moral character. During this epiphany, he eventually concluded that integrity, empathy, and loyalty are more important than the accumulation of priceless antiquities.

As the truck heads toward Ko-erh-mu, Marlowe sits silently, lost in his thoughts. Alex helps Trevor by recalling critical incidents as he tries to scribble notes in the bouncing truck.

A few miles west of their destination, Alex looks at Trevor. "Thank God this misadventure is nearly over. It was a complete fiasco. I hope this calamity has permanently squashed Dad's obsession for collecting. It's time he starts tending to business."

Trevor responds ruefully, "I'm afraid that's wishful thinking, Alex. Marlowe is Marlowe. This venture was a blip in his view of the world. Though I must admit that in the last few hours he's become almost an enlightened human. Nonetheless, if I may be so bold, I advise you to take complete charge of his business conglomerate. Manage it with the skills I know you have."

Alex muses. "You're correct. I don't recall ever seeing him happier." After a few seconds she responds, "If I'm going to be the hands-on manager of Dad's empire, I can't continue running the Composite Press Service. Come with us to New York. Be my executive editor of the Press. Make it the hallmark of the oncoming revolution in communication services."

"What revolution? We've had enough revolution for now." Trevor, after some reflection, adds, "Are you proposing to become my boss?"

"In a word, yes. But not in the traditional sense. You'll have complete control to accomplish the guidelines that we'll set together. I need someone with your talents, energy, writing skills, and foresight. Someone who understands the international situation. The world is quickly moving into an era of political upheavals, and I suspect that another world war is on the horizon. The Composite Press Service needs to lead with the most accurate, fastest, and most comprehensive coverage, and must embrace the nascent technology that will transform our profession."

"I'm not sure your offer is a tolerable idea, Alex. Nonetheless, I'm flattered that you've asked. Thanks."

"The job comes with unwritten perks."

"Define, please." He smiles.

"They're also under wraps." She takes his hand and looks him in the eyes. "Join me. Let's make a great team."

"I'm intrigued. However, I won't make a decision now. I need time to sort out my life."

Alex looks at him with a questioning eye. "I understand. Should you choose not to join me, I'll respect your decision. But it will be with deep regret."

"Thanks, Alex." Trevor muses on her congenial companionship, her intellect, her logical reasoning, her femininity, and the sensuous pleasure he's experienced with her. He's inclined to accept her offer but wonders if it's his ripening protective instinct or something far deeper. Could it be possible that he, the freewheeling Trevor Pryce, is in love?

Alex interrupts Trevor's pondering. "Whatever you decide, you've got an amazing story on what happened at Yumin. I'll publish it with the terrific photographs you've taken. A Pulitzer Prize is waiting for you."

"Sounds great. However, I don't relish dodging the NKVD for the rest of my life."

"Perhaps you won't have to. Dad has contacts in the upper echelon of our government. He's a strong supporter of President Roosevelt—with money, influence, and intelligence. He has had several visits with Roosevelt during the campaign, and he was a special guest at the inauguration last January. I think the president would be strongly inclined to use whatever resources he has to protect Dad and his family." She has Trevor's attention and sees that he is impressed. Emboldened, she continues. "In fact, the Secretary of State, Cordell Hull, is Dad's pal. Write your story under a pseudonym. We'll give it to Mister Hull for safekeeping with the Department's Bureau of Intelligence and Research."

"To what end?"

"William Bullitt, our newly appointed ambassador to the Soviet Union, will call on their foreign minister, Maxim Litvinoff. Bullitt will deliver your story to Litvinoff, and request that the NKVD stand down. Our recognition of the Soviet Union is tenuous. Roosevelt favors recognition, but even most of his own party and supporters advise him against it. They cannot excuse the Soviets for the senseless regicide of the Czar and his family and the Comintern's aggressive brutality."

"But, I don't understand what is to keep the NKVD at bay."

"Bullitt will make it clear that should any of us—Dad, you, or me—meet with an accident or an undue medical crisis, the United States and most of our Western allies will withdraw their recognition. Trade deals will collapse. Aid will be withdrawn. And Comintern agents worldwide will be identified and expelled. The Japanese will provoke incidents in Mongolia, Manchuria, and Sakhalin." She smiles slyly. "Frankly, it's diplomatic blackmail."

After some reflection, Trevor takes Alex's hand, and with a wry smile says, "Okay. I'll write the story and you publish it. Deal?"

"Deal."

Near Ko-erh-mu, Chinghai Province, China
19 September 1933

It is the second day of travel for the Occidentals in the back of one of Chen's captured Soviet trucks. The sky is clear, and the intense afternoon sun heats their compartment uncomfortably. The truck bounces along a dirt road en route to Ko-erh-mu. There, the Occidentals will either charter an aeroplane or board a train to Peking. Chen is the driver, and his youngest brother is riding shotgun, holding a Soviet submachine gun at the ready. Bandits are known to roam in this area. Earlier, Chen and his brothers had painted over all insignia identifying this truck as having belonged to the USSR.

52

Headquarters Building, Composite Press Service, New York
30 September 1938

Trevor Pryce is reviewing the lead story for this evening's newspaper. It has just arrived from his senior reporter in London: "Neville Chamberlain, Great Britain's Prime Minister, returned to England this afternoon from his meeting in Munich with Adolf Hitler, Chancellor of the Third Reich. Chamberlain waved the agreement he signed with Herr Hitler that approved the Germans' demand to occupy the Sudetenland area of Czechoslovakia to resolve the 'German question.' With self-satisfaction, Chamberlain announced, 'Peace for our time.'"

Multiple pings on his private teletype machine announce an incoming FLASH message. The clickety-clacking teletype slowly prints:

MOSCOW, 30 SEPTEMBER 1938. THE MINISTER OF JUS-
TICE OF THE UNION OF SOVIET SOCIALIST REPUBLICS
RELEASED A STATEMENT TODAY THAT SAID LAVRENTI
BERIA, HEAD OF THE PEOPLE'S COMMISSARIAT FOR IN-
TERNAL AFFAIRS, THE NKVD, HAS CHARGED COLONEL
GENERAL YAKOV YUROVSKY WITH ANTI-SOVIET ACTIV-
ITIES. YUROVSKY WAS THE FORMER COMMANDER OF
THE NKVD FOR ALL OF SIBERIA AND THE EXECUTION-

ER OF THE RUSSIAN ROYAL ROMANOV FAMILY IN 1918.
THIS MORNING, YUROVSKY WAS TRIED, CONVICTED,
AND EXECUTED AT LUBYANKA PRISON.

FIN

Saint Catherine's Crown

Дцтног's Иотеs

The basis of this yarn lies in the aftermath of the Bolshevik Revolution in Russia, and the murder of Czar Nicholas II and his family on the night of 17 July 1918 at Ekaterinburg. To add authenticity, I used the real names of key Russian characters, historical facts and dates, and geographical accuracy, and set the narrative in the milieu of the times. Any story dealing with Russian history is convoluted. Accordingly, to assist the reader in understanding, I have added to this chapter the following commentary about key elements: historical background, the book's protocols, and Russian and Soviet intelligence and police organizations.

Historical Background

Grand Duchess Anastasia Romanov (5 June 1901 to 17 July 1918). Since the early 1920s, rumors had flourished that Anastasia was alive and living in Paris, Florence, Montevideo, New York, or Peking, under assumed names. Films, tales, imposters, and flimflam artists have exploited the Anastasia myth. In 1991, amateur archeologists found a bone fragment thought to be from one of the royal family in an unmarked grave in Ekaterinburg. Russian and British pathologists confirmed conclusively, through mitochondrial DNA analysis, that this bone fragment was Anastasia's. This evidence counters the legend that she mysteriously survived the regicide, and proves Anastasia died with her family. Nonetheless, the legend is too ingrained, too intriguing, too vital to let die. Consequently, I exercised my author's prerogative to pen this tale that she did survive the regicide.

Catherine the Great (1729 to 1796). Empress Catherine reigned over Russia from 9 July 1762 to 17 November 1796. The "MacGuffin" in this story is the magnificent crown that Catherine wore during her reign. She became Czarina on the death of her husband, Czar Peter III. Her reign is a study in contrasts. Legend has it that she organized a plot to have some of her sycophants murder Czar Peter III, and that her sexual proclivities were unusual. On the other hand, the actual historical record is replete with accomplishments. In 1757, Voltaire called her an "enlightened despot." For example, Catherine established the Free Economic Society in 1765 to encourage the modernization of agriculture and industry. She promoted trade and the development of under populated regions by inviting foreign settlers, and she founded new towns. Catherine patronized the arts, letters, and education. She permitted the establishment of private printing presses, and relaxed censorship rules. Under her guidance, the University of Moscow and the Academy of Sciences became internationally recognized centers of learning; she also increased the number of state and private schools. Finally, Catherine greatly expanded the Russian empire—prizes from two successful wars with Turkey. After her death, the Russian Orthodox Church proclaimed her a saint.

Russia in World War I. By the autumn of 1916, Imperial Russia was losing badly its war with Germany/Austro-Hungary. The Bolsheviks and other insurrectionists were in armed revolution and close to capturing Saint Petersburg and overthrowing the Romanov monarchy.

China. Peking was the capital of China through the Ming and Manchu dynasties. In 1928, the Nationalist Kuomintang government moved the capital to Nanking because it was the center of General Chang Kai-shek's power base; it reduced the power of the northern warlords; and it was Doctor Sun Yat-sen's burial place. To reflect this capital relocation, "Peking" became "Peiping." Nonetheless, for consistency I use "Peking" throughout the novel.

In the 1930s, China was seriously underdeveloped and beset with chaos. Warlords controlled many of the provinces, bandits roamed freely, Japanese patrols sallied on reconnaissance missions, Communists fought Nationalists, and foreign imperialism hamstrung China's economic, social, and political growth.

Austrian Maria Theresa schilling. This one-troy-ounce, 24-carat-gold coin is fictional. There is an Austrian Maria Theresa silver 25-schilling coin.

Sinkiang Province. In 1933, this Chinese province was one of the most remote parts of our planet. Northwest Sinkiang is contiguous with the USSR. It was largely unexplored by Occidentals and only marginally by the Chinese.

Yumin, Sinkiang Province. Yumin, abandoned many years ago, is about five miles from the USSR border and about eight miles from the closest USSR town, Duzhba.

Kirgiz tribesmen. The Kirgiz, spelled "Kirghiz" after 1990, and also spelled "Kyrgyz," are the predominant nomadic tribe in northwest Sinkiang Province.

The Czechoslovak (Czech) Legion. When World War I started in August 1914, the ethnic Czechs living in the Russian Empire petitioned Czar Nichols II to permit them to establish an armed militia to fight the invading Austro-Hungarian Army. He agreed.

The Czech Legion was formed in February 1915 and became a Division of the Russian Army. The Legion consisted of 6,500 soldiers, including ethnic Czechs, prisoners and deserters from the Austro-Hungarian army, and volunteers from France and England. After the Treaty of Brest-Litovsk was signed on 3 March 1918, the Kerensky provisional government agreed to evacuate the Legion to France via the Siberian port of Vladivostok. By this time, the Legion's ranks had swollen to approximately 68,000 armed, well-trained soldiers, and it had become an independent Czechoslovak army operating inside Russia.

The Legion, in six groups, started its evacuation through Siberia on the Trans-Siberian Railway. Lenin's Bolshevik government made increasing demands on the Czechs to disarm and surrender. For example, on 25 May 1918, Leon Trotsky, People's Commissar of War, sent telegraphic orders to Bolshevik army units scattered along the Trans-Siberian Railway to shoot on sight any Czech with arms.

Fully aware of the duplicity of the Bolsheviks, the Czech leaders decided to fight their way to Siberia. The Legion quickly occupied large areas around the railroad east of the Volga River. In the ensuing fighting, the Legion captured considerable amounts of military and civilian equipment, including eight railroad freight cars full of gold bullion from the Imperial reserve in Kazan. Although not a formal element of Admiral Kolchak's White Army, the Legion fought a running battle with the Bolsheviks all the way to Vladivostok. By 1920, the fight was over, and the Legion's main body had embarked on Allied transports. Others faded into China.

Protocols

1. I use aeroplane and aerodrome purposely. England had significantly more influence in China than did the United States. Also, in the 1930s, the use of these two words was not uncommon in the U.S.

2. I use the Wade-Giles Romanization method for the spelling and pronunciation of Chinese names—the standard at the time of our story. In 1958, the Chinese Communist government instituted the Pinyin Standard Mandarin Romanization spelling and pronunciation. For example, Peiping became Beijing.

3. The Bolsheviks captured all of the state and Orthodox Church jewelry that was in Saint Petersburg and elsewhere. To maintain clarity, I emphasize "personal" when I discuss the Romanov jewelry.

4. In the Saint Petersburg settings, the dates are set in the Russian Julian calendar. The Julian calendar is thirteen days behind the Gregorian calendar used in Western Europe and the Americas.

5. When spelling Russian names, I used the Romanized spellings (for example, Ekaterinburg instead of the Russian transliteration spelling Yekaterinburg, and czar instead of the lesser-used variation tsar).
6. The geography, on the whole, is exact: town and feature names are spelled as they were in the 1930s.
7. Distances are approximate.

Intelligence and Police Organizations

Okhrana (Okhranka). Okhrana is an acronym for the Department for Defense of Public Security and Order. The Okhrana were the secret police of Imperial Russia; their primary task was to combat political terrorism and left-wing revolutionary activity. Czar Alexander III created the Okhrana in 1866 after the assassination of Czar Alexander II.

Cheka is an abbreviation for Vecheka, itself an acronym for the All-Russian Extraordinary Committee for the Struggle against Counter-Revolution, Sabotage, and Misuse of Authority. On December 20, 1917, Vladimir Lenin appointed Felix Dzerzhinsky as People's Commissar for Internal Affairs, which included the Cheka. It operated free of any independent review. It was the Cheka that kept the Soviet government, the Communist Party, and the Third International in power during these extraordinary times. Cheka troops ran the gulag labor camps, suppressed peasant rebellions, crushed riots by workers, and vanquished mutinies in the Red Army. The Cheka was the spearhead of the Red Terror and murdered an estimated twenty to thirty million Soviet citizens: those associated with the Romanovs, the intelligentsia, kulaks, Ukrainians, Poles, and anyone else the Cheka considered a threat to the Soviet state—or just anyone they wanted to eliminate. They were responsible for the regicide of Czar Nicholas II and the royal family.

GPU is an abbreviation of the State Political Directorate. In 1922, at the end of the Civil War, Lenin transformed the Cheka into the State Political Directorate (GPU) with Dzerzhinsky as its head. The GPU was under the control of the Council of People's Commissars of the USSR and continued the policies of the Red Terror.

NKVD is an abbreviation for the People's Commissariat for Internal Affairs; it later became the Main Directorate for State Security (GUGB). In early 1933, Josef Stalin was chairman of the Communist Party Secretariat and the leader of the USSR. Lenin and Dzerzhinsky were dead. Stalin dissolved the GPU, formed the NKVD, and appointed Genrikh Yagoda to head this burgeoning organization.

The NKVD was the public and secret police organization of the USSR. It continued the reign of terror started by the Cheka and the GPU. The NKVD's authority encompassed the USSR's internal and foreign intelligence activities. Its authority also included the regular police force, firefighters, border guards, and the state archives. The NKVD conducted espionage and political assassination abroad; for example, an undercover NKVD agent murdered Leon Trotsky in 1940, while he was in exile in Mexico City. The NKVD ran the gulag system of forced labor, suppressed underground resistance and political opposition, and conducted mass deportations of various nationalities and social groups to unpopulated regions of the country. Its agents in the Comintern influenced foreign governments and enforced Stalinist policy within the Communist Party in the USSR and in other countries.

Using the NKVD as his strong arm, Stalin—much afraid that someone might challenge his leadership—focused on purging his old Bolshevik comrades and the senior officers of the Red Army. In late 1934, Yagoda arrested Lenin's former Bolshevik comrades—Lev Kamenev, Grigory Zinoviev, Ivan Smirnov, and thirteen others—and accused them of being involved with Leon Trotsky in a plot to murder Josef Stalin and other party leaders. These men were all found guilty and were executed on 25 August 1936.

FIN

Рнотоɡгарнıс Ɋаɭɭeгч

I have posted the following photographs in the order in which each subject was first mentioned.

Chapter One

Grand Duchess
Anastasia Age 15

Grand Duchess Olga
Age 22

Grand Duchess Tatiana
Age 20

Grand Duchess Maria
Age 18

Empress Alexandra
Feodorovna Romanov

Czar Nicholas
Romanov II

Colonel Baron
Gustaf Mannerheim

King George V

Chapter Two

Roman Malinovsky (Dmitri)

Chapter Four

Tsareavich Alexei
Nikolaevich Romanov

Chapter Seven

Vladmir Illyich Lenin

Leon Trotsky

Alexander Kerensky

Chapter Eight

Grand Duke Nikolai

Felix Dzerzhinsky

Chapter Thirteen

Gregory Zinoviev

Chapter Fourteen

Yakov Yurovsky

Chapter Nineteen

Colonel Chiang
Kai-shek

Warlord General
Wu Pei-fu

Chapter Twenty-One   Chapter Thirty-One

General Aleksei
Brusilov

Comrade Joseph Stalin

General Anton Denikin

Admiral Vasily Kolchak

Chapter Thirty-Two

Yen Hei-lan
(Black Ordhid)

Chapter Thirty-Nine

Gennikh Yagode

Chapter Forty-Five

General Chiang Kai-shek

Chapter Fifty-Two

Neville Chamberlain

Adoph Hitler

Author's Notes

Catherine the Great

Czar Peter III

Voltaire

Czar Alexander III

Czar Alexander II

Lev Kanenev

Дбоцт тне Дцтног

Captain S. Martin Shelton retired from active and reserve naval service with an extensive background in Soviet and Chinese studies. Shelton served in the Korean and Vietnam wars and spent many years traveling in the Far East.

After obtaining a Master of Arts in Cinema from University of Southern California, he produced a host of information motion-media shows, and won over forty awards in national and international film competitions and festivals. Shelton is a Fellow of the Society for Technical Communication and of the Information Film Producers of America.

Shelton has published several historical action-adventure novels whose *mise-en-scène* is the Far East and Africa. The characters in his novellas and short stories comprise a mélange of aviators, assassins, and adventurers. His professional book, *Communicating Ideas with Film, Video, and Multimedia,* garnered the Best of Show award in the Society for Technical Communication's Spotlight Publication Competition.

The details of Shelton's literary work are posted on his website:
sheltoncomm.com.